THE PLINY THE YOUNGER MYSTERIES

†

"The author brings to the reader the many cultures that were yoked under the politics and power of ancient Rome.... The colorful characters, both fictional and historical, are well blended to reveal the sordid web of money, greed, and ruthlessness hidden behind the façade of civilization. One hopes to see Albert Bell's Pliny again in the future."

—*Historical Novels Review* [on *All Roads Lead to Murder*]

"Outstandingly researched and laden with suspense, this journey into ancient Rome by history professor Bell could be one of the masterpieces of the historical mystery genre. ...Highly recommended for all collections."

—*Library Journal* [starred review of *The Blood of Caesar*, which it named as one of the five Best Mysteries of 2008]

" Pliny the Younger, nephew of the naturalist Pliny the Elder, proves a natural at detection in Bell's third whodunit.... Bell deftly blends clues and period details in this worthy alternative to the Roman historicals by such better known authors as Steven Saylor and Lindsey Davis."

—*Publishers Weekly* [on *The Corpus Conundrum*]

DEATH
IN THE
ASHES

ALSO BY ALBERT A. BELL, JR.

HISTORICAL FICTION

All Roads Lead to Murder:
A Case from the Notebooks of Pliny the Younger

The Blood of Caesar:
A Second Case from the Notebooks of Pliny the Younger

The Corpus Conundrum:
A Third Case from the Notebooks of Pliny the Younger

The Flute Player (e-book)

CONTEMPORARY FICTION

Death Goes Dutch

CHILDREN'S FICTION

The Secret of the Bradford House

The Secret of the Lonely Grave

NONFICTION

Perfect Game, Imperfect Lives

Exploring the New Testament World

Resources in Ancient Philosophy (with James B. Allis)

DEATH
IN THE
ASHES

A FOURTH CASE FROM
THE NOTEBOOKS OF
PLINY THE YOUNGER

✝

ALBERT A. BELL, JR.

MMXIII
PERSEVERANCE PRESS · JOHN DANIEL & COMPANY
PALO ALTO / MCKINLEYVILLE, CALIFORNIA

A Perseverance Press Book
Published by John Daniel & Company
A division of Daniel & Daniel, Publishers, Inc.
Post Office Box 2790
McKinleyville, California 95519
www.danielpublishing.com/perseverance

Distributed by SCB Distributors (800) 729-6423

Book design by Eric Larson, Studio E Books, Santa Barbara, www.studio-e-books.com

Cover: Ruins, House of Neptune, Herculaneum

10 9 8 7 6 5 4 3 2 1

LIBRARY OF CONGRESS CATALOGING-IN-PUBLICATION DATA
Bell, Albert A., (date)
Death in the ashes : a fourth case from the notebooks of Pliny the Younger /
by Albert A. Bell, Jr.
pages   cm
ISBN 978-1-56474-532-3 (pbk. : alk. paper)
1. Pliny, the Younger—Fiction. 2. Tacitus, Cornelius—Fiction.
3. Rome—Fiction. 4. Historical fiction. 5. Mystery fiction. I. Title.
PS3552.E485D45 2013
813'.54--dc23
2013003898

For Judy Geary
in appreciation of her friendship
and strong encouragement

AUTHOR'S NOTE & ACKNOWLEDGMENTS

I am ambivalent about author's notes. Sometimes I read them, often not. I wanted to write this one, though, because I am working with a new publisher and deeply appreciate the opportunity Perseverance Press has given me to continue this series.

As any author discovers when writing a series, there are positives and negatives. I like Pliny and Tacitus and would hate to miss the chance to continue telling their stories. I welcome the opportunity to develop some of the characters, even minor ones, who have appeared in earlier books.

But how do I use characters from earlier books without giving away their plots? One mystery author whom I will not name gives away so much of the plots of her earlier books that I find I can start reading at any point in her series and not have to read the previous books. So, how do I make this story stand alone while, at the same time, making it feel connected to the other books—previous and yet to come—in the series? I hope I've succeeded.

For the first time I'm including a list of characters. I hope it will help readers keep the characters clear but will not give away any "spoilers." Please see the end of the book for the Cast of Characters, both real and fictional, and a Glossary of Roman Terms.

As I always do, I need to express profound thanks to my writers' group, the West Michigan Writers' Workshop, for their penetrating critiques each week. In no particular order, just visualizing them around the table: Steve, Dan, Roger, Vic, Norma, Jane, Dawn, Carol, Lisa (both of them), Sheila, John, Sarah, Paul, Bill, Karen, Nathan, Christine, Alyssa, and Joyce. The regulars and not-so-regulars have all had a hand in making me a better writer than I was twelve years ago, when I joined the group.

I also owe a long-standing debt of gratitude to my wife, Bettye Jo, for her patience and support. Someone once said, "A writer's hardest job is to convince his wife that he's working when he's sitting back with his feet propped up." My wife, I'm glad to say, understands how much my writing means to me.

DEATH
IN THE
ASHES

I

I'M AFRAID WE'RE going to be late," I said to the throng of clients gathered in my atrium for the morning *salutatio*. "And we cannot be late."

My servant Aurora, who attends to my personal needs, put her hand on my cheek, which she had shaved half an hour ago. Running a finger along the narrow, dark red stripe which she had sewed on herself, she adjusted my new toga one more time. Her hand rested for a moment over my heart, which seemed to surge toward her. "Good fortune, my lord..." she said aloud, then added in a whisper, "Gaius."

Aurora is the daughter of my late uncle's mistress, Monica. She and I have been friends since she, along with her mother, came into our household when we were both seven. Until she began her monthlies, she called me Gaius. From the day she arrived in our house, though, my mother has tried to insist that she address me properly, as *domine*, "my lord." The first time Aurora called me that, we both broke out laughing. But as my voice changed and my beard began to grow, she fell into the habit of addressing me as a slave should address her master, no matter how many times I told her she didn't have to if no one else could hear us.

My clients chattered around me, pleased with the extra donative I'd given them this morning, but I hardly noticed. How could I notice anything with Aurora standing this close to me, with her olive skin and dark eyes complemented by her yellow *stola*?

As children Aurora and I played together. As we matured, though, my mother made certain we became more aware of the gulf between us. Mother deeply resented her brother's relationship with Monica,

13

and has sometimes done things to hurt Aurora, especially after her mother died. I recognize Aurora's feelings for me, and I can't deny mine for her. But I don't know what to do about them.

"Gaius!" my mother called from across the atrium where she and her servant and friend Naomi were observing us. My clients fell silent. "Gaius, your mother-in-law is waiting in the Forum."

I knew she was talking more to Aurora than to me. And Pompeia wasn't my mother-in-law—not yet. My fate might be sealed, as surely as the fate of a sacrificial animal being led to the altar, but I wasn't going to give up. The priest's hammer hadn't fallen on my forehead yet, and sometimes the victim breaks away and throws the crowd into a panic as it flees.

But who was I kidding? The victim is always caught.

From her left hand Aurora removed a ring and dropped it into the *sinus* of my toga. "For luck," she said. We had found the ring on one of our adventures in Laurentum when we were eleven. A large, chunky thing made of bronze, it bears an image of the goddess Tyche, the Greek version of Rome's Fortuna. We have a custom of passing it back and forth between us when one of us feels the other one needs a bit of luck, even though neither of us believes in such a thing.

"Thank you," I said, suddenly aware of an intense longing for this dark-haired Venus.

"Gaius, you mustn't disappoint Pompeia." Mother was stalking across the atrium, her blue *stola* billowing around her, with Naomi in tow.

I touched Aurora's hand and held her dark eyes with mine for another moment. Then she bowed her head and stepped aside, and I started for the door, inhaling one more whiff of her perfume, imported from Egypt, which I had given her on her last birthday. My steward Demetrius held the door open as I led a crowd of thirty men out into the street. "Good fortune, my lord," he said as I passed him.

I patted the *sinus* of my toga. "I believe I have it."

Looking over my shoulder as the door closed and we gathered on the sidewalk, I made certain my scribe, Phineas, was close to me and carrying his writing case on a strap over his shoulder. He had designed it himself so that he could carry it under his arm, as he was now, or rest it on his belly to make a writing desk. The red-haired young man, the son of Naomi, is adept at the rapid writing known as Tironian notation. This morning he would take down my speech and my opponent's in the case I would be prosecuting in the Centumviral Court. I had dictated a copy of my speech as I worked on it. That copy I had in the *sinus* of my toga and intended to read it over as I walked, but I sometimes get flashes of inspiration while I'm speaking, so I wanted to have a record of exactly what I said during the trial. Some of my friends would enjoy reading it. And being able to read my opponent's speech at my leisure would allow me to see what points in my own speech were vulnerable to attack.

"How many clients do you think Cornelius Tacitus will bring with him, my lord?" Phineas asked.

"He said he can muster fifteen or so." With Tacitus coming from his house on the other side of the Aventine Hill, I wouldn't know the size of his retinue until we met them in the Forum.

The curl of Phineas' lip told me what he thought of Tacitus' reinforcements. "Oh, that many?"

"Being Agricola's son-in-law," I said, "has put Tacitus in an awkward position, and he knows he shouldn't put pressure on his clients to appear with him in public. I'm sure they'll be vocal, though, whatever their number."

"Do you think it wise, my lord, to have someone so closely associated with Agricola supporting you so visibly?"

Phineas doesn't like Tacitus. I've known that for some time. But Tacitus and I are friends, and not in the sense of people to whom I've granted my formal *amicitia*. "Tacitus and I will stand by one another," I told the scribe, "no matter what anyone thinks of his father-in-law."

Of course, all that matters is what the *princeps* thinks of Agricola, and Domitian makes no secret of his jealousy and hatred of his most successful general.

I started down the hill toward the Forum. The largest men among my clients stepped in front of me to clear a path on the crowded sidewalks. After several days of rain the morning was clear and crisp, even a bit cool for the Kalends of October. As I took out the copy of my speech, for some reason an image came to my mind—Pompey, leaving the safety of his trireme, in the little boat taking him to shore, reading over the speech he intended to give before Ptolemy, the Egyptian boy-king, but murdered before he could set foot on shore.

"At least you'll be able to speak outside, sir," one of my clients said on my left. I was glad to be snapped out of my unhappy reverie.

"Yes. That will make everything more bearable." When the court has to meet inside, the basilica is divided into sections by heavy curtains. The air becomes oppressive and the only light is from torches and the clerestory windows. Speakers' voices are muted, so that we have to strain to get our points across.

I unrolled the small scroll containing my speech, but all I had on my mind right now was Aurora. Many men of my class would simply force themselves on a female slave. I could never do that. If I freed her, I still would not be able to take her as my wife. My mother would never speak to me again if I even suggested such a thing. She must suspect that I've thought about doing it, though. That's why she arranged a marriage for me, even though I am, at just past twenty-three, still somewhat young to marry. I suppose Aurora could become the sort of mistress or common-law wife that Monica was for my uncle, but, as independent-minded as she is—for which my mother says I'm to blame—I don't think she would accept that role, or that it would suit either one of us.

We had just come to the next corner when I heard a voice calling from my right, "Gaius Pliny! Gaius Pliny!" I didn't want to stop, but my clients must have assumed I did. I turned, peering through the crowd of men who surrounded me like the palisades of a fort, and saw Valerius Martial waving his hand and running toward us.

Martial holds a place on the periphery of my friends. Two years ago I gave him a piece of property, a small farm north of Rome, because he has a child by a woman who is a former slave of Marcus Aquilius Regulus. I am indebted to the woman and the animosity between my family and Regulus is deep-seated, so I was pleased to be able to assist them—her, really. Martial divides his time between the farm and his apartment here in the city. His poetry is all the rage among my circle, and he has flattered me in one of his poems. At times he does amuse me, but overall I find him abrasive. I would never trust him or work with him the way I do with Tacitus.

"Gaius Pliny! Thank you for stopping." He caught his breath. "I was afraid I would miss you." He held out a small green bag with the handle of a scroll protruding from the end. "For you. My latest collection."

"Thank you." I took the scroll from him. "I've got some more urgent reading right now"—I held up my speech—"but I will give this my full attention when I return home." I handed the scroll to Phineas, who put it in his writing box.

"You're on your way to court?"

I nodded. "The Centumviral Court. My future mother-in-law is prosecuting a man who stole some money from her late husband's estate."

"Future mother-in-law? I hadn't heard. Who is she?"

"Pompeia Celerina, widow of Livius Macrinus. My engagement to her daughter was announced three days ago."

"Congratulations. When is the wedding?"

"The date's not set, but it'll be after the Saturnalia." I was going to be adamant about that.

"How did this all come about?"

I didn't really have time for this small talk, but some things I couldn't say at home. "My mother and Pompeia are cousins. They've apparently been planning the marriage for some time, without bothering to inform me or ask my opinion in the matter."

"Well, congratulations or commiserations, whichever is appropriate."

"I'll let you know when I decide. In either case, thank you. You'll get an invitation to the wedding." I hadn't planned to invite him, but now it would be awkward not to. "Would you like to accompany us?"

Martial glanced up the hill. "I'm afraid I have another obligation this morning, and I'm late." He is among Regulus' clients, a fact which does not endear him to me.

"Regulus has already gone down to the Forum," I told him. "He went past my house a short while ago." Regulus' house is only a short distance from mine, higher up on the Esquiline. I don't have to spy on his movements because he always makes a great show when he passes my house—everything short of blowing trumpets and pounding drums.

"Oh. Then I guess I…need to go this way." Martial turned and started down the hill toward the Forum.

"Come for dinner tonight and read your book for us," I called after him.

"I'll plan on it. Thank you."

"My lord," Phineas said at my elbow, "we really are going to be late. Your future mother-in-law will be most displeased."

"And out a good bit of money if she has to forfeit her case because I'm not there." I glanced at the sun, now fully visible over the peak of the hill. "All right, we need to make up some time."

The usual route from my house to the Forum would be down the hill, past the Iseum, the temple of Isis, and turning right to go past the Ludus Magnus, the gladiators' training ground, and the Flavian Amphitheater. While not the most direct route, it is the safest. Looking down the hill this morning, though, I could see what looked like a crowd already forming on the street that ran past the Ludus Magnus.

"Are games being held today?" I asked.

Several of my clients nodded. I pay so little attention to the games and chariot races and other such shows that I wasn't aware any were scheduled. I knew my clients would rather be there.

"We'll never get through that crowd in time, sir," one of my clients said.

"Then we'll have to go through the Subura."

The clients who were closest to me gasped. "The Subura? That's awfully dangerous, sir."

"We're a large enough group," I assured them, "and it's daylight now. I think we'll be safe if we keep moving. Phineas comes down here every few days with your mother, don't you, Phineas? And you've even brought *my* mother on occasion." I was horrified when I first heard that my own mother had come down here with her slaves to attend some religious ritual.

"Yes, my lord," my scribe replied with his head down, "but we don't attract the kind of attention this group will."

"It can't be helped. I have to get to the Forum quickly. This is the shortest way. We just need to keep moving."

We took the street leading behind the Portico of Livia, dedicated by the deified Augustus to his wife, turned left onto the Clivus Suburbanus, and followed it until it ran into the broad street known as the Argiletum. The Argiletum cuts directly through the Subura, the lowest point in Rome in more ways than one. In the Subura the city's human dregs settle as inevitably as the lees at the bottom of an amphora of wine. Today, as we came down the hill toward it, the place had a particularly fetid smell from all the water that had collected there during the last few days' rain, washing the garbage from higher spots down with it.

We were making good time, but with each step I felt more doubts about my decision. Even though the Argiletum is broad, it is a channel that holds as many dangers as the strait Odysseus had passed through. We were now surrounded by no mythological Scylla and Charybdis waiting to snatch sailors off their vessels. Every man lurking in an alley looked like a thief or a cutthroat. The merchants shoving their shoddy wares under our noses were just more blatant about their thievery.

The prostitutes were the biggest distraction, though. With their breasts bared and their cheeks and nipples rouged, they leaned out the second-story windows of their *lupanar*, singing songs I'm sure no Siren ever dreamed of—or perhaps they were the very songs that lured ships onto the rocks. One raised her gown and thrust her hips toward us. A few of my clients looked like they were eager to be drawn in. Whores can be found all over Rome, but none as brazen as those in the Subura. Our progress slowed. I wished I could plug my clients' ears with wax.

One of them held up his money pouch and jingled it in the direction of a window full of women. It made a substantial noise because I had been especially generous to them this morning to insure their most enthusiastic support in court.

Phineas jerked the man's arm down. "Don't do that, you fool."

"Watch your tongue, lad! Your master hears you talking like that to a free man and a client of his, he'll take the whip to your scrawny back."

I grabbed the man by the shoulder of his tunic. "If you don't put that money away, you'll be no client of mine. You might as well wave raw meat in front of a wolf." I raised my voice to address all of my *clientela*. "Our destination is the Forum, not a brothel! Let's keep moving."

"Yes, sir," they groused, bumping into one another as they tried to walk with their necks craned upward.

"But after you've applauded my speech, you're free to go where you please."

"Thank you, sir!" They waved to the prostitutes, who waved back. One of the women gave a long, piercing whistle which seemed to echo or to be answered by someone up ahead.

As we rounded a bend in the street I could see some sort of obstacle in the next block. It looked like scaffolding had collapsed where some-one was working on a building. A large crowd had gathered between us and the scaffolding, but they faced us and not the heap of wood. Our way was completely blocked. I sensed, rather than saw, people filling in the road behind us.

"We can turn left here, my lord," Phineas said, glancing to each side, "and make our way around it."

I was reluctant to leave the Argiletum. Once off the main road, I was afraid we would find ourselves in a labyrinth with a Minotaur at every turn.

"How well do you know this area?" I asked Phineas.

"This is where my synagogue is, my lord. We go down this street for a block, make a couple of turns that I can show you, and we'll be back on our way."

By now we had no choice. The crowds in front of and behind us were growing larger with each moment we hesitated. My clients were already outnumbered. Turning around was out of the question. My case would be called at the Basilica Julia in less than an hour, by my best estimate. Phineas did come down here regularly. I had to trust him.

I touched the Tyche ring in my toga's *sinus*. "All right, let's go. Every-one stay together and keep moving!"

The street onto which we turned was narrower, but there were no obstacles between us and the next corner. We reached it and turned onto a block entirely taken up on one side by a two-story building with what looked like one large commercial area on the ground floor—it had only one door—and apartments above it. Several men with beards sat in the doorway, one reading from a scroll as the others listened. There was something odd about the picture, but it took me a moment to realize that the reader was unrolling the scroll from the back. He looked up at us and I thought I caught an exchange of glances of rec-ognition between him and Phineas.

"Do you know him?" I asked Phineas.

"Yes, my lord. This is my synagogue. He's the rabbi, our teacher and leader."

Before Phineas could say any more, one of my clients cried out in pain. I turned to see him crumble to the ground, struck in the head by a roof tile. Another quickly followed him. Pieces of tile and brick rained down on us from the roof of the building across the street. We instinctively pulled our togas over our heads and crouched down. Bystanders scurried for cover. The bearded Jews gathered up their scrolls, in no particular hurry. They must have known the attack posed no danger to them.

Phineas broke through my wall of retainers. I thought he was going to try to save himself, but he shouted something I couldn't understand to the man who'd been reading the scroll. The man nodded and opened the door behind him.

"Hurry, my lord!" Phineas shouted. "Get everyone inside."

We picked up our wounded and scrambled to enter the synagogue as the gang of Subura thugs rushed up the street toward us. Two of the bearded men closed the heavy doors and barred them. I suddenly knew what Odysseus must have felt like when the Cyclops rolled the stone over the entrance to his cave. Would we ever get out of here alive?

II

THE SYNAGOGUE ECHOED with the angry pounding of fists on the doors.

"My clients and I are in your debt, sir," I said to the man Phineas had identified as the rabbi. He had deep-set eyes in a long, mournful face. I wondered if he would have opened the door without Phineas' intervention, but some questions are best left unasked. The man looked at me without comprehension until Phineas translated my Latin gratitude into something he could understand.

"You welcome stay until danger pass," he replied in choppy, heavily accented Greek.

I shifted to that language and spoke more slowly. "I hope we don't defile your holy place." My comment was sincere but ironic. This place didn't look any holier from the inside than it did from the street, but gods don't like to have their territory invaded by people they don't recognize. Or so I'm told. On the far wall one small section was enclosed by a railing and something in a niche behind it was covered. I might have suspected it was a cult image, but I know that Jews don't make images of their god.

Aside from that niche I had the feeling I was in a lecture hall, the sort of place one could rent for a literary reading. It had benches arranged in rows, with an aisle down the center, and a speaker's platform. Only this one was much plainer than most such places, the walls decorated only with geometric patterns in subdued colors.

I surveyed the injuries among my clients as they huddled together as far from the door as they could get. One man had a severe gash on his head. Two others had less serious cuts. I found the man with the cleanest tunic in the crowd and told him to tear some strips off it and bandage the wounds. "Your toga will cover the damage and I'll replace the tunic when we get out of here."

"Wait." The bearded man who had let us in said something to Phineas, who translated. "He's sent someone upstairs to get supplies to treat the injured."

"Thank you," I said. "I am Gaius Pliny. Phineas said you are a... rabbi?"

His face gave me the impression I was talking too fast for him. "Yes. Teacher of our laws. My name is Malachi."

"Is this a temple?" I asked.

"It's not a temple, my lord," Phineas said. "For us Jews there is—or was—only one temple. We meet here to encourage one another and to keep our knowledge of our holy books alive."

"So this rabbi is your priest?"

"Not exactly, my lord."

"How can one be 'not exactly' a priest?"

"Our priesthood was tied to the Temple." Phineas struck me as impertinent, but in this place, I realized, he didn't think of himself as a slave. And his Greek was better than Malachi's. "A rabbi helps us to observe our laws, but this is not a holy place in the sense that the Temple was. Your presence poses no problem for us."

"That is true," Malachi said. "On all our sabbaths we have in here *goyim.*"

"'*Goyim*'?" My tongue could hardly shape the ungainly word.

"That's what we call non-Jews in Hebrew," Phineas said. "It's like the Greeks calling non-Greeks barbarians."

I knew I needed to get out of here quickly, but the pounding on the door told me I would not be going out that way any time soon. As long as we were safe and as long as I was losing Pompeia's case *in absentia*, I might as well take advantage of this opportunity to try to understand my mother's interest in these people and this place. Malachi seemed to be the only one of the men who was willing to talk with me. The others who had been listening to him read appeared to have duties to attend to. One crossed the building and came back to whisper something in Phineas' ear.

"Why do non-Jews come here?" I asked.

"Many Greeks, many Romans, they like our way to live," Malachi said, looking to Phineas to expand on what he said.

"We call them 'God-fearers,'" Phineas explained. "Like your mother, my lord."

Malachi's face brightened as he made a connection. "You are son of lady Plinia? Of course. She is wonderful woman, most generous. She gave us this Menorah." He pointed to a large, multi-branched candlestick like the small one Mother had given Naomi as a Saturnalia gift.

My mother has her own money, inherited from her husband and her brother. She does not have to account to me for how she spends it, but I planned to have a conversation on this subject when I returned home.

"Is there any way out of here, other than through that door?" I asked Malachi.

I must have been talking too fast for his limited comprehension of Greek. When he squinted in confusion, Phineas stepped in with the answer.

"There is a back way." He pointed to the opposite side of the building. "But they've got someone watching it, too. They're trying to keep themselves hidden, but Barak spotted them."

"Then we need a distraction that will draw everyone to this door. Money is what they're after, so we'll give it to them." I went over to where my clients were huddled—as afraid of the strangeness of the place, I suspected, as of the mob outside.

"Give me your money." Their apprehensive looks almost made me laugh. I must have sounded like one of the thieves outside. I waved my hands at them impatiently. "Give it to me. I'll reimburse you when we get home. And this is the only way we're going to get home."

A patron is supposed to protect his clients. My decision to walk through the Subura had undermined their confidence in me. I had led them straight into an ambush and several were injured. I could see on their faces that they were unsure whether they owed me any further loyalty, but they grudgingly complied with my demand. When I had half a dozen money pouches, I picked the smallest of my clients, Marcus Fulvius. He wouldn't be of any use in a fight in the streets, but he might be able to help me avert one. "Come with me."

We walked over to Malachi and Phineas.

"My lord, what—" the scribe started to ask.

"You said you can get to the second floor of this building?"

"Yes, we can, but—"

"This is Fulvius. He's going to throw money out of a window on this side of the building—a few coins at a time. While the mob is fighting over them, we're going to make our escape out the back."

My client's eyes grew big. "But, sir, what will happen to me?"

"After things settle down I'm sure Malachi can provide an escort for you, at least to a safe spot out of the Subura." Phineas translated all of that for the priest, who nodded. "And," I added, "I'll make sure you get an extra donative tomorrow—quite a large one."

Fulvius' expression told me he wasn't sure he would live long enough to receive the money, no matter the amount. But I knew he was a heavy gambler, and gamblers can be bought more easily than most men. I hoped the odds didn't seem prohibitive to him.

I put a hand on his shoulder. "The crowd is just trying to frighten us. They don't want blood. They want money. Once they've got it, they'll go away." At least that was my plan for them.

Fulvius took the money bags and I clapped him on the back.

"Good man. Remember, only a few coins at a time. Make them last as long as you can. Throw them toward the north end of the building."

Malachi picked Barak to take Fulvius to the upper floor.

"All right," I told my other clients, "we are going to move toward the back door and be ready to leave on a moment's notice."

Because of the slope of the ground the back door of the building, on the south end, was on a lower level than the floor we were on. We grouped ourselves at the stairs leading down to the door and listened intently. From the excitement of the crowd at the front door we could tell when the money started raining from the sky. Caligula used to stand on the balcony of his house, Tacitus tells me, and throw gold coins to the crowd in the street below him. Although it looked like an act of generosity, he just enjoyed watching people trample one another in the fight for the coins. It sounded like our money was having a similar effect. A shout went up from the street and we could hear people running away from the door. A few voices were raised outside the back door and then they, too, faded away.

Phineas opened the back door and looked in both directions. He waved for us to go.

"Stay together," I said. "It's our only hope. Walk fast but don't run."

I managed to keep the group together for the first block. We heard nothing behind us. Then someone shouted from a window above us, in a language I didn't recognize. The sound scattered my clients like a flock of birds startled by the snap of a dry stick. I grabbed the two men closest to me and, with the promise of a reward, made them stay with me. Phineas, of course, remained steadfast. Him and his mother, Naomi, I count among my most trustworthy servants.

The shout from the window, it turned out, was a warning from a woman about to empty her family's chamber pots. She must have had one in each hand because the first load hit me and the second one simultaneously hit the man on my left. Phineas and my other client were splattered as well. By the time I could look up she was gone.

"You'll be richly rewarded tomorrow," was all I could promise. "And I'll buy you each a new toga and tunic." *And Martial will probably write a poem about this*, I thought.

Martial would certainly know about it. All of Rome would hear about it because I had to go to the Basilica Julia in this condition. There was no time to go home and clean myself up.

†

My pitiful entourage had no trouble clearing a path the rest of the way into the Forum. No one wanted to stand in our way. We entered through the open space between the Forum of Vespasian and that of Augustus. Domitian has announced plans for yet another forum to fill that space. The Cloaca Maxima, Rome's largest sewer, runs directly under it. We looked and smelled like we had been for a swim in the cloaca. People stepped away from us, gagging and laughing at the same time.

Tacitus must have been looking for me. He saw us as soon as we entered the Forum and got as close as he dared. "Please forgive me, Gaius Pliny, if I don't greet you as a friend should."

I held my arms out as though I would embrace him. He stepped back in horror.

"Don't worry," I said. "I wouldn't touch my worst enemy right now."

"Speaking of Regulus, he's in the basilica."

"I wonder which case he's involved in. But first I have to put things right with Pompeia."

My prospective mother-in-law was waiting for me on the steps of the basilica. Her eyes widened and she put her hand over her mouth as I drew near. "Gaius Pliny! By the gods. What happened?"

Her question must have been rhetorical. What I had experienced was not a unique event. Most people in Rome have had it happen to them or knew someone who had. "I'm sorry, Pompeia. Let me see if the court will give me a few minutes—"

"The court is already hearing the next case," she said sharply.

"Without a decision in your case?"

"Unfortunately not. My spokesman wasn't here, so I forfeited my case. Your friend Cornelius Tacitus offered to step in, but I knew he was not familiar enough with the details and I did not wish to have an enemy of Domitian speaking on my behalf. I have lost the chance to recover a great deal of money this morning."

The first thought in my mind was that she might decide to cancel the engagement, but I knew my mother would be determined to keep the arrangement in place. I would probably have to make up Pompeia's loss from my own funds to placate both women.

"As you can see, dear lady, my absence was not voluntary or intentional." I flapped my toga in her direction to give her a good whiff. "Let me go in and talk to someone."

With Tacitus alongside me I trotted up the steps to the central entrance of the basilica, stepping over the idlers who were playing games on the "boards" scratched into the steps. A case was being heard outdoors to my right. To judge from the applause I was hearing, the speaker had brought an impressive group of clients. Inside another case was in progress. When the building isn't divided by curtains, a speaker whose voice makes the chamber resonate can draw an audience on the main floor and in the balconies that run around the second floor.

The man holding forth was Marcus Aper, one of the foremost jurists of our day, a man under whom Tacitus had studied. He seldom appears in court now because of his age. I couldn't help but look and listen as I hurried across the vast floor of the basilica. Everything Tacitus had told me about him was true—the power and sweep of his voice, his economical but effective gestures.

"He's a majestic figure," I said.

"I'll bet he wins this case," Tacitus replied. "I'd vote for him and I don't even know what it's about."

The Centumviral Court, in spite of its name, is made up of 180 members, who divide into four panels to hear cases that are mostly financial in nature. Disputed inheritances are a common topic here. The entire court is presided over by a praetor, and that was the man I was looking for now. "Who is the praetor?" I asked Tacitus. This was the first time I had appeared in this court this year.

"It's Larcius Macedo. He's over there." Tacitus pointed me in the right direction and the crowd began to divide in front of me like water yielding to the prow of a boat.

"Can you tell what sort of mood he's in today?" I asked Tacitus quietly.

"More arrogant than cruel, I think."

I nodded. Those two words described Macedo most of the time. His father was a former slave who had made a fortune after his manumission. Some say Macedo doesn't remember his servile origins, but I think he's too aware of them. Even though he holds one of the highest offices in Rome and will enter the Senate as an ex-praetor in a few months, he is entirely untrustworthy among his social equals and brutal in his treatment of his slaves. He considers his female slaves his harem and even boasts about the herd of bastard children he's siring on them.

"I shudder to think that I have to plead for leniency from this man," I said.

"And you get to do it in a shit-stained toga." Tacitus couldn't help but chuckle. "Sorry, I know this is serious, but...."

Macedo, a tall man with broad shoulders, had his back to us, talking to someone we couldn't see until we were right up on them. Then Regulus looked around Macedo and said, "Why, there he is. Gaius Pliny, we were just talking about you."

If Regulus was talking about me, it could not mean anything good. Martial and several of Regulus' other clients clustered behind him. Martial tried not to meet my eyes.

"Good morning, Marcus Regulus. Forgive me for interrupting your conversation. I need to talk to Larcius Macedo."

Macedo had been looking at me over his shoulder. Now he turned around to face me. "That was quite a downpour you got caught in."

"My clients and I were attacked on our way here."

"By a mob wielding chamber pots?"

"I wanted to be certain I was on time, so we came through the Subura."

Macedo's face seemed fixed in a sneer. "You took that big a risk and you were still late."

"Yes, and I want to ask if the case can be rescheduled. My delay in getting here was unintentional, as you can see—"

"And smell." Behind Macedo, Regulus laughed.

"I don't think Pompeia Celerina should be penalized because of circumstances beyond her control, or mine."

"You're wasting your breath, Gaius Pliny."

"But—"

"Marcus Regulus here has already graciously asked that the hearing be rescheduled."

"Regulus asked? What does he have to do with it?"

"He's defending the fellow you're prosecuting. We're going to put it off until the middle of this month. The Ides will be given over to the rites of the October Horse. Let's hear the case the day after that. Is that agreeable to you?"

My mouth moved a couple of times before words came out. "Why, yes. Of course."

"Regulus explained to me that you are prosecuting on behalf of your future mother-in-law. He did not want you to start your marriage on such an inauspicious note. You are in his debt," Macedo said as he waved to someone and began to walk away. "I hope you realize that. *Deeply* in his debt."

I stood before Regulus in utter humiliation. "You're defending in this case? Why?"

"Because you're prosecuting."

"But your client had already won the case. Why did you ask for the postponement?"

He leaned close to me, in spite of the smell. He kept a smile on his face, but his voice dropped to a low snarl that only Tacitus and I could hear. "But I had not *beaten* you, you insolent pup. You beat me when you pled your first case. No one has let me forget it. This is my chance to even that score. I'm not going to let people say the only way I can win against you is by default."

Regulus had hated my uncle, and that enmity had become part of my inheritance. If he was doing this just to settle a score or avenge his honor, I didn't see how I could be in his debt. I drew my shoulders back with a bit more confidence. "So you managed to persuade your client to forgo victory in the case, however obtained, in order to satisfy your hatred of me? What if you lose? The evidence against your client is substantial. We're demanding a stiff fine on top of the restitution."

Regulus waved his hand. I wasn't sure if he was dismissing me or trying to get rid of the smell emanating from my clothes. "Evidence be damned. I'm *not* going to lose." He gathered up his toga and turned away.

†

Tacitus dismissed his clients and I sent my two remaining ones home as well. That left us with a retinue of three of Tacitus' slaves and Phineas. I apologized again to Pompeia Celerina and assured her that I was confident we would win the case when it came to trial. I must have looked to her like Odysseus in his beggar's rags claiming that he could string the bow. Through the scented cloth she held over her nose and mouth she accepted my apologies but did not offer to embrace me. Her litter-bearers and her clients started her on her way home.

"Now I must get home as soon as possible and get cleaned up," I said. "This is disgusting."

"You act like you're the first person it's ever happened to," Tacitus said. "I know it's not even the first time it's happened to you."

"You don't get used to this, no matter how many times it happens." I touched the Tyche ring in my *sinus*. The events of the morning seemed to make a mockery of the whole idea of the thing bringing me any good fortune. And yet, the case had been postponed. I had made a bad decision when I led my clients into the Subura, but we had escaped, almost unscathed, and I hadn't lost Pompeia's case. Was it my good fortune today that Regulus hated me enough to let go of an assured victory just to have a chance to humiliate me?

Opting not to return through the Subura, we were cutting through the crowd with ease and passing the Ludus Magnus when Phineas said, "My lord, I believe that's Demetrius approaching us."

I looked where he was pointing and saw my steward, accompanied by a man I didn't know. Phineas waved to attract Demetrius' attention and we gathered off to one side of the street.

"My lord, what happened?" Demetrius asked.

Tacitus made a motion of someone turning a pot over to empty it.

"Isn't it obvious?" I snapped. "What do you want?"

Demetrius brought the stranger forward. "This man, my lord, is Thamyras, a messenger from the lady Manilia Aurelia. He arrived just a short while ago."

"Arrived? From Naples?"

"Yes, my lord," Thamyras said.

"Are they well?" I had met Aurelia in Smyrna. At the time she was a slave, but I helped her learn her true identity and take her place with her family. I had not seen her since her wedding a year ago. Her husband's sister was a friend of my mother. Though they had property in Rome, Aurelia and her husband preferred to stay at their house south of Naples. They were overseeing the restoration of their estate after the destruction wrought by Mount Vesuvius. Even after five years, there was still much work to do.

"No, my lord, they aren't. They sent me to ask your help."

"Help? With what?"

"The noble Calpurnius has been accused of murder, my lord."

III

CALPURNIUS? ACCUSED of murder? That's preposterous."
I didn't know Aurelia's husband well, but I knew he was rich
enough not to have to kill anyone for money and—even though he
was almost twenty years her senior—too smitten with Aurelia to be
involved in any sort of affair.

"My lady asked me to give you this, my lord." Thamyras held out
a tablet sealed with a signet featuring a ram's horn, which Aurelia had
inherited from her father. As we walked along I broke the seal and read
quietly so that no one but Tacitus could hear me.

Manilia Aurelia to her friend Gaius Pliny, greetings.

*I hope you are well. I am in dire need of your assistance. My dear
husband has been accused of killing one of our freedwomen. He
will not defend himself. He won't even tell me what happened.
The servant who brings you this note will tell you the details. I
cannot bear to write them. You have done so much for me in the
past that I hate to ask for your help again, but I don't know where
else to turn. Everyone is convinced he's guilty, but I swear to you
that my husband could not have done such a horrible thing.*

Given two days before the Kalends of October.

I looked up at Thamyras, really seeing him for the first time. He was
a man of about forty, thin and with a tanned, weathered complexion
that suggested he worked mostly outside. Although he had an honest

face, with eyes that did not turn away from mine, the fact that he hadn't been shaved in a couple of days made him look disreputable. He wrinkled his nose as the stench from my drenching wafted over him.

"She says you will provide the details."

"Yes, my lord."

I saw Phineas take out his stylus and a wax tablet. Making notes while we were walking would be tricky, but I was glad he'd thought of it without my having to call attention to it. I could wait until we got home to begin questioning the man, but I sensed urgency. My uncle used to criticize me because I liked to walk rather than be carried in a litter. He would have a scribe in the litter with him, reading or taking notes, to make use of time spent in travel. With Phineas' writing box, I could emulate my uncle and still walk.

"Well then, what details do you know?" I asked Thamyras.

"I'm the one who found Calpurnius standing over the woman's body, my lord."

"When was this?"

"Two days ago, my lord. Early in the morning."

So, Aurelia had written the note and dispatched Thamyras immediately after the body was found. He had made good time getting here. "Did you see him kill her?"

"No, my lord. No one did."

That much was encouraging. "Where did you find him?"

"In the orchard beside our house, my lord."

"And he was just standing over the woman?"

"Yes, my lord. Standing over her, looking down at her."

We turned and started up the Esquiline Hill. It was hard to hear over the noise of the crowd around us, but I didn't want Thamyras to have to stand too close to me.

"How would you describe the expression on his face?" Tacitus asked.

"He looked very…puzzled, my lord."

"What did he say when he saw you?"

"He told me to get some help, my lord."

Something a man might say if he was concerned about what he thought was an injured person…or something a killer might say to get rid of a witness. "Did you see any injuries on the woman?" I asked.

"I saw blood on her chest, my lord." He touched a spot that would have been just above a woman's left breast.

"Was the woman clothed?" Tacitus asked.

"Yes, my lord, but her gown was bunched up. You could see quite a bit of her legs." He touched his own leg high on the thigh.

That might suggest she had been coupling with a man, whether willingly or not. "You say there was blood on her chest?" I asked. "Did you see blood anywhere else?"

"No, my lord."

"Who examined her?"

"The freedman who cares for our sicknesses, my lord."

"And what was his conclusion?"

"She'd been stabbed, my lord."

"How many times?"

"Only once, my lord."

That made me pause. To kill a person with only one thrust of a blade, someone had to know what he was doing. Someone attacking in anger or fear would likely inflict multiple wounds. "Did anyone see a knife?"

"Yes, my lord. Calpurnius was holding it."

"A knife with blood on it?" Tacitus asked.

"Yes, my lord."

That made me stop for a moment in the shadow of the temple of Isis. Even the greenest prosecutor could convict a man found standing over a dead woman with what was probably the murder weapon in his hand. When we resumed walking, I asked, "Where is the woman's body now?"

"When I left, my lord, the lady Aurelia was trying to think of a place to put her until you could get there. She said you could tell what happened to her if you could examine the body."

I looked at Tacitus and could see he knew what I was thinking. The woman had already been dead for two days and it would be at least a couple of more days before I could get down there. I wasn't sure how much I would be able to learn from a body that had been decaying for that long. And she would be moved, so anything I might have gathered from the spot where she was found was already lost. I muttered an oath.

"The lady Aurelia says the woman was a freedwoman. Would Calpurnius have had any reason to kill her?" A reason such as a love affair that had turned sour.

"No, my lord!" Thamyras seemed appalled that I would even ask such a thing. "She worked in the kitchen. She'd been in my lady Aurelia's household for years."

"All right. Can you tell me anything else? Any little detail you might have forgotten?" I knew I would interrogate him again to see if his story was consistent, but I asked the question anyway.

"No, my lord. I've told you all I know."

"Where is Calpurnius now?"

"He's being held at the *vigiles'* headquarters in Naples, my lord. He won't say anything, won't even deny killing her. The lady Aurelia is nearly hysterical. We're afraid it may have some effect on her unborn child."

"She's carrying a child?" That was news to me.

"Yes, my lord. Her nurse says she could give birth at any time now."

†

When we arrived at my house, I sent Thamyras to the kitchen to get something to eat and gave orders for water to be heated and brought to the bath. "Make it practically boiling," I told the servant. I didn't think the water already in the bath would be hot enough to make me feel clean again.

Tacitus sat on a bench beside the soaking pool as I dropped my stinking clothes and kicked them as far away from me as possible. I wrapped a towel around me as a loincloth.

"You didn't really get much on yourself," Tacitus said, "except in your hair. Most of it ended up on your clothes."

As much as I hated to think of it, those clothes—with the stripe sewn by Aurora and worn only once—would have to be burned or cut up into cleaning rags. No matter how much they were washed, I couldn't imagine myself wearing them again. Before I got into the pool I used a sponge to scrub myself with water from a basin brought by one of my servants.

"How can I possibly help Aurelia?" I asked Tacitus as I worked on my arms, forcing myself to endure the scalding. "I don't know if there's a body to examine, and the place where she was found has most likely been trampled over and cleaned up by now."

"You can't even be sure that's the spot where she was killed."

I looked at Tacitus with a raised eyebrow.

"Don't look so surprised," he said. "I've learned something from you by now. Things are not always what they at first appear. And I've learned something *about* you. I know you will go down there and give Aurelia whatever help you can, no matter how hopeless the situation seems right now."

"'Hopeless' is the right word. If Calpurnius was found standing over a murdered woman with a bloody knife in his hand, you don't have to be Regulus to make him appear guilty."

"It's possible that he *is* guilty, isn't it?" Tacitus slipped off his sandals and sat on the edge of the bath, with his feet dangling in the water. "Maybe that's why he won't defend himself."

"Anything's possible, of course. Ow! Ow!" I poured water over my head and shuddered at the color of it as it ran onto the floor. Without breaking off the conversation, I put the sponge to work. "But Aurelia's grandfather chose Calpurnius as her husband, and you know how protective he is of her, since she's his only living descendant. I'm sure he knows Calpurnius better than Calpurnius knows himself."

"You were surprised, though, at his choice. You told me so at the time."

"Yes, I know. I thought Manilius might have chosen someone from a more distinguished family. That branch of the Calpurnii haven't held an office in my lifetime. They retired from public life when Nero was *princeps*. There was some sort of accusation against the elder Calpurnius, I believe, but nothing came of it."

"Your uncle retired from public life at that time."

"True, but he resumed his career when Vespasian took power and it was safe for decent men to be active again. Calpurnius and his family have continued to live apart from society."

"Is that such a bad thing?" Tacitus asked.

"No, of course not. I'm sure Aurelia's grandfather was satisfied with the younger Calpurnius' character. My mother counts his sister among her friends. They are respectable people."

Tacitus shook his head slowly. "The passing of time can change a man, or bring out a nature he's been hiding all along."

I was ready to discard my towel, but I'm never comfortable being nude in Tacitus' presence because of his indifference to the gender of his sexual partners. He has never expressed that sort of interest in me, and yet the thought occurs to me in a situation like this.

"Should I turn my back?" he said. "Or close my eyes?"

Embarrassed that he could read my thoughts, I dropped my towel, stepped into the pool and soaked my head for a moment. When I surfaced I said, "I simply can't make any assessment of Calpurnius' character until I get down there and talk to him."

"Are you ready to go back there? I thought you still dreaded the area around Vesuvius."

"I do, and I wouldn't go back if I had any choice."

Tacitus focused his gaze on his feet in the water. "If you don't go down there, how do you keep up with your estate at Misenum?"

"I get regular reports from my steward there. I keep a minimal staff, just for friends who may need a place to stay when they're in the area."

"Who is your steward?"

"I put Damon in that post."

"Damon? After all you learned about him in Smyrna?"

I shook water out of my hair. "In spite of that, I've learned that he is absolutely trustworthy."

It had been four years since I'd been back to the Bay of Naples. After Vesuvius destroyed Pompeii and several other towns along the eastern end of the bay I had stayed at the villa at Misenum where we were living at the time. It had been damaged by the earthquakes that accompanied the eruption. My mother was so terrified of the place that she demanded we leave immediately. I could understand her fear. Her brother died in the eruption and she and I barely survived. I sent her up the coast to our house at Laurentum while I oversaw the repairs to the villa and tried to understand what it meant to be my uncle's heir and adoptive son. I had not wanted to rush back to Rome until I understood my own position better. Once I'd left the bay, I did not want to return.

"There's a time problem, too," Tacitus reminded me. "Pompeia's case was postponed, but not for long. You have to get to Naples, do whatever you can for Aurelia, and get back in ten days or so."

I got out of the pool, picked up a clean towel, and gave myself an invigorating rub. One of my servants was ready with a fresh tunic. "I know that's a problem. Travel alone will take a couple of days in each direction, even with the fastest horses I can find. But I won't ask for another postponement. I won't give Regulus that satisfaction."

"We can get there faster if we go by ship."

"'We'?"

"Of course. If nothing else, I want to see what Vesuvius did."

My shoulders slumped. "Do we really have to go by ship?"

"If we can find one leaving Ostia tomorrow morning, we can be in Naples by sundown." The prospect—of a voyage or of my discomfort—seemed to make Tacitus quite happy.

"Really? That fast?"

"With the wind behind us. Even if the wind's not favorable, we'll make it by the middle of the next day at the latest. And it's so much less tiring than going by horse or carriage."

Tacitus knows how much I hate being in boats. I have a scar on my head from the last time I was in one. It throbs occasionally to remind me of my aversion to things nautical. "That will mean going down to Ostia this afternoon and staying in an inn so we can be ready to leave at dawn."

"Do you know anyone in Ostia that we could stay with?"

I shook my head.

"Nor do I, unfortunately. Well, it'll be for only one night."

"I'll send a couple of servants down there to find us rooms and to see if there's a ship sailing for Naples tomorrow."

The servant who brought me the clean tunic began to gather up my soiled clothing. Suddenly I remembered the Tyche ring.

"Wait," I told the servant. "Shake the toga." I thought that would relieve me of the necessity of touching the filthy garments again.

He shook it, but the ring didn't fall out.

"What are you looking for?" Tacitus asked.

"A…a personal item. I suspect it's hung up on something." The ring is large and the image of Tyche is raised, with a couple of rough spots on it, so it could easily have gotten caught in the cloth. As much as I hated to touch the garments, I had to find the ring. So much for being cleaned up. I took one end of the toga and told my servant to move back and straighten the material out.

"There's something," Tacitus said, pointing to an object.

"That has to be it." We put the toga down and, without touching anything else, I managed to lean over and reach the ring, which was caught in the cloth. I untangled it and rinsed it off in the pool.

"What have you got?" Tacitus, with his feet still in the pool, reached for the ring, but I wouldn't let him touch it.

"It's a ring. A talisman, I guess you'd say. Something…precious." I put it on the little finger of my left hand, the only finger it will fit on.

"Now that's something I didn't know about you. You believe in magic charms? That wouldn't happen to be the ring of Gyges, would it? The one that Plato talks about?"

"No, it doesn't make me invisible." I twisted the ring around, as Plato says Gyges did to render himself invisible.

Tacitus gasped and looked around, waving his hands like a man trying to find something in the dark. "Gaius Pliny! Where are you?"

I laughed in spite of myself. "I wish it would make me invisible, so I could walk out of here without having to tell my mother we're going to Naples."

"Why would she object? You're helping a friend, and the brother of a friend of hers. It's what we're expected to do."

"She's planning all sorts of things for the rest of the month to announce my engagement."

Tacitus got up from his seat on the edge of the pool and a servant dried his feet. "I know you said 'engagement,' but it sounded like you meant 'execution.'" He stepped into his sandals. "Marriage isn't the end of the world, my friend."

"Oh, and this comes from the man who, just a few months ago, was quoting Hipponax: 'A woman makes a man happy on two days— when he marries her and when he buries her.'"

"My wife was having a particularly difficult day. Oh, wait!" Tacitus clapped his hands in glee. "By the gods! You're in love with somebody."

I felt myself getting warm. "No, I'm not."

"Yes, you are. Is it—"

I held up my hand to silence him and turned to my dilatory servant. "I believe you have some clothes to burn."

"Yes, my lord. At once." He bundled up my stained toga and tunic and hustled toward the door of the bath.

I drew Tacitus into a corner, under a mosaic of Diana and her nymphs bathing, with Actaeon's face barely showing in the brush behind them. It's hard to have a private conversation in a bath when every sound bounces around as though you're talking in a cave. The presence of a pool of water doesn't help.

"It's Aurora, isn't it?" Tacitus said in a whisper. "You're in love with your slave."

"No... Yes... I don't know." I twisted the Tyche ring. "All I do know is that I don't want to marry this girl my mother has chosen." For the life of me, I couldn't remember her name at that moment.

"You're eventually going to marry." Tacitus put a hand on my shoulder, the way a man encourages a wavering comrade as they're about to go into battle, knowing that one of them might not return.

"My uncle never married."

"There are exceptions to almost every rule. He had you to carry on the family name. You have no siblings and thus no nephews. If you don't want your family to die out, you have to marry someone. And it's not likely to be one of your servants."

"I realize that. Right now I'm not ready to marry anyone. And my mother has nothing but a wedding on her mind."

"Then going to Naples can be your escape."

"Nothing will change by the time I get back."

Tacitus slapped me on the back. "Who knows? The whole world could change by then. You saw the eruption of Vesuvius. On the day before it happened, did anybody suspect anything?"

"No, of course not."

"I'm sure at least one poor bugger down there was dreading something he'd have to do in a day or two. But he didn't."

I threw up my hands. "I don't want to *die* just to get out of marrying."

"That's not my point. All I'm saying is that you never know what's going to happen tomorrow, so why worry about it? The lady Aurelia needs your help. That's all you need to know right now. Let's go talk to your mother."

"That can be a daunting prospect," I said.

"My friend, you have a pair of balls. I've just seen them. That suggests that you're a man. Now act like one."

IV

WE FOUND MY MOTHER in the garden, selecting herbs and discussing a menu with our cook. As forthrightly as I could, I explained to her what I was going to do and reminded her of her friendship with Calpurnius' sister, Calpurnia Hispulla.

"Naples?" She screwed up her face. "But, Gaius, I'm planning a dinner with Pompeia Celerina and Livia."

"Livia?"

"Your betrothed," she said through clenched teeth. "The dinner is to introduce them to our friends. It's tomorrow night."

"And you invited Martial to read tonight," Tacitus reminded me.

Mother groaned. "Why did you invite that dreadful man to dinner?"

"He amuses me," I said. "Just feed him and send him on his way."

"I don't want to insult him. He might write something salacious about us."

"Mother, you can't insult Martial. Stick him in a corner somewhere. That's what I was going to do."

She straightened her shoulders into what I call her legionary stance. "Gaius, I think you must be here tomorrow night."

"My friends already know me, so it won't matter if I'm not here." I rubbed the Tyche ring, disappointed that it could not, in fact, make me invisible.

"But everyone needs to see you with Livia, to let them know this engagement has been settled and the marriage *will* happen."

I couldn't look at my mother while I struggled with myself. *Aurora knows the marriage is going to happen,* I wanted to say. *You don't have to keep waving it in front of her like some trophy you've taken from a fallen enemy.*

"Aren't you satisfied with this arrangement?" Mother asked.

I turned toward my room. "I have to go to Naples, Mother, to help your friend's brother." It wouldn't hurt to reinforce that point.

She started to follow me. "What about Pompeia's case? Aren't you going to defend her?"

"I'll be back by the Ides, regardless of how things stand in Naples. I promise you that," I said over my shoulder. "I wouldn't want to miss the October Horse." I had no intention of watching one of the most inane, barbaric rituals we Romans practice. No one even knows what it means, if it ever meant anything.

I dispatched three servants to Ostia to find us rooms and to see if any ships would be sailing for Naples the next morning. Tacitus sent his servants to his house to get him packed for the trip. He oversaw the packing of our provisions while Aurora helped me get ready. I found it particularly difficult to talk to her.

"It's very noble of you to go to all this trouble to assist the lady Aurelia," she said breaking the silence as she folded several tunics and placed them in my bag. "Especially after everything you've already done for her."

Most people would say I had no obligation to help Aurelia any more than I already had. Her husband might very well be guilty of murdering the freedwoman. With only a badly decayed body to examine and with the spot where she was found trampled by any number of people by now, I had little hope of determining what had happened. But I felt an obligation to try.

†

We hired horses and a cart and took the Via Ostiensis down to the port. Thamyras came with us to direct us when we landed because he knew where Calpurnius' villa was. Our progress was slow, since the road was as heavily traveled as any street in Rome. About the tenth hour of the day we met my servants in the forum in Ostia, as we had arranged to do. They showed us to the inn where they had found rooms.

"These will be…serviceable," Tacitus said.

"They've got four walls, a door, and a bed," I said. "For tonight that's all we need." I would have liked beds that smelled a little cleaner and plaster that wasn't so cracked, but I wasn't going to upbraid my servants in front of Tacitus.

We left an order for our evening meal and headed down to the docks. The innkeeper had told us several ships were tied up there, notably a trireme from Misenum, the *Jupiter*. "Quite a sight to see, that is."

"Too bad we can't book passage on it," Tacitus said. "With sails *and* oars, we'd make Misenum by late afternoon. We could stay at your villa there."

"But I know that ship," I said. "That was the name of the ship my uncle took when he went to rescue people during the eruption."

Our inn was only three blocks from the harbor, which, in the late afternoon, was bustling with activity. Some ships were being loaded and prepared for their departure the next morning while the crews of others, just arriving, hurried to get their cargo unloaded before dark. A crowd had gathered to watch one transport ship unload animals bound for the amphitheater in Rome. My uncle had described many of them—lions, giraffes, apes—in his *Natural History*, but, recalling some of his descriptions, I don't think he had ever observed the animals themselves.

"This is something you don't see every day," Tacitus said, craning to look over the woman in front of him.

While the crowd oohed and ahhed as each cage was set on the dock, the sight of the magnificent beasts, lethargic from a long voyage or frightened by the noise engulfing them, filled me with a sense of pity. "They'll all be dead within a few days," I said.

"You're right," Tacitus conceded, "but it'll be quite a show. Too bad we'll miss it."

"We need to be more concerned about booking passage on a ship," I reminded him. The shows in the arena repulse me. Watching a helpless animal—or person—being butchered while the crowd went insane was a sight I would gladly miss. Tacitus revels in it.

Leaving our servants to gawk at the spectacle, we walked along the wharves, looking for someone we could talk to on a ship. I glanced over my shoulder, trying to look like I was just taking in my surroundings.

"What's the matter?" Tacitus asked.

"I think somebody's following us."

"In a port town I'd be surprised if somebody wasn't. The place is crawling with thieves and cutthroats. The stripes on our tunics are practically a challenge to those lowlifes."

"But I think somebody has been following us since we left Rome."

"Well, you think Regulus has a spy behind every tree and door."

"Not more than every other one."

Our route took us alongside the *Jupiter*. It was indeed the king of the gods among the ships in the fleet stationed at Misenum, which my uncle had commanded for several years before his death. I paused on the dock beside it, falling silent, and looked up at it.

"Is something wrong?" Tacitus asked.

"The last time I saw my uncle alive, he was boarding this ship."

"That memory weighs heavily on you, doesn't it?"

"Sometimes it's so vivid it doesn't feel like a memory."

A man leaned over the bow of the *Jupiter*. "Do my eyes deceive me? Is that young Pliny?" he called.

I looked up to see someone I recognized. "Marcus Decius. Is that really you?"

Decius, a burly man with a long scar on his left cheek, had been captain of the ship under my uncle. He was the one who brought us the news that my uncle had been overcome by fumes and died on the shore near Stabiae. I could still see my mother collapse on the floor and hear her wail when Decius told us.

"It most certainly is, sir," Decius called. "Would you like to come aboard?"

After a ladder was extended, Tacitus and I boarded the ship and I made introductions.

"It's such a pleasure to see you, sir," Decius said. "What brings you to Ostia?"

"We need to get to Naples. We're looking for a ship that's leaving tomorrow."

"Well, then, you've found her," Decius said. "I just brought a load of prisoners up here. They're headed the same place as that cargo of animals. We'll be under sail again tomorrow at dawn. How many in your party?"

"The two of us, and we have four servants each. And one more."

"Eleven." He nodded. "That's no problem, then."

"But you're a military ship," I said. "You're not supposed to carry civilian passengers."

"Would you like to lodge a complaint with the captain of the ship?" Decius asked with a grin that raised the right side of his mouth more than the left. "I couldn't make a special trip for you, but as long as we're both going the same way, I'll take whom I like on board."

"How long a voyage do you think it'll be?" Tacitus asked. "Our friend here isn't exactly an Odysseus when it comes to ships."

"I know, sir." Decius was unable to suppress a smile. "He never did like to go out with us. His uncle would drag him onto the ship once in a while. Thought it would toughen him up."

If there was one thing for which I could not forgive my uncle, it was the memory of those humiliating voyages across the Bay of Naples. I spent most of my time vomiting over the side of the ship. The sailors couldn't laugh at me because I was the commander's nephew, but I knew what they were thinking and what they said after I was gone. When he was leaving to rescue survivors from Vesuvius, he asked me if I wanted to go along. I declined the invitation.

"Don't worry, sir," Decius said. "With any kind of wind at all, we'll be in Naples before dark. It'll be an easy voyage. No worse than getting bounced around in one of those litters you city folks ride in."

"How much will our fare be?" I asked.

Decius snorted. "Please, sir. Don't insult me. I'm happy to do a favor for my old commander's heir. Just be here when the sun's coming up."

We thanked him, retrieved our servants, and made our way back to the inn. I had asked for some fish, and it proved to be fresh and quite tasty, as fish should be in a port town. Tacitus had the innkeeper's specialty, a rabbit stew. I was leery of it because I did not notice an abundance of rabbits in Ostia. I suspected the meat in the stew came from some other small animal that one finds in large numbers in any town and that resembles a rabbit only in its penchant for gnawing on things.

When Tacitus and the servants got up to go to bed after dinner, I remained at the table.

"Aren't you coming?" Tacitus asked.

"I'm going to walk around the block," I said. "I hate eating while sitting up. It doesn't allow a meal to settle the way reclining does. I'll feel better after a walk, I think."

"You may find yourself running to keep away from the thieves and brigands."

"It'll be a short walk. I'll be fine." When his back was turned I picked up a knife and tucked it into my belt. The weapon I've taken to carrying was in my room.

The sun had set and darkness was deepening over Ostia, the air offering a hint of autumn's coolness. I left the inn, walked to the corner, and turned onto the cross-street. Earlier in the day I had noticed a recessed doorway just a few paces past the corner. It was part of my plan. I ducked into it and waited.

I wasn't disappointed. I had barely gotten out of sight when a figure turned the corner. As he walked past my hiding place, I grabbed one of his arms and pulled him into the recess, shoving him face-first up against the door and pinning his arms behind him so he couldn't draw a weapon.

"Who are you?" I snarled into his ear. "And why are you following me?"

"My lord Gaius, let go. You're hurting me."

I could not mistake Aurora's voice.

†

"By the gods! What are you doing here? And in that disguise?"

I released her and stepped away. She turned around and pulled off the head-covering she'd been wearing. She had disguised herself as a young man in Eastern garb, in a brown robe and scarf drawn over part of her face. When I had glimpsed her twice earlier in the day, I thought she was an Arab. She had darkened her olive complexion even more with makeup.

"I was concerned about you, my lord, so I followed you."

When we were children Aurora and I went out into the streets of Rome and listened in on conversations, at first playing at being spies but soon discovering we might stumble onto information my uncle found useful in his investigations for the *princeps* Vespasian. In the last few years I've given Aurora permission to leave my house without answering to anyone but me. She sometimes disguises herself, saying that every household should have eyes and ears in all sorts of places. This was the first time I'd known her to range so far.

"Concerned about me? Why?"

"Even before you left Rome, my lord, Dorias was on her way to Regulus' house."

I recognized Dorias' name, but her duties in my house kept her in the laundry or the kitchen most of the time, so I had trouble recalling her face. "And you think she's Regulus' spy?"

Aurora nodded. "Or one of them, my lord."

"But why would Regulus care if I'm going to Naples?"

"He cares about every move you make, my lord. He's looking for any little misstep that will enable him to destroy you."

I couldn't dispute her. Regulus had given up a sure victory in a court case just to have the opportunity to defeat me. We stayed in the recess, standing close together. I glanced out to see if anyone else was on the street. "How did you get here?"

"I hired a horse, my lord." She smiled and lit up the darkness around us. "I kept you in sight all the way down here."

I give Aurora small sums of money now and then, to enable her to buy drinks for people to loosen their tongues or even to bribe them outright. She must have been saving some of it, if she had enough to hire a horse.

"You're not as clever as you think, young lady," I said. "I knew someone was following me."

"But you didn't know who, did you?" I noticed that she dropped the *domine*, but I didn't care. This was just the two of us, and I felt as close to her in my heart as I was to her physically.

"Well, no… Does my mother know you've left the house?"

"No. I waited until she was in the *latrina*. Demetrius knows I have your permission to leave as I wish, so he did not try to stop me."

I was torn between my pleasure at seeing her—and knowing she cared this much for me—and a feeling that she had taken advantage of the liberty I'd given her. I decided I had to be her master right now. "I appreciate your concern for me, but…you've gone too far. You have to go back to Rome."

She looked down and then back up at me. "Are you going to punish me?"

We were standing close to one another, too close perhaps. Her shoulder pressed against mine, her breast caressing my chest. She wasn't wearing her perfume, but my awareness of her had never been keener. I had trouble keeping my breathing under control. "You know I could never punish you…or hurt you in any way."

She looked straight into my eyes. "Could you ever love me, Gaius?"

I was stunned by the impertinence of her question and just as much by my inability to answer it immediately. It was the question I'd been asking myself since the moment my mother informed me that she had arranged a marriage for me. Now Aurora had given voice to it. Until a question is put into words for another person to hear, it can be mulled over, even ignored. Once it's been heard, though, it has to be answered, no matter how difficult or painful the answer might be.

But how could I answer it? My mouth moved, but no words came out.

"That's what I thought," Aurora said.

"No, you don't understand."

"Yes, I do understand, *my lord.*"

No servant had ever dared speak those last two words to me in that tone.

She put the head scarf she'd been wearing back on and started to step around me. "I'll be on my way back to Rome tomorrow morning—or tonight, if you wish, my lord."

"Don't be ridiculous. Let me get you a room."

"I don't think it's a good idea for anyone else in the household to know I've done this, my lord. It obviously was a mistake, my lord." She wiped her face with the tail of the scarf. "I'll find my own room, my lord."

"Aurora, please…let me explain." I grabbed her arm, but she jerked away from me and was gone before I could decide what I ought to do.

†

As the first rays of the sun fell on the docks Tacitus and I, with our servants, stood beside the *Jupiter,* waiting to be called aboard. The oars on the dock side of the ship had been pulled in to allow the vessel to be tied up. There was a great deal of activity on the ship as last-minute supplies were laded, the crew of rowers took their places, and a dozen armed legionaries found their positions on the deck.

"You look like Dawn stuck one of her rosy fingers in your eye," Tacitus said.

"I didn't sleep well."

"Something bothering you?"

"Just anxiety…about this voyage," I lied, "and the bed bugs." The last part wasn't a lie. I had spent the night scratching and recalling my last meeting with Aurora. At one point I even got up and was about to go out into the streets to search for her. Then I reminded myself that she had money and a horse. She could be anywhere.

"Well, this is a big ship," Tacitus assured me. "Once we're underway you won't notice any more bouncing or bobbing than you do in a litter. Decius was right about that."

"How big do you think it is?"

Tacitus eyed the *Jupiter* like a potential buyer. "I'd say…forty paces long and perhaps six paces wide."

Decius appeared at the bow of the ship and waved to us. "Come aboard, sirs. We're ready to leave."

We climbed the ladder that was extended from the ship to the dock and stowed our belongings where Decius showed us. In addition to the three banks of oars, the ship had a large sail mounted on a mast a bit closer to the bow than to the stern and a smaller sail on the bow. The deck was covered and flat, so we would be left open to the elements for the whole day. On each side of the deck a row of shields had been mounted vertically for protection during a battle. Below them a protective cover extended farther out as a kind of wooden awning over the rowers' seats.

Decius offered us the use of the small tent set up at the stern that was the captain's quarters. "You can go below if you need to, but it's crowded down there, and the air gets a little ripe as the day goes on. The most important thing to remember is, when you need to relieve yourself, be mindful of the wind."

Two smaller boats tossed lines to the ship so they could pull us away from the dock and out into open water. The ship creaked and pitched slightly from side to side. I clutched the rail and tried to appear comfortable, in spite of having been on a ship this large only once since I was fourteen. That was when my uncle gave up trying to make a sailor of me.

After seeing that all was in order, Decius came back to stand beside us and watch the operation. "These harbor rats know their business," he said with a nod of approval. "They'll have us out of the port in no time. We've got a good following north wind, so I'm going to use the sails *and* the oars. I've a mind to see just how fast we can make this trip. You'll be having dinner in Naples this evening. I guarantee it."

When we were clear of the harbor we came to the mouth of the Tiber. Several things happened at once. Sailors released the tow lines and dropped them into the water. The harbor rats scrambled to pull them into their boats. The belly of the ship rumbled as the rowers slid their oars into position and turned the ship to the left, heading south.

"Brace yourself," Tacitus warned me, but I wasn't quick enough.

At Decius' command the sails were unfurled and caught the breeze with a crack so loud I was afraid the mast had snapped. The ship seemed to leap ahead. My grip on the rail was too loose and I was thrown down on my backside. Tacitus laughed and extended a hand, but I couldn't grab it before I rolled through a gap in the row of shields, slid down the wooden awning protecting the oarsmen, and tumbled overboard.

V

A FALLING MAN grabs at anything, even the air. I was fortunate to wrap my arms around one of the oars before I hit the water. Using the strength that panic gave me, I pulled myself up and threw my legs around the shaft as well. Orders were shouted, a horn blew, the sails whipped back up the mast, and the ship came to a stop.

Decius leaned over the railing. "Are you all right, sir?"

A weak "I think so" was all I could muster. I could already feel the bruises that were going to show up all over my body.

"We're going to raise that oar and bring it in toward the ship. A couple of men will help you back on board. Don't let go."

Don't let go. As if I would seriously consider doing any such thing. I tried not to look down as I hung about five paces above the water. Although the ship had stopped its forward motion, it bobbed and pitched from side to side. The oar wiggled as the men on the other end of it tried to counter my weight.

"Here we go, sir!" Decius shouted.

I didn't think my grip could get any tighter, but it did as the oar slid back into the ship. Two of the legionaries, with ropes tying them to the rail, stood on the wooden awning over the rowers. When they reached out to me, I had difficulty at first persuading myself to let go of the oar and take their hands.

"There you are, sir," one of them said, taking my hand and peeling it off the oar. "We've got you. Let's just swing back up here, nice and safe."

The awning didn't look any safer to me than the oar I was clinging to, but the legionaries were tied to the ship. I reached up to them and

51

unwrapped my legs from around the oar. They lifted me back onto the wooden awning and over the rail as though I was a child. Tacitus put an arm around me before I collapsed on the deck and led me to the prow of the ship. I knew he could feel how much I was trembling, and I was ashamed of that.

"Just sit down," he said, dropping me in a spot at the bow where I could sit down and lean against the side. "Maybe we'll tie you here."

Decius knelt beside me. "Any injuries, sir?"

I stretched my arms and legs. "Just a few bruises. Nothing serious."

"Good. And don't be embarrassed. You aren't the first man to fall overboard, though you are the first I've seen do such a trick as catching an oar. If you want to get to Naples today, though, you're going to have to stay on deck."

At his command the oars bit into the water again and the sails were lowered. The ship surged ahead. I felt like Bellerophon must have felt on the winged horse Pegasus. No ship I'd ever been on before had moved this fast. The sail on the bow flapped and snapped over my head. Its three vertical blue stripes matched those on the larger main-sail, which billowed as it tried to break free from the rigging. Looking over the side, I could see the banks of oars digging into the water, pro-pelling the ship with the precise timing of a centipede's legs.

As a man recovers from a bad shock, some kind of energy seems to drain out of him, leaving him as limp as an old man's virile mem-ber. When I gave into that sensation, the warmth of the sun and the rhythmic movement of the ship lulled me into some of the sleep I had not gotten the previous night. The sun was almost overhead when I woke up to find Tacitus and the servants breaking out provisions for lunch.

"Oh, now we'll have to share with *him*," Tacitus said.

We had brought along a good supply of cheese, bread, fruit, and wine mixed with water. Decius approached and we invited him to eat with us.

"I'm glad to see you're doing so well, sir," he said. "A couple of your servants haven't had so easy a time of it."

Tacitus pointed to Thamyras and one of my servants. "They spent some time hanging over the rail this morning. Are you feeling better now?"

Both men nodded sheepishly but declined to take any food or drink.

After we had eaten and drunk a bit Tacitus turned to Decius. "I understand you were stationed at Misenum when Vesuvius erupted."

"Yes, sir, I was." Decius did not volunteer any more.

"What can you tell me about it? I've heard Gaius Pliny's account once, but he's very reluctant to say any more than that."

The sailor's stern face couldn't hide the pain that the memory aroused. "Well, sir, for those of us who lived through it, it's troubling to remember, but we can't stop remembering it. Talking about it only makes it worse, at least for me."

"That's how I feel, too," I said when Tacitus questioned me with a raised eyebrow. "That's why I haven't said much about it. No matter what we tell you, you'll never really understand the fear we felt, the sense that the world was coming to an end."

"But how are others going to learn anything about it—probably the greatest disaster Rome will ever know—if those who were there won't tell the story?" Tacitus was at his oratorical best. "How can anyone write the history of it if the people who were there don't share what they know?"

Decius tore off another piece of bread and seemed to be thinking while he chewed. When he had swallowed and drunk some wine he said, "Historians never get it right, sir, because they weren't there. Why don't we wait until we reach the bay? Gaius Pliny and I can't help but think about it then, and you'll understand a lot more if you can see it while we tell you the story."

"Forgive me, my lord," Thamyras said from his spot by the rail. "May I speak?"

"Certainly," Tacitus said.

"I lived on the bay, too, my lord, when Vesuvius erupted. What these gentlemen are saying is true. I see the results every day. Unless you were there or you've seen what the place looks like now, you can't possibly understand.... Meaning no disrespect."

"All right," Tacitus said, slapping his hands on his thighs. "I guess I'll have to wait."

†

After lunch Tacitus went below to study the structure of the ship.

He'd heard the story of the collapsible barge Nero built to drown his mother, Agrippina, and wanted to see if such a thing was even feasible. I declined his invitation to join him. I'd seen enough of the belly of a ship when I was a boy. Stepping around coils of rope and trying to keep out of the sailors' way, I wandered to the stern and looked at the coastline gliding by us. The ship throbbed with the steady beat of the drum that set the pace for the rowers. Even as short as it was, my hair blew in the wind.

Like Decius, I did not want to talk about the eruption. Five years had not dimmed the memory in the least. I had stayed away from the Bay of Naples for a reason. Fortunately, Aurelia's wedding had been at her grandfather's house in Rome. Now I was being drawn back to Naples by her letter. Her need for help and my friendship with her had to override my reluctance to return.

But, if I were honest with myself, what could I do to help her? In other cases where I'd been able to identify a murderer, I had been able to examine the victim's body within a few hours after the crime was committed. Thanks to what I had read in some unpublished scrolls my uncle left me, I had developed some small skill in deducing information from the examination of a dead body. But this time what I would have to examine would be little more than a rotting corpse.

Also, in other cases I had investigated, people who were accused of killing someone protested their innocence and tried eagerly to explain why they weren't guilty. Now the man who was found standing over the victim, with what might have been the murder weapon in his hand, refused to say anything, even to his wife. What reason did I have to think he would talk to me?

I had to admit, at least to myself, that part of the reason I was making this trip was my desire to run away—away from a marriage I didn't want and away from Aurora, because I couldn't decide how to deal with my feelings for her.

Both of those problems would still be there when I returned. If I couldn't help Aurelia, this whole trip would be a waste of time. I had to accomplish something down here, even if I did no more than comfort Aurelia. I touched the Tyche ring, which I was wearing on a leather strap around my neck. Sometimes I wished I actually believed in luck.

I needed to concentrate on the task at hand. The only way I could examine the scene of the murder was through the eyes of a person who had been there. I called Thamyras to join me in the captain's tent near the stern, which Decius had offered for my use. It might provide a modicum of privacy and it would get me out of the sun, which was beginning to bother my sensitive eyes. I took one of the stools that was fastened to the deck and motioned for Thamyras to sit on the other one. He seemed uncomfortable with this breach of master-and-slave etiquette and kept his back straight when he did sit down, as though he were standing from the waist up.

"Yes, my lord, what can I do for you?"

"Tell me if you've remembered anything about this murder that you didn't tell me yesterday." I found myself falling into a rhythmic speech pattern, keeping time with the drumbeats as the oars dug into the water. "It doesn't matter how small a detail, or how seemingly insignificant. Just tell me and let me judge whether it's important."

Thamyras shook his head and looked at me as though pleading with me. "That's all I've been thinking about, my lord, and I can't remember anything else. Calpurnius was standing over the woman, with the knife in his hand. As soon as he saw me, he told me to go get help. That's all I can tell you."

I wanted to get him thinking differently about what he had seen. Often, when a person witnesses some dire event, he can recall it only from the perspective from which he viewed it. Someone has to coax him to look at it from another angle, to imagine himself standing somewhere else in the scene.

"Who was the woman who was killed?"

"She was called Amalthea, my lord."

"What were her duties in the house?"

"She worked in the kitchen, my lord. She was one of the lady Aurelia's people."

"What do you mean by that?"

"When Calpurnius and Aurelia married, my lord, they moved into Aurelia's house, because Calpurnius' villa had been buried in the eruption. Some of the servants are Calpurnius' people that he brought with him, like me, but most are Aurelia's people."

"How are you getting along? Is there any animosity between the two groups?"

"No, my lord. I think we've mixed well, like water and wine."

At least he didn't say water and olive oil. "Did Calpurnius even know Amalthea before the marriage?"

"No, my lord, I'm sure he didn't."

I couldn't detect any telltale signs of lying. Everyone has them—a blinking of the eye, an inability to look at a person—but Thamyras seemed straightforward. "Do you know of anyone who had argued with Amalthea or had any complaint against her?" I asked.

"No, my lord. She was quiet, minded her own business."

"Have Calpurnius and Aurelia had any arguments recently?"

He seemed surprised by the leap I had made. "No, my lord. They're very happy and so pleased about the child. I haven't heard a cross word between them."

He seemed to be relaxing. His back wasn't quite as straight and he was looking around at the gear stowed in the captain's quarters. I felt it was time to shift attention back to the murder scene. "You said you found Calpurnius in an orchard behind the house?"

"Yes, my lord."

"What were you doing there?"

"It's my job, my lord. I take care of the garden and the orchard."

So he had every reason to be there. I was sorely missing Phineas and his notes. "Why was Amalthea there, if she was a kitchen servant?"

"She went out every morning for some sort of religious ritual, my lord."

"Religious ritual?"

"Yes, my lord. She had carved a mark in one of the trees. I guess she worshiped it. She did it before my lord and lady got married. She went into a kind of trance. The morning I spoke to her, she didn't know I was there until I touched her arm. I told her not to go carving up any more of the trees."

"Can you show me that tree when we get there?"

"Certainly, my lord."

"Now, what can you tell me about Calpurnius when you found him there?" I realized that was too vague a question. "What about the expression on his face? Did he seem frightened? Surprised? Angry?"

"I would say more like…confused, my lord. He looked at the knife, at me, then back at the knife."

"How much blood was there on his clothing?"

Thamyras brushed his thinning hair out of his face and pondered a moment. "That's interesting, my lord. Now that you mention it, there wasn't any blood on him that I could see. I hadn't thought about that."

Now I had a trail I could follow, like a hound picking up a scent for the first time. "How was he standing when you saw him? Was he facing you?"

"Not entirely, my lord."

"Show me."

Thamyras stood and turned so that I was looking at him from the side. "Well, my lord, he was like this when I came up to him. Then he turned partway toward me."

"You were looking at him from the right side, the side where he was holding the knife?"

Thamyras nodded.

"So you saw at least that side of his tunic."

"Yes, my lord, and there was no blood on it." He blinked as he took in the meaning of what he'd just said. "Does that mean he didn't kill her?"

"It's not conclusive proof, I know, but if a man was standing close enough to stab someone, I would expect to find blood on his clothes."

"Certainly, my lord. That's what happens in the arena, when the gladiators fight." His face showed excitement, either at the memory of the slaughter he'd seen or the realization of some slight hope of proving his master innocent.

"Don't put too much weight on one little observation," I cautioned him.

He sat back down, arms resting on his legs. "It's a relief to have *any* hope, my lord, no matter how small. I can see why the lady Aurelia sent for you."

"You seem quite devoted to your master and lady."

"I've served Calpurnius since I was a boy, my lord." He straightened his back with pride. "He's always been kind and fair with me—and with all his servants. And now the lady Aurelia has brought him much happiness, long overdue happiness. For that I owe her loyal service."

I cocked my head. "'Overdue happiness'? Was Calpurnius not happy before his marriage?"

Thamyras' face told me that he knew he had said too much. "Excuse me, my lord, but I think I'm going to be sick again." He bolted out of the tent, leaned over the rail, and began to make retching noises, but only noises, like a storm that never brings rain.

†

At about the tenth hour Decius found me standing by the rail. "Sorry to disturb your musings, sir, but we're about to come into the bay."

I saw what I had been looking at without paying any attention. "Oh, yes, that's Cumae, isn't it?" I wondered if the Sibyl could give me any advice on the questions I'd been pondering.

"Yes, sir, and Misenum is just ahead." Decius pointed to the promontory looming larger with every stroke of the oars. "Once we're around it, we'll strike the sails. With the wind from this direction, they won't do us any good when we're crossing the bay."

"I'd better get Tacitus," I said.

"Yes, sir. And I'm sure he's going to want to hear our stories about the eruption."

"You know more about it than I do, Decius. You sailed right into the teeth of it. I sat back and tried to read while the world was falling apart, just because I didn't want to get on a ship. I've often wondered if it would have made any difference if I had gone with my uncle. Could I have saved him?"

"Don't trouble yourself with thoughts like that, sir. The commander always had trouble with his breathing. You know that. He just couldn't get a breath in that hot air. You're more likely to have died with him than to have saved him. Don't trouble yourself."

He put a hand on my shoulder. Something about the gesture made me feel twelve years old again. I wouldn't have been surprised if he'd called me "lad."

"Don't trouble yourself about what?" Tacitus asked as he came up behind us.

"Things that can't be changed," I said.

"That's good advice indeed." Tacitus leaned on the rail beside me. "In all areas of your life. Is this Misenum ahead of us?"

"Yes, sir," Decius said. "We'll slip between the point and the island of Prochyta over there and turn east into the bay."

"Will we be able to see your villa?" Tacitus asked me.

"If we look behind us. It's on the east side of the point, at the top of the hill. That's why we could see the eruption so clearly."

"Do you want to stop there, sir?" Decius asked.

"No. Let's just go on to Naples. Thamyras will still have to show us where Aurelia's house is once we get there. I want to arrive before dark, if at all possible. If we have time, I might stop here on the way back."

"A surprise inspection will keep them honest," Tacitus said.

Once we had passed Prochyta and were turning into the bay I pointed out my villa to Tacitus. Misenum is a cape with the Tyrrhenian Sea on one side of it and an inlet of the bay on the other. Puteoli sits on that inlet, rather than on the bay itself.

"Didn't I hear you say once that you were born in Puteoli?" I asked Decius.

"Yes, sir, I was. That part of the bay was spared the worst of it, thank the gods."

Passing the inlet gave me the feeling of being on completely open water, too far away from land. I'm a competent enough swimmer that, if I had to, I could make it from where most ships sail to the shore, but not to the other side of the inlet. I was glad to get past it and see a coastline again.

"The land still has a gray cast to it," Tacitus said, "even under the canopy of leaves."

"Yes, sir," Decius said. "The ash still gets into everything, even this far away. Some days I feel like I'm eating it and breathing it."

I had turned my back to the coast and leaned against the rail. "It's amazing how light the ash feels, like warm snow, when you pick up a handful of it, but when it piles up, the weight can crush you."

"That's what almost happened to you and your mother, wasn't it?" Tacitus asked.

"I've not heard that part of the story, sir," Decius said.

Now that we were here, there was no way to avoid thinking and talking about those days. I'd known from the start that was how it would be. "After you and my uncle left, the ground began shaking so badly I ordered everyone to gather in the garden, so we wouldn't be crushed if the house fell. Even that didn't seem safe, though, so I decided to leave the house and move north, as everyone around us was doing. We couldn't get the wagons to stay still to board them, even with the wheels chocked, so we started walking. A servant helped me hold my mother up. She told me to leave her behind so that she wouldn't be the cause of my death."

"You would never do that, sir," Decius said.

"No, of course not. We got several miles up the road when my mother simply couldn't go any farther. We took shelter behind a milestone so we wouldn't be trampled by the crowd. It was dark as night and people were crying, looking for those they'd lost and wailing in despair. Some thought it was the end of the world, and I wouldn't have argued with them.

"After we'd been sitting down for a bit I tried to move and that was when I discovered that the ash was burying us. I couldn't see it happening because it was so dark, but I felt it. I managed to get up and get my mother on her feet. We stayed there, getting up often to shake off the ash, until a bit of light returned to the sky. Then we turned back to home. If we had fallen asleep, we would still be buried there. You know how tall milestones are."

"Oh, yes, sir," Decius said. "Usually taller than a man."

"Exactly. That's how this one was when we sat down. When we left, the top of it was even with my waist."

Decius shook his head in disbelief. "And you were that far from the mountain! Speaking of the accursed thing..."

I dreaded looking ahead, but Tacitus pointed and said in awe, "By the gods! So that's Vesuvius."

VI

W E COULD NOT YET see the eastern coast of the bay, but the mountain was already looming on the horizon, as though jutting out of the sea like an island, or like the Pharos lighthouse as you approach Alexandria.

"It looks like it has two peaks," Tacitus said.

"It used to be almost a cone." Decius tented his hands to show the shape. "The eruption tore the top off."

"There's a wisp of smoke coming out of it now," I said, drawing a deep breath to try to steady myself.

"It does that now and then." Decius didn't seem concerned. "We've gotten used to it. Some folks around here say it's just old Vulcan belching—or farting, if you're inclined to be earthier about it."

"The eruption started one afternoon in August, didn't it?" Tacitus asked.

"Yes, sir. Nine days before the Kalends of September."

My stomach tightened as more of Vesuvius' mass rose into the sky. "My uncle, my mother, and I were sitting on the terrace after lunch when my mother spotted the cloud," I said.

Decius' voice softened and deepened. "The commander sent me an order to get a ship ready—this ship. He wanted to investigate. But by the time I could round up the crew and get them on board, we had a message from a friend of his, Rectina, the wife of Tascus, begging for help. So, instead of satisfying the commander's curiosity, we got several ships ready to go rescue people."

Tacitus looked puzzled. "If people could send messages, why did they need rescuing?"

"Rectina sent one of her servants by land," I said, "before the eruption got really bad. She was elderly and given to hysterics. Her house was right at the foot of Vesuvius. At the first sign of trouble she went into a panic. Most people didn't realize how serious the situation was until it was too late."

"And you didn't want to go?" Tacitus asked me.

Before I could answer Decius said, "It seemed a good idea to have a man in charge back home, especially since we didn't know quite what lay ahead of us."

Tacitus looked at me with something like pride. Someday I would have to tell him the truth. I simply had not wanted to get on a ship, and no one had any idea how vast a disaster we were facing. He turned back to Decius. "What did you see as you crossed the bay?"

"The cloud kept rising from the volcano. We couldn't believe how high it got. Have you seen the Parthenon, sir?"

"Yes, I have."

"You know how you feel when you stand at the feet of that image of Athena? Your eyes are barely at a level with her toes, and you almost fall over backwards as you try to see the top of her."

Tacitus chuckled. "Yes, I've done that."

"Well, that's what it was like as we got closer to the end of the bay. I never imagined anything could go that high."

"I think the cloud was probably two miles high," I said

Tacitus whistled in disbelief.

"Oh, it was at least that," Decius assured him. "The wind was behind us. The cloud was drawing the air up with it, so we made good time. The commander told us to get in close to shore, but we couldn't. It was as though the water in the bay had drained out through some hole in the bottom of the sea."

The eastern coast was emerging now, a gray line that ran all the way across the horizon, with Vesuvius brooding above it.

"Many times I had sailed up to the docks at Herculaneum," Decius said, "but that day we couldn't get any closer than, say, the length of the Circus Maximus."

"That far?" Tacitus said. "That's almost half a mile."

"Yes, sir. I saw it—still see it in my dreams—and I can't believe what I saw. Fish and sea creatures were flopping around on the rocks and in the shallow water between us and the shore."

"That's what we saw at Misenum, too," I said. "It was worse than a nightmare. At least with a nightmare you can wake up. This was real, and we didn't know when, or how, it was going to end."

"People were standing on the shore," Decius said with a shudder, "their arms raised, pleading for help, and there was no way we could get to them. That's what I still have nightmares about—the people on shore. Some of them tried to launch their boats and get out to us, but they crashed on the rocks. They were desperate to get away from the cloud behind them. As Gaius Pliny said, it went up into the air for what seemed forever."

"It went straight up," I said, raising my eyes, "then flattened out at the top, like the branches on a pine tree, one that looks like a mushroom. Then it collapsed, and dust and ash came rushing down the sides of the mountain. I could see that much even from Misenum."

"And the heat, sir." Decius shook his head slowly. "We felt it all the way out on the water. Even at that distance it was like having your face in a blacksmith's forge. That's what made us turn away to Stabiae." Decius pointed to the south side of the bay. "I don't know how anybody on shore could have survived."

"Stabiae was where your uncle died, wasn't it?" Tacitus asked, turning to me.

"Yes. He tried to calm everyone in the house where he went ashore by having a bath and dinner, but they had to leave the house during the night. Two days later they found him on the shore, dead." The coastline was clear before us now and suddenly I wanted to get away from the retelling—and reliving—of this horrible memory. "What is it like living down here now?" I asked Decius.

"There's been a lot of cleaning up." Decius pointed at several spots on shore. "Naples and the towns and villas along the north shore of the bay are back to something like normal. People have shoveled the ash out from their houses and streets."

"Where do they put it?" Tacitus asked.

"That's the problem. There's so much of it that there is nowhere to put it all. Buildings that used to be level with the ground, you now have to step down to get into."

"The place looks like a gray desert," Tacitus said.

Decius nodded. "Everything has changed—utterly changed. I can't recognize *anything*, and I've lived on this bay all my life. It's been reshaped, just like a sculptor took his chisel to it. The volcano threw out so much ash that the coastline is farther out than it used to be. Herculaneum sat right on the coast. As I said, I've sailed up to its docks many times over the years. It was at the foot of Vesuvius—a little to the right as we're looking at it now—so I guess I know generally where it was, but there's nothing to tell you a town used to be there. And you would never know that a busy and prosperous town like Pompeii even existed just a few miles farther down the coast."

"Has anyone tried to get back into the towns that were destroyed?" Tacitus asked. "Are people going in to reclaim their property?"

"Many of the owners were buried along with their property, sir. We've caught some looters, especially in the villas outside the towns, ones that aren't so deeply covered. Some of them were in the batch of prisoners I transported to Ostia. The magistrates are doing everything they can to stop them. But there are temptations. The roofs of a few buildings—especially ones with two floors or more—are still visible in spots where the ash wasn't so deep. Some of the buildings have collapsed from the weight of the ash. It's very dangerous to go poking around over there."

"Poking around in deserted houses is definitely not what I'm here for," I said. Poking around in a murder was my objective, and that could be just as dangerous.

†

We still had a couple of hours of daylight left when we sailed up to a dock on the south side of Naples, just where the coastline bends south. Thamyras told us it was the closest that we could land to the villa of Aurelia and Calpurnius. Because of the size of the trireme we couldn't actually tie up at the dock. Our ship had only one small boat in tow for use in an emergency. Thamyras was rowed to shore in that and made arrangements for a larger boat to come out and ferry us in to shore. Transferring our gear didn't take long.

"How long will you be here?" Decius asked.

"I have to be back in Rome on the Ides. I'm concerned about whether I can make it. My mother and my future mother-in-law will crucify me with their own hands if I'm late."

"Well, what a coincidence," Decius said as we cast off. "I'm going to Rome on the day before the Ides. If you need transport, just let me know."

"Thank you," I said with great relief. I hoped respect for my uncle would open other doors for me as easily around the bay. I took a seat so I could face away from the memory of death and destruction spewing out of Vesuvius.

Tacitus couldn't seem to get enough of the view, though. He cocked his head back, open-mouthed in awe. "The slope of the mountain is quite gentle. Makes it feel like it covers the whole end of the bay."

Thamyras nodded. "There were villas all up the sides of it, my lord. It was covered with vineyards, the most beautiful sight you ever saw. Now it looks like—well, if there are mountains on the moon, like some of those old Greeks said there are, I suspect this is what they look like."

When we reached shore I was the first one out of the boat, almost knocking Thamyras over.

"You really couldn't wait to get your feet on *terra firma*, could you?" Tacitus laughed.

"Human beings don't have wings or fins," I said. "That's proof enough for me that dry land is where we belong."

Thamyras found a carriage and driver to take us to the villa. "It'll take about half an hour to get there, my lords. I'll arrange for your gear and servants to be sent along."

"All right," I said. "We'll see you all there later this evening."

I didn't like going alone into unfamiliar territory, but finding transportation for nine more people and all that we were carrying would take time. I wanted to get started on my investigation of whatever had happened before any more evidence was lost or destroyed.

The villas on the shore of the bay looked like people were rebuilding after a war. As Decius had said, those that had been on the water were now inland—some only a few paces, but others, as I looked south, a considerable distance. What had happened, I wondered, to the water supply in those houses? If they depended on springs or wells, as my house at Laurentum does, had those been covered by the eruption?

"Are people still living in these villas?" I asked our driver, a stolid man whose age I couldn't determine, but whose left eyelid drooped.

"For another mile or so to the south, yes, sir. Your friends Calpurnius and Aurelia have one of the last villas that's still fit to live in. After that, most of them have been abandoned. Even if the houses weren't badly damaged, the ash was just too heavy to clear out."

"My uncle died at Stabiae," I said. "I was at Misenum when the eruption occurred. The ash was heavy and we felt severe shaking of the earth. I can't even imagine how bad it was over here."

He looked at me with a bit more respect, as though we were soldiers who had fought in the same horrific battle. "Yes, sir. Those of us who survived can't believe that we did. Some places collapsed. Others had to be torn down afterwards because they weren't safe anymore. In Naples itself the shaking did as much damage as what the volcano was throwing out."

"Why don't people leave?" Tacitus asked.

"Where can we go, sir?" the driver said with a fatalistic shrug. "All we can do is get out of doors if the mountain so much as rumbles."

†

The road we were on ran close to the shore, with room for houses but not much else between it and the water. There were no cliffs here, just a gentle slope into the bay. What was a beach five years ago was regaining that character, just farther out than it had been.

"Here we are, sirs," the driver said as he pulled off the road.

In the dim light of early evening it seemed the color had drained out of this part of the world. Trees, buildings—everything—looked like a statue before it's painted, except that it was all gray. We climbed down from the wagon and retrieved the two bags we'd brought with us. I gave the man a bit more than we'd agreed on, and he touched his cap in appreciation.

Aurelia's estate appeared to have recovered from the eruption as well as any property we'd seen since we touched land, which wasn't saying a lot. The vegetation around the house was beginning to reestablish itself, but the overall impression of the place reminded me of being on the edge of a desert, like the one I'd seen when I served in Syria.

The doorman admitted us with some surprise. "We didn't expect you so soon, my lord."

I didn't want to waste time on explanations. "Where is your lady?"

"She's in the garden, my lord."

He was about to lead us to her, but an older, heavyset Nubian woman with a bright, multi-colored cloth wrapped around her head stopped us in the atrium.

"Welcome, my lords. I am Bastet, the lady Aurelia's midwife," she said in accented but elegant Latin with a slight bow of her head. "Forgive me, but I think it would be better if you saw her in the morning. I'm very concerned about her health and about the baby, because of all this…disturbance. She's less than a month from the time when she should deliver the child, and it has not been easy for her all along. I'm afraid it may be an early birth and a difficult one."

"It might be best to wait then," Tacitus said. "We don't want to do anything to harm the child."

I knew he was thinking back to earlier in the year when his own wife had lost a child, but I couldn't waste any time. "We need to see her right away. If you don't talk to people immediately after a crisis, their memory of it starts to change. Sometimes their first recollections are inaccurate, but they're important none the less. It's already been several days."

"My lord, please," the midwife said, "if you will only—"

"Gaius Pliny, is that really you?" Aurelia stood in the doorway leading from the atrium to the back of the house, bracing herself with one hand on the doorpost. "I can't believe you got here so soon." She rushed to me and embraced me—or clung to me. I expected tears, but she wasn't shedding any.

When I felt her arms relax a bit I held her shoulders and stepped back, looking at her for the first time in over a year. Her face was puffy and she had gained weight, as women will do when they are bearing a child, but she was no less beautiful. I couldn't look away from her eyes. They were still as green as young acorns, just like the first time I saw her. Now, though, I saw dark circles around them and a Maenad's madness in them. Her golden hair—the origin of her name—was unpinned, lying loose around her shoulders. It looked so natural I had to remind myself it was a wig, covering the fact that her hair had been whacked off the first time I saw her and hadn't yet had time to grow back to its full length.

"Thank the gods you're here, Gaius Pliny," she said. "And Cornelius Tacitus, it's wonderful to see you again." She took Tacitus' hand and squeezed it. "You two are my only hope."

"Lady Aurelia, please don't expect too much of us," I said. "We'll give you all the help we can, but there may not be much we can do."

She wrung her hands. "If you can just get my husband to talk, you'll have done more than any of us."

"Where is Calpurnius now?"

"He's being held in the *vigiles*' quarters. They won't let me see him. They say he doesn't want to see me."

"Tacitus and I will go there first thing tomorrow." I deliberately did not promise her that I would talk to him because I didn't know if they would let me, or if he would want to.

"My lady," the midwife said, "you should sit down. You need to rest."

Aurelia slipped her arm through mine and let me escort her to the *exhedra* at the end of the garden. The garden itself must have been quite lovely at some time, but now it showed signs of a lack of care. Shovels and rakes leaned against the walls at random, as though waiting for someone to put them to use. The scraggly plants were struggling to recover from neglect as well as from the effects of the eruption. The plaster on the walls of the rooms surrounding the garden was cracked in places. Here and there a few chunks had fallen out. In the fresco to my right Venus, cradling the dead Adonis, was missing her face and her right shoulder and breast. In a far corner of the garden ash had been piled up more than half as high as the wall.

"This was one of my father's houses," Aurelia said, "the one where I grew up. Since I was his only child, he left it to me when he died. It's very dear to me. My husband's house was farther south. It was buried in the ash by the eruption. He lived with his father west of Naples for a few years until we married."

"So Calpurnius has lived in this house for only a year or so?" I asked.

"Yes. Is that significant?"

"I'm not sure. Before he came here, would he have had any contact with the woman who was murdered?"

"None that I know of. Bastet, you've served my husband's family for so long. Did Calpurnius know that poor woman?"

"No, my lady. None of us who came here with him knew her."

While I was weighing what I had just learned, Tacitus said, "I take it you've combined households since your marriage."

Aurelia nodded. "The arrangement has worked well, I think. We are one family now."

Out of the corner of my eye I tried to study Bastet's face for a reaction to what Aurelia had just said, but I couldn't read anything. I wished I could keep my face that impassive when I was playing *latrunculus*.

"I'm sorry for the appearance of the house," Aurelia said. "We just haven't gotten everything repaired, even yet. Calpurnius did a lot of work right after we married, but he seems to have given up now. My father had to pile up that ash just to get it off the plants. Calpurnius keeps telling me he's going to have the rest of it removed, but no one has touched it in months."

"It's clear the damage was extensive," I said. "At least you didn't have to abandon the place, since it means so much to you."

"Sometimes I wonder if that wouldn't have been the wiser thing to do." Aurelia sighed heavily, then gathered herself. "Now, I suppose you need to see poor Amalthea."

"As soon as possible, yes." I hadn't wanted to rush her, but I couldn't have let her go on talking much longer.

"I'll have her brought up here."

"Is there a room you can put her in?"

"That would be better, wouldn't it?" Aurelia said. "It will give you privacy to work and spare poor Amalthea from being made a spectacle. You can use that last room." She pointed across the garden. "It's empty. And we'll make sure you have plenty of light."

"Maybe it would be better to examine her where she is now," Tacitus said, "just to avoid moving her any more than we have to."

"I put her in a little cave, like a cellar, below the house," Aurelia said. "You would find it much too cramped to work in." She summoned her steward and told him to have the woman's body brought to us.

While we waited Aurelia offered us bread, cheese, and wine. I wasn't sure I wanted to eat much, considering the condition I expected the woman's body to be in. Normally the sight of a body doesn't make me queasy, but I still wasn't entirely recovered from an entire day spent on the water.

"How old was she?" I asked.

"About thirty-five, I think," Aurelia said.

"Had she been in this house all her life?"

"According to his records, my father purchased her and her mother when Amalthea was about ten."

"Do you know of any diseases or other problems she might have had?" Knowing such things beforehand helps me to understand what I'm seeing in a situation like this.

Aurelia shook her head. "As far as I know, she was in good health."

In a few moments two servants entered the garden from the direction where I thought the kitchen must be, carrying a woman's body between them. She was limp, V-shaped. The death rigor had already passed. That would make our work easier. Aurelia directed them to the room where we would examine her. Two lampstands were set up and Tacitus closed the door.

VII

L YING BEFORE US on the bed was the body of a nondescript woman of medium height. I doubt that I would ever have noticed her if we'd passed one another on the street. She was still wearing the gown she'd had on when she was killed, the front of it soaked in blood.

"There's dirt all over her," Tacitus said. "It looks like she was buried and dug up."

I pinched some of the dirt between my fingers. "It's clay. Very dry. We'll have to ask Aurelia about that."

"I thought she would be much more…decayed," Tacitus said.

"I did, too. It looks like she hasn't been dead more than a few hours." I raised one of her arms and found it limber. "I wonder if this clay has dried her flesh and prevented it from rotting. The death stiffness has passed, though."

"Should we…take her gown off?" Tacitus' hesitancy—almost a sense of decency—surprised me. I also felt much more reluctance to undress the woman than I had ever felt about undressing the body of a dead man. But it had to be done.

"Do you have your knife on you?"

In light of our experiences the last two years Tacitus and I have taken to carrying a weapon at all times, something that men of our class don't ordinarily do. Tacitus carries a knife. My weapon is the short legionary sword I used when I was a military tribune in Syria. In spite of some discomfort, I keep it strapped under my tunic. I'm not particularly adept at using it, but I feel safer having it at hand. I wasn't wearing it at the moment because I hadn't figured I'd need it on the trireme. Tacitus gave me his knife and I began cutting Amalthea's gown off of her, starting at the top and working down.

The first thing I noticed was the red marks around her neck. "Someone grabbed her by the throat," I pointed out to Tacitus.

"From in front or from behind? Can you tell?"

"Not immediately, but we'll have to figure that out."

As I got to the bottom of the gown we discovered that Amalthea had soiled herself, as people often do in the agony of a violent death. We raised her body and slipped the gown out from under her, dropping it in a wad beside the door.

"Not what you'd call a pretty woman, was she?" Tacitus said. "She might have been at one time, though. You know, Herodotus said that Egyptian embalmers weren't allowed to work on the women until they'd been dead for several days. Apparently they caught one of them coupling with a fresh corpse."

At my look of dismay, he raised his hands and said, "I'm merely reporting what Herodotus said. Surely you don't think I'm *that* depraved."

"I know you have lines you won't cross. Some of them, I've learned, are pretty far out on the frontier."

I pulled a blanket from under Amalthea and laid it over her, covering as much as I could. The wound in her chest was the only thing we needed to look at.

"Aurelia didn't say anything about her having a child," Tacitus said.

"What makes you think she had a child?"

Tacitus raised the blanket. "Her belly. Those silvery marks are where the skin stretched when she was pregnant and then didn't return to its normal size."

"How do you know that?"

"You really should get out of your house and go to the baths, Gaius Pliny. Now that Domitian encourages men and women to bathe together, there's much to be learned. I should think you would have, shall we say, a scientific interest."

"My only interest right now is in finding out how this woman was killed." I pulled the blanket back over the lower part of her body.

"There's not much to puzzle over, is there?" Tacitus said. "A knife wound near the left breast, just as Thamyras said."

"It's above the breast, not below it. That means the blow was struck down. Let me have your knife." I inserted Tacitus' knife slowly into the wound, not pushing but letting it follow the path made by the knife that killed Amalthea.

"What are you doing?" Tacitus cried.

The knife handle was pointing upward, toward the woman's face, and toward her right side. The blade ran down into her chest.

"I think whoever killed her was standing behind her," I said. "He grabbed her around the neck and reached over her and drove the knife in."

"Couldn't someone standing in front of her have stabbed her with a downward motion?"

I turned Tacitus so we were standing face-to-face. "See how the knife is angled to the woman's right? If the person who killed her was standing in front of her, as I am standing in front of you, he would have had to be left-handed to inflict that sort of wound. And remember, he's holding her by the throat, so his own right arm might get in the way. Someone stabbing her from the front would be more likely, I think, to use an underhand motion. The wound would be below her breast and would go straight in."

Tacitus put his right hand on my throat and pretended to stab me. "It is awkward," he said.

"And, even though you're stabbing downward," I pointed out, "the blade would go in straight, not angled the way Amalthea's wound is."

Tacitus mimed stabbing me at that angle. "Yes, it is quite a bit more awkward. So you think the killer was standing behind her?"

"I'm certain—well, reasonably certain—of it. You're taller than I am." I turned my back to Tacitus. He put his hand on my throat and acted like he was reaching over to stab me.

"This could also explain why there was no blood on Calpurnius' tunic," he said, "if he attacked her from behind."

I hadn't intended to strengthen the case against Aurelia's husband. "But Calpurnius knew her. Would someone who knew her approach her from behind? I think he'd be more likely to walk up to her, face-to-face. She wouldn't be surprised to see him. And he would plunge the knife straight in, even with an upward thrust, not downward. The wound would be below the breast, probably in her stomach."

"You're saying 'he,'" Tacitus observed. "Have you ruled out a woman as the killer?"

"Not necessarily. The so-called fairer sex is just as capable of mayhem as we are."

"What do you make of the fact that there's only one wound?"

I had to think about that question for a moment. "If someone was angry at Amalthea, I would expect him to stab her multiple times." I repeated a stabbing motion. "This one wound was precisely placed. When I put my blade into the hole, it went between the ribs, straight to the heart." I removed and wiped the knife.

"So the killer knew what he was doing."

"I wouldn't be surprised if he had killed someone before." While I was talking I picked up Amalthea's left hand, as if I might comfort her or apologize for the indignity to which we were subjecting her. "Look at this."

"What do you see?"

"Under her fingernails. Is that blood? Bring one of those lamps over here."

Tacitus removed a lamp from one of the stands and held it close to Amalthea's hand. "Are you sure it's not just grime? She worked in the kitchen, Aurelia said. One can hardly imagine what she might have had her hands in."

"Her hands are clean." I used the point of Tacitus' knife to scrape material from under the dead woman's fingernails. When I put a speck of it in my mouth, Tacitus groaned.

"It's blood," I said, spitting it out.

"Whose blood?"

"The blood of the person who killed her, I think."

"That's a big leap."

"If someone grabbed you by the throat, what would you immediately do?"

"Kick him in the balls."

I rolled my eyes. "Wouldn't you try to get his hand off your throat? If you were a woman, smaller than the man who was attacking you and he was behind you, wouldn't you scratch at his arm?"

Tacitus put one hand on his own throat and mimed clawing at it with his other hand. "I guess so. Does this mean you're going to go around tasting people's blood to find someone that matches? Can you identify blood, like a wine vintage?"

"No. Blood is blood. But we're going to see if Calpurnius has scratches on either of his arms."

†

We found Aurelia and Bastet in the *exhedra*, at the end of the garden near where we were examining Amalthea. As was common in villas in this area, the *exhedra* had sloping couches made of concrete and arranged like a *triclinium*, with blankets and cushions covering them. At Aurelia's invitation Tacitus and I reclined, but Aurelia sat on the edge of one of the couches, like a matron of the old republic. She put a hand on her belly and almost smiled. "It's more comfortable for me to sit now. Bastet recommends it." Bastet sat in a chair near her mistress. Both women's arms were bare, and I could not stop myself from glancing at them. Neither bore any scratches.

"What did you learn from your examination?" Aurelia asked, almost as if she were afraid of the answer.

"I'm still weighing the results," I said. "But I have to ask about the condition of the body. She was killed four days ago, wasn't she?"

Aurelia nodded.

"There's no way to say this delicately, but I would expect the body to be decomposing by now."

"There's something about the soil in that little cave," Aurelia said, "that preserves flesh. I learned about it when I was ten. Amalthea got pregnant. She knew my father would be angry. He didn't like the expense of raising slave children—except his own. With the help of a few other servant women she managed to hide her condition until late in her term. Then the baby was born dead. She was frightened." Aurelia put her hand on her own belly. "She didn't know if she would be accused of killing the child. The night the child was born she and another servant dug a grave in that cellar and buried the baby. When it was discovered several months later, it looked like the child had been born only a few days before. So, when this awful thing happened, I decided to put Amalthea's body there. I didn't know if it would work with an adult, but it was the only hope I had of preserving her until you arrived."

I tried to ignore Tacitus' smug expression, but he had been right about Amalthea having a baby. "The soil down there must dry the body out and prevent putrefaction."

"Like making mummies in Egypt," Tacitus said. "Or drying a piece of meat. It's all a matter of getting the moisture out."

"Yes. You should put her back down there," I said, "in case we need to examine her again."

Aurelia summoned a servant and gave the order for Amalthea to be returned to the cellar. Before the man turned and left, Tacitus stopped him.

"Hold out your arms," Tacitus said. "And turn them over."

The man looked at Aurelia, who, in spite of the confusion on her own face, reinforced Tacitus' order. "Do as he says."

Both of the man's arms were unscathed. With a last quizzical look at Tacitus and at Aurelia, he left to carry out his assigned task.

"What was the meaning of that?" Aurelia asked, looking from one of us to the other, when the man was out of earshot.

Tacitus started to say something, but I cut him off. I was sorry he had said anything. I didn't want to reveal all that we knew. If Amalthea's assailant was in Aurelia's household, he could be forewarned, and that could make him dangerous. "Tacitus has a theory about the size of a man's forearms and his…intelligence," I said. "He tries to take samples whenever he can."

The answer clearly didn't satisfy Aurelia, but she let it pass. Once we were settled on our couches, her servants brought us dinner, placing a small table where Aurelia and Bastet could reach it. The meal was simple, as a guest might expect when arriving earlier than anticipated: dried fish in garum, beans, bread, cheese, and wine.

Aurelia sighed deeply. "Thank you again for coming, Gaius Pliny. And so quickly. I feel safer just having you here."

"Safer? Do you think you're in some danger?"

"I'm not sure. Something has been bothering Calpurnius lately, but he won't tell me what it is. As good and kind as he is, he's never been a man to share what he's thinking with others. In recent days he'd be gone for hours and I didn't know where he was or what he was doing. I suppose he's seeing another woman. I can hardly blame him. Look how fat and ugly I am right now."

"Now, my lady," Bastet said, laying a comforting hand on Aurelia's arm, "you know that's not true. Calpurnius would never betray you like that."

"And you certainly aren't fat or ugly," Tacitus said before I could get the words in. "You're bearing his child. A woman can never be more beautiful to her husband than when she's bearing his child."

"Thank you, Cornelius Tacitus. You're a very sweet man." Aurelia dabbed at her eyes. "I'm sorry I keep crying. I seem to be doing that a lot lately."

"Sweet" wasn't a word I would use to describe Tacitus, but I'd never heard him express such a tender sentiment.

"You said 'in recent days' he would be gone for considerable periods of time. How long has he been doing that?" I asked.

Aurelia closed her eyes and pondered for a moment. "For at least six months, actually. The first time I remember is last March."

"Has anything happened that would explain the change in his behavior?"

"At first I thought it might be me. Once I was pregnant, I began to have trouble controlling my temper. And I cry over the smallest thing."

Bastet patted Aurelia's arm. "That happens to many women when they're carrying a child, my lady. I never saw your husband upset by anything you said or did."

"Only because he's so patient with me."

Bastet drew Aurelia closer to her and put Aurelia's head on her shoulder. Aurelia's wig fairly gleamed against Bastet's black skin. With both of her parents dead and her husband under arrest, she had no one but her nurse to turn to. But the gesture struck me less as comforting than as confining.

I wished the solution to Aurelia's problem was as easy as letting her lay her head on my shoulder. I was beginning to suspect, though, that the murder of which Calpurnius was accused might be just one part of a much larger question, a question that might be related to the change in Calpurnius' behavior. If a man begins, at some point, to act differently than he acted before that point, then something happened to provoke the change. It might help to know if it was something Calpurnius did or something that someone did to him. Did Thamyras' unguarded comment that Aurelia had finally brought her husband some long overdue happiness have any connection with this change in the man's behavior?

Aurelia groaned and put her hand on her belly.

"Is something wrong, my lady?" Bastet asked.

"The baby's moving. She has been since I first heard Gaius Pliny's voice."

I was surprised by her choice of a pronoun. "She? How can you know it's a girl?"

"Bastet can see signs." Aurelia drew in a sharp breath.

Bastet nodded. "The women of my tribe, my lord, can recognize clues as to whether the unborn child is a boy or a girl. We've been doing it for ages. I'm sure my lady is bearing a little Calpurnia."

And I was sure that would be a disappointment to Calpurnius, as it would to any man.

†

As we ate, Tacitus, Aurelia, and I reminisced about the circumstances under which we first met. Recalling what had been a perilous few days seemed to distract Aurelia from her current worries. Bastet had not heard the story. She asked questions with a freedom that made me wonder about her standing in this household. She wasn't old enough to have been Calpurnius' nurse when he was a child.

When Bastet went to use the *latrina*, I decided to satisfy my curiosity. "Is she slave or free?" I asked Aurelia.

"She is freed. Calpurnius emancipated her several years ago after she cared for his mother for a number of years. She was the only one with his mother when she died."

I pondered that but said, "She's been in the household for a time then?"

"Calpurnius brought her back with him when he returned from his service with the army in Egypt."

"She seems to have a favored status in your house." Sometimes a favorite servant is treated like a family member—given the privilege of sitting with the family or speaking without being spoken to. We spend so much time with our servants that it's difficult not to regard some of them as special friends. Seneca claimed that he allowed his servants to recline at meals with him. I treat mine humanely, I believe, but I do try to maintain a sense of separateness between us. Without that, we would have anarchy. With it, we have a dilemma such as Aurora presents to me.

"I suppose she is a favorite," Aurelia said. "She was a princess in her own tribe, she says. That's why she wears that scarf around her head. No one has ever seen her without it."

"Not even when she bathes?" Tacitus asked.

"She doesn't bathe with the other servants. She says that, among her tribe, it is improper for a woman to bare herself before anyone but her husband. She bathes in her room." There was something guarded about Aurelia's voice.

"I think you don't quite trust her," I said.

"I've never been able to relax around her." Aurelia glanced to see if Bastet was within earshot. "There's something imperious about her that sometimes feels…sinister. Even though she's been freed, she still calls us 'my lord' and 'my lady,' as though she were still a slave. It feels… sarcastic. She's a very wise woman, and I'm not sure I could have gotten through this child-bearing without her by my side. I appreciate her, but I'm uncertain how much I trust her."

"Just be careful that you don't create resentment among your other servants. While I treat my servants kindly, I don't believe it's a good idea to allow one to assume a much higher position than the rest. It can create jealousy and resentment among those who aren't favored."

Tacitus snorted. "Interesting, coming from a man who gives one of his female slaves more freedom than most men give their wives."

Bastet's return from the *latrina* put an end to the exchange. And what could I have said? Tacitus knew that Aurora served as my eyes and ears in places where I could not go, but I didn't want to announce that to the world. A spy isn't of much use if everyone knows she's a spy. And yet, could I admit that, at that moment, I did not know where Aurora was or what her intentions were? If she had run away, I would have to find her and bring her back, to punish her and to warn all my other slaves. The typical punishment for a fugitive slave was to have FUG branded on the forehead. Could I do that to Aurora?

When Thamyras arrived with our servants and other belongings we concluded our dinner and tended to unpacking and getting everyone fed. Or, more precisely, we left Aurelia and her servants to see to those tasks.

"Before it gets completely dark," I told Thamyras, "I want to see where Amalthea's body was found."

"Certainly, my lord. It's this way."

Taking a torch, he led us out the front entrance of the house and turned left. The orchard occupied all the space between Aurelia's house and the next one up the road.

"We grow apples up here, my lord," Thamyras said, waving a hand, "and olives closer down to the shore, though they're farther from the water than they used to be. That's true all around the bay, of course. There's grapevines on the other side of the house. It was all planted before I came here," he added as though to forestall any criticism of the arrangement that we might make. "And the trees are much closer together than they should be. The one that Amalthea marked is over here."

He led us to a tree—one of the oldest in the orchard, to judge from its size—that was far enough away from the house to be out of sight due to all the intervening foliage. Only a few paces from it sat a grotesque herm marking the boundary between Aurelia's land and the neighbor's. The ash had been dug away from around the ugly little statue so that it didn't have to be moved. His spot was now the lowest in the orchard.

"There's what she carved, my lord." He rubbed his hand on the trunk of the tree.

"All right. Thank you." I took the torch from him. "You can go on back to the house now. Tell the lady Aurelia we'll be in shortly."

"Do you not need me to show you anything else, my lord?"

"This is all we need. Go back to the house."

"Yes, my lord."

Tacitus gave me an odd look and started to say something, but I held up my hand to stop him until I was confident Thamyras was far enough away not to hear us.

"Why didn't you want him here?" he asked.

"We just arrived. Our luggage isn't even unpacked. I'm not sure yet whom to trust. You know how servants spread tales in a house. I don't want everyone to know what we know, almost as soon as we know it, especially if someone in this house is involved in whatever's going on."

"Do you think someone might be?"

"I think we'd better assume that anyone in this house could have wielded a knife out here. Now let's look at this mark."

The mark was on the east side of the tree. Logical enough, since

Amalthea came out here in the early morning. With the sun now low
in the sky to the west, though, it was difficult to make it out, even with
the torch. I ran my finger over it and then Tacitus did the same. The
carving was the simplest outline of a fish one could make.

"Why would somebody carve a fish on a tree?" I asked.

"And what's that below it?" Tacitus ran a hand down the trunk of
the tree. "Is it writing?"

I had to peer in closely to make out the letters carved vertically beneath the symbol. "It's the Greek word for fish. If you've carved a fish,
why would you then carve the word for fish right below it?"

"I'm surprised she even knew it," Tacitus said.

"A woman who worked in a kitchen in this part of Italy would have
heard it, I imagine."

"But was she literate?"

"Not highly." I traced the word with my finger. "The letters are
crude."

"This is an odd place to practice her writing."

"We'll ask about her education when we get back to the house.
Now I want to look around this spot before it gets dark."

The ash from Vesuvius had made the ground crusty, so we could
see the footprints of the people who had carried the dead woman away,
but everything close to the tree, where she must have been killed, was
a confused mess of impressions made by people milling around and
moving the body.

"Widen the search," I said. "Make larger circles around the tree."

"What are we looking for?" Tacitus asked.

"If someone other than Calpurnius killed the woman, there should
be footprints leading to and away from this spot from another direction."

"But there aren't any," Tacitus said after making a few circuits
around the tree and its neighbors. "It's as though he flew in and settled
in a tree until he was ready to attack."

"We know that's impossible, so we just have to find how he did get
to her. Look farther out."

We fanned out, moving away from Aurelia's house, until I spotted
a footprint at the base of one tree, then other footprints leading up to
that tree and away from it. "He walked this far," I said, "climbed this

tree, and moved from tree to tree until he was over the spot where he knew Amalthea came."

"Wouldn't she have heard or noticed him?"

"Thamyras said she became so enraptured in her prayers that she was practically in a trance. The morning he spoke to her, she didn't notice him until he touched her."

Tacitus studied the footprints. "The killer didn't come from inside the house, but he knew Amalthea would be here. The only way he could know that was if someone in the house told him."

"Or," I said, "if he's someone who used to be in the house but isn't anymore. I think we've demonstrated Calpurnius' innocence."

"But, if it's that easy, why won't Calpurnius say anything?"

VIII

BY THE TIME we got back to the house darkness had settled in. Showing us to our rooms, Aurelia walked between Tacitus and me and put her arms through ours, drawing us close to her.

"Thank you again, both of you, for coming to help me. I think I will sleep better tonight than I have in several days."

"We'll do everything we can for you," I said, "but it's not going to be easy."

We stopped in front of the two rooms where Tacitus and I would be sleeping. I had to move a shovel to open my door. As Aurelia kissed each of us on the cheek she groaned, put her hand on her belly, and bent over.

"Are you all right?" I asked.

She nodded quickly and drew a deep breath. "I think this baby is eager to meet you, Gaius Pliny. She's been kicking since the moment I heard your voice in the atrium. I'd better get her to bed."

We watched as she made her way across the garden to her room, where Bastet stood waiting for her. Some women, when they are carrying a child, get fatter all over, to put it unkindly. Others seem to carry the child out in front, as though they have it in a basket. Looking at them from the back, one can hardly tell they're pregnant. Aurelia was one of the latter. Watching her cross the garden, I couldn't see any difference from the way she looked the first time I saw her. When she had closed the door behind her, Tacitus and I wished one another a good night and entered our rooms.

I heard Tacitus close his door, but I left mine partly open. Before the eruption of Vesuvius I had never thought about how we build our houses. I doubt if many Romans had. When the eruption started, many people sought shelter inside—a natural enough response. After a few hours, when it showed no sign of letting up, they decided to leave but couldn't because our doors are hinged so they open outward, away from the room. Several feet of heavy ash piled up against the doors kept many people from opening them. I was told by Decius that my uncle almost died that way in a house in Stabiae, before the fumes finally killed him on the shore of the bay. My mother and I had to flee our house at Misenum to avoid being buried.

While I stayed at Misenum after the eruption, I would not close the door of a room all the way. In the years since, being away from this area, I thought I had overcome that fear. Now that I was back here, with the jagged peak of Vesuvius looming over me in the moonlight, I could not bear to think of closing a door.

†

I was awakened by a woman's scream, cut short as though someone had clamped a hand over her mouth. For a moment I thought I might have been dreaming—reliving the catastrophe—but then I heard the muffled sounds of a struggle, coming from the garden.

Putting just enough of my head through the partly open door to be able to look around, I saw two men carrying someone toward the rear of the garden. In the moonlight I could see a swollen belly that could belong to only one woman in this household. One man had his hand over Aurelia's mouth and his other arm around her throat. The second man had picked up her feet. Since she wasn't using her arms to fight them off, I thought her hands must be tied behind her back.

My first impulse was to shout at them, but I decided on a surprise attack. I couldn't find my sword quickly in the dark, so I grabbed the shovel that was propped against the wall beside my door. The men were having too much trouble controlling Aurelia to notice me until I was right upon them. I aimed a blow at the head of the man carrying her feet, but in his attempt to keep his hold and avoid her kicks, he bent over at the last instant and I could only land a solid blow on his back. As soon as his grip loosened, Aurelia kicked him in the groin. He crumpled to his knees.

The second man dropped Aurelia and I could see a gag stuffed in her mouth. The man pulled a short sword from under his cloak and took a stance like a gladiator preparing to fight. We circled and feinted, but he wouldn't get close enough for me to strike a blow. I yelled for Tacitus, to no avail. The man sleeps like the dead, and his door was closed.

"Somebody! Anybody!" I called. "Help!"

"I'm here, my lord," Bastet's voice sounded from somewhere in the garden.

As unfamiliar as I was with the garden, even with the moonlight, I tripped over a bench and fell backwards. I managed to keep my grip on the shovel, ready to ward off a blow. Instead, the intruder pulled his companion to his feet and they scrambled up the pile of ash and over the back wall. A piece of pottery, thrown by someone behind me, crashed against the wall, barely missing the men. One of them let out a cry of surprise or pain as he went over the wall.

Even though my yelling hadn't penetrated Tacitus' dreams, I had awakened several servants. They began lighting lamps as I knelt over Aurelia and removed the gag and the cord binding her wrists. As soon as her hands were free she threw them around my neck, grasping me so tightly I had trouble breathing.

"Just lie still," I said, loosening her grip. "Let's make sure you're all right."

"I think…I am," she choked out between sobs. "Thank you, Gaius Pliny." She grimaced and put a hand on her belly.

"Is it the baby?"

"No more…than usual. Don't let…"

"I'm right here, child," Bastet said over my shoulder.

Where had she been during the attack? I wondered. I had heard her voice but never saw her. Had I awakened her or had she already been in the garden?

With the help of two of the female servants Bastet got Aurelia back into her bed. The intruders didn't seem to have disturbed anything in the room. Aurelia was all they were after.

Tacitus finally stumbled out of his room. His eyes widened as I recounted the evening's adventure.

"Was Aurelia harmed? The baby?"

"I think she's all right. Let's look at how they got out."

"And how they got in, I imagine," Tacitus said, rubbing his eyes.

We climbed up the pile of ash, which had hardened over the years until it was practically a stone staircase, and looked over the back wall. The intruders were long gone, but the trees growing close to the wall must have provided them a means of entry. They were old trees, hardy survivors of the ashfall from the eruption. A broken branch hung down from one.

"I want to look around out there in the morning," I said.

"Why not do it now?" Tacitus asked.

"We could easily miss something in the dark, or trample over something important."

"You're right. Sorry I wasn't any help to you," Tacitus said as we climbed back down to the garden. "I was more exhausted than I realized."

"With at least one of them armed, I'm not sure what you could have done. I had to choose between chasing them and looking after Aurelia."

"You made the right decision. Following them in the dark, in unfamiliar territory, would have been risky, to say the least. And there might have been more men out there."

I nodded. "In the morning we can examine the ground outside the wall to see if they left any signs that would help us identify them or tell us which way they went."

When we returned to Aurelia's door Bastet had put herself on guard, sitting on a stool in front of it, holding a short knife.

"No one gets in for the rest of the night, my lord," she said. "No one."

Surely she didn't mean me. "May I talk to her?" I wanted to ask her if she recognized either of the men, or if they said anything to her.

Bastet's eyes narrowed to slits and her hand tightened around the handle of the knife. "No one gets in, my lord. I gave her something to help her sleep and forget all of this."

I hoped she could sleep, but I didn't want her to forget even the smallest detail of what had happened.

"I wish you had consulted me before you did that," I said.

"My lord, you are an honored guest, but you are not part of this house. With my lord Calpurnius gone and my lady in the condition she's in, this house is my responsibility."

†

At first light the next morning Tacitus and I unbarred the door in the back wall of the garden. The wall around the door was painted to represent a house, so one had the feeling he was about to step indoors but instead went outside. The whole effect struck me as whimsical. We stepped out to examine the spot where the intruders had made their entry and exit.

"I suspect this is where they planned to take Aurelia out," I said.

Tacitus yawned and nodded. "I can't imagine them hauling her up over the wall."

The barren stretch of ash between the house and the bay looked like a ghostly desert, broken only by random bits of greenery that struggled to grow wherever the wind or the birds happened to have dropped the seeds. Close to the house a layer of the ash had been removed to save the trees and other plants, but the ground still had a gray tinge to it and crunched under our feet as we walked. At least the smoky smell that had lingered over the area for so long had dissipated. The air was as fresh as it should be on the coast in the early morning.

"Here's the tree with the broken branch," I said.

Tacitus tugged at the branch. "It's fresh. One of them must have grabbed it as he jumped from the wall last night and broken it."

"That would explain the yell I heard. Watch where you step. If the branch broke, the man who was holding it must have hit the ground harder than he expected. He might have left an imprint."

The man had apparently managed to land on his feet. Below the broken branch we found two deep footprints and a handprint where he reached down to steady himself. I knelt to examine them.

"So we know he had two feet and at least one hand," Tacitus said. "Beyond that, can you learn anything?"

"It's a right hand, and the small finger is missing."

Tacitus knelt beside me. "Missing? Are you sure? Maybe it just didn't make an impression."

"No. The other fingers and the palm all made a clear impression. He must have landed hard and leaned forward with a bit of force. There's definitely a stump where the small finger was cut off." I pressed my hand into the ground next to the intruder's print. "See, that's about the same depth as this print, and all five of my fingers show clearly." I put my hand in the intruder's print. "He's about my size, I think."

Tacitus snorted. "The size of one portion of a man's anatomy doesn't necessarily tell you anything about his overall size. Anyone who's been in a public bath should know that."

I couldn't dispute him.

"Could you tell anything about either man last night? How tall they were? How heavy?"

I shook my head. "So much happened so fast. It was dark, and I was concerned about Aurelia. I had a sense that both men were bigger than I am, but it's not as though they were legionaries standing for inspection. We were all moving, and one of them was bent over after Aurelia kicked him."

"Maybe she can give us some description of them."

"I hope so, if whatever Bastet gave her didn't actually make her forget everything. I wanted to talk to her last night, while her memory was fresh." I stood, straightened my tunic, and made sure no one was around. "That woman bothers me. Does she seem awfully protective of this family, or am I reacting too strongly?"

"No, you're right." Tacitus brushed ash off his hands. "The way she blocked Aurelia's door surprised me. But I'm not sure protective is quite the word. Her attitude strikes me more as possessive. She seems to regard them as hers, rather than herself as theirs."

"I definitely want to talk to Aurelia some more without Bastet being there. She's already expressed some misgivings about the woman. I want to know more." I looked around and up at the wall the intruders had climbed over. "I guess we've done all we can out here for now."

"At least we know something about them," Tacitus said as we went back into the garden and dropped the bar in place across the door. "They were both agile. One of them was heavy enough to break that branch and was missing a finger on his right hand."

"As a clue, that may not help much. How many butchers, farm hands, and retired soldiers do you know who have all ten digits?" I rubbed my unshaved chin as I glanced around the garden. "And another question we can't answer is how they knew which room Aurelia was in."

"Why do you think they knew that?"

I counted doors. "There are ten rooms opening off this garden. No one else reported anyone coming into their rooms. The only door those men opened was the door to Aurelia's room. They didn't have to search for her. She was the one they wanted and they knew exactly where she was."

With the sun fully up, I could see the thin column of gray smoke still rising from Vesuvius, like the last breath of a fire that has been extinguished. Or the smoldering of a fire that is just waiting to flare up again.

"I don't like the looks of that," I said.

"At least the ground's not shaking," Tacitus reassured me. "That's not…what it looked like when it erupted, is it?" He seemed to need my assurance now.

"No. There was no smoke at all until it erupted. I guess this is nothing to worry about." Then why was my stomach starting to tighten?

"Let's see if we can talk to Aurelia," Tacitus said.

We crossed the garden to Aurelia's room. She was still asleep, and Bastet refused to allow anyone to disturb her. The Nubian woman's eyes were glazed from lack of sleep, but her grip on the knife was still firm.

"An exhausted woman with a knife in her hand isn't someone I want to confront," Tacitus said as we stepped away from Aurelia's door like rejected lovers.

"We need to talk to Calpurnius anyway," I reminded him. "Let's get someone to guide us."

"Do you think it's safe to leave Aurelia alone after last night?" Tacitus asked.

I looked over my shoulder at Bastet. "She's hardly alone, but even the most determined guard can have momentary lapses. And someone in this house may not be trustworthy. Let's get a couple of our men and post them to guard the guard."

We summoned one of my servants and one of Tacitus', armed them, and instructed them not to let Aurelia out of their sight, no matter what Bastet might say.

†

Feeling somewhat more secure, we set out on horseback, accompanied by Thamyras and three of our servants, for the headquarters of the *vigiles* in Naples. With the sky clear and the air cool, it would have been a beautiful day, if not for the gray pall hanging over everything.

Thamyras rode between us, with me on his left and Tacitus on his right. In a bag over his shoulder the servant carried a change of clothing for Calpurnius. Away from his household, with no one except our men around to hear what was said, I took the opportunity to question the man again, based on what I had learned from Aurelia.

"I understand the house you live in now belongs to the lady Aurelia," I began.

"Yes, my lord. Calpurnius' house was covered by the ash."

"Did he try to dig it out?"

"We tried, my lord, but the ash was just too deep. We couldn't do much more than dig tunnels in it. By the time we gave up it looked like a gang of miners had been in the place. And the roof had collapsed over part of the atrium. It wasn't safe to be in there. We recovered a few pieces, especially a bronze statue that stood in the atrium. The master was particularly keen to get that out."

"The one that's in the atrium now, the satyr with the Pan flutes?"

"Yes, my lord."

"I can see why he went to the trouble," Tacitus said. "It's a beautiful piece."

"He prizes it, my lord."

"How long have you been in Calpurnius' household?" I asked.

"I was born in the house, my lord, just two months after my master. He and I grew up together." He said it with the kind of pride that *vernae*—slaves born and raised in one house—often display. They consider themselves as much a part of the family as the master's children.

Tacitus jumped back in. "You and Calpurnius' other servants must resent having to move into Aurelia's house and take second place to her servants."

"Why, no, my lord." Thamyras seemed genuinely surprised. "There's no first or second place. Because of the way she grew up, I guess, the lady Aurelia won't let anyone act superior to the next one. And besides, there's…well, there's not many of us left from Calpurnius' house."

"Why not? Has he sent some to his other estates?"

"He's been selling some of his slaves, my lord, starting with the ones he bought most recently. It's brought…a great sadness into…the house."

"When did he sell your woman?" I asked softly.

Thamyras drew his horse to a halt. Tacitus and I stopped beside him.

"How did you guess, my lord?" I could see the pain on his face.

"I didn't have to guess. Your voice fell. Your shoulders sagged. That great sadness was written all over you."

"I can't help it, my lord. I fell in love with her the day she came into the house. It was about six months before the eruption. And she loved me. I thought we would be together for the rest of our lives."

"What was her name?" Tacitus asked.

"She was called Proxena, my lord."

"Did Calpurnius allow you to marry her?" I grant my own slaves the right to marry and to make wills. I would never sell a slave who was the spouse of another of my servants.

"No, my lord, he didn't. But we lived together as man and wife."

"Where is she now?" I asked.

"I don't know, my lord. Calpurnius sold the first batch of his slaves to a dealer…a few months after the eruption. They were the ones he'd bought most recently. She could be anywhere by now. I just hope she's in a household and not in a…a whorehouse." His voice broke as he said the last word. The memory of Proxena must have been as fresh to him as though she had gotten out of his bed that morning, not five years ago.

How does the memory of a certain woman insinuate itself into a man's mind so deeply that he cannot eradicate it? And yet other women leave no impression. I had met my bride-to-be, Livia, several times, but at this moment I could not recall the color of her hair or eyes, only that she had a high forehead. And yet I could see Aurora as though she were standing in front of me and the light pressure of the Tyche ring on my chest made her seem all the more real. I had not willed myself to think this way about Aurora—no man of my class, in his right mind, falls in love with a slave—and I knew I had to marry Livia. There were other women with whom I had been intimate. I had never even come close to that with Aurora, but she was the only woman I could picture at the moment, or imagine myself spending my life with.

I patted Thamyras on his shoulder. While he lowered his head and wiped his tears I studied our surroundings, to get my mind off Aurora. Even in the few miles we had traveled the world had turned greener, though still a pale green, like the merest hint of color a modest woman would put over her eyes.

"You must really hate Calpurnius," Tacitus said.

"What, my lord? Hate him?" Thamyras fought to recover his composure. "No, I can't do that. You masters…have the right to sell…your property."

I kicked my horse in the ribs to get him moving again. The other horses followed his lead. "It sounds to me as though Calpurnius needed money. Is that why he started selling his slaves?"

Thamyras shook his head. "I don't know, my lord. My work is in the gardens. I'm not one he consults about his finances."

"Whom does he consult?"

"No one, really, my lord. He's very close about his money. There is one freedman, Diomedes, who assists him."

So Diomedes would be a man we'd have to talk to when we returned to Aurelia's house.

"Why hasn't Calpurnius freed you?" Tacitus asked. It was the question I was about to ask. Emancipating a slave who has grown up alongside the master is a common practice—something I should consider for Aurora—and freedom might have taken some of the sting out of Thamyras' loss of his woman, just as it might make it easier for Aurora to accept that I cannot marry her.

"I've not…asked him to, my lord," Thamyras said. "I'm sure he will when the time is right. All in all, he's a kind man. I wouldn't want to be anywhere else, whether I was slave or free."

†

We were on the outskirts of Naples now, passing the Necropolis with its tombs and monuments. Some of the older ones were still partially covered by the ash, probably because the deceased had no more family to care for the tomb. Ashes covered by ash—the image struck me as ironic, though I meant no disrespect to the dead.

"I need to stop for a moment," Tacitus said. "And there's a stone I can use to mount again."

He dismounted and stepped behind one of the larger tombs. It's common practice for travelers to relieve themselves in the shadows of a Necropolis. This one was unusually large, offering lots of privacy. Tacitus returned with a smile on his face.

"I must have found the favorite spot for people around here. On the back of that big limestone monument someone has scratched, 'Stranger, please don't piss on my grave.'"

"That one does provide the most cover," I said.

"Some of these tumbled ones look rather old," Tacitus said, "even older than the time of the eruption."

"There was a huge earthquake in this area the year I was born," I said. "That was seventeen years before the eruption. Those monuments must have been damaged then."

"I wonder if there was any connection between that earthquake and the eruption," Tacitus said.

"How could there have been? Seventeen years is a long time."

Tacitus looked over his shoulder at Vesuvius. "I suppose you're right."

Where people had uncovered their stones they had piled some of the ash against the neglected burials. The newer tombs sat higher, some as much as a cubit.

With our journey nearing its end I wanted to ask some more questions of Thamyras while I still had the time. "The lady Aurelia says she has noticed a change in her husband over the past few months. He often goes away for hours, and she doesn't know where he is or what he's doing. Do you know where he goes? What he does?"

Thamyras pondered before he replied. "No, my lord, I don't. As I said, my work is mostly in the garden and the grounds, so he doesn't confide in me about his comings and goings."

"Does he walk or ride?"

"He rides, my lord. At least when I've seen him leaving."

"So he must be going some distance. Which direction does he go?"

"Toward Naples, my lord. There's no point in going south."

"Does he take anyone with him?"

"Not that I've seen, my lord."

Tacitus and I looked at one another in surprise. For a man of Calpurnius' class—our class—to venture out unaccompanied would be most unusual, not to mention dangerous.

IX

WE ROMANS have controlled Naples for several hundred years—the city withstood a siege by Hannibal—but it still feels like the Greek city it originally was—Neapolis, Newtown. It was laid out on the grid pattern that makes most Greek cities in southern Italy so attractive and so easy to get around in, unlike Rome, which grew up randomly, without any planning except what was driven by greed.

The *vigiles'* headquarters where Calpurnius was being held sat on the main road by which we entered the southernmost gate of Naples. Just ahead of us I could see a bath, which I intended to visit after we talked to Calpurnius. We hadn't bathed yesterday on the ship, and it was too late to bathe when we arrived at Aurelia's villa. This morning I had washed off and put on a clean tunic, but that was no substitute for a real bath.

The *vigiles'* building must have originally been a large *taberna*. The main room had been cut up into smaller rooms, but the counter at which food had been sold was still visible and the bits of wall paintings that I could see were the sort of thing one finds in a food-shop. The commander of the day watch—a gray-haired and grizzled former legionary, to judge by his demeanor—introduced himself as Novatus but greeted us with something less than enthusiasm.

"Why do you want to see *him?*" he asked when I told him what we wanted. "He won't talk to anybody."

"I promised his wife I would talk to him," I said, "and we've brought him some fresh clothes."

"That'll be welcome," Novatus said, "for him as well as for us. The tunic he was wearing when they brought him in is getting a bit ripe."

"His servant also brought a razor. A shave might make him feel better."

Novatus shook his head. "You'll have to leave that here. I can't let you shave him unless it's done in front of me. And your other men will have to wait out here."

Thamyras deposited the bag containing the razor on the counter where people used to get their food. I hoped Tacitus and I did not give away, by our expressions, the fact that we were armed. Novatus made the assumption that people always do—that men of our class depend on our servants to protect us and so don't carry weapons.

Swinging the short rod that was the symbol of his office, Novatus led the three of us through what had been the kitchen to some storage rooms at the back of the building. The buckets used to fight fires were stacked along one wall. On the opposite wall stood a collection of swords and spears. The doors of three of the storage rooms had been removed and replaced with iron bars that ran from top to bottom of the door frame, with a small opening at the bottom to allow containers to be passed through. Only one of the cells was occupied.

Calpurnius, his head in his hands, sat on a rickety bed. If the covering on it had ever had a color, it was lost under dirt and stains that I would not want to try to identify.

"Visitors," Novatus said, rapping the bars with his rod.

Calpurnius looked up slowly, as though trying to comprehend the word. "I don't want any visitors."

"Well, you've got 'em."

"Where can we talk to him?" I asked.

"Right here," Novatus said.

I looked around. "But there's no privacy."

Novatus grasped one of the bars. "We'll open this door when we're told to bring him to trial. Until then, he stays on that side and you stay on this side...sir."

When Novatus was out of sight I told Thamyras to watch and let us know if anyone came into this part of the building. Calpurnius was standing up now. He was a tall, thin man in his forties, whose natural gauntness was heightened by his need for a shave and a good meal.

"Gaius Pliny? Is that you?"

"Yes, Calpurnius. I've come to help you."

"No, no. This is terrible. You've got to leave right away." Shaking his head, he grabbed the bars, more to hold himself up than to try to force them open.

"Look at his arms," I told Tacitus. "No scratches."

Calpurnius looked at his own arms and back at me. "What? What are you talking about?" His voice was thick and slow.

"Amalthea scratched the person who killed her. I didn't think you did it, but now I know for certain that you're innocent."

"Get out of here!" Calpurnius waved an unscathed arm to send us away. "You've got to get out of here before they know you've talked to me."

"'They'? Who are 'they'?"

"The people who will harm my wife and child if they find out you've been here."

"Someone tried to kidnap her last night," Tacitus said. "Fortunately we were there and stopped them."

I glared at him but didn't say anything about the "we."

"No, don't you see?" Calpurnius' voice was growing desperate. "They tried *because* they knew you were there. Oh, gods, it's hopeless."

"Calpurnius," I said, "you're not making any sense. What's going on?"

"I can't tell you, Gaius Pliny. If I did, you would be in as much danger as my family and I already are. Just go away. That's the best thing you can do for us. The only thing."

I took a step toward the bars and waited until Calpurnius' eyes found mine. Then I asked, "Do you know a man who is missing the small finger on his right hand?"

Calpurnius sank to his knees, still gripping the iron bars. "It's too late, then."

"No, it isn't, Calpurnius. I can help you. I know you didn't kill Amalthea. There are no scratches on your arms, no blood on your clothes—"

"Of course I didn't kill her, but that doesn't matter." With his head down, I could hardly hear him.

"What were you doing out in the orchard so early in the morning?"

He looked up, like a man pleading for mercy. "I'd had a message

the day before, telling me to be there, where the herm is, at the first
hour."

"A message from whom?"

"I can't tell you, Gaius Pliny. I really can't."

I decided not to press that point for now. "Why would you do what
the message said?"

Calpurnius got up off the floor and sat on the bed, with his hands
clasped between his knees, his head down. "Because I'm being blackmailed."

"Blackmailed? By whom?"

"I can't tell you."

"Can't or won't?" Tacitus asked.

"I can't, because I don't know who's doing it."

"But you knew the message was from the blackmailer?"

"Yes."

"How did you know that?" I asked.

"Because it contained a code word that only they and I could know."

I knew there was no point in asking him what the code word was.
"What did you do when you got to the herm?"

"I called quietly, but no one answered. Then I saw a pair of feet
sticking out from behind the statue. When I looked more closely, I
saw Amalthea."

"Where was the knife?"

"On the ground beside her."

"You picked it up. Why did you do that?"

"Because I heard a noise—a movement, I guess. I was afraid and
the knife was the only weapon at hand."

"You don't carry a weapon?"

He snorted. "In my own house? Why would I?"

"Do you know who made the noise?"

He gestured to his servant. "It turned out to be Thamyras, coming
out to work." The slave nodded.

"Could you tell if Amalthea was still alive?"

"I don't believe she was. She didn't move or make any sound."

"Thamyras says you sent him to get help. Why did you do that?"

"It just seemed the thing to do. There was blood all over her."

"Did you know—"

"Gaius Pliny, I barely knew the woman." His patience was wearing thin. "She was part of my wife's household. Are you aware that I'm living in my wife's—"

"Yes. Aurelia explained the situation."

"So, you see, a woman like Amalthea—a kitchen servant—is someone I haven't spoken to more than half a dozen times in the year I've been living in the house. I have no idea why she was out there."

"She was in the habit of going there every morning," Tacitus said, "before she began her work in the kitchen."

"Well, I wouldn't know about that." He straightened up as he seemed to gather some last bit of resolve. "Now, you simply must leave. And I mean leave my house, leave Naples. Leave my family alone before you do more damage than you've already done."

"We're only trying to help," I said. "If you'll tell us—"

"I will not say another word to you." Calpurnius flung himself on the bed, with his face to the wall.

Tacitus and I looked at one another. "I guess we've gotten all we're going to get out of him," Tacitus said. "And I don't think he wants a shave."

"If you decide to tell us any more," I said to Calpurnius' back, "ask your jailer to send a messenger to us. I'll leave him something that should make him amenable to such a request. Oh, and Thamyras brought you a clean tunic." I draped the garment over one of the bars. Calpurnius did not respond.

We worked our way back to the front of the jail and retrieved Thamyras' razor. Novatus' face brightened into a crooked smile as I placed some coins in his hand. "Make sure he's comfortable," I said.

"This should buy a lot of comfort, sir."

"For Calpurnius." I clinked a last coin into his hand.

"Of course, sir." His hand closed around the money, into a fist that I would not want to have aimed at my jaw. "For Calpurnius."

"Has he said anything to you about what happened?" I asked, leaning back a little.

"No, sir. He won't say a word. Won't even deny that he killed the girl."

"He didn't. You can be sure of that. Has anyone else tried to see him?"

"His father did come by here." Novatus fished a key on a leather strap from around his neck and unlocked a box sitting on the counter. He opened the lid enough for me to see that my coins would not be lonely in there.

"His father is still alive?" I hadn't heard anything more about Calpurnius' father since the wedding. He'd seemed elderly then.

"Yes, sir. Old Fabatus is along in years, but still active. He lives a couple of miles west of town, on the road to Puteoli."

"Did Calpurnius talk to him?"

"No, sir. He told me not to let the old man come back there." As Novatus returned his key to its place of safety I sensed, from the set of his jaw, that he had closed the conversation as securely as he had his strongbox.

"Thank you…for your assistance."

We squinted at the bright sunlight as we emerged from the jail. Our servants brought our horses and helped us mount. Tacitus turned his horse toward the gate through which we had entered Naples. I followed him until I thought we were out of earshot of the jail, then stopped.

"Did you forget something?" Tacitus asked. "Oh, yes, you wanted a bath."

"No, that will have to wait. As long as we've come this far, I think we should go visit Calpurnius' father."

"Why? He wasn't there when the girl was killed. And he didn't talk to Calpurnius."

I nodded. "But he may help us understand why Calpurnius is behaving so oddly. Thamyras, I assume you know the way to the house."

The slave's face darkened. "Yes, my lord, but I don't think you should bother the old man."

"Why not?"

"Meaning no disrespect, my lord, but there's some things I'd rather not talk about."

I turned my horse so that I was facing Thamyras. "By the gods, man! I've gone to considerable trouble and expense to respond to the lady Aurelia's request for help. But every way I turn, someone says they won't tell me something or there's something I can't know or somebody I can't see." Passersby were starting to stare, so I lowered my voice. "The more you tell me that I can't see him, the more determined I am to do precisely that. Now, we are going out to Calpurnius Fabatus' house. And you are going to show us the way. Is that clear?"

"Yes, my lord." Thamyras turned his horse onto a street leading west and the rest of us followed him. "Very clear."

†

Our route took us through a tunnel over seven hundred paces long. Augustus built it to make the route between Naples and Puteoli shorter and more direct. The hills around Naples run down to the coast and the old road to Puteoli winds along the shore. The tunnel cuts through the hills and rejoins the road as it begins to straighten out. It's the longest of three tunnels Augustus built in this area. It's wide enough for two carts to pass one another, and the slope of the roadway from end to end is so gentle as to be hardly noticeable.

By the time we reached the western end of the tunnel I was regretting my outburst. But my impatience had not abated, even if my anger at Thamyras had. Never had I known people so reluctant to answer questions, let alone volunteer information. Were they trying to protect someone? If so, whom? Against what?

It was difficult to keep my focus on the problems before me, though, because the scenery along the road was so enticing. Over the roofs of the houses to our left I could see the bay itself, as placid as though it had never been roiled by earthquakes or eruptions. The foliage on the trees we passed did not yet show any signs of autumn. This far south in Italy that season comes late and practically undetected, slipping in like a wayward servant in the middle of the night. You wake up one morning and wonder how it got there without your noticing it. I prefer the crisp decisiveness of autumn farther north, in my native Comum at the foot of the Alps.

After we had ridden a mile or more I decided to see if I could get Thamyras to open up about someone he probably didn't know well as Calpurnius. Maybe he wouldn't be so protective.

"Can you tell me any more about why Amalthea would have been out in the orchard so early in the morning?" I asked. "Did she pray to the herm?" People sometimes make little offerings to a herm, but I'd never known anyone to go to the trouble of getting up early to ask a favor of one, which is what prayers usually amount to.

"No, my lord. She went out to pray to her god."

"Which god was that?"

"I don't know, my lord."

"Did you ever ask her what the fish meant? Was it a sign of her god?"

"I believe it was, my lord. I chewed her out good for putting it there. I don't like people carving in my trees, even if she did it before I came here with my lord Calpurnius. I told her not to do it anymore. It's not good for the trees, and they're having a hard enough time recovering from the eruption."

"Why carve a fish on a tree?" Tacitus asked.

"I don't know, my lord. To worship Neptune perhaps."

"Were others in the household aware of what she was doing? Was the lady Aurelia aware of her strange behavior?"

"I think so, my lord."

"Did she do anything about it? Reprimand her?"

"What should she do, my lord? Amalthea did her work and didn't cause any trouble. She was a bit simple, but she worked hard."

"Do you pray to any gods, Thamyras?" I asked.

He didn't seem startled by the question. "No, my lord. For a while I prayed to Venus and to Mercury to bring Proxena back to me. Since they watch over lovers and travelers, they seemed a likely pair. But it did no good, so I don't do that any more. The gods, if there be such, don't seem to have much interest in what we humans do."

I certainly sympathized, but I didn't say anything. It's not a good idea to reveal too much of what one thinks to a slave. But, if you can't reveal to her what you're thinking... An intense longing for Aurora suddenly surged over me, so strong I had to tighten my grip on the reins and squeeze my knees against the horse's sides. Where was she? Was she safe? Perhaps I should offer prayers to Venus and Mercury.

"Are you all right?" Tacitus asked, reaching over to put a hand on my arm.

I shook my head to clear it. "I'm fine. How much farther is it to Fabatus' house?" I asked Thamyras.

"We turn at the next road, my lord. Then it's just a short bit."

X

FABATUS' HOUSE sat close to the road, as though inviting visitors. The trees shading it appeared to have survived the eruption as well as any in the area. The plaster and paint on the two-storied walls were fresh. As soon as we turned off the road we were spotted by two boys playing in front of the house. One called out, "Papa!" bringing a heavyset servant to the front door.

"May I help you, sirs?" he asked.

We dismounted, handing the reins to our servants. "I'd like to speak with Calpurnius Fabatus," I said. "I'm Gaius Pliny and this is Cornelius Tacitus."

"Please come in," the servant said, standing aside. "I am Stentor, doorkeeper for Calpurnius Fabatus."

I wondered if his voice was as loud as the mythical character for whom he was named. Servants are sometimes given names based on a characteristic which they embody, and sometimes on a characteristic which they noticeably lack, if the master has an ironic sense of humor.

"Greetings, Thamyras," Stentor said quietly as we entered the house. "It's been a while since we saw you here." Then he addressed us. "Now, if you gentlemen will wait here, I'll inform my master of your arrival."

We had only a moment to admire the decorations in the atrium. The typical Roman exterior of the house did nothing to prepare one for these frescoes, which depicted scenes from Egypt. The Nile seemed to flow around the atrium, with pyramids and a sphinx in the background on the wall to our left and boats and river creatures on the wall to our right.

"Is Pliny really here?" a jovial voice said just before Fabatus came into view, with Stentor on his heels. Calpurnius' father looked just as I remembered him from the wedding—old but robust, with a full head of white hair and his skin unwrinkled. His tunic, though Roman in style, had a border of Egyptian symbols.

"What a pleasure to see you again, sir," I said. "May I introduce my friend, Cornelius Tacitus?"

"Welcome," Fabatus said, extending his hand to Tacitus and then to me. "Please, let's go sit in the garden and have something to drink. The way this damned ash gets into everything, I feel like I'm always thirsty. Stentor, be sure their servants and horses are tended to." He walked ahead of us toward the back of the house.

Fabatus' house was small, the home of a man who did not want to draw attention to himself. The second story served as an extra level of protection to shield the interior from prying eyes. The garden, though, showed that, within the safe confines of that modest house, he paid close attention to details. Each plant had been chosen and placed not only to show it to best advantage but also to draw the eye to the few pieces of sculpture that decorated the garden. They all looked Egyptian.

"I don't think these are copies," Tacitus muttered to me.

Fabatus' hearing was not that of an old man. He turned back toward us, a smile playing on his lips. "No, I don't buy copies. I've been fascinated by Egypt since I lived there when my father was on the governor's staff. Have either of you ever been there?"

Tacitus and I shook our heads. Fabatus' family came from near my hometown of Comum, but they had traveled much more widely than my family had, or Tacitus' for that matter.

"You really must go. And by Egypt I don't mean Alexandria—that cesspool of bastardized Greeks. Go up the Nile. See the real Egypt. Their skill in building astounds me. The pyramids, by the gods, the pyramids—you simply cannot fathom them until you've stood in front of them."

"We passed the tomb of Cestius as we left Rome," Tacitus said.

About a hundred years ago Gaius Cestius' heirs had built, in accordance with his will, a pyramid for his tomb on the outskirts of Rome. At that time Egypt, which had just recently been conquered, was all the rage in the city. Augustus even hauled a huge obelisk across the Mediterranean and erected it in the Circus Maximus.

Fabatus chuckled. "Ah, yes, Cestius' tomb. An amusing trifle. The grandest pyramids in Egypt are four times that size." He stretched his arms as far apart as he could.

My eyebrows arched. Cestius' tomb is one of the tallest structures in Rome. I could not visualize something four times as large. It must rival Vesuvius.

"And the antiquity of Egypt," Fabatus continued to rhapsodize, "is almost incomprehensible. Herodotus was there five hundred years ago. I'm sure you've read his account. When he stood in front of the pyramids, they were at least *two thousand* years old. The Egyptians built those pyramids when we Romans were hardly more than wild animals, still shitting behind bushes and dragging our bottoms on the ground to clean ourselves." He placed his hand on a statue that occupied the center of the garden, where the walkways crossed. "The man who sold me this assured me it was carved over two thousand years ago. Could a Roman—or a Greek—have produced anything like this at that time? Can we really equal it today?"

The statue of which he was so proud showed a man and a woman standing side by side. The woman had her right arm around the man at his waist. The man's left arm went around the woman's neck and draped down so that his hand covered her left breast. The woman wore a gown that reached from her shoulders to below her knees and clung to her figure. The man wore a garment that looked like what I would wear in the bath, a towel wrapped around his waist and extending to his knees. The whole piece, including the base, which bore Egyptian symbols, came to just above Fabatus' own waist.

"Isn't it magnificent?" Fabatus said.

To me the statue looked crude, the poses stiff and awkward. "There is certainly an…elegance to it." That was as close to a compliment as I could honestly come.

Tacitus stepped closer to the piece and bent over to examine it. "It's interesting to see that men were groping women two thousand years ago. Some things never change, I suppose."

Fabatus' displeasure at the insult to his treasure flashed across his face. If we were going to get anything helpful from him, I had to get back on his good side. I slapped Tacitus on the shoulder. "If it's not a statue or a picture of people coupling, you don't think it's art, do you?"

Fabatus' eyes twinkled. "Now, if that's your style, Cornelius Tacitus, the Egyptians were just as frank as we Romans. I keep that part of my collection inside, though, so as not to offend my sister. I'll show it to you later. Even if you can't read the writing, you'll especially like the books, I think. They're illustrated."

We followed him to the *exhedra* at the end of the garden and took our places on the couches. His servants were setting fruit, bread, and wine on the table under the supervision of a woman of about thirty-five. Her dress, made from linen and adorned with some of the same symbols we'd seen on the statue, was even more Egyptian than Fabatus'. It revealed the outline of a lovely figure. From the way she carried herself, I knew the woman was not a servant.

"This is Sabina," Fabatus said.

I was surprised by the lack of any identification. Was she his wife? A freedwoman?

Sabina acknowledged us with a nod of her head. "Welcome, gentlemen. Gaius Pliny, I'm sorry I did not get to meet you at Calpurnius' and Aurelia's wedding. I was ill at the time."

"I'm glad to see you looking so well now," I said. She was indeed attractive. Her makeup, done in the Egyptian style with dark coloring around her eyes, gave her a seductive quality. Her hair was cut in a style one sees in images of Cleopatra—straight across the forehead and squared around the neck. She sat on the foot of Fabatus' couch and put her hand on his leg. The glance that passed between them could have been one Cleopatra gave Caesar—or Marc Antony.

Sabina poured some wine for us and I took a sip. Fabatus was right about the ash; my throat was dry.

"Now," Fabatus said, "it is a pleasure to see you again, Gaius Pliny. My daughter tells me that she misses seeing your mother, now that you don't spend as much time in Misenum as you used to."

"My mother's reaction to the eruption of Vesuvius is what keeps us away. She was delighted to see your daughter at the wedding last year. She was much relieved that it was held in your house in Rome so she did not have to come down here. Frankly, so was I."

"Unfortunately, you're not the only one. Our changed conditions down here have made the area much less enticing to visitors than it was five years ago. The mineral baths and such places that depend on traffic from Rome are suffering. I'm sorry that my son's difficulties have made it necessary for you to make the trip."

"Considering the friendship between our families, I'm only too willing to offer whatever help I can." I was exaggerating a bit. Except for my mother's friendship with Fabatus' daughter, Calpurnia Hispulla, there was no close connection between our families.

"It's kind of you to say so." Fabatus raised his cup to me. "But for you Aurelia is the one who really matters, isn't she?"

I felt myself blushing.

"It's all right. Her grandfather told me the whole story. You risked your life to save her and reunite her with her family."

I didn't want to drag that story out again. "Aurelia sent and asked me to help her husband."

"I'm glad she did. And I'm glad you're here, for whatever motive. My son seems to have no interest in helping himself. I'm not sure he even wants to live to see his child born. I'm certainly looking forward to having a grandchild. A grand*son*, I hope. That's our only hope for keeping the family name alive."

I didn't want to tell him that Bastet had predicted the child would be a girl. No sense dashing his hopes.

Tacitus put his cup down. "Her nurse predicts the child will be a girl."

"Oh, yes," Sabina sneered. "Bastet and her nonsense."

"That's exactly how I feel," I said, glaring across the table at Tacitus, a wasted gesture since he was dividing his attention between a bowl of figs and Sabina's body.

"I've never understood my uncle's devotion to that woman," Sabina added.

"Nor do I," Fabatus said. "He brought her—and little else—back from Egypt when he served as a military tribune there. Beyond tending to my wife in her last days, she contributed little to the household. She claims to be some sort of princess and still acts like one. She's not Egyptian, you know; she's Nubian."

"Is there a difference?" Tacitus asked. "I thought Nubia was a province of Egypt."

"And Egypt is a province of Rome," Fabatus said, "but that doesn't make Egyptians Roman. When Calpurnius married, she was the first of the slaves that he picked to move with him to his new household, and she chose the others he would take. I was relieved to see her go." He picked up a date.

Sabina stepped in while Fabatus' mouth was full. "On a more pleasant topic, I trust my aunt Aurelia is well."

"Yes, she is. She's anxious for her husband, but otherwise well."

Fabatus was ready to get back into the conversation. "I tell you, that girl is a prize. I was overjoyed when Manilius Quadratus asked me to consider a marriage between our children. Puzzled, too, though. My family is far less distinguished than his and has been under a shadow since Nero's day."

"Some of us are proud to say that we offended Nero, sir. My uncle withdrew from public service rather than hold office under him."

"Yes. I've always admired old Secundus for that. But he wasn't accused of knowing something about Calpurnius Piso's plot against Nero and about the infidelities of Nero's aunt Lepida."

"Is there a connection," Tacitus asked, "between your family and Piso's?"

"We're only distant relatives," Fabatus said. "But to Nero's mind one Calpurnius was as good as another."

"The charge against you wasn't pursued," Tacitus said. "At least that's what I've read in the history that Gaius Pliny's uncle wrote."

Fabatus watched the memories swirl around in his cup and sighed heavily. "You're right. It became clear that witnesses had been bribed or coerced. Nero would have been embarrassed to prosecute me on such flimsy evidence and have me acquitted. But I learned that I had no stomach for public life."

"Your son hasn't pursued a career either," I said, hoping to get us back to my main concern.

"He's never shown the inclination or the aptitude," Fabatus said. "He's done a good job of running our family enterprises, though. The boy does have a head for business."

"But you're the *paterfamilias*," Tacitus said. "Don't you oversee what he does?"

"I emancipated him and handed everything over to him six years ago, when my wife died. I felt like a fire went out in me when that happened. Now I'd rather be free to travel. We were planning another trip to Egypt until this dreadful business came up." He squeezed Sabina's hand.

We were almost back on track. "So you don't know the current state of your son's business affairs?"

"All I know is that he maintains my household at a level that satisfies me, so things must be going well for him."

Or, I thought, *he's siphoning money from somewhere else to make it appear that everything is all right.* "Can you think of any reason, then, for Calpurnius to be acting the way he is?"

Fabatus shook his head slowly, like a man who wishes he could explain the course of human history but can't even understand what happened to him yesterday. "He baffles me. He wouldn't even talk to me when I went to visit him in jail yesterday."

"Do you know of any reason he might have had to kill that woman?"

"Gaius Pliny, I've looked at it from every angle I can imagine, and I cannot come up with an explanation, not even a far-fetched one."

"Has Calpurnius' behavior changed recently? Has he acquired new friends?"

"To say 'new friends' would imply that he had old ones. He's always been a solitary sort of man."

"Do you know of any problem—"

I froze and my eyes widened as the earth shook. The four of us looked at each other. Then we felt another shock, stronger this time. Fabatus' servants came pouring out of the house into the open garden, like ants when a child pokes their hole with a stick.

"We'd better get away from these walls," Fabatus said, putting a protective arm around Sabina. "We don't want them on top of us."

Another shock made it hard to keep our balance as we joined the servants in the center of the garden, where they were holding to one another. A few were crying. It took all my strength not to join them. My heart was pounding, my hands shaking. I found it difficult to breathe. All the memories of five years ago were trying to crowd into my mind at once—the walls of our house shaking, the wagons rolling back and forth so uncontrollably that we couldn't even get into them, the look of terror on my mother's face.

"Stentor, have someone take a look," Fabatus ordered. His calm voice helped me pull myself out of near panic.

Stentor tapped a young man on the shoulder and he quickly climbed the tallest tree in the garden.

"What do you see?" Fabatus asked.

"The mountain's quiet, my lord."

"No smoke or anything belching out of it?"

"Nothing more than usual, my lord."

With Sabina huddled close to him, Fabatus addressed his servants. "It's all right. You all know that we get these little rumblings now and then. This won't be the last one. Let's look for cracks and see what got tossed off the shelves."

My eye happened to fall on Thamyras, standing on the other side of Fabatus and Sabina from where I was. I couldn't understand the scowl on his face. I would have to ask him about it as we rode back to Naples.

We were beginning to relax and return to what we had been doing when another shock coursed through the house, raising a cloud of dust. I was standing beside a door into one of the rooms off the garden. To steady myself I grabbed a wall bracket designed to hold a torch. As I was knocked off my feet by the shaking, I felt the bracket give under my weight.

"Look out!" Fabatus cried as a huge stone crashed to the ground behind me.

†

"Are you all right, Gaius Pliny?" Fabatus said, extending a hand to help me up. Tacitus, on the other side of me, patted me on the back as I stood.

I moved a bit and was not aware of any injury. "I'm fine. What happened?"

"Well, you discovered one of my little secrets," Fabatus said.

I brushed myself off and looked at where the open door had been. It was now blocked by a large, carefully hewn slab of rock. "*Little secret?*...Did the earthquake dislodge that?"

"No, you did."

"What?... How?"

"It's a trick I learned in Egypt," Fabatus said with some pride.

"When they constructed a tomb to conceal a king and his treasure, the Egyptians often rigged up a mechanism by which the last man out of the tomb could cause a large stone to drop into place, blocking access to the treasure chamber."

"And this is your treasure room?" I said.

Fabatus cast his eyes down modestly. "'Treasure' would be too grand a word. It's where I keep my strongbox. I designed it in case someone broke into the house. In these country villas we are more vulnerable than we like to think."

I ran my hand over the stone. "No one's going to get in there now, including you."

"Don't worry. The stones in the Egyptian tombs can't be moved once they've been dropped into place. They're too large and there's no room to use a lever. But my servants will lift this one and reset the mechanism."

I studied the device beside the door, peering into it as best I could. "So this is the lever that operates it. Do any of the other wall brackets mask surprises?"

"Now, Gaius Pliny, you're asking me to reveal too many secrets." Fabatus put a hand on my shoulder as though I was an annoying child.

Standing back, I examined the door and the wall around and above it. The house was two stories high, so it was easy enough to conceal the large block of stone in the wall of the upper story. Plaster and paint covered any cracks as effectively as they would on a Roman matron's face. I was already thinking about how I could have such a thing built into any of my houses.

"My uncle would have found this fascinating," I said. "Did you use this device in any of your other homes?"

"I hope you never have occasion to find out." Apparently reluctance to answer questions was a trait that ran in the family, like red hair or a crooked nose.

The earth had been still for a long enough time now that I thought the danger was over. "I think we need to leave," I said. "We should check on Aurelia."

"By all means," Fabatus said. "I don't want anything to happen to that grandchild of mine. Thank you for trying to help my son. Let me know if there's anything I can do."

As we left the garden I turned to wave good-bye one more time and saw Sabina kiss Fabatus. His hand rested on her breast, like the figures in his prized sculpture.

†

"What an amazing device," I said as we turned onto the road back to Naples. "I wonder what other secrets he has hidden in that place."

"One was right in front of you, my lord," Thamyras said from behind me.

"Is something bothering you?" I asked over my shoulder. "You didn't want to bring us out here, and while you were there your face looked like you were sucking on something sour."

"It's that woman, my lord."

I stopped my horse and turned to Thamyras. "Watch how you talk about her," I said sharply. "Remember who you are, and who she is."

"I can't forget who she is, my lord. She's his great-niece, his sister's granddaughter."

"His great-niece?"

"Yes, my lord. And she's been his concubine since she was fourteen. That's twenty years now."

"What? But Fabatus had a wife. She died just a few years ago."

Thamyras nodded.

We sat in silence for a moment while I tried to understand what he was saying. This was a shock as severe as the trembling of the earth that we had just experienced. I had to remind myself that Thamyras had been born in that household and grew up in it. "Did his wife know?"

"Everyone in the house knew, my lord."

"But I've never heard a word of it," I said. Something of that sort would be hard to keep secret in our circle.

"It's the real reason why Fabatus never tried to have a public career, my lord. And it's why Nero tried to implicate him in that plot with Junia Lepida."

"Yes," Tacitus said. "Nero accused his aunt Lepida of incest with her nephew. I've read about that. I never understood why he accused Fabatus of knowing about it, but now it all makes sense."

"The man's living like some Egyptian king."

"Yes, my lord. That's why my lord Calpurnius hasn't been back in that house since Fabatus emancipated him."

"And perhaps it's why he wouldn't talk to his father in the jail yesterday."

XI

WE RODE FAST on our way back to Naples, growing more anxious. At each milestone along the road the earthquake damage seemed to be worse.

"I hope the tunnel is still open," I said.

"It's survived for a hundred years," Tacitus reminded me. "I think it can take the little jolt we got today."

"I wonder if Augustus' engineers ever came up with a device like Fabatus'."

"I haven't heard of one," Tacitus said, "but his family certainly were no strangers to coupling with close relatives."

We had to pick our way around a pile of rocks in the road just before we got to the tunnel. From the western end of the tunnel, though, we could see light at the eastern end. All the same, I picked up the pace to get through the tunnel as quickly as possible. What we found as we emerged from the tunnel brought us to a halt.

"This area was hit a lot harder than where we were," Tacitus said as we surveyed the damage.

A pall of smoke lay over the city. When buildings shake, lampstands fall over, spilling burning oil across wooden floors. Charcoal braziers, which the poor use for heating and cooking, tumble and their contents scatter. Pieces of clothing or bedding, left on the floor, burst into flames. Within moments, an apartment can become an inferno.

On this day several buildings had collapsed. Others, judging from the size of the cracks in their walls, would have to be knocked down. Naples, not entirely rebuilt from the eruption of Vesuvius, now had more work ahead of it.

"What if the jail was damaged?" I said.

"We'll be going very near there, my lord," Thamyras reminded me, concern for his master clouding his face.

"Let's check on it then."

As we drew closer to the south side of Naples the damage seemed to be more severe and a sense of foreboding crept over me. Some of the streets were blocked by the debris of damaged buildings. People were digging to find family and friends trapped beneath the rubble. I felt heartless for ignoring their pleas, but we had urgent business of our own. When we turned onto the street where Calpurnius was imprisoned, I breathed a sigh of relief. The buildings on that street appeared to have been spared. But when we reached the door of the *vigiles'* headquarters Novatus met us, covered in dirt.

"Sirs, you're a welcome sight! The back part of the building has collapsed. One of my men was back there with Calpurnius when it happened. I need help."

"Where are your other men?" I asked.

"After the first shock I sent them out to assist where they were needed. Then we got a bigger rumble."

"Let's get to work," I said. We dismounted and tied our horses. They pranced nervously, jerking at the reins.

"I don't like the looks of that," Novatus said.

"What's the matter?" I asked.

"Haven't you noticed how animals can sense things when we can't? I think your horses are telling us there's going to be another jolt."

"Shouldn't we stay outside then?"

"I've got a man trapped back there, sir, along with your friend Calpurnius. Alive or dead, I don't know. If the earth shakes again, I doubt they'll survive."

We entered the building and began digging through rubble. Novatus had started a path back to the cells but had made little progress by himself. The back wall and part of the roof had collapsed. We could see the sky and the walls of the buildings behind us, which had also crumbled. We'd gone only a short distance when we heard a groan.

"At least someone's alive," Novatus said. "Steady, lad! We're coming!"

"What was your man doing back here?" Tacitus asked.

"He was trying to persuade Calpurnius to eat a little something, clean himself up, and put on that tunic his servant brought. He's just a young fella that helps out around here."

"There's an arm!" Tacitus said. "And it's moving."

Novatus grasped the hand that was sticking out of the rubble. "We'll have you out in no time, lad." He gave orders as though all of us were his subordinates. "Start down there. Make sure you're not loosening something else when you move a piece."

With our coordinated effort it didn't take long to free the man, who was indeed hardly more than a boy. He was bloodied around his face and shoulders, but his worst injury seemed to be a broken leg, to judge from the odd angle at which the limb was turned. The bars of one of the cells had fallen across him and leaned against the wall behind him in such a way that they kept him from being crushed by anything heavier. We carried him to the front of the building and laid him on a small bed.

"I've got to set this leg," Novatus told him. "It won't feel good, but I've got to do it."

"I know, sir," the boy said.

I turned my crew toward the rear of the building, "We've got to get back there and find Calpurnius."

The injured boy raised himself up on an elbow and called after me. "He's not there, sir."

I came back and stood beside his bed. "Not there?"

"When the second shock hit—the big one—the bars of his cell came loose." He winced and groaned as Novatus straightened his leg. "Calpurnius…pushed them onto me…and ran out through the hole… in the back wall."

"Well, at least he saved your life."

"Yes, sir, I guess he did." The young man gritted his teeth and drew in a sharp, hissing breath.

"But an escaped prisoner is a blot on my record," Novatus muttered as he applied a splint and wrapped the leg. "I'm responsible for him."

"Let's see if we can find a track," I said.

That proved easier to do than I would have hoped. Calpurnius must have been injured because he had left a trail of drops of blood out the back of the jail. We followed it through the rubble of the next block before we lost it.

"It just stops," Tacitus said, "right here at the street."

†

As we rode out south of Naples on the road to Aurelia's villa, with Thamyras and our servants leading the way, I studied the paving stones on either side of us.

"Looking for blood?" Tacitus asked.

I nodded. "I know it's unlikely we'll pick up the trail again, but it's worth keeping an eye open."

"Why do you suppose it stopped like it did?"

"I think it means he found a horse wandering around loose. Or maybe someone in a cart picked him up."

"Or someone pounced on an injured man and carried him off." Tacitus always looks on the darker side of things.

"In that case," I said, "I would expect to see a larger amount of blood. If he was struggling, the wound would have bled more freely."

"You don't seem overly concerned about his escape," Tacitus said. "The man was injured seriously enough to bleed."

I slowed my horse so that I dropped farther behind our servants. Tacitus kept his mount beside mine with some difficulty. The animals were still nervous, and that made me nervous. "I am worried about his injury, but I know where he's going," I said in a low voice.

"How can you know that?"

"He'll do what any man would do in a moment of crisis. He'll go home."

Tacitus couldn't hide his confusion. "Home? Won't that be the first place anyone would look for him?"

"He won't go to Aurelia's villa. That's not home to him."

"So you think he's going back to—"

I cut him off before any of the servants could overhear him. Thamyras especially seemed to be sitting up straight on his horse, with his head cocked to one side. I had to admire the fellow's devotion to his master. At least I hoped that's what accounted for his interest. "Yes, I think he's going…home."

"How will he get there?"

"It's not that far."

"But he's hurt."

"I think he'll be determined enough to get there that he'll crawl if he has to. His injury wasn't bad enough to prevent him from bolting when he had the chance. If someone picked him up, they'll likely care for the wound. If he can't get any help, we may find him somewhere along this road. If we don't, I think it's safe to assume he got home."

Tacitus swatted a fly that seemed particularly interested in his face. "So all we have to do is go down there and pick him up. We could even be waiting for him when he gets there. I'd like to see the look on his face when—"

"No. It'll be better to let him get home and think no one is looking for him there. Give him a little time to recover, or to realize he needs help. Remember, Thamyras said they dug tunnels all through the house when they were trying to recover some of his possessions. After a day or two, when he's hungry and thirsty enough and trying to deal with his injury, he'll be glad to see us, and I expect, more cooperative."

We fell silent and moved in single file to the side of the road as a cart drawn by an ox approached from the other direction. Whatever it was carrying was covered by a large blanket with straw sticking out from the sides. The driver, a man of fifty or so with leathery brown skin and his jaws sunken in, wore a tunic made from the same dingy fabric as the blanket.

"Good day, sirs," the driver said. "What's the damage up ahead?" He was missing enough teeth that he whistled when he spoke.

"It's worst in Naples itself," I said, turning my horse to ride along-side the cart for a moment. "Quite a few buildings were toppled."

The driver nodded sadly. "That's what my wife feared. I'm on my way to see about her sister and her husband."

"I hope you find them well."

"Thank you, sir. I just wish we knew what has made the gods so angry at us."

We exchanged a wave and I turned my horse south again. Pulling up beside Tacitus, I looked out over the bay, as calm and innocent now as a boy after he's pulled a trick and knows you can't fix the blame on him. Maybe that's why we invented gods, so we would have someone other than ourselves or mere chance to blame for our misfortunes.

Tacitus pulled me back to the matter at hand. "What if Calpurnius' injury proves fatal?"

"Then we'll be back in Rome long before the Ides, won't we?"

"Why, Gaius Pliny, I didn't know you were such a callous bastard."

"I don't mean to sound that way, but if Calpurnius is in such serious trouble that he poses a threat to his wife and child, his death might remove that threat."

"And you're more concerned about Aurelia's safety than about Calpurnius' fate?"

"Frankly, yes. The man won't give us any help in trying to defend him. All we've learned so far is that his behavior in recent months has been very odd and that he claims someone is blackmailing him."

"You don't believe him?"

"I don't know what to believe right now. I can't see any connection between the death of a servant in the orchard and an attack on Aurelia and this alleged blackmail. Until I can make a connection, the only thing I'm concerned about is protecting Aurelia."

"But you have to get back to Rome in a few days. Are you going to come back down here afterwards if you haven't resolved this matter?"

I shook my head. "If we can't settle it in the time we have, I doubt we'll ever get to the bottom of it. Trails grow cold. People's memories fade."

"What about the threat to Aurelia?"

"I'll take her back to Rome with me if I have to."

"As close as she is to giving birth?" Tacitus threw his head back and laughed. "You might find yourself playing midwife on the journey."

†

Earthquakes seem to have a center, where the most damage occurs, and then to be weaker as the waves spread out from that center, much like a whirlpool. In this case the south side of Naples was the center. The farther we rode away from there, the less damage we saw and the more we—and our horses—began to relax.

"Did your uncle write anything about earthquakes in his *Natural History*?" Tacitus asked after we had ridden in silence for a few moments.

"As a matter of fact, he did, and it's in one of the parts of the book that I happen to have read." People expect me to have practically memorized all thirty-seven scrolls of my uncle's greatest work, but it's so vast and so oddly organized that it's the sort of thing one consults rather than reads.

"What did he say about them?"

"Following a long list of authorities—all the way back to Aristotle and Anaximander—he believed they're caused by wind blowing into underground chasms, just as the wind causes thunder."

Tacitus pondered for a moment. "I can see how that could be the case."

"He mentioned Naples as a spot that's particularly vulnerable to them."

Tacitus looked around, nodding. "There certainly are a lot of grottoes around here, like Tiberius' on the isle of Capri, where the wind could get underground."

I shook my head. "At the risk of disagreeing with my uncle and those other eminent authorities, I don't find it a satisfactory explanation. How much wind would it take to shake the earth? Thunder is one thing. It has no physical substance. Moving the earth the way it was shaken today would take more wind than I can imagine."

"But the wind can tear a large tree out of the ground. And in Syria we saw how it could move sand and reshape the landscape overnight."

"But there was no wind to speak of today." That silenced Tacitus.

†

By the time we reached Aurelia's villa there was hardly a sign that anything had happened. Our horses were easier to control as we turned off the road onto the grounds of the villa. We were spotted long before we reached the entrance to the house. Aurelia, Bastet, and the servants we had appointed to watch Aurelia were waiting for us. Most of her other household servants hovered behind them.

"Did you see Calpurnius?" Aurelia asked as soon as my feet touched the ground.

"Yes, we did."

She waited for me to say more, but I didn't. "Well? What did he say?"

"Let's talk inside."

"It's bad news, isn't it?" She grabbed my arm. Her other hand rested on her belly, as though she would cover her child's ears.

"I just want to talk privately, with as few people listening as possible."

I wished I could erase the anxiety from Aurelia's face, but I didn't want to say any more in front of the whole household. Thamyras would spread the tale soon enough, probably with Calpurnius ripping the bars out of the wall and flinging them aside, like Hercules. I just wanted to be sure Aurelia had the most accurate version.

The library seemed the most private place and large enough for several of us. I steered Aurelia in that direction. Bastet, with her arm through Aurelia's, got into the room before I could close the door. Once she was in I didn't feel I could tell her to leave without causing an earthquake of sorts in the room. The woman did carry herself like a princess, even in the way she held her head, wrapped with the multi-colored scarf that could serve as a crown.

"Gaius Pliny," Aurelia said, seating herself on a scribe's workbench, "you're frightening me. Why all this secrecy? Is my husband all right?"

"I believe he is, as I'll tell you in a moment. First I need to ask you about something he said when we talked to him."

"You can ask me anything. You know that."

I didn't think Aurelia would be able to answer this question, but I had to ask it. In some families the women manage the money or at least know how it is being managed. I even knew of cases where wives had diverted money for their own use from their husbands' accounts. Cicero divorced his wife for doing just that. I didn't think Aurelia was devious enough or knew enough about handling money—but an idea jolted me. What if someone in Calpurnius' own family was blackmailing him? And what if he knew—

"Gaius Pliny," Aurelia said, "why are you looking at me like that? What do you want to ask me?"

No, it couldn't be. I took a deep breath and asked, "Did your husband tell you about any financial problems he'd run into lately?"

Aurelia seemed genuinely surprised by the question. "Why, no. Calpurnius handles his own affairs and doesn't share his dealings with me. Since his father emancipated him, he's had complete control of his money and doesn't like anyone looking over his shoulder. Why do you ask that?"

"Just because of something he said."

"Well, I'm sure it doesn't matter. Now, tell me if he's all right."

Her eyes widened and her hand went to her mouth as I told her the story of the earthquake and Calpurnius' escape, putting as little emphasis as possible on the trail of blood. "As of a few hours ago," I concluded, "he was alive and well enough to take advantage of his opportunity to flee. Beyond that I can't say anything for certain."

"Where do you think he'll go?" she asked. "Will he come here?"

"I doubt he'll risk that. He was very concerned about putting you and your child in danger. I believe he'll go back to his own house."

Bastet cleared her throat. "You're very wise, my lord. He loved that place like it was his own child."

I tried to ignore the woman's intrusion and her attempt at flattery. "Tomorrow morning Tacitus and I will go down there and find him."

But would we be bringing an injured husband back to his wife or a dead man back to his widow?

XII

"ARE YOU SURE you don't want to go out to Calpurnius' house now?" Tacitus asked as we sipped some wine on a bench in a shaded corner of the garden. "He might need our help."

I shook my head. "I'm willing to wait until morning. It's late enough that I don't want to be prowling around the place in the dark. While we have the time, I want to look at his financial records. They might give us some clue about what he's hiding."

"I doubt that blackmailers give receipts."

I didn't dignify that comment with a response. "Something's wrong around here. For one thing, a man with Calpurnius' wealth shouldn't keep this poor a wine in his house."

Tacitus swirled his wine around in the cup. "You noticed it, too? I thought perhaps all this ash was making things taste bad."

"No, it's the wine. It's wretched. The spices they've put in it don't even help."

Even more than the wine, the garden gave the impression of a household living beyond its resources, on the verge of ruin. In addition to the damaged and unrepaired fresco of Venus and Adonis that I had noticed earlier, I could now see missing or cracked roof tiles. If they weren't replaced, water would find its way into the beams under them. Probably it already had and the beams were rotting, soon to collapse. The few flowering plants around us seemed to be struggling to stay upright as well. Their colors did little to dispel the air of gloom that hung over the whole place.

"Here he comes," Tacitus said.

A man, not as tall as I am, approached us across the garden. His hair was gray but still thick, his back hunched as though from poring over accounts for a long time. Stopping in front of us, he bowed his head. "My lady said you wanted to see me, sirs."

"Are you Diomedes?" I asked. Aurelia had said she would send us the one servant—a freedman—whom Calpurnius trusted to help him keep track of his money.

"Yes, sir, I am."

"We want to examine Calpurnius' financial records. The lady Aurelia says the room where they're kept is always locked and only you and her husband have keys."

"That's correct, sir." He touched the leather strap that ran around his neck and under his tunic. I recognized the gesture—because I made it often to feel the Tyche ring—of a man reassuring himself that something precious is still close to his heart.

"Which room is it?"

Diomedes pointed to the middle door across the garden, the only one closed at the moment. "All of my lord's records and his strongbox are in there."

"Then we need you to open it for us."

"But, sir, I've been given strict orders not to open that room or the strongbox. I have the keys only in case something happens to Calpurnius."

"Something *has* happened to him," Tacitus said. "And we need to know why it's happened."

Diomedes held out his hands as though pleading a case in court. "But, sir, what do his records have to do with it?"

"We won't know until we look into them," I said. "You can stand there and watch us."

"Forgive my boldness, sir, but I've received explicit orders from Calpurnius, and I don't believe it is your place to countermand them. I understand he's no longer in prison, so I cannot violate his order until I know what has actually happened to him."

"What if your mistress told you to unlock the door?"

Diomedes folded his arms over his chest. "I don't believe she would do that, sir."

This household seemed to have more than its share of bold servants. I wondered if Aurelia, because of her own background, was too lenient on them, or if they still saw her as one of them. But the two boldest ones I'd met so far were from Calpurnius' household and had been with Aurelia for only a year. This particular servant had just issued a challenge that I had to accept.

"Let's find out if she will."

With Diomedes sulking along behind us, Tacitus and I crossed the garden to Aurelia's room. The door was open and we heard a woman's moans coming from inside. She sounded as though she was in considerable pain.

"By the gods!" Tacitus said. "Is she having the baby?"

But the moans came from a servant woman, we discovered when we reached the room.

"She cut her hand," Aurelia said as she stepped out of the door. "It's not as bad as she thinks it is. Bastet is sewing it up."

"So the woman is a princess *and* a doctor?" I said.

Aurelia looked back into the room. "She seems to have many talents. A year ago she cut off the finger of one of the servants." She waggled the little finger on her right hand. "It wasn't recovering from an injury. It was red and swollen, and the redness was spreading. Bastet said the finger would have to be cut off or he would die."

I tried to keep my face from showing too much of the shock I felt. "Where is that servant now?"

"Calpurnius sold him, along with some others, about six months ago. Why do you ask?"

I didn't know what to say. Tacitus and I had agreed not to reveal the detail of the missing finger so the men who had attacked Aurelia wouldn't suspect we had any way to identify them.

"It's just his infernal curiosity," Tacitus said. "He's never satisfied until he knows the full story. I'm surprised he didn't ask you the man's name."

"Oh, it was Sychaeus."

"Well, that's neither here nor there," I said. "I hope Bastet doesn't have to take this woman's hand off. Now, can we talk with you out here?"

Aurelia joined us and we moved to the center of the garden beside a fish pond now filled with ash. The sea creatures decorating the mosaic tile must have been choking. "What is it?" she asked.

"Diomedes refuses to open the door to Calpurnius' money room."
I felt like a child tattling on another.

"Oh, is that why you wanted to see him?"

"Yes. Why did you think we asked for him?"

"You said you wanted to talk to him. I thought you just…wanted
to ask him some questions." Her hesitation flowed over into the way
she glanced at Diomedes, who was standing behind me.

"We won't know what questions to ask," I said, "until we know
something about your husband's finances."

"But he's accused of murder. What do his—our—records have to
do with that?"

"If we're going to find out who killed Amalthea, we need to understand why. An affair might be a likely motive. You suggested as much
yesterday."

Aurelia dabbed at a tear. "In spite of what I might have said, I will
never believe Calpurnius could have been unfaithful to me."

"Then money is the next likely motive for someone to be murdered.
From what Calpurnius said when we saw him in Naples, we think
money might somehow be involved here."

Aurelia took a step toward the servant. "Diomedes, please unlock
the door."

When I could get her aside I would have to tell her that a master
must never say "please" to a servant. It means you're asking a favor, not
giving an order.

Diomedes shook his head slowly. "You know that my lord Calpurnius gave me explicit instructions. I have served in his household
faithfully for years—"

"You will *not* address me in that tone." Aurelia drew herself up and
seemed to come alive, surprising me as much as she did Diomedes,
who flinched. She walked over and stood by the door to the records
room. "Calpurnius is my husband. There is no 'his household' or 'my
household.' We are one *familia*. I told you to unlock this door. If you
don't do it, I'll tear that key from around your neck and do it myself."

"Yes, my lady." Clearly cowed, Diomedes drew two keys from under his tunic, inserted the larger one into the lock, and opened the
door. But he still stood in front of it.

"Move," Aurelia said, thrusting her face close to Diomedes'. "Let these gentlemen get in. You are to do what they ask you to do and answer any questions they may have, just as you would for me or my husband."

Diomedes stood away from the door, his head hanging. "Yes, my lady."

But he was talking to her back as she returned to the room where Bastet was stitching up the servant's hand.

†

Calpurnius' storeroom could have belonged to any man of our class, except that it hadn't been decorated as a storeroom. It was a bedroom which he had taken over when he married Aurelia and moved into this house. The lock was new enough that it still gleamed, the only thing in this part of the house that anyone appeared to be taking care of. With the light coming through the door I saw frescos showing scenes from the *Odyssey*—the Cyclops on the wall to our left and the slaughter of the suitors on our right. They were partially obscured by tables and boxes of writing materials set against each wall. A strongbox with a large lock on it sat under one of the tables. The wall in front of us was covered by shelves holding sheets of papyrus and some wax tablets.

"We need more light," I told Diomedes.

"Yes, my lord. Right away." He left to get a candle or lamp. From his pace I suspected that "right away" didn't mean to him what it meant to me, but I didn't mind at the moment. Tacitus and I needed time to talk.

"I told you the men who attacked Aurelia knew this house," I said.

Tacitus nodded. "We just need to know to whom Sychaeus was sold."

"But we can't ask outright and draw attention to him. He may still have an accomplice in the house, somebody who could get word to him that we're looking for him."

"There might be a clue to his whereabouts in here." Tacitus pointed to the shelves of papyrus documents. "Calpurnius probably kept a receipt for the sale of a slave. You or I certainly keep those kinds of records."

"We'll soon find out," I said, gesturing with my head to Diomedes, who was strolling across the garden with a candle.

"Here you are, my lords." He lit the oil lamps hanging from a stand in one corner.

"That's much better," I said. "How are these papers organized?"

"The oldest are on the bottom shelves, my lord. The newer ones, higher up."

"That's helpful," Tacitus said, reaching up to pull some papyrus pages off the top shelf. "Are they gathered by subject?"

"No, my lord, just by date."

"Well, that's better than nothing." Tacitus began shuffling through the first batch of pages he had picked up.

As he watched us, Diomedes rubbed his hands on the sides of his tunic, like a man who couldn't stand the sight of strangers pawing his most precious possessions—the way I would react if I saw another man touch Aurora.

"Wait outside," I told him. "We'll call you when we need you."

Tacitus sighed with relief when Diomedes was out of sight. "Thank you. The fellow was starting to irritate me."

"I don't see what he was so edgy about. These are nothing but receipts and reports from the stewards on some of Calpurnius' other estates."

Tacitus held up one page. "Here's the receipt for that wretched wine. But he didn't pay for all of it. He still owes for half."

"If he's lucky, somebody will come and take the rest back." I stooped to get some pages off a bottom shelf. "I wonder if that's the sort of wine he's always bought."

We spread some sheets out on one of the tables. Most of them were scrap pieces of papyrus, larger pages that had been cut up and were written on the reverse side. They went back no more than four years. "His records from before the eruption of Vesuvius must have been destroyed when his house was buried by the ash," I said.

"Here's a receipt for some Falernian," Tacitus said. "It's almost three years old."

"If he could afford Falernian then, why is he buying swill now? When did he make the change?"

As we laid receipts out on the table, going from oldest on the left to newest on the right, I could see that Calpurnius' spending habits began to change about two years ago. He started purchasing cheaper varieties of wine, olive oil, garum—all essentials for a Roman household.

"He and Aurelia have been married for only a year," I said, "so this would appear normal to her. She must think her husband is just thrifty."

"'Miserly' would be my word for him."

"Do you see any references to the sale of slaves?" I asked.

Tacitus shook his head.

"I'm not seeing any recent reports from stewards on other estates," I said. "These are all two or three years old."

"The newer ones could be in the strongbox. Let's get Diomedes back in here and see what he knows."

I reached for the door. "What he knows and what he'll tell us might be two different things, no matter what orders Aurelia gave him."

Diomedes was not forthcoming at first, but we gradually coaxed some general information out of him. He had helped Calpurnius keep his records for over twelve years. For the first six years Calpurnius had still been under his father's *potestas*, so the old man had to see everything. During that time, Calpurnius' spending habits were unremarkable. When Fabatus emancipated his son six years ago, Diomedes noticed, Calpurnius began to spend more than he accounted for.

"Do you have any idea where the money was going?"

"My lord, I have opened this room for you and told you as much as I can. Please don't ask me to betray my lord Calpurnius any further."

"I'm not asking you to betray anyone," I said sharply. "Don't talk to me in those terms."

Diomedes cringed.

"Do you understand that Calpurnius is accused of murder? If convicted, he could be put to death."

"Yes, my lord, I understand that."

"Do you also understand that we're trying to help him? And the only way we can do that is if the people in this household will help us."

Diomedes nodded several times.

"If you're not going to help us," Tacitus said, "we might as well go back to Rome in the morning and leave you people to fend for yourselves."

"No. No, please don't do that, my lord." The dismay on Diomedes' face seemed genuine. "It's just that…these last couple of years have been so…so difficult for this family. And now this. I don't know how we're going to survive it."

"The only chance you have of surviving," Tacitus said, "is to tell us everything you can, no matter how unimportant it might seem."

With a sigh Diomedes seemed to decide to step over whatever line he had been shying away from. "Very well, my lord… I asked him about the money, but he said he would not be held accountable to me or to anyone else, any more than Pericles was held accountable to the Athenian assembly."

I nodded. In the glory days of Athens, Pericles had set aside large sums under a miscellaneous item in the budget. Only after his death did people learn that the money went to bribe Sparta not to attack Athens—a kind of blackmail, and all it did was postpone the attack, not prevent it.

"We need to see what's in the strongbox," I said.

"Of course, my lord." Diomedes pulled the box out from under the table without much effort and unlocked it.

"It doesn't seem very heavy," Tacitus said.

"No, my lord, it's not," Diomedes admitted. "Not nearly as heavy as it was six years ago."

"Is this the only box he has here?" I asked. Like most men of my class, I have money stored on each of my estates, entrusting the steward of each place with the key and the accounting. In my house in Rome I have two strongboxes.

Diomedes looked at the fresco of the Cyclops and then back at me. "It's the only one he has at all, my lord."

"He doesn't have money stored on his other estates?"

"He doesn't have any other estates, my lord. Not anymore."

And, I realized, he didn't have this one. It belonged to his wife's family.

"This is all the money he has, my lord." Diomedes raised the lid of the strongbox and stepped away from it. "I'll be in the garden if you have any more questions."

†

Tacitus and I lifted the strongbox onto a stool so we wouldn't have to bend over every time we took something out of it. The box contained gold and silver coins and pieces of papyrus, most of them rolled up and tied with cord but not sealed. We put the documents on the table and made a quick count of the money.

"This won't last a household of this size more than a couple of months," I said, wondering if Aurelia knew her husband was teetering on the precipice of financial ruin. Did she have the money to keep the household solvent? I looked around the storeroom as though we were missing something. "He must have more somewhere else, no matter what Diomedes says."

Tacitus untied and unrolled one of the documents. "Let's see if these tell us anything."

The first little scroll proved to be the receipt for the sale, three years ago, of a house and land on the road from Naples to Capua. Without knowing the exact location of the property or its size or condition, I couldn't speculate on whether Calpurnius had made a good deal. To judge from the other scrolls, he had made a number of similar sales in the past three years—properties in Naples and Misenum, an estate on Sicily.

"This box ought to be more than full," Tacitus said, dropping the record of another sale on the table. "Or at least there should be receipts for what he's spent. He seems pretty careful about that with household expenses."

"It's as though the money just disappeared," I said, "washed away like the waste in a *latrina*."

"Could he have loaned it to someone?" Tacitus asked.

"If he did, he didn't get anything in writing. His father said he has a good business sense, so I would expect more careful records."

"Maybe he has a gambling habit he's managed to keep hidden from his wife. Or a mistress. Or both, if he's a really lucky bastard."

"Whatever the reason, he is desperate for cash."

Tacitus unrolled another scroll—a larger one—glanced at it, and handed it to me. "He said he was being blackmailed. That's not an expense you would record."

"In order to blackmail somebody, you have to know something about them that they don't want anyone else to know." I ran my eye over the document Tacitus had given me.

"We haven't found a confession to a murder or to a plot against the emperor," Tacitus said. "What would someone have to hold over him?"

I didn't answer because my attention was focused on the papyrus in my hands. It was a list—several lists, actually, made over a period of four years—of the sales of slaves, usually in groups of up to a dozen. At the beginning of the document was the first group of slaves Calpurnius had sold, over four years ago, to a man in Puteoli. In that group I saw the name Proxena, Thamyras' woman. She was described as "blond and short." The most recent sales came at the end of the document. And there was the name I was looking for—Sychaeus, sold to a man in Capua six months ago. He was even described as "missing small finger on right hand."

"How far is Capua from here?" I asked. Tacitus has a much better sense for directions and distances than I do.

"No more than twenty miles. It's northeast of here. Why?"

"That's where Sychaeus was sent." I tapped the papyrus.

"Then it wouldn't be difficult for him to get back here."

"No more difficult than it would be for us to send someone up there to see what he's up to." I found a scrap piece of papyrus that was blank on one side. The ink in the pot on the table was a bit dry, but I managed to write down the name of the man to whom Sychaeus had been sold. Then I added another name.

"Who's that?" Tacitus asked, reading over my shoulder.

"That's the man who purchased Proxena."

Tacitus smiled and clapped me on the shoulder. "And you, the incurable romantic, are going to try to find her, aren't you?"

"What harm would it do? It might even make someone happy."

Somebody ought to be happy, I thought. If I couldn't make myself happy, the next best thing would be to bring a bit of joy into another man's life by reuniting him with the woman he loved.

Would I ever know what that felt like?

XIII

THE NEXT MORNING dawned gray, with a misty drizzle. An October chill was settling over us, creeping into my bones. I put on a second tunic when I got up.

I didn't like dispatching servants in such unpleasant weather on a journey I would not willingly make, but I could see no way around it. Two of my men would be going to Puteoli. One of Tacitus' men and a servant of Aurelia's would ride to Capua. Aurelia supplied horses and leather cloaks to protect the men from the rain. I supplied only the vaguest of explanations to her for why they were being sent. "We just have some questions about what we read in Calpurnius' records. This will help us clear up a couple of things."

Aurelia, professing not to understand finances, seemed to accept my reasons, but not Bastet. The Nubian, I thought, wanted to bore a hole in me with her narrowed eyes and reach in and dig out the truth, like a bear scooping honey from a beehive.

"Is your need so urgent, my lord, that you have to send these messengers out on a day like this?" she asked. "Perhaps you just haven't asked the right questions to the right people in our house."

I refused to be drawn into a debate with her. With her arms folded over her ample chest, she seemed formidable, even malevolent. I dictated letters, using one of my own servants as a scribe instead of Aurelia's household scribe so no one could report on the contents of the letters. The names of the men they were being sent to were written on the outside of each letter.

"Find these men," I instructed each set of servants as they prepared to mount. "The letters will provide an introduction and explain what

I want. This man Furius, in Puteoli, will probably know my uncle's name and recognize my seal." I use my uncle's seal ring, bearing a dolphin with his name, now mine, around it—G. PLIN SEC. "The fellow in Capua, Marcus Jucundus—well, I don't know. Whatever you learn, each of you should be able to get back here by tomorrow evening. Just don't linger along the way."

"The sooner you get back," Tacitus said, "the larger reward you'll get."

Once the servants were gone, we turned our attention to getting ourselves down to Calpurnius' house. We decided to take a wagon, in case Calpurnius was injured badly enough that he couldn't ride a horse.

"If you're going to take the wagon," Aurelia said as we walked out to the barn where the family's equipment was kept, "let me go with you."

I shook my head quickly. "No. As close as you are to delivering your baby, I won't take that risk."

"My husband needs me."

"We already have one person in danger," I said. "I'm not going to expose someone else to this kind of risk."

"I was attacked in my own house two nights ago. Am I any safer here than I would be with you?"

The argument broke off when a servant opened the door of the barn and Aurelia looked into it. "Where's the other *raeda?*" she asked.

"I don't know, my lady," the servant answered. "We haven't traveled much lately, so no one's been out here in a while...."

The cobwebs and the mustiness of the place testified to the truth of his statement.

"Could someone have stolen it?"

"I doubt it, my lady. The lock wasn't broken. Someone must have been able to open it."

"You had two *raedas* in here?" I asked.

"Yes. The other one was newer than this one and quite nice."

Tacitus and I looked at each other. A decent *raeda* could fetch enough money to warrant selling it, if a man was desperate for cash. We hadn't seen a receipt, but that didn't mean the transaction hadn't taken place.

"Who has a key?" Tacitus asked.

"There's only this one key," Aurelia said. "My steward has charge of it. He would not use it without consulting Calpurnius or me."

"So no one could have opened this door without you or your husband knowing about it."

Aurelia nodded, then turned to me. "Please take me with you, Gaius Pliny. I have to ask Calpurnius what's going on."

I put my hands on both her shoulders. "No. I doubt that he's going to want to talk about a missing wagon right now. We'll bring him home and get him tended to, then we both have a lot of questions to ask him."

"I should go with you," Bastet insisted. "No one here knows that house—or its master—as well as I do."

Before I could object, Aurelia said, "That's true. Take her with you, Gaius Pliny." She put her hand on Bastet's arm, as though she would push her toward me.

"But what if you should deliver the child before we get back?"

"There are other women here who've helped with a birth. I'll be fine. Take Bastet with you."

When I looked into her eyes I realized she was pleading with me.

†

We took only one servant with us, one of Aurelia's, to drive the *raeda*. I wanted to leave as many men of my men and Tacitus' as possible to protect Aurelia, even though I was sure we would be back before dark. As much as I would have liked to have more protection on the road, there was no room in the wagon, since we had to take the Nubian princess and still have room for Calpurnius on the return trip. Something about Bastet—something I could only call her manner or her presence—seemed to fill the interior of the wagon and left little room for anyone else. I hoped we could squeeze Calpurnius in on the return trip.

Aurelia's *raeda* was old and had never sported much decoration. It must have belonged to her father, but it had been kept in good condition. It was completely closed in, with only a small window on one side, and covered with a rounded roof to let the rain run off. The driver sat in front, outside, and drove a team of two horses. This particular *raeda* was about three paces long and less than two paces wide, with the entrance on the side opposite the window. The three of us could sit comfortably, Tacitus and me on each side and Bastet in the seat behind the driver, facing to the back. Between her feet she had the baskets of food and medical supplies that Aurelia had prepared.

"How long will the trip take?" I asked.

"At this pace, perhaps half an hour, my lord," Bastet said. "This wagon is a little heavy for only two horses, but they were all we had left, after you sent your messengers…here and there." She waved her hand to show her opinion of the errands I had assigned the servants.

We rode in silence—Tacitus even closed his eyes—until the wagon stopped. I heard the driver talking to someone.

"Are we there already?" Tacitus asked, jerking awake.

"It seems too soon," Bastet said.

"I hope the horses are all right." I got out of the *raeda* and was surprised to see a boy standing in front of the horses. He couldn't have been more than ten and was as gray and ash-covered as the terrain around him, like a statue come to life—an emaciated statue. His tunic was too long, a cast-off from someone older, ragged at the hem and badly patched in several places.

I glanced around, my unease growing as I saw the mounds on either side of the road, formed by structures buried by Vesuvius. Titus, the *princeps* at that time, had sent soldiers and slaves to clear the roads as soon as possible after the eruption. They could do little more than pile the ash up on either side. At some places the roads were as narrow as mountain roads, with barely room for two vehicles to get past one another. At this particular point they had created a narrow pass that offered perfect cover for an ambush. I got between the *raeda* and the mound on the side of the road only with some difficulty.

"What's the matter?" I asked.

"The boy's begging for food, my lord," the driver said. "Says he hasn't eaten in three days."

"I can believe that," Tacitus said, standing on the steps of the *raeda*. "Don't you think we could spare him a bite?"

Before I could answer, someone grabbed me from behind and I felt a knife at my throat.

"Don't nobody move," a desperate voice said in my ear, "or I'll slit him from ear to ear. You, driver, get down."

When the driver hesitated, I was afraid he might be an accomplice, but then he tied the reins to the railing beside him and dropped to the ground.

"Now I don't want to hurt nobody," my assailant said. "Really, I don't. Just do what I tell you. I'm only tryin' to feed my boy."

"We'll give you—"

The knife pressed against my throat. "You'll give us your scraps, I know. But we need more than that. And we need a few coins. In fact, all your coins. All right, boy, tie 'em up."

The boy reached into a cleft in the rock beside the road and pulled out several lengths of cord.

"Get the big one first," the man said, gesturing with his head toward Tacitus. "Tie him to the railin' on the wagon. If you please, sir."

"Please," I managed to gulp. I wasn't actually frightened because I could tell the poor man was leaning on me to support himself. I felt confident we could overcome him at some point, but I wanted to wait until the knife was not so close to my throat.

Tacitus did as the man ordered and the boy trussed him up expertly. This was not their first robbery.

"Now the driver."

In a moment the driver's hands were securely fastened near Tacitus'. Then the man pushed me toward the wagon. When I offered the least resistance, the pressure on the knife increased.

"I will slice you, sir, much as I don't want to."

Cicero said you can't defeat an enemy who has nothing to live for. I decided this wasn't the time to test the truth of that axiom. I let myself be tied to the front wheel of the *raeda*.

When the boy got into the carriage I heard him gasp. "Papa, there's a woman in here."

"Please don't hurt me," Bastet cried.

"Get out here, woman," the man said, leaning on the back wheel.

Bastet climbed out of the *raeda*, with her shaking hands drawn up to her mouth and tears running down her face. "Please don't hurt me."

"Should I tie her up, Papa?"

The man shook his head and pointed his knife toward the Nubian. "Sit down and keep still, woman." Bastet, quivering, moved toward the back of the wagon.

The man turned to his son. "See, she's afraid but she knows we're not goin' to hurt nobody, so she won't hurt us. And we need somebody to untie these gentlemen after we're gone." He slipped his knife into his belt. "Now let's see what's for lunch."

The boy climbed into the *raeda* and pushed the baskets toward his father, who remained at the door. They were so absorbed in unwrapping their bounty that I saw what was going to happen before either of them did. Bastet picked up a rock, took two steps toward the man, and brought it down full force on his head. I had my mouth open to cry out, and the boy saw her coming and yelled, "Papa!" But the man had barely turned before the stone crushed his skull. Blood splattered on the *raeda* and on the boy, bright red against the gray.

"Papa!" the child screamed. "Papa!"

Bastet drew the rock back again, but I cried out. "Don't! If you harm that boy, it will cost you your life. I swear it!"

As the boy hugged his father and wept, Bastet was clearly weighing her options. Was she thinking that she could kill us all and disappear? I had made a threat that I was in no position—literally—to enforce.

Bastet's eyes met mine as she hefted the bloodstained rock. She might even have half smiled. Then she threw the rock as far as she could into the desolate landscape beside the road. Pulling the boy off his father, she shoved him toward Tacitus. "Untie them, you worthless little wretch!"

With tears making tracks down his dirty face, the boy untied the three of us. As soon as my hands were free, I knelt beside the man, but I could not detect any signs of life.

"He's dead, ain't he?" the boy said as he dropped to both knees beside me.

"Yes, I'm afraid he is. I'm sorry." It felt odd to say that about a man who, just moments before, had had a knife pressed to my throat, but I was truly sorry. I put a hand on the boy's shoulder. He jerked away from me and threw himself on his dead father, crying.

"We'd best get going, my lord," Bastet said.

I jumped up and turned on her, as angry as I had ever been at another human being. "Why did you do that?"

"I had to protect you men, my lord." She crossed her arms over her chest and drew herself up in her best regal manner.

"He wasn't going to hurt us!" I've never had a slave whipped or tortured. At that moment I could have. "He was so weak he could barely hold the knife."

"Are you certain of that, my lord?"

I thrust my face into hers. "I've had a knife at my throat before, held by a man who could have taken my head off. I know what it feels like. This man was leaning on me just to keep himself standing. I didn't do anything because I didn't want to hurt him in front of his child."

"I had no way of knowing that, my lord." There was no remorse or humility in Bastet's voice. "It looked to me like you were in danger."

"You could have just knocked him out, stunned him for a moment. He was so weak you could have pushed him over with one hand. You didn't have to kill him right in front of his child."

"I did not know how weak he was, my lord, and I did not know how hard I hit him. My only thought was for your safety."

Why did I find that so hard to believe?

"We were not in any immediate danger. The poor man was just trying to feed himself and his son."

"You may believe that if you wish, my lord, but you were defenseless. He could have killed you in any of a dozen ways." She seemed to be picturing them.

The boy, still kneeling beside his father, piped up between sobs. "My papa never killed nobody."

Out of the corner of my eye I saw the boy jump up.

"But you killed my papa!" he cried as he lunged at Bastet with the knife he'd taken from his father's belt.

I grabbed his thin arm and had no trouble twisting the knife from his hand. He kicked and lashed his fists at me. "Are you gonna kill me now?"

I took a breath to calm myself and embraced the boy to hold him still. There was no reason to frighten the child any more than we already had. "Nobody's going to hurt you. This is all a terrible mistake, but we're not going to hurt you. I promise you."

I handed the knife to Tacitus. Still holding the boy's wrist, I asked, "Did you and your father live around here?"

He jerked his head to indicate some place behind me. "Over there, just a ways, in a cave."

I released the boy and let him drop back to his father's side. "We can't leave this man here," I said. "We'll take him home."

Leaving Tacitus to guard the *raeda* and clean up the blood, I made Bastet and our driver carry the man's body through a ravine created by the mounds of ash to the place where the boy directed us. He and his father had worn the beginnings of a path.

"How do you know there's not a band of them waiting for us, my lord?" Bastet protested.

"There's nobody but me and my papa," the boy said, walking beside his father and holding his hand. "Now, it's just me." He started crying again.

The "cave" the boy led us to was actually part of a rural villa that had been covered in the eruption. Stopping at the entrance, the boy fished a flint and a lamp out of a niche someone had carved into the ash.

"We keep this here 'cause we need a light to get out and back in again," he said.

When he had lit it, he led us into one of the rooms off the atrium. Ash had filled the atrium, falling through the opening in the roof, but had left a couple of the rooms off it accessible to anyone willing to do a little digging. The opening that the man had cut out was low enough that we had to stoop to enter. It was braced with timbers, which looked none too sturdy. To one side of it were a fire pit and a hole which, from the smell, was used as a *latrina*.

Standing up inside the room, I saw that the man had scrounged up enough utensils and bits of furniture—a small table and two beds—to make a nest for himself and his son. Because the ground shook so badly during the eruption, most of the plaster and the frescos painted on it had cracked and fallen off the walls.

"That's Papa's bed." The boy pointed to a sleeping couch.

"Put him there," I told Bastet and the driver. "Cover him with that blanket."

Before they covered his father, the boy kissed him one more time and smoothed his filthy hair. Then he looked at me. "What do I do now? Where do I go?"

"You'll come with us." I ignored Bastet's gasp. "How long have you and your father lived here?"

"As long as I can remember."

Probably since just after the eruption, I realized. The boy must have been four or five when that disaster happened. "Did you live in this villa before the eruption?"

"I don't know, sir. Papa said everything looked so different, he wasn't sure where we were."

"Was your mother here with you?"

"No, sir. Papa said he couldn't save her."

"What was your father's name?"

"Ferox. His name was Ferox. That's what it says." He pointed to the table beside the bed.

"The fierce one." The name hardly fit the trembling man who had threatened me. I picked up a bronze slave bracelet, still intact, off the table. It would have fit the man's wrist snugly at some point, but he was so thin now that it must have slipped off easily. It said FEROX SERV GN LUC.

"He was a slave of Gnaeus Lucullus," I said to Bastet. "Do you know that family?"

"No, my lord."

Why did I not believe her? Was it just because I found it difficult to trust her in anything? Or because she did not look me in the eye when she spoke?

I turned to the driver. "Do you know them?"

"No, my lord."

The boy's soft crying brought my attention back to him. I put my arm around him and pulled him to me. "What's your name, son?"

He ran his arm across his mouth and nose and wiped it on his tunic. "Papa called me Philippos, 'cause I love horses so much." He pointed to the other bed, where a section of a fresco showing two horses pulling a chariot still clung to the wall.

"Well, Philippos, how would you like to help drive our horses?"

"Yes, sir, I'd like that."

His face didn't exactly brighten up, but I couldn't expect it to. He had seen his father murdered right before his eyes. The man's blood was on his tunic. He would never forget that. I had lost my father when I was too young to know what was happening. Then I lost my second father—my uncle—when I was old enough to realize that death was the ultimate end for all of us. But this boy wasn't old enough to understand any of that. All he knew was that he had lost the one person in the world who loved him and cared about him, the person he had depended on for the last five years.

"Is there anything here you'd like to take with you?" I asked the boy.

He took his father's slave bracelet out of my hand and laid it on the shrouded body, then looked around the grim room. "No, sir. Nothing."

"Well, there's one more thing we need to do before we leave," I said. "I'm sorry we can't provide a proper funeral, but we can do this."

I had noticed the fire pit where they cooked outside the door as we came in. The ashes were heavy in it, and a few pieces of wood stuck out. I picked up one, and with the charred end, wrote on the wall above Ferox's corpse, in large letters: D M FEROX.

Since I assumed Philippos couldn't read, I pointed to the first two letters and said, "That stands for 'Dis Manibus—To the gods of the underworld.'" Then I ran my finger along the second line. "That's your father's name. This will protect him"—from imaginary monsters, perhaps, but not from the animals and insects that would descend on the body by the time we were back at the raeda. I took a coin out of the pouch under my tunic, placed it in the dead man's mouth, and pulled the blanket over his face. "That will pay his passage across the Styx."

"Thank you, sir," Philippos said, choking back a sob.

He need not know that I didn't believe a word of it. I had stopped believing it before I was his age.

I wished I could have done better by Ferox and provided him with a funeral pyre. Even if he was a slave, he should have some kind of reward for keeping himself and his son alive for five years under such difficult circumstances. I doubt many men of my class would have survived. To judge from their physical condition, he had been giving Philippos the larger share of whatever food he found. However, there was nothing in the room or nearby to fuel a pyre. Ferox's tunic and the covering on his bed would burn, but not nearly long enough or hot enough to consume the body. Leaving the corpse half-burnt would be an even worse indignity than leaving the man untended and unprotected.

When we were outside the room again I noticed that the chunks of hardened ash that Ferox had chiseled out were piled up not far from the entrance to his "home," probably as far away as he could move them in his weakened condition. If I couldn't dispose of the body properly, I decided, I could at least keep anyone from disturbing it.

"Help me," I told the driver. We piled the larger pieces over the low opening until it was completely blocked. When Philippos saw what we were doing, he pitched in. I did not turn my back on him, for fear that he might pick up a rock and try again to take his vengeance on us. But he seemed to have accepted what had happened—one more tragedy in a young life already too familiar with them.

Once we had the opening blocked, I picked up a charred stick from the fire pit and scratched on the flattest piece of stone: FEROX MORTUUS

"That means Ferox is dead," I told Philippos. "If anyone should find this place, I don't think they'll want to disturb him. And this will be one more bit of protection, I hope." I rubbed enough of the soot in one place that I could then press my seal ring into it.

†

We returned to the *raeda* and gave Philippos something to eat. We finally had to stop him from eating so there would be something left for Calpurnius. The apple crop was just in and Aurelia had packed several in our basket. I sliced one in half and let Philippos feed each of the horses. In spite of the tragedy he'd just been through, the boy's eyes showed a spark as he petted one of the horses on its haunch.

As we packed up and prepared to get back in the carriage, Bastet said she thought we had another half mile to go before reaching Calpurnius' house. "Look for the tops of two pines sticking out of the ash," she told the driver. "They're dead, of course, but you'll see the branches."

"I know that place, sir," Philippos said, wiping his mouth on his arm. "My Papa and me's been in there 'cause it was dug out so well."

"Why didn't you live there?" Tacitus asked.

"We was afraid somebody'd come back, sir. It didn't look like they was finished with the place. We never took nothin'," he added quickly.

"Nobody's going to punish you, boy," I said. "But I want you to ride in front with the driver and show him where to stop."

The driver didn't dare object, even though his eyes showed his annoyance. The boy's presence would make the driver's platform crowded, but making him our lookout provided a good excuse for him not to sit with Tacitus and me, staring at the woman who killed his father. It also meant we wouldn't have to smell him.

"What do you mean to do with him?" Tacitus asked as we settled ourselves and the *raeda* picked up speed.

"I don't know, but I couldn't leave him in that hole to die."

"No, of course not. His legal status will be difficult to sort out, though. He's the son of a slave, so that means he's a slave. You'll have to find Gnaeus Lucullus or his family, if there are any left, and return the boy to them."

"All in due time. For now, he's safe and has had a good meal. Obviously his first in a long time."

"I'd say it's been even longer since he had a bath," Tacitus said.

"We'll get all of that taken care of when we get back to Aurelia's house." I looked at Bastet, daring her to contradict me—even to open her mouth.

"For a boy, he certainly cries a lot," Tacitus said.

"By the gods, man! He's a child. He just saw his father killed right in front of him. How would anyone react in that situation?"

Bastet stirred and spoke softly, looking at a spot in the rear of the *raeda*, or perhaps seeing something beyond that. "They might mourn for the rest of their lives. As I have done, since I saw my entire family slaughtered by your Roman soldiers." She broke into a chant, in a language I had never heard before, and began rocking back and forth.

I knew little about our presence in Egypt. It's not a province but the personal possession of the *princeps*. "In what battle was your tribe defeated?" I asked.

Bastet broke off her chanting. "Our last battle. I don't know what you Romans call it."

"Who attacked first?" Tacitus asked.

"My people had taken the head off a statue of your Augustus. It stood on the boundary between Roman land and ours, on top of the graves of our ancestors. We buried it. When the soldiers demanded its return, we refused."

"That was a grievous insult," Tacitus said.

"I suppose it was. Almost as much of an insult as placing the statue over our graves." She lapsed back into her chanting and rocking.

A few moments later the wagon slowed and the driver called, "We've come about half a mile, my lords, like the woman said. The boy says we've arrived."

"Is this the place?" I asked Bastet, placing a hand on her arm.

She blinked her eyes, like someone awaking from a dream, and collected herself for a moment. "I'll see, my lord."

We got out of the *raeda* and found ourselves in a landscape even bleaker than we had confronted a few miles back up the road. We were closer to the volcano than I had ever been, close enough to feel the weight of its mass. I wondered how anyone could tell the location of one house from another. It all looked like desert dunes made of stone. Five years of rain had hardened the ash and shaped it into unpredictable lumps and depressions. Wind-blown dirt and debris had settled in some of those depressions. The lack of any vegetation taller than my waist made me feel, for a moment, like a Titan.

"This is it," Bastet said. "A place even more dead than the African desert. The shaft that Calpurnius' servants dug when they were trying to recover things from the house should be just over here."

With Philippos trailing after us, she led us to a place where we could climb up the ash on the side of the road toward the bay. A few steps had been cut into the ash. I nudged Tacitus and pointed to a small spot that appeared to be blood—fresh blood. He nodded.

When we got to the top and were standing between the skeletal tips of the dead pines, I paused to look out toward the water. "Was this house on the shore before the eruption?"

"Yes, my lord," Bastet said. "Right on the shore. You could hear the waves from anywhere in the house."

I turned to Tacitus. "What would you estimate the distance to the water is now?"

Tacitus put his hand up to shade his eyes. "At least a quarter of a mile."

I looked up at Vesuvius, in awe that the mountain could have spewed out so much and still be standing. How much more did it have stored up to unleash on us when we least expected it?

"Here's the opening, my lord," Bastet said.

It was a relief to see that the shaft was on a slant. That was how Bastet had described it to us, but I had still feared that we would have to use ropes and lower one another into the ruins. That would mean leaving one person above ground to stand guard. It could also make it difficult to get Calpurnius out if he was seriously injured. I was glad to see we could work our way in—and back out—with little trouble, even if we had to carry Calpurnius.

I crouched to look down into the shaft as far as the sunlight would let me. The size of the tunnel surprised me, but then I realized that Calpurnius had wanted to bring out pieces of furniture and statuary, like the satyr with the flutes. "We may have to stoop or crawl," I told Tacitus, "but it looks manageable."

"It's not hard to get around in, sir," Philippos said. "You'll see."

I turned to Bastet. "Wait here."

As I expected, she disagreed with me. "My lord, I think it would be better if my lord Calpurnius heard my voice. He knows he can trust me—"

"Are you implying that he can't trust me?"

"Don't be so damned sensitive, Gaius Pliny," Tacitus said. "The woman has a point. Calpurnius wasn't exactly overjoyed to see us when he was in jail."

I threw up my hands in surrender. "Fine. Let's light some torches and get on with this."

From the supplies in the *raeda* we lit a torch for each of us. Tacitus carried a bag with several more torches and a flint. Bastet took a bag filled with skins of wine and water, a bit of food, and some medical supplies. I stationed Philippos at the entrance to the shaft and gave him a torch and a flint. He could show a light or call to us if we needed help finding our way out. I hoped the confidence I was showing in him would allay what I was sure was his hatred and suspicion of us—and well-deserved it was.

The boy hugged me. "Be careful, sir."

I was more surprised than I would have been if he'd hit me. "All right then…let's go."

Before I could set foot in the opening, though, Bastet stepped in front of me.

"I should lead the way, my lord. Unlike you, I have been in here since the digging was done. I think I know where he might be. There will be some twists and turns."

There was no point in fighting her any more. Feeling like Aeneas entering the underworld with Bastet playing the part of the Sibyl, I crouched down and followed the Nubian into the opening. Tacitus, being larger than either of us, had to crawl behind us.

"My knees will never recover from this," he muttered.

All I could think of was the Sibyl's warning that the descent to the underworld was easy; it was the return that was so difficult.

The shaft angled down for about twenty paces. The hard gray ash had a porous appearance and seemed to absorb the flickering light from our torches like a sponge, rather than reflect it. The walls of the tunnel gave off a strong sulfur smell. At one point the floor of the shaft felt and looked different.

"I think we're going over the wall of the house," Tacitus said.

The surface I felt under my hand was masonry, a different texture than the rest of the tunnel. "Which part of the house are we going into?" I asked Bastet.

"The peristyle garden, my lord. Calpurnius reckoned that was the most open part. He wouldn't have to worry about breaking through the roof."

"How many men did he use in this digging?" Tacitus asked.

"Fifteen of his strongest, my lord. We had to wait almost a year after the eruption before the ash cooled down enough. As it cooled, it hardened. The men worked for nearly a month. The ash hardened even while they were working." She ran her hand over the wall. "I think it's more solid now than it was then. But some of the men began to get sick. They had trouble breathing. Three of them eventually died."

Like my uncle at Stabiae. I wondered if the volcano threw out something poisonous—a vapor of some kind—that could still be seeping out of the rocklike ash around us. Maybe that was why I was having trouble getting my breath. I felt like the wall of the shaft was getting closer to me, so I put out my hand to push it back.

Behind me Tacitus asked, "Gaius Pliny, are you all right?"

XIV

I DON'T KNOW," I said, breathing rapidly, with my mouth open. "It's so...damnably dark in here." The light from my torch flickered even more because the hand holding it was starting to shake. "How much farther?" I asked Bastet.

"I think we're almost down to ground level, my lord," the Nubian said, looking over her shoulder at me with an expression that I couldn't read. In the dim light, against the dark background of the tunnel her black skin seemed to disappear. All I was aware of was her multi-colored head-covering swirling in the torchlight, and her eyes. Those eyes seemed to grow and shine.

Within a few more paces we did reach a point where the tunnel leveled out and we could stand a bit straighter. The sense of panic I was feeling ebbed a bit, but only a bit. My desire—an almost frantic need—to get out of this place was making my head throb and my stomach tie into a knot. I didn't understand what was happening to me. I'd been in a few caves when I was younger—Aurora and I explored some around Laurentum—and never felt anything like this. But those caves had been larger, and I had been smaller. I could turn around in them. These tunnels were so narrow I couldn't even straighten my arms out to each side and my head almost scraped the top. And Aurora wasn't beside me.

"That's the fish pond," Bastet said, pointing to a mosaic edge worked in a meander pattern, blue and red against a white background—a welcome splash of color.

From there the tunnel branched in three directions. I pointed to our left. "That would take us to the atrium, wouldn't it?"

"Yes, my lord. And I think that's the way my lord Calpurnius would go."

"Then let's get moving."

Walking more quickly on level ground, it took only a couple of moments to reach the front of the house. To my great relief I saw that one side of the roof over the atrium had collapsed in a single large section. Because of the way the piece of the roof was sitting at an angle, supported by fallen columns and other debris, it had prevented the ash from filling in the rooms on that side of the atrium. We could stand up and move more freely. I took a deep breath and was able to stop my hands from shaking. Our torches had more effect here, easing the knot in my stomach.

"You look like you're feeling better," Tacitus said, patting my shoulder.

I nodded. "I just wish there were more light."

Tacitus reached into the bag of torches he was carrying and pulled out two. "The man wants more light. Well then, *fiat lux*." He placed the torches in the wall brackets and lit them from the one he was carrying. "Is that better?"

"Yes. I hope we don't need them on the way back. That tunnel was unbearable with some light. I couldn't do it in the dark."

"We've got a few more, so don't worry about it. And if we have to, we can set your tunic on fire."

As my rational faculties took control, I glanced around me. The upheaval of the earth during the eruption had made the mosaic floor we were standing on wavy, like the water coming into the shore. Much of the plaster on the walls had been dislodged, taking the frescoes with it, but I thought I could make out a pyramid.

"Is that what I think it is?" I asked Bastet.

"Yes, my lord. Calpurnius Fabatus built this house after one of his trips to Egypt."

I looked at the brackets where Tacitus had placed the torches. His eyes followed mine. "Why did Fabatus leave this place?" I asked.

"When he fell into disfavor with Nero, my lord, about twenty years ago, he gave this one to his son and built himself a smaller house in a less conspicuous place."

"That's the one we saw, west of Naples?" Tacitus asked.

"Yes, my lord. And now, forgive me, but I must find my lord Calpurnius."

She began calling in the language I'd heard her using in the *raeda*, a concoction of words almost overwhelmed by the rhythm. She could have been a bard singing.

"What are you saying?" I asked.

"I'm calling him in my native Nubian, my lord. I taught him some of it. When he hears it, he will know for certain it's me."

All I could do was trust her. For all I knew, she could have been warning him, telling him to get ready to kill us—I simply did not know. I put a hand on the sword under my tunic.

We finally heard a noise, a groan, from up ahead and quickened our pace.

"He's here, my lord," Bastet said as she entered one of the rooms off the atrium with Tacitus and me on her heels.

Calpurnius had propped himself up on a bed against the wall opposite the door. He held a knife in his left hand but dropped it as soon as he saw us. "Thank the gods," he muttered, letting himself collapse full-length on the bed.

"It's all right, my lord," Bastet said in the soothing tone a nurse would use to calm a frightened child. "We're here. Everything's going to be all right." She unstopped the skin of water and Calpurnius drank greedily.

"Gaius Pliny," he said, wiping his mouth, "I'm not even...unhappy to see you."

"That's not the most gracious welcome I've ever had," I said, "but it's an improvement over the last time we met."

"I'm sorry, but you must understand—"

"Where are you hurt, Calpurnius?" I had no patience for revisiting our conversation in the jail. The only thing that mattered to me now was to tend to this man and get him—and myself—out of here. We lit the lamps hanging from a lamp tree in a corner and the room felt almost bearable, if I could just stop thinking about the pile of ash on the roof above us and how deeply we could be buried beneath it.

"It's my arm." Calpurnius held out his right arm, which had a long gash in it. He had tried to wrap it. "The bleeding has pretty well stopped, but it has left me weak. And I think I may have a broken rib."

Bastet took some oil and an ointment from her bag and began to clean the wound on his arm. "It may need to be sewn up, my lord, but I don't have what I need to do that right now. At least we can clean it and bind it tightly."

Calpurnius nodded. "Tying a knot on one's own arm is virtually impossible, I've discovered."

"Do the best you can with it," I told Bastet. "Then we'll get him out of here."

"I'm not leaving," Calpurnius said abruptly. "Let me die here. It would be better for everyone."

"He's not making sense because of his injury, my lord," Bastet said. "I'll stay here with him. Give him a couple of days to recover. You can send food and water to us under cover of darkness."

I did not want a servant telling me what to do, not even a servant who had been a princess in some earlier part of her life and was making good sense now. Turning to Calpurnius, I said, "I will not agree to that arrangement unless you tell us exactly what's going on. The friendship between your sister and my mother obligates me to try to help you. Tacitus and I have inconvenienced ourselves a great deal to come down here. Our presence has resulted in the death of an innocent man at the hands of this servant of yours." Calpurnius did not seem surprised to hear that, nor did he ask for details. "If you won't tell me what you're afraid of, I'll…I'll—"

"We'll post notices all over Naples," Tacitus said, "revealing where you are."

"Exactly," I said.

"Oh, surely you wouldn't," Calpurnius moaned.

"Yes, I would. That is the extent to which you have exhausted my patience."

Calpurnius bowed his head and lay back on the bed. "All right, but you must swear to me that this secret will remain buried here, as deeply as this house is buried."

And yet people can dig around in it, I thought. He might want to rethink his analogy because I was going to dig around in whatever he told us. "I will not reveal to anyone what you tell us in here."

"What about your friend? Can he be as silent as his name suggests?"

Tacitus pinched his lips together and nodded once, drawing a chuckle from Calpurnius, followed by a grimace. Bastet held his hand.

"The story goes back about fifteen years," Calpurnius began, "and I'm afraid it's somewhat complicated."

"Keep it as simple as you can," I urged him, casting a nervous glance toward the ceiling, where the light failed to penetrate.

"Yes, I'm not exactly Odysseus telling his tale to the Phaeacians over dinner. Well, have you heard of Aelius Lamia?" Calpurnius asked. "Ah, I can see from your faces that you have."

"I know the name," I said, and Tacitus nodded. "Are you talking about the Aelius Lamia whom Domitian executed a few years ago?" I hated that I had to be the one to introduce the name of the *princeps*. If Domitian was involved in whatever was going on, it was more than somewhat complicated.

Calpurnius nodded and sadness crept into his voice. "The very same. He and I were friends from the time we were boys."

"Wait," Tacitus said, "didn't Domitian seduce Aelius' wife?"

"Seduced her, my not-so-silent friend, and stole her away from him."

I wished I could sit down, but the room had been stripped of all other furniture. We hovered around the lamp tree, like soldiers gathered around a campfire to exchange tales. "Are you talking about Domitia Longina, his current wife?"

"Yes. It all happened during the chaos after Galba's death, that year when there were four emperors. No one knew who the next *princeps* was going to be."

"It was a frightening time," Tacitus said. "Gaius Pliny was seven, too young to remember much of it, but I was twelve."

"I was twenty-one," Calpurnius said. "Aelius, a year older. No one could believe it. Civil war in Rome, after a century of peace. Roman troops even burned part of the Capitoline Hill. Not barbarians, mind you, but Roman troops."

"My father said it felt like the end of the world," Tacitus said quietly. "But how does Aelius' wife figure into this?"

"Longina, in case you've forgotten or didn't know, is a direct descendant of the deified Augustus, in the fifth generation."

I shook my head slowly. "By the gods, the man's seed has spread like weeds in a wheat field."

"Perhaps we should set fire to the field to cleanse it," Tacitus said. It was a dangerous thing to say, even when we could be sure there were no spies to hear us.

"The men have all been killed off, I think," Calpurnius said, "but there could be dozens of women out there, ready to breed the next generation. They don't brag about their descent because some man who craves power will come seeking them. And you can't spot them easily because they have their fathers' names, not the Julian family name. Longina's father was Domitius Corbulo, the general whom Nero forced to commit suicide. Her connection to Augustus came through her mother."

"And any man who was married to her could have some chance to claim power," I said. Even though Augustus' last recognized descendant had been dead for fifteen years, his name and any connection to it, no matter how remote, gave a man a status that mere mortals such as myself could not hope to equal.

Calpurnius nodded. "Exactly. In those chaotic times several of Aelius' friends thought he might put himself forward. He had held high offices. His ancestors had held consulships and governorships. He was not unworthy, we thought, to become *princeps*. Better an educated, cultivated man like him than the brutish generals who were competing for power."

"But he had no troops under his command," Tacitus pointed out.

"That's correct. What he had, though, was a descendant of the deified Augustus by his side, and their children would carry that same blood. They would not establish a new dynasty but would revive Rome's first dynasty, the empire's rightful rulers."

Even in the dim light I could see Tacitus take a deep breath to steady himself. The idea of Rome having a ruler of any kind, let alone a "rightful" ruler, is repugnant to him. He longs, with all his being, for the restoration of the Republic.

"So how did Domitian end up with Aelius' wife?" I asked.

"By the end of that summer it was clear Vespasian and his sons would win out," Calpurnius said. "Vitellius had taken Rome, but nobody wanted that drunken lout as our ruler. Vespasian and Titus were still in the east, trying to squelch the revolt of the Jews. Domitian was in Rome, claiming to represent his family's interests."

Tacitus snorted. "He still likes to say that *he* took the empire from Vitellius and gave it to his father when Vespasian got to Rome."

"What he did take," Calpurnius said, "was Longina. He seduced her by promising her that she would play Livia to his Augustus."

"Why would a woman yield to that sort of blandishment?" I asked. From what I'd read, Livia had been a manipulative, conniving shrew who stopped at nothing—possibly even murder—to clear the way for her son Tiberius to succeed Augustus. In her old age she had supplied Augustus with virgins to deflower. What sort of woman would want to be compared to her?

"Longina is very aware of her ancestry," Calpurnius said. "She has always been deeply embarrassed by her father's suicide and the eclipse of her family. She married Aelius and had resigned herself, I think, to remaining in obscurity, even though she chafed at it. But Domitian offered her the chance to claim what she saw as her rightful place."

"She gives him a modicum of legitimacy," Tacitus said, "in an otherwise illegitimate system." Calpurnius raised his head as if he would object, but said nothing as Tacitus went on. "Plus, their children would be descendants of Augustus."

Calpurnius nodded and again took Bastet's hand in his. "That's exactly what Domitian was thinking, I'm sure. He is obsessed with his inferiority to the Julian bloodline."

I barely kept myself from laughing. Based on my own experience, I could have told Calpurnius that "obsessed" was far too kind a way to describe Domitian's interest in Augustus' descendants.

"Ironically," Calpurnius said, "the only child they've had died." Even in the dim light I could see that he couldn't suppress a smile.

"What does any of this have to do with you being blackmailed and Amalthea being killed?" I asked.

"It's the reason behind it all," Calpurnius said. "What Aristotle would call the prime mover, the thing that sets everything else in motion." He took a moment to gather himself, then went on. "Several of us—friends of Aelius—decided we would not sit idly by and let this pretender take Aelius' wife from him. His father Vespasian comes from a family of tax-collectors and rag-merchants. They barely qualify for the equestrian stripe. They had over-reached themselves and needed to be dealt with."

Calpurnius' tone of voice, along with the tilt of his head, revealed his arrogance. Even though his family wasn't in the top rank in Rome, he thought himself better than he was and everyone beneath him worse than they were. That sort of snobbery can cause a man to underestimate those he considers his inferiors. Vespasian and his sons may have over-reached, but they had grasped the prize, pushing Calpurnius and his ineffectual friends aside in the process.

"How did you propose to deal with them?"

"I wrote a short letter to Aelius telling him we were going to 'rectify the wrong that had been done' to him."

Tacitus and I gasped. "You put that in writing?" Tacitus said before I could form the question.

"Why are you so surprised?" Calpurnius said. "It's perfectly innocuous. I didn't say we intended to kill Domitian, although that was precisely what we were planning."

"I don't think anyone could miss your meaning," I said. "If you were foolish enough to write that, was Aelius foolish enough to keep the letter?" I knew I was being harsh, but this man had gotten himself into this predicament by violating the first rule of survival in Rome: never say anything that could be misunderstood—inadvertently or deliberately—and never write anything down. If it's on papyrus, somebody will find it.

"Yes, he kept it. He wanted to write a history of that period, so he kept everything. There's no more dangerous urge than the itch to write history. I hope neither of you is ever afflicted with it."

"When did the blackmail begin?"

"About the time I was emancipated I received the first demand for money. They—or he, or she, I don't know—said they would reveal the contents of the letter if I didn't pay."

"That was six years ago, wasn't it?"

"Yes. A little over a year before this disaster." He waved his hand as though showing off the room. "Someone knew I had access to money that I didn't have to account to my father for. And they knew a particular phrase that was used in the letter. They couldn't have known that unless they had seen the letter."

"You don't have *any* idea who it was? Not even the most unlikely suspicion?"

"None whatsoever. I talked to Aelius, of course. He said he still had the original copy of the letter."

"So someone had read it or made a copy." Once again I wished I had Phineas along to take notes.

"They had to have seen the original or they wouldn't have seen the word we used as a code. It was embedded in the text, rather cleverly if I must say so myself. I told Aelius to destroy the thing immediately. He told me that he burned it."

"After it was too late," Tacitus said.

Calpurnius nodded. "Epimetheus always sees things more clearly than Prometheus, doesn't he?"

"If you didn't know who was blackmailing you," I asked, "how did you pay them?"

"Once a month I rode into Naples and left the money with the owner of a book shop on the south side of town. He had been told that I was paying off a gambling debt and was trying to remain discreet."

"Could he have been the blackmailer?"

Calpurnius shook his head. "He was nobody. He couldn't have had access to the letter."

"So he delivered the money to someone, or someone picked it up," Tacitus said.

"He must have," Calpurnius said.

"Did you watch to see what happened after you left the book shop?" Tacitus asked.

"The first time I left the money I did hide nearby and kept watch for the rest of the day. I did not see anyone I recognized going into the place, and no one coming out was carrying my money pouch."

"It would be easy to conceal," I pointed out.

"I know, but I couldn't search everybody who left. The next day, I received a message warning me that I had been spotted."

"That suggests that someone with a connection to the book shop was collecting the money."

"There are apartments on the two floors above the book shop. I had no way of knowing where somebody was watching me. The note said, if I was seen again, the consequences would be dire. I decided it was safer just to let the matter rest."

I couldn't believe a man would have so little interest in finding out who was blackmailing him, especially a man described as having good business sense. "You could have hired someone to watch the place." A spy like Aurora.

"I wasn't sure I wanted to know who was behind it. I didn't think it was Domitian or Longina. If they had found out about the plot, I was sure they would have taken more direct action. If I pressed the issue, I was afraid the blackmailers might actually go to Domitian. There was no serious threat, just the demand for some money. Bribes and payoffs are part of doing business. I could absorb the expense."

"Until the eruption?"

Calpurnius sighed heavily. "Yes. After the eruption my sources of income were greatly diminished. The shops I owned around here, the estates, they were all gone. I went through my reserves in just a couple of years."

Bastet held a skin to his lips and Calpurnius took another swallow of water. He laid his head on the Nubian's bosom and closed his eyes. For a moment I was afraid he was dead.

"He needs rest, my lord," Bastet said, caressing his forehead, "and food. That filthy child didn't leave enough. You and Cornelius Tacitus should go back and get some more supplies."

I did not want a slave giving me instructions, especially one who showed no remorse whatsoever about killing a boy's father. "I think one of us should stay here," I objected.

"Do you think I'm going to run away, Gaius Pliny?" Calpurnius said without opening his eyes. "If it hadn't been for the good fortune of a stray horse, I would never have gotten this far. And the horse is gone now. I'll be here any time you want to talk to me. I'm very tired and very hungry."

Tacitus took me by the elbow and steered me out of the room. "Let's go," he said. "It won't take us that long to get to Aurelia's house and back here. If the man's stomach is full, he'll be able to talk longer, and perhaps be in a more voluble mood."

I didn't like the idea, but it would give me a chance to think over what I'd heard so far, and I needed to get out of this place.

†

When we emerged from the tunnel I took a deep breath. "Well, at least the Sibyl was wrong."

"But you have to go back down there," Tacitus reminded me, picking up on my allusion as though he were reading my mind.

Like a good sentinel, Philippos stood on duty. I explained our mission to him. "We're going to get some food and lamps and other supplies for the man who's down there. I want you to conceal yourself and keep an eye on this entrance. If that Nubian woman or a tall Roman man comes out, you watch which way they go and tell me when I get back."

"But, sir, you want me to stay here…all by myself?"

His eyes conveyed a scroll's worth of expression. I realized he had never been completely alone in his life, and he had no reason to believe that we—the people who had killed his father—would return. I took the leather strap with the Tyche ring from around my neck and placed it around his.

"This ring is quite…quite precious to me. It's the goddess of good fortune. If I leave it with you, she will protect you and you know I'll come back for it, and for you. And we'll bring you some more to eat."

"And a clean tunic," Tacitus said.

"How long will it take, sir?"

"Not long at all. I promise you that. You just keep a sharp eye on that entrance. It's a very important job."

Fingering the ring, he seemed reassured enough to smile at me. I tousled his hair and Tacitus and I climbed down the bank of hardened ash to where the *raeda* was waiting. The driver had showed some forethought by turning the contraption around, no easy task on the narrow roadway.

"Don't spare the horses," I told him.

Tacitus chuckled as he climbed into the *raeda*. "That's easy to say when they aren't your horses."

The noise of the carriage covered our conversation, but we sat at the back anyway, as far from the driver as possible, and side-by-side so we wouldn't have to raise our voices.

"What sense do you make of all this?" Tacitus asked as we bounced on the *raeda*'s hard, uncomfortable seats.

"Not much. I can't see any connections. Fifteen years ago Calpurnius wrote a letter containing an implicit threat to kill Domitian. But the blackmail began only six years ago."

"And one of the first things Domitian did when he took power three years ago," Tacitus said, "was to kill Aelius, the recipient of the letter. But he didn't lift a finger against Calpurnius. Pity, really. There would be one less king-loving bastard in the world."

I had to let him release his republican anger. "If Aelius told Calpurnius the truth, he destroyed the letter when the blackmail began. I don't think Domitian knew about the letter or the plot. He simply seized his first opportunity to get rid of his wife's former husband."

"Perhaps she'd come to her senses and wanted to go back to Aelius."

I gave that some thought before rejecting the suggestion. "Knowing Domitian, he was probably consumed with jealousy of another man who'd coupled with his wife. Remember what Ovid says: 'Propose a toast, "Good health to the fellow she sleeps with," while you're thinking, damn his eyes.'"

"But blackmail is a kind of torture," Tacitus said, "and we both know Domitian is capable of tormenting someone. It's his nature. They say, when he's by himself, he catches flies and pulls their wings off."

"If he's by himself, how does anyone know what he does?" I certainly didn't mean to defend the *princeps*, but fallacies in logic annoy me.

"From all the dead, wingless flies in his room?"

That would have been funny, if I'd been in a mood for humor. "This kind of anonymous blackmail just doesn't seem Domitian's sort of crime. He wouldn't get to watch his victim suffer or have the satisfaction of his victim knowing who was hurting him. For him that's the greatest pleasure he derives from tormenting people."

"So, if Domitian's not behind the blackmail, who is?"

"I'm not as ready as Calpurnius to dismiss the owner of the book shop where he dropped off the payments. A place like that wouldn't be chosen at random. The blackmailer would have to be confident he would get the money."

"You're saying 'he.' Do you think it's one person—a man?"

I had to brace myself to keep from sliding into Tacitus as the *raeda* took a bend in the road. "Oh, I was just saying 'he' for convenience. But it's more likely to be a man, isn't it?"

"I'm not so sure. Blackmail is a woman's game. Wives do it to their husbands in subtle and not-so-subtle ways every day, as you'll soon find out."

"Please, don't remind me." I had almost managed to forget the bride looming in my future back in Rome. "If it is more than one person, though, I suspect it's a small group—a leader and a couple of thugs to do the dirty work."

"Namely, the two men who attacked Aurelia?"

"Yes, Sychaeus and his companion. I'm certain they're also the ones who killed Amalthea."

"What was her involvement in the blackmail?"

"I don't think she was involved at all. She was the bait in a trap. She had a routine that brought her outside the house alone, so they knew where and when to find her. They killed her, then they lured Calpurnius out to the spot using the code word from his old letter."

Tacitus rubbed his chin in thought. "Does that mean Sychaeus has the letter? Is he the leader?"

"I doubt it. He's a slave. How would he get access to Aelius' papers? And he was sold to someone else six months ago."

"But he was in Aurelia's garden two nights ago."

I nodded. "We can't get around that, can we? Not with that hand-print. So he must be a runaway. That will make him difficult to find."

"And whoever is behind this has the letter or saw it before Aelius destroyed it—if he did in fact destroy it."

†

Aurelia met us at the door of her house, peppering us with questions before we could even get inside. I assured her that Calpurnius was safe. "What he needs is food and some medical items that Bastet requested."

"What he needs is his wife beside him," Aurelia insisted, "not that conniving Nubian 'princess.'"

"Why do you talk about her that way?" I asked, since I shared her mistrust. "She seems genuinely concerned about Calpurnius and very solicitous of your health."

"I don't know. Maybe it's just because I'm bearing a child. That makes a woman—well, I don't know how to explain it to a man. I've known, since the moment I became aware of this child, that I will do whatever I must to protect her." Aurelia placed her arms over her belly. "And I've felt a menace ever since Bastet came into this house."

I led her into the atrium and got her seated on a bench. "Has she threatened you?"

"No, but she's always hovering over me and telling me what to eat and when to rest. I feel like she wants to control everything I do. She gives me potions to take—to relax me, she says. I hide them or spit them out when she's not looking."

"Hasn't she been in Calpurnius' family for some years?"

"Yes," Aurelia snapped, unable to mask her resentment.

"And she's of noble birth."

"Do we really know if she is? All we have is her word on that. Though her arrogance might prove her claim."

"Calpurnius seems to trust her implicitly," Tacitus said.

"Or to be completely under her spell," Aurelia insisted.

"We don't have time to discuss this," I said. "We need to get back to Calpurnius."

"Oh, and we need a child's tunic," Tacitus said, holding his hand out to show Philippos' approximate height.

Aurelia's brow wrinkled. "A child's tunic? What do you need that for?"

"You'll see," I said, "in due time."

†

We made the trip back to the ruins without much conversation, eating a bit ourselves as we rode. When we climbed up the bank of hardened ash, carrying three bags of food and supplies, I did not see Philippos immediately. So much for trust, I thought.

"Sir, you came back!" a small voice called before the boy stepped into view from behind an outcropping.

"Why do you sound surprised?" I asked. "I told you I would come back, didn't I?"

"And we brought you something to eat," Tacitus said, handing Philippos one of our bags. "There's also a clean tunic in there. Put it on and we'll bring out a torch and burn that rag you're wearing."

Philippos looked down at his tunic.

"Have you seen anyone come out of the tunnel?" I asked.

"No, sir."

We started for the entrance.

"But," Philippos said from behind us, "I did see somebody go in."

XV

WE STOPPED in our tracks and turned back to the boy. "Somebody went in?" Sychaeus was my first thought—my first fear. "How long ago?"

Philippos looked like I'd spoken in a foreign language. Time was a concept, I realized, that had never figured very largely in his life. Anything less than a day must be meaningless to him. "After…after you left, sir." His eyes brightened as he offered what he thought was helpful information.

"Did you know him? Was it a him?"

"Yes, sir, it was, but I didn't know him. He looked like one of us—me and my papa, I mean."

So, another scavenger. That was not the worst news we could get. But the man might be desperate enough to attack Calpurnius for the little bit of food we had left with him.

"We'd better hurry," Tacitus said. "Calpurnius is no condition to defend himself."

"I imagine Bastet can take care of him," I said.

"Like she did…my papa." Philippos' soft voice was filled with pain.

"She won't have the advantage of surprise this time," Tacitus said.

"But there's plenty of rocks around, sir." He pulled the clean tunic out of the bag and put it to his face. It looked like he was sniffing it, but I saw he was hiding his tears.

We lit two of the torches we'd brought and started for the shaft.

"Sir, wait," Philippos called.

I turned back to see him taking the Tyche ring from around his neck.

"You may need this, sir."

I bent over so he could slip it over my head.

"I may indeed. Thank you."

As Tacitus and I passed from the gray light of the upper world into the tunnel, darkness engulfed us. This time, though, a sense of urgency overcame my anxiety about going back into this underworld that seemed to suck the life out of everything that entered it—even the torches. My eyes are more comfortable in dim light than in bright, but this place was several levels below dim. I hadn't experienced such thick darkness since the first night of the eruption five years ago.

"Be quiet," I cautioned Tacitus. "We need to hear any sound an intruder might make."

"I have a feeling he's more accustomed to the place than we are," Tacitus whispered, "and less likely to make any noise."

Without saying anything else, we made our way down to ground level and were about to turn toward the front of the house.

"No sign of any intruder," Tacitus said. "Maybe the boy was imagining things."

A flicker of movement came from our right, toward the back of the house. It couldn't have been more than the flapping of a tunic as someone moved, a speck of something noticeable just because it wasn't entirely black.

"I'm not imagining *that*," I said, "are you?"

"No. We'd better go see who's there."

Tacitus started toward the movement, but I put a hand on his chest to stop him. "We can't leave Calpurnius completely unprotected. This is the only way in or out. You stay here, in case somebody tries to sneak by. I'll go." I pulled my sword from under my tunic.

"He's probably more scared of you than you are of him," Tacitus said.

"Which could make him fight even harder."

I stepped into the tunnel leading to the back of the house. I could still see Tacitus' torch behind me when I passed a tunnel diverging to my left. Sticking my torch into it, I could see only blackness, with no sign of anyone's presence. After a few more steps a tunnel opened off to my right. This time I took a couple of steps into it, only to find that it ended abruptly, as though someone had changed his mind about digging it.

Ten paces farther on, the main tunnel turned sharply to the right. I estimated I was close to the back wall of the house by now. If I made the turn, I would lose sight of Tacitus' torch, but I had to know who else was down here with us and what danger he might pose. With one last look at the speck of light shed by Tacitus' torch, I turned the corner.

Calpurnius' crew must have been looking for something valuable in this area, or scavengers had been hard at work here. Side tunnels opened off the main one, left and right, every few paces. When I saw some scraps of animal bones in a tunnel to my right, I turned into it. Kneeling over the bones, I thought I detected teeth marks on them. Was someone so hungry that he gnawed the bones?

I heard the movement behind me but did not have time to react to it before a blanket dropped over me and someone shoved me into the side of the tunnel. My head struck the hardened ash and I collapsed. Although I never lost consciousness, I was stunned long enough for the attacker to run away. The blanket smelled like someone slept in it or wiped his bottom with it, or both perhaps. When I whipped the stinking thing off me, my torch was extinguished.

Or had the blow to my head caused me to go blind?

The darkness was so complete I could not see my hand in front of my face. I pulled my hand closer and closer until it touched my nose, but I could not see it. The Sibyl must be laughing now, I thought. When she told Aeneas that the journey back out would be difficult, at least he had whatever kind of murky light would exist in the underworld, if the underworld existed.

Groping around me, I could not find the torch but I found my sword. I had that much comfort, even if I couldn't see anything to use the weapon on. The metal blade didn't even glimmer. Someone could be looming over me right now, ready to strike, and I would be oblivious. I stood and shook my head to clear it. That only made me dizzier.

My breathing was labored as I felt the darkness embracing me, smothering me. I didn't know where I was or which way to turn. Had I spun around when I was pushed into the wall? Or was it just my head that was spinning? Was I still in the side tunnel? Or was I back in the main tunnel? If I was in the main tunnel, which way should I turn to get back?

An odd thought raced through my mind. A blind person would actually have an advantage over me in such a situation. He or she would not notice the deprivation of sight but would be accustomed to depending on feeling or hearing. Such a person would probably have had a better chance of surviving the eruption of Vesuvius.

"Tacitus!" I yelled, but the sound seemed to die a few feet in front of me, absorbed into the porous ash. I redoubled my effort. "Tacitus!"

I thought I heard something. Was it a response to my call? Where was it coming from? I turned in one direction, then another. Something furry scurried past my foot. I yelled in revulsion when it brushed against me.

A rat! And the damn thing nipped me.

I moved forward, swinging my sword hand back and forth like a peasant harvesting grain with his scythe or—more heroically—a legionary cutting a swath through the ranks of the enemy. My hand banged into the wall and the weapon clattered to the floor of the tunnel. Falling to my hands and knees, with panic constricting my throat, I felt around until I found it. The rustling of the rats seemed to be getting louder. Did they think I was going to be their next meal? Once my hand gripped the hilt again, my breathing slowed.

As I stood up I decided that I needed to take a different approach to getting out of here, a more reasoned approach. If I couldn't see where I was going, I would have to feel my way. With my left hand on the wall of the tunnel, I inched forward, still moving my right hand back and forth with the sword, just not as vigorously as before. All the time I kept calling Tacitus' name. If only I could be sure I was moving toward him and not away from him.

After a few steps I felt nothing with my left hand. That was an opening, but how many openings had there been? Was this opening the main tunnel back to the front of the house? I peered into it and called Tacitus.

Nothing.

Unless I was in fact blind, I should see his torch. I had seen that torch until the main tunnel took that sharp turn to the right. How many paces had I gone after I made that turn?

Finding the wall on the other side of the opening, I continued my slow progress until I came to another opening. Were there two openings on this side as I was coming in? Was this the direction I was going when I came in?

By now it didn't matter. I just wanted to keep moving. I found the wall on the other side of the opening. Leaning more heavily against the wall, as though it would afford some protection from the rats, I took a few more steps. Before I was ready for it, the wall ended and I fell. When I looked up, I saw a speck of light—Tacitus' torch! I felt like a sailor must feel when he catches his first glimpse of the light glinting off the tip of Athena's spear as he rounds Cape Sunium. Wiping tears from my eyes, I scrambled to my feet and walked as fast as I dared in the dark toward that beacon of hope.

"Whoever you are, stop right there!" Tacitus called.

"It's me!" I shouted back.

"Gaius Pliny?" He took a few steps toward me. "What happened? Where's your torch?"

I reached out and touched Tacitus' arm, needing that reassurance that I was in fact safe. "Someone jumped me and knocked it out of my hand."

"So there is somebody back there. Do you want me to go back with you and help you find him?"

"Maybe later and with reinforcements. There are too many places he can hide. There are rats back there, too. One of them bit me." In the light of Tacitus' torch I could see the mark on my foot. "Let's see if Bastet has anything for that."

"She'll probably want to cut your foot off," Tacitus said.

As we entered the collapsed atrium I called out, "Calpurnius! Bastet!"

"We're here, my lord," Bastet responded, stepping out of Calpurnius' room. "My master is asleep, so please lower your voice."

"Have you seen anyone else down here?" I asked, not lowering my voice.

She took my elbow and guided me away from the door to Calpurnius' room. "Why, no, my lord. Were you expecting someone?"

If I'd had a piece of bread, I could have sopped up the sarcasm dripping from her voice.

"No. I wasn't expecting to get bitten by a rat either." I held up my foot. "Can you do something for me?"

"Have a seat, my lord. I'll get an ointment."

I recalled what Aurelia had said about spitting out potions that Bastet gave her. But, if the woman was getting something she intended to use on Calpurnius, I had to assume it was harmless. Otherwise I would have been dubious about letting her take care of me. Her entry into the room must have awakened Calpurnius. He came to the door and watched as Bastet tended to my foot.

"You didn't see anyone come down here after we left?" I asked Bastet.

"No, my lord."

"What's that?" Calpurnius said. "You saw someone else down here?"

"Yes. Someone is hiding at the other end of your house."

Calpurnius scrunched his face in anxiety. "Do you think he poses a threat?"

Salving my foot and wrapping a bandage around it, Bastet said, "I doubt there's any harm in him, my lord. He's likely just one of the slaves whose masters were killed in the eruption. No one knows how many there are. They have no place to go, unless they want to be someone else's slaves, so they live like rats, burrowing into these houses and scrounging for whatever they can find."

"What can be left, after five years?" I asked, wondering what would keep even real rats alive.

"There's no food left, my lord, but they forage off the countryside, catch fish in the bay, and retreat to whatever kind of hole they can dig for themselves in the ruins."

That described Ferox's life perfectly.

"She's right," Calpurnius said. "My estate on the south side of Pompeii was destroyed. I lost almost a hundred slaves. How many died and how many ran away, I'll never know. I'm sure many who did survive have died by now. Bastet tells me she reduced their number by one this morning." His voice displayed a touch of pride.

"Gaius Pliny had a little run-in with this fellow," Tacitus said. "I think we should hunt him down."

Calpurnius shook his head. "I think Bastet's right. He won't hurt anyone. His greatest fear is being caught. Some of them get too bold— or too hungry—and go into houses closer to Naples. Occasionally the magistrates will round up a batch of them, especially a short time before the elections, to show they're dealing with the problem."

"The captain of the ship who brought us down here said he'd delivered some to Rome," Tacitus said.

"It's a problem that will correct itself in another year or two," Calpurnius said dismissively, "as the last of them die off. Now, I hate to be rude, but have you brought me something to eat?"

Arrogant people don't really hate to be rude. They just say that so they can get their way. "Yes, we have," I said, "but the food comes with a price."

"I know, I know. More questions. I hope what you've brought is worth humiliating myself."

Bastet began taking out the cheese, bread, dried fish, apples, and other items Aurelia had hastily assembled. Calpurnius sighed as he took his first bite. I gave him time to savor it and wash it down with a bit of his wretched wine.

I decided not to ask him about his father and Sabina, at least not now. "You were telling us earlier that you were able to absorb the cost of the blackmail until Vesuvius erupted."

"Yes. The bastards weren't particularly greedy, or they were particularly stupid. They really weren't asking for much."

The sum he mentioned made me suspect the blackmailers were very poor people to whom such a small amount would seem significant. Or perhaps they knew they had to suck the life out of Calpurnius slowly, like a tick on a dog, or he might try to find out who they were. I could see how Calpurnius, with his resources, might have tolerated the blackmailers, the way a dog can become so accustomed to a tick that he hardly even scratches. Until disaster struck.

"So after the eruption you had to start selling pieces of your property."

Calpurnius nodded as he bit into an apple. "I started with pieces that were the farthest away."

"The estate in Sicily." His head came up when he heard that. "We've gone through your records."

"Over Diomedes' vehement protests," Tacitus added.

Calpurnius grunted. "He's a good man. Very loyal."

"Did your marriage have financial motives?" Tacitus asked.

"I have to confess that it did. My father is old and I thought I could wait until he died to start selling off properties closer to home, but he shows no sign of wearing down. He must have absorbed some power of longevity from his beloved Egypt. Nothing in that place ever dies. It just gets older and drier. I finally decided I had to get married. Aurelia was the ideal match. Her father is already dead, and her grandfather can't live forever."

"You bastard!" I said. "All you wanted was her money?"

Calpurnius held up a hand to calm me. "At the time I thought so, but I have come to love and adore her. I would lay down my life to protect her."

"That's easy for a desperate man to say."

"Gaius Pliny, Bastet tells me that my child will be a daughter. She's never been wrong about that. To show you how much my wife and family mean to me, I will ask you right now, in front of a witness. Will you marry my daughter Calpurnia when she comes of age?"

I was already being herded into one marriage I didn't want. But at least this one wouldn't happen for fifteen years or so. I might be dead by then. "We can talk about that once we're out of here."

"I don't think I'm coming out of here. I need an answer now."

Taking on such an obligation meant I would have legal responsibilities to Aurelia and her daughter—if the child was a daughter, but that was only an even chance. Her survival to a nubile age was also doubtful. Half the children born in Rome die before they're five. Placing no trust in Bastet's ability to foretell the gender of an unborn child, and needing to keep Calpurnius talking, I held out my hand. "I agree to your proposal. If your child is a daughter, I will marry her when she comes of age."

Calpurnius shook my hand with surprising firmness for an injured man who hadn't eaten in several days. Tacitus placed his hand over ours. "Thank you, Gaius Pliny. Thank you, Cornelius Tacitus. That takes an enormous weight off my mind."

"In return," I said, not releasing his hand just yet, "I expect you to tell me the rest of this story, so I can protect my future wife and mother-in-law."

Calpurnius shook my hand again and chuckled. "Funny how it sounds when you put it in those terms. Almost like Caesar referring to Pompey as his son-in-law when they were the same age."

It sounded funny to me, too, to imagine Aurelia as my mother-in-law when she was five years younger than I am.

Calpurnius drew a deep breath until the pain of his broken rib made him grimace. "But you're right. You need to know everything I know. The problem is, I don't know much more."

"I gather that marrying Aurelia gave you the money you needed," I said to prompt him.

"It allowed me to sell off more of my property. It made sense to reduce the size of my household when I combined it with Aurelia's. But then the blackmailers deceived me."

"You just can't trust criminals these days," Tacitus said.

"Unlike in the glorious days of the Republic." I jabbed him. "What did they do?"

"They left a note at the book shop, raising the amount of money they were demanding and threatening Aurelia if I didn't pay. The marriage that I thought would relieve my burden ended up increasing it. And they demanded even more when we learned Aurelia was bearing a child."

"If they know that much about your family, they're getting information from someone in your house." I looked at Bastet, but she met my gaze without blinking.

"Was it Amalthea?" Tacitus asked. "Is that why you killed her?"

Calpurnius sat up as far as he could. "Why do you even suggest that?"

I knew that line of inquiry would lead nowhere. Calpurnius had not killed anyone. By now I was sure of that. "Have you failed to pay the blackmailers?"

"Yes. This month I just couldn't do it."

"So they killed Amalthea as a warning, a way of showing you that they could attack your household whenever they chose."

"But why her? I barely knew the woman's name. She meant nothing to me."

Even Bastet flinched to hear her master say that about a servant.

"She had a routine," I said. "They knew where she would be at a certain time, and they knew they could lure you out there, using the code word from your letter. The attempt to kidnap Aurelia was another, more direct, warning because they thought you had sent for us."

"Bastet tells me Aurelia is all right," Calpurnius asked, his voice rising in anxiety. "And the child."

"They're both fine," I said. "Aurelia is frightened, of course, but she seems to have suffered no ill effects."

Calpurnius slumped back on the bed and blew out a long breath. "Thank the gods for that."

"Better to thank Gaius Pliny, my lord," Bastet said. "He drove them off. I didn't see any gods fighting them."

"Yes, of course. Thank you, Gaius Pliny. My debt to you is far deeper than I can ever repay."

"I'm not worried about getting repaid," I said. "What does concern me is that the attackers knew precisely where to find your wife, the very room she was in. That information could have come only from someone who knows your household well and has some grudge against you—some reason to betray you."

"The first name that comes to mind," Calpurnius said, "is Sychaeus."

"Your former slave who's missing the small finger on his right hand?"

Calpurnius blinked like a man with a bright light shining in his face. "How did you—"

"That doesn't matter. You sold him six months ago, didn't you? In a group of slaves, to a man in Capua."

"Yes. You really have been through my records, I see. Sychaeus was one of those slaves that you tolerate because he works hard, but you wish he weren't such an unpleasant fellow. And after Bastet had to take off his finger he became openly hostile and resentful."

"He couldn't accept that we did it to save his life," Bastet said.

"How long had you owned him?" I asked.

"Almost seven years. I got him from Aelius. I had a horse that Aelius admired, so we traded—the horse for three slaves."

"What? Sychaeus was a slave in Aelius' house? Why didn't you mention this before?"

Calpurnius looked at me in genuine surprise. "How is it relevant here?"

"It could be the most relevant thing you've told me yet. The letter that someone is using to blackmail you came from Aelius' house and Sychaeus was a slave in Aelius' house." I held up my index fingers and brought them together. "It's the first connection we've made."

Calpurnius didn't appear impressed by my logic. "But Sychaeus couldn't have known about the letter. He's a common laborer, more valuable for his back than for his brain."

"Can he read?"

"A bit, but he wouldn't be able to make sense of the letter."

"If he can read at all, he could recognize—"

"He can read Latin, Gaius Pliny. The letter was written in Greek."

While Calpurnius tore off some more bread, I had to stop to consider that bit of useful information. Many people in Rome, even slaves, are fluent in both Latin and Greek. In this case someone who could not read Greek was eliminated as a potential blackmailer.

"That means we're looking for another person in addition to Sychaeus," I said as Calpurnius took a sip of wine, puckering his face.

"I'd forgotten how awful this stuff is," he said." My apologies to you if you've had to drink it."

"I've had worse," I lied. "But back to Sychaeus. He has to be working with—or for—someone who knows an *omicron* from an *omega*."

"Perhaps it's the other man who attacked Aurelia," Tacitus suggested.

"We do have to consider that," I said, pacing from one side of the small room to the other and back again. "But something tells me those two were, as Calpurnius so aptly put it, more valuable for their backs than for their brains."

What unnerved me was the unspoken possibility that the person who did have the brains might be connected to Domitian—might even *be* Domitian, toying with Calpurnius until he decided to kill him. If Domitian had seen the letter, he knew that Calpurnius was the one who suggested killing him. That alone would seal Calpurnius' fate. The only question would be when Domitian felt he had exacted enough revenge—or had tired of the game—and was ready to finish Calpurnius off.

"Let me see if I have the chronology straight." Picking up one of the torches that had gone out, I made a black line on the wall in the blank space where a chunk of plaster had fallen off and wrote *hodie* beside it. "That's today, where we are now. Domitian put Aelius to death three years ago." I put marks to count off those years and wrote *Ael mort*.

Calpurnius nodded. "As soon as I heard about it, I thought my days were numbered. Maybe they are, in Domitian's mind."

"But the blackmail began six years ago, based on a letter that you wrote fifteen years ago." I counted off those time spans and made marks and notations, *crimen* for the blackmail and *epist* for the letter.

"Yes."

"And you purchased Sychaeus from Aelius seven years ago."

"Yes. Swapped the horse for him, to be precise. It was a magnificent creature."

"You said you received three slaves," Tacitus put in. "What happened to the other two?"

"I put both of them to work on my estate south of Pompeii. I haven't seen either of them since the eruption. For all I know, the fellow Gaius Pliny ran into back there could be one of them. Or they could all be dead."

The last mark I put on the wall was for the arrival of Sychaeus in Calpurnius' house. "As you can see, the two events that are closest in time are your purchase of Sychaeus and the beginning of the blackmail. And we know that Sychaeus was one of the men who attacked Aurelia. He is woven into the very fabric of this plot, the thread we have to find to unravel it."

"But he's been in Capua for the past six months," Calpurnius said, "since I sold him."

"He wasn't in Capua two nights ago, when he tried to kidnap your wife."

"Are you absolutely certain it was Sychaeus?" The look in Calpurnius' eyes told me he was growing weary of the discussion.

"He left his handprint in the ash outside your garden." I held up my right hand and turned the small finger down. "He might as well have signed his name."

"And he knew which room was your wife's," Tacitus said.

"You shouldn't be surprised, my lords," Bastet said. "He was a difficult man. And he hated my lord Calpurnius—and Aelius—for separating him from his sister."

"He had a sister?" Calpurnius said in surprise.

"Yes, my lord. You may not have heard him, but among the servants he did talk about her. She even wrote him a letter now and then."

I took a step toward Bastet. "Was she a servant of Aelius'?"

"Yes, my lord. She was younger than Sychaeus, and he felt very protective of her."

Turning to Calpurnius, I asked, "What became of Aelius' household after Domitian put him to death?"

"His second wife was allowed to keep some of the property," Calpurnius said. "To show his clemency, Domitian left her with an estate north of Naples and a few bits of property in the city—an *insula* and some *tabernae*, I think. He confiscated the rest, mostly estates north of Rome."

"Who was this second wife?"

"A woman named Fabia. Aelius had a daughter by her, as he did by Longina."

"By the gods! Aelius fathered a child who was a descendant of Augustus?"

"Yes, but she died when she was three."

"So the execution had nothing to do with Aelius possibly claiming power on the basis of his wife's and daughter's connection with Augustus."

"I don't see how it could have. The daughter was dead and Domitian had taken Longina some years before. His family had a secure hold on the *imperium*. He executed Aelius simply out of spite. I suppose Longina may have prodded him."

"Is Fabia still living on the estate?"

"I believe so. I haven't heard from her since Aelius' death. You know how it is. Sometimes it's better to step away. Especially in this case...I mean, with the letter."

I could not condemn Calpurnius as a coward. When a man is put to death by the *princeps*, his surviving family is often shunned by former friends, anxious about their own safety. A ruler's enmity can spread like leprosy, from one person to the next, and it's every bit as painful and deadly as that disease. Sometimes men seek their own deaths to escape the pain and avoid spreading the plague any farther.

Calpurnius leaned back and closed his eyes. "Have I answered enough questions to pay for my meal? Or must I, like Odysseus in the palace of Alcinous, tell you my entire life story?"

"No," I said. "This has been very helpful. And I'm thankful you didn't precede the tale with a pack of Odyssean lies."

"Reluctant I may be to talk, Gaius Pliny, and very tired, but never a liar."

Bastet pushed past Tacitus and me and put her arm around her master.

Not giving the Nubian a chance to order us out, I said, "We're going to leave now. We'll come back tomorrow or send someone to bring more supplies. Are you certain you'll be all right? Do you feel any threat from whoever else is down here?"

"I sense no threat from him at all, my lord," Bastet said.

"I'm sure Bastet is right," Calpurnius said. "Thank you for all you've done—all you *are* doing—to help my family. You'll make a good son-in-law."

†

When Tacitus and I reached the point where the tunnel turned to go back to the surface, we paused and peered into the darkness where I had followed the intruder.

"Do you want to go back there and find him?" Tacitus asked.

My gaze darted from that section of the tunnel to the branch that would take us out. "I have a feeling Calpurnius is right. The poor man is hungry, but more frightened. I imagine he knows places to hide where we two would never find him. We'll bring some reinforcements tomorrow and do a thorough search. For now I just want to get out of this place."

Tacitus nodded. "It does feel like we've been down here for a long time. It took Virgil only one scroll to get Aeneas into and out of the underworld."

"But Aeneas didn't have a pack of rats gnawing on his leg."

"Now, Gaius Pliny, a nip on the foot from one rodent hardly qualifies as a gnawing horde. Are you sure it was a rat and not a tiny little mouse?"

XVI

WHILE WE WERE in our own underworld the sky had grown overcast, but my sensitive eyes still found even the softened light almost blinding. Philippos popped up from behind a rock, sporting his new tunic, which was brown with a dark green trim. He had used some of the water we brought him to scrub the top layer of dirt off his face. As my eyes adjusted to the soft sunlight I thought, he could be a handsome lad, almost pretty, but maybe the light was playing tricks on me.

"Fortune protected you, sir," he said. "I'm glad to see that."

"I guess you could say she did." I touched the Tyche ring on the strap around my neck.

"We Romans have been saying it for hundreds of years," Tacitus said, "from the days of Ennius and Terence. *Fortes fortuna adiuvat.*"

"Does Fortune help the brave? That's what my uncle said as he was boarding his ship to sail toward Pompeii and look what happened to him."

Tacitus lowered his head. "Sorry. I didn't mean to dredge up that memory."

"You couldn't have known, and it doesn't lie deep enough to require much dredging."

"What happened to your uncle, sir?" Philippos asked.

"He tried to rescue people during the eruption, but he died. He was like a father to me."

"What about your father, sir?"

"He died when I was very young."

"So you've lost two fathers."

"In a manner of speaking, yes."

174

"I'm very sorry for you, sir."

A destitute orphan pitying me! The boy displayed a maturity far beyond his years. He had had to grow up even faster than most Roman children.

"And I'm very sorry," I said, "for what happened to your father. I promise you that I will take care of you. You don't have anything to worry about."

He drew his shoulders back. "Will I be your slave, sir?"

"I don't intend for you to be anyone's slave, but we'll have to work all of that out. Now we need to get back to the lady Aurelia's house before it gets dark."

"Can I ride with the driver, sir?"

As we stowed our bags in the *raeda* I noticed that the one we'd given Philippos still seemed to have something in it.

"What's that?" I asked, touching the bag.

"It's my old tunic, sir." He drew the bag toward himself. "Please don't make me get rid of it."

"Why do you want to keep that old rag?"

"It has my papa's blood on it, sir. That's all I have left of him."

✝

Because we weren't in such a hurry this time we weren't bouncing around in the *raeda* and the metal rims of the wheels didn't make such a deafening noise on the road's paving stones. Something close to normal conversation was possible.

"I suppose we'll be off tomorrow morning," Tacitus said, "to find Fabia and ask her about this sister of Sychaeus."

"Yes. I don't see how she could have anything to do with the blackmail, but she's the only one who might know where Sychaeus is. We could spend days trying to locate him, and we don't have that kind of time. And along the way I want to stop at the book shop where Calpurnius left the money for the blackmailers."

"Do you think you'll learn anything there?"

I shrugged. "I just want to see the place. It could have more of a connection to this matter than Calpurnius assumes."

"And what do you intend to do with this boy?" Tacitus jerked his head toward the front of the *raeda*, from where squeals of delight were emanating. "You've made him a rather large promise."

"I felt I should, given what happened to his father—to be more accurate, what someone in our party did to his father. I'll ask Aurelia to put him up for a time, until I can sort out his legal status."

"That could be another burden on her, and she's already so anxious about her baby."

I felt my tone hardening. "Don't forget, it was one of her husband's servants who killed poor old Ferox."

"True. But one more mouth to feed—that's all Aurelia needs."

"I can leave her some money. That's not my main concern now."

As the *raeda* turned into the drive to Aurelia's villa I was surprised to hear a young voice call, "Whoa! Whoa, boys!" We stepped down from the carriage to find Philippos holding the reins and beaming.

"I let him drive the last little bit, my lord," the driver said. "I hope that was all right."

"He didn't wreck us, so no harm done." For a servant it's always easier to ask forgiveness than permission.

"He's got a nice touch with the horses, my lord."

Aurelia, with several servants, came out to meet us. One hand was cupped under her belly, as though she was already cradling her child—my future wife? "Well, Gaius Pliny," she said, "where did you find—"

"This is Philippos. We encountered him on the road." I did not want the boy to start telling the story. "Due to an unfortunate incident this morning, the child is an orphan. I didn't feel I could leave him behind."

"No, no. You're quite right," Aurelia said, sympathy welling up in her eyes and voice. "We'll see what we can do for him. Obviously, the first thing we can do is make sure he has a bath." She motioned to the woman on her right, who stepped forward and took Philippos' hand.

"A…a bath?" the boy said, pulling back. "I don't want a bath, sir. You didn't tell me I'd have to take a bath."

"When was the last time you had a bath?" I asked, half expecting "never" to be the answer.

Philippos shrugged. "Sometimes, after it rained, my papa and me would find a pool of water and wash ourselves."

"It's time you had a proper bath," Aurelia said. "This is Chaerina. She'll help you."

"I can bathe myself," Philippos insisted. "I washed my face a while ago."

"And that just shows us how dirty the rest of you is," Aurelia said, wincing and putting her other hand on her belly. "Now, go along with Chaerina."

Chaerina took one of Philippos' arms and another servant woman took the other. Between them, they pulled the boy, protesting all the way, into the house.

"How did you end up with him?" Aurelia asked.

I dismissed the rest of the servant women and told her the story, concluding with my evaluation that Bastet did not have to kill Ferox. "The man was so weak, she could have easily overcome him without really hurting him."

"I told you, Gaius Pliny, I have felt a menace since the day that woman came into this house. I'm relieved she's not here now, but I'm afraid to have her out there alone with my husband."

Over Aurelia's shoulder I saw Chaerina hurrying toward us. "We can talk about that later, I suppose." I indicated Chaerina, and Aurelia turned around.

"My lady," the servant called. "My lady!"

"What's wrong?" Aurelia asked. "Is the boy all right?"

"My lady, the child isn't a boy."

"What? Well, what is he?"

Chaerina looked at her mistress as though Aurelia had asked something as obvious as what color the sky was. "He isn't a 'he,' my lady. She's a girl."

"Of course. I mean…. Well, as soon as he's…she's cleaned up, get her a more suitable garment and bring her into the garden."

"I told you that child cried an awful lot for a boy," Tacitus said as we entered the house and made our way into the garden.

"Didn't you notice, Gaius Pliny?" Aurelia asked as we settled ourselves.

I didn't know whether to laugh or to blush at my lack of perception. "It's odd how one can see what one expects to see. Ferox called the child his son and that's what I saw."

"What did you see the first time you saw me?" Aurelia asked.

"Certainly not the daughter of a noble Roman family. Knowing this child is a girl changes a lot of things. With a boy we could think of training him for a trade. I'm not sure what to do now, and I don't want to burden you."

Aurelia patted my hand. "We don't have to settle everything today. You've done a very generous thing. For the moment, that's enough."

Less than half an hour later Chaerina brought the child—what were we to call her now?—to us. Her hair was still wet and she was wearing a blue *chiton*, a Greek garment worn by women in this part of Italy, where the Greeks had established themselves long before we Romans blundered onto the scene. She was pulling at the unfamiliar gown, which came almost to her ankles.

"Sir," she said as soon as she saw me, "do I have to wear this? I can hardly walk in it. And it smells funny."

"That's because it's clean," I said. "I think what you're wearing or what you smell like is the least of our concerns right now. Why were you disguised as a boy?"

She stopped in front of my chair and folded her arms over her chest, standing legs apart like a man. "My papa told me to pretend to be a boy because people weren't as likely to bother me if they thought I was a boy."

I glanced at Tacitus but didn't say anything.

"He kept my hair cut short. He said someday people would see I was a girl, but he wanted to keep me safe as long as he could." She tugged at the *chiton* again. "What are you going to do with me, sir?"

"For now you're going to stay here." Aurelia had agreed to that.

"Am I a slave of this lady?"

"No. This is the lady Aurelia. You are now…well, part of her household. You will address her as 'my lady' and you will do whatever you are told to do."

"That sounds like being a slave, sir."

"You are an impertinent child," I said.

"Thank you, sir."

Over Tacitus' laughter I said, "That's not a good thing. Remember that your father was a slave. That makes you a slave. Until we can determine whether your master died in the eruption or is still alive, we cannot know what to do with you. For the time being, you'll stay here."

"But, sir, can't I go with you?"

"You can't go anywhere until we find out what happened to your master."

"Sir, I thought—"

"Would you like to help take care of my horses?" Aurelia asked. "That can be your job."

"Oh, that would be wonderful." When I gave her a hard stare, she said, "I mean, that would be wonderful, my lady."

"A *chiton* is not a suitable garment for working in a stable," Aurelia said. "You can wear a tunic out there." The girl beamed. "The only other matter to settle, I think, is what to call you. Philippos doesn't fit anymore. Did your father call you by any other name, perhaps when it was just the two of you?"

"No, my lady. I've been Philippos as long as I can remember."

"Well, then, let's keep what's familiar to you and just make it Philippa. Yes, the girl who loves horses."

The girl didn't smile. I wondered how long it would be before she could smile again, but she bowed her head. "Thank you, my lady. I'd like that."

†

When we woke the next morning I was pleased to learn that our servants had already returned from Capua. They had ridden into the evening and arrived during the second watch of the night. We brought them into the atrium to hear their report. Tacitus sat beside me but was not awake enough yet to participate much in the conversation.

"You made excellent time," I said.

"Yes, my lord," the older man answered. "The moon was full enough that we had no trouble seeing the road, so we just kept riding. My lord Cornelius Tacitus did promise us a bit extra if we got back in a timely fashion."

"You'll certainly have that." And I would make certain it came out of Tacitus' money pouch. "Now, what did you learn?"

"Marcus Jucundus told us that he sold the man Sychaeus four months ago, my lord."

That opened Tacitus' eyes. "Sold him?" he said. "To whom?"

"To a lady named Arria, my lord. He said she came to his villa and inquired about Sychaeus by name. She told him her husband had sold him several years ago over her objections and she wanted to have him back."

"Why would a woman go to that much trouble to track down a former slave?" I said.

"Perhaps he had a...talent that she particularly valued," Tacitus suggested.

"Begging your pardon, my lord," the servant said, unable to suppress a smile, "but that was what Marcus Jucundus suspected as well. He said she paid a handsome price for him and invited him to sit in the *raeda* with her as they left. He was surprised because he hadn't found Sychaeus to be of much use."

"I wonder if his wife had," Tacitus muttered.

Sometimes it's better just to ignore Tacitus. "How did he know who the woman was?"

"He said she arrived in an elegant *raeda* and she signed this." He handed me a document, a single sheet of papyrus, which I read quickly. It acknowledged the sale and was signed by Marcus Jucundus and Arria. Jucundus had also affixed his seal.

"But there's no seal for this Arria, not even her husband's ring. Anyone could write a name on a piece of papyrus. What did she look like?"

He screwed up his face in the manner of a servant who wants to make himself look good but isn't sure he has done or can do what his master wants. "Jucundus said she was quite refined, my lord, like a noble lady. Never even got out of the *raeda*. Just told him what she wanted and gave him the money. Didn't even try to talk him down on the price."

"What color was her hair? Did she have any features that might help us recognize her?"

"I'm sorry, my lord. Jucundus didn't say and we didn't think to ask about that."

Aurora would have, I thought. She'd never miss such details.

We dismissed the servants and read over the document again. "I assume this was written by Jucundus' scribe," I said. "It was done hurriedly."

Tacitus took the document and eyed it from several angles. "I agree. Arria's name is written in an entirely different hand."

"A better hand, I would say." I took the papyrus back. Even when women do write, they seldom develop as fine a hand as the one I was looking at. "The *Ar* is oddly made, though. I've never seen it done quite like this, the way the *r* comes right out of the cross-bar for the *A*."

"Looks like an affectation," Tacitus said. "Who could this woman be? Why would she have been asking for Sychaeus by name? Who goes shopping for a particular slave by name?"

"Someone who knows him and knows where he is. That's the only possible answer."

"But he'd been sold just a couple of months before this woman bought him. Why didn't she come looking for him when he was in Calpurnius' house? He'd been there for six years."

I gave that some thought. "I suspect it's because she didn't want Calpurnius to know that she was interested in this particular slave. But we can't answer those questions until we find out who this Arria is. Let's take this document with us. Maybe Fabia can tell us who she is. Sychaeus was her husband's slave. She might know something about him."

†

Accompanied by four servants—three of ours and Calpurnius' man Thamyras—we set off on horseback for Naples. On the north side of town we would turn east on the road to Nola. Fabia's villa, we'd been told, was three miles up that road. As we rode into Naples Thamyras said, "My lord, you mentioned that you'd like to visit the book shop which my lord Calpurnius...frequented."

"Yes, that would be interesting," I said. "We should have plenty of time to get to Fabia's villa and back." We had agreed not to spread the word of Calpurnius' true difficulty among his servants. They knew he was accused of killing one of them. I was confident now that we could disprove that accusation. If we could find out more about Sychaeus, I hoped we could identify the real killer. Once accused, a man is never completely exonerated until the guilty party is found. Last night we had told Aurelia that her husband was being blackmailed and that we didn't know any more details than that. It was easier to do without Bastet in the room.

"The shop is just ahead, my lord. Turn left at the next corner."

After the turn Thamyras directed us one more block. "That's it, my lord."

We stopped in front of the shop where Calpurnius had dropped off the blackmail payments. A wooden sign hung beside the door with the Latin and Greek words for *Books* painted on it.

The building in which the shop was located stood three stories high, with living quarters on the top two floors. It appeared to have suffered some damage in the earthquake which had enabled Calpurnius to escape. A crack in the wall above the door looked new to me, with no dirt accumulated in it and the edges of the crack still sharp. We left our servants to mind the horses and moved far enough away from them so we could talk as we surveyed the surrounding buildings.

"It would be difficult to keep an eye on this place without someone spotting you," Tacitus said. "There aren't many places nearby to conceal yourself. I wonder if there's a rear door."

"Or maybe a door that connects to one of the upper floors. Whoever picked up the money might never have left the building." I took one more look around. "Well, we can't barge in and start making accusations."

"Maybe there'll be a box with a sign that says, 'Deposit blackmail payments here.'"

"Ever the optimist, aren't you? There's a lot we still don't know. If we move too soon, we could alert anyone who might be connected to the blackmail. They could go to ground, like a hunted animal, and we would never find them."

"So we're just going to look?"

"For now, yes, just look."

The shop was larger than I expected, with two good-sized rooms. The owner must have bought a neighboring shop and knocked a door through the wall at some point. Shelves laden with scrolls covered three walls of the first room and as far as I could see into the second. It was the largest book shop I'd ever seen outside of Rome. I'm never more comfortable than when I'm surrounded by books. That was the one deficiency in Aurelia's otherwise charming house: the library was quite small. Aurelia herself was not broadly educated, and most of Calpurnius' library was entombed in his villa.

A heavyset man, mostly bald with a white fringe around his head, sat at a table in one corner, with scrolls, pens, and inks surrounding him. He appeared to be putting the finishing touches on a scroll, making the last corrections and erasing any extraneous marks. The pumice stone whispered as he rubbed it back and forth over the papyrus. One of the first Greek words I learned described that smoothing action: *psao*. I found it easy to remember because it sounds so much like what it means.

"Good day, gentlemen," the man said in Greek, looking up but not rising from his work. "Is there anything I can help you find?"

I hadn't actually thought of what reason I would give for visiting the shop. We had none, except to get a feel for the place. Then inspiration struck. "A friend of ours, Calpurnius Fabatus, suggested we stop by here while we were in Naples."

He raised an eyebrow. "Do you share the old gentleman's enthusiasm for Egypt then?"

"He has…other enthusiasms," Tacitus said, "that appeal more to me."

"Indeed he does," the man said, rolling up the scroll and inserting it into a red bag. "Indeed he does. You need to look in the other room, sir, on the wall to your left, on the top two shelves."

While Tacitus browsed in the other room, I asked the shopkeeper, "How are your books arranged?"

"Poetry, philosophy, and more exotic books, such as your friend is interested in, are in the other room, sir. Anything else is in here. Latin on that wall, and Greek over there."

I looked at the *tituli*, the tags hanging from some of the scrolls. My uncle's history, continuing the work of Aufidius Bassus, occupied a prominent place. I wondered if I would ever see my name in a book shop or library. Having one's work published amounts to achieving immortality—the only kind of immortality there is, to my way of thinking. My uncle has been dead for five years now, and yet people can still know what he thought, almost as though they were talking with him. I picked up one of the scrolls and unrolled a few pages. As I read the words I could hear his voice. A wave of sadness swept over me and I lowered my head.

"Do you fancy history, sir?" the shopkeeper asked from behind me.

I put the scroll back on the shelf and took a deep breath before I turned around. "My taste runs more to oratory."

The shopkeeper pointed to a spot to my right. "We have some nice copies of Cicero. We finished a copy of his speech on behalf of Archias just the other day."

"That is one of his best," I said. *And we're still reading it over a hundred years after his death. If that's not immortality, I don't know what is.*

"Gaius Pliny!" Tacitus called. "Come here. You have to see this."

The shopkeeper's eyes widened as he looked at me. "Gaius Pliny?"

I've lost track of how many times I've had to explain to people. "He was my uncle. He adopted me in his will."

"This is an honor, sir," the man said, standing and bowing his head slightly. "I never had the privilege of meeting your uncle, but everyone around here speaks highly of him. It was a brave thing he did, trying to rescue people from Vesuvius."

"Thank you—"

"Gaius Pliny," Tacitus repeated. "Get in here."

"Excuse me," I told the shopkeeper and stepped into the other room.

"What is so important?" I asked Tacitus, not masking the irritation in my voice. "You know that I have no interest in looking at pictures of—"

"Forget that. Look at this." He laid a partially unrolled book on the table in the center of the room and pointed to the top of the first page.

The scroll contained a copy of the last book of Ovid's *Ars Amatoria*, the frankest and most explicit of the three books which make up the work. I could see from the illustrations why Tacitus' attention had been drawn to it.

Tacitus tapped the page. "Do you see that?"

"How can I not?"

"Not the picture, the script."

I let my eyes follow his finger. The poem begins *Arma dedi Danais*. The *Ar* was formed in the same way as on the bill of sale for Sychaeus, with the *r* running out of the cross-bar of the *A*.

Tacitus had trouble keeping his voice down. "The person who wrote that also signed that bill of sale."

"Yes, I see that." I picked up the scroll and started to the other room of the shop.

"What are you going to do?" Tacitus asked.

"I'm going to buy a book. And find out who copied it."

The shopkeeper stood up when we came back into the main room. "Did you find something you liked, sir?"

"This is an exquisite copy of the *Ars Amatoria*," I said, drawing my money bag from under my tunic. "Did you do it?"

"No, sir. I can't take the credit. I don't do much copying anymore. My hand's a bit unsteady." He held out his right, still ink-stained, and I could see the slight tremor. "I supervise the men that work for us, put the finishing touches on—that sort of thing."

"'Us'? Does someone own the shop with you?"

"Oh, I don't own the place, sir. I work for my lady Plautia. She's the owner. Owns this whole building, in fact."

I couldn't imagine that the owner of this much property would dirty her hands to copy books. "Is there by chance a woman among your copyists?"

"No, sir, but my lady Plautia keeps a close eye on the men. She writes a fine hand herself, and she expects them to come up to her standards. You're holding the result, sir."

I didn't feel I could ask any more questions about this Plautia without arousing the man's suspicions. "How much is the book?"

"Don't you want the others, sir? I'd hate to break up a set."

It made sense to get on his good side. I might want more information from him at some point. "All right, I'll buy all three."

"Very well, sir." He told me the price and I counted out the money.

†

When we rejoined our servants on the street I handed the scrolls in their bag to Tacitus. "An early Saturnalia gift," I said.

"And much appreciated."

"I do want to compare that writing to the bill of sale," I reminded him.

We retrieved the document from the servant who was carrying it and held it next to the third book of Ovid. "There's no question," I said. "The same person wrote these."

"So the shopkeeper must have been lying," Tacitus said. "They must have a woman among their copyists."

"Or a woman taught this scribe. The shopkeeper said this Plautia keeps a close eye on the men."

"But her name's Plautia, not Arria."

Even though he's older than I am and more experienced in many ways, Tacitus can still be exasperatingly simple. "You're assuming that the woman who purchased Sychaeus was scrupulously honest. She could have signed any name she pleased as long as she paid the price Jucundus was asking. Your servant said she didn't haggle, just paid the first sum Jucundus mentioned. I wish we had a description of Arria, even just her hair color. Then, if we saw Plautia, we would know if they could be the same person."

"Women can wear wigs," Tacitus reminded me. "When I saw your Aurora in her blond one, I didn't recognize her."

"All right, I'll grant you that. I don't think we can accomplish any more here. Let's get out to Fabia's place so we can get back before dark."

†

The road to Nola was level, skirting the north side of the range of hills that rise to their summit in Vesuvius. The eruption had not affected this area at all. Seeing green, living things and trees as tall as trees should be restored my spirits. We rode the two miles at a quick pace. At a crossroads we found a *taberna* where we could get a drink and directions to Fabia's house.

"It's not much more than a stone's throw up that road," the innkeeper promised. His lack of education and his lack of teeth made him difficult to understand. "But you'll find nary welcome there."

"We have some connection with her family," I said.

The innkeeper shook his head. "Won't matter. She ain't let nobody in the house in over two year. Keeps it sealed up."

"Why?" Tacitus asked.

"Says she and the women of the house are devotin' themselfs to some god. To let a man in the place would cause 'em to lose their purity."

"But how do they keep themselves alive? How do they feed themselves?"

"One of my lads goes up there now and then and finds out what they needs. We bring it to 'em and leave it outside the door. They won't open up until we're outta sight."

"If they won't open the door," I said, "how do they tell your man what they need?"

"They cut a little hole in the door and put bars over it. They talks to him through that."

We paid for our drinks, thanked the man for the directions and the warning, and set off up the road he indicated.

As we brought our horses to a halt in front of the house Tacitus shook his head and said, "It's a bit shabbier than I expected. Aelius' family was quite prosperous."

"Domitian wouldn't let her keep the nicest of her husband's properties, I'm sure."

"No, but she's not even taking care of this one."

Tacitus' criticism was true. The lane leading from the road to the front of the house was overgrown with trees in need of pruning and brush that should have been cleared entirely. I had the feeling Fabia was trying to discourage visitors by letting the house be hidden behind all the vegetation. In a few more years the house would disappear from view. We dismounted and found plenty of places to tie our horses.

When I approached the door I saw that a small opening had indeed been cut into it, at about my head height, and bars had been placed over the opening. I knocked, and when there was no immediate response, I called through the opening, "Good day! Is this the house of the lady Fabia?"

I was surprised to see a woman, not a doorkeeper or a steward, crossing the atrium in response to my call. She stopped a step or two from the door but did not open it. From the simplicity of her dress it was difficult to tell whether she was a servant or someone of higher rank who disdained ostentation. She wore a gown of unbleached wool, with a scarf of the same material covering her hair. Without any makeup, she looked worn and tired, as drab as her garments. Behind her the house was quiet.

"Who is asking for the lady Fabia?" Her tone let me know that she did not wish to be bothered.

"Good morning. I'm Gaius Pliny." I held up my hand so she could examine my signet ring. "This is Cornelius Tacitus. We would like to see the lady Fabia."

"What is your business with her?"

"We're trying to assist Calpurnius, son of Calpurnius Fabatus, a friend of Fabia's late husband. We believe she might be able to help us."

"Why does Calpurnius need any help?"

"He's being blackmailed and is accused of murder."

The woman's eyes widened. "We know nothing here that would be of any use to you. No one here has had any contact with Calpurnius in several years."

"My lady"—I had guessed by now and she did not react—"we pose no danger to you or to your house. We think a former slave of yours is involved. May we come in and talk for a few moments?"

"No." The answer was curt, but sad rather than rude. "We do not allow outsiders in the house anymore. If you have questions, I will try to answer them here and now."

I had to accept what she was willing to offer. "Very well. We—"

"Would you please step away from the door, so I can get a good look at you? And you said there were two of you?" Fabia waved her hand to back me away.

I stepped back and Tacitus stood beside me and leaned over so he could see through the opening, which struck him at chin level.

"Thank you," Fabia said. "I thought you might be sent by Domitian to finish what he started three years ago, but I don't see any weapons."

"No, my lady," Tacitus said. "The *princeps* didn't send us. I'm the son-in-law of Julius Agricola. If you know that name, you'll understand our relationship to Domitian."

"Yes," Fabia said with a nod, "that does give me more confidence in you. Death looms over you as heavily as it does over me. Now, what do you want to know?"

I could see one other woman behind Fabia. There was no activity and no sign of anyone else. "You once owned a slave named Sychaeus," I began.

Fabia's shoulders slumped along with her voice. "What has that scoundrel done now?"

"That's what we're trying to determine. Your husband sold Sychaeus about seven years ago, didn't he?"

"Traded him and two other slaves for a horse, to be more accurate."

"We've been told that Sychaeus had a sister in your household."

Fabia sighed so heavily I wondered if she was still in mourning for her husband. "Canthara was her name, and it pains me to speak it after some years."

"She's not still in your house?"

"No. My husband freed her six years ago."

"Freed her?" That was as surprising a bit of information as any we'd picked up this morning.

"If you'll spare me the interruptions, Gaius Pliny, I'll tell you the story as succinctly as I can, for it is truly not something I like to remember." She looked up as she gathered herself, like a bard seeking inspiration. "I always suspected that Canthara was my husband's child by a slave woman. Even though she was born with a misshapen foot, Aelius refused to get rid of her."

"Was Sychaeus also his child?"

"I asked you to spare me the interruptions," Fabia said. "I saw no evidence that Sychaeus was his child, though he was born of the same woman. Aelius never showed any particular interest in Sychaeus. He used Canthara as his assistant scribe because she couldn't do much other work around the house. She was clever with figures and she did write a beautiful hand. She knew that Aelius favored her and flaunted herself in my face. You know how arrogant a pampered slave can become if you don't keep control of her."

Yes, I thought. *She can rent a horse and ride off to…somewhere.*

"Canthara became bitter after Sychaeus was sold. They were very close. I finally insisted Aelius sell her. I told him that she and I could not live in the same house. He refused and emancipated her instead, giving her a large sum of money in the bargain."

"From your tone, I suspect you weren't happy with that arrangement."

"I certainly was not. I accepted it only so long as the girl was not allowed to stay in the household or have any contact with anyone here. I suspect he may have seen her when he was away from here, though."

Freed slaves often remain in a house, doing the same tasks they had done as slaves but with a different status. It would be unusual for a man to send a freed slave away, especially if she was crippled, and I couldn't imagine him sending her away if she might be his own daughter.

"Do you know where she went, or where she might be now?"

Fabia's face turned grim. "I hope she died in the eruption. No one here has heard anything from her since the day she left. I gave strict orders to the other servants that no one was to have any contact with her. Now, is that what you needed to know?"

Tacitus leaned in toward the opening. "Could Canthara read Greek?"

Fabia nodded. "Aelius had her taught alongside our own daughter, over my strenuous objections. He said he needed for her to know Greek and Latin if she was to be useful to him."

I wasn't sure what my next question should be, but I wanted to keep the conversation going. "Did Canthara—"

"Gentlemen, this conversation is causing me great distress," Fabia said. "I have nothing more to say. At the risk of seeming rude, I must ask you to leave." She turned and walked quickly toward the interior of the house.

We could do nothing but return to our horses for the ride back to Aurelia's villa. Lacking a mounting stone, we had to rely on our servants to boost us up and then help one another onto their horses. We had just mounted when a woman, hiding behind a tree, motioned to get our attention. I rode over as close as I could get to her. She kept the tree between herself and the house, partially hiding herself from me as well. All I could tell was that she was in her middle years and had covered herself the same way Fabia had.

"What do you want?" I asked.

"Forgive my boldness, my lord, but I heard you asking about Canthara."

"You were the woman I saw behind Fabia."

"Yes, my lord."

"Do you know something that the lady Fabia didn't tell us?"

"Yes, my lord."

"I suspected she was hiding something," I said.

"No, my lord. Not hiding. She couldn't tell you because she doesn't know it."

XVII

IGUIDED MY HORSE as close to the woman as I could manage in the midst of all the trees and brush. "How can you know something—"

The woman edged closer to me but kept a hand on the tree, as though anchoring herself. "Forgive me, my lord, but I must speak quickly, before I'm missed. Please send your servants down the lane, so they can't hear us." She motioned with her arm, revealing splotches on her skin, which she quickly tried to cover up.

Studying her as we waited, I noticed that she was holding a piece of papyrus at her side. I thought I saw a seal on it.

When the servants had ridden thirty paces or so, the woman finally nodded with what seemed to be satisfaction. Then she began to speak rapidly and in a low voice, with the diction of an educated slave from a noble house. "I am Xanthippe, my lord. I was the midwife twenty years ago when two girls were born in my lord Aelius' house, within an hour of each other. The daughter born to my lord Aelius and his wife, the lady Longina, had a badly misshapen foot. The other daughter, born to a slave woman, was whole. My lord Aelius told me to switch the two children. He did not want his wife to be disappointed in her firstborn child or to blame him for her misfortune. But that healthy child died when she was three. And then Longina left him for Domitian." She spat out the second name, winning a degree of my respect.

Tacitus and I looked at one another in amazement, and the woman read the glance.

"Yes, my lords. That means exactly what you think it means because you know who the lady Longina was descended from, don't you?"

191

We certainly did know what it meant. Aelius had raised his daughter, a direct descendant of the deified Augustus, as a slave in his own house, passing off a slave's child as a descendant of Augustus. Canthara thought Sychaeus was her brother when, in fact, he was no kin to her at all. Her kinsmen included names like Caligula, Claudius, and Nero.

"How could a man so callously condemn his own child to a life of slavery?" I asked.

"Both of the girls were his, my lord. The servant woman died after the birth. My lord Aelius said he knew the girl with the misshapen foot could never take the place in society that she ought to have. It would be better for him to keep her close and care for her. Eventually he could make things right. It didn't matter to him which child was called slave and which free."

"I'm certain it would matter to his wife."

Xanthippe snorted. "She was a haughty woman, my lord. She was holding the healthy child to her breast when she first saw the child with the misshapen foot—her own daughter! She called her 'a wretched little thing' and said my lord Aelius should put her out to die. He told me that he knew then he had made the right decision."

Tacitus leaned back on his horse. "Why are you telling us this? Why should we believe a word of it?"

"I heard you say you were the son-in-law of Agricola, my lord. That, I think, makes you someone I can trust." Since she was closer to me, the woman reached up and handed me the document—a single sheet of papyrus, folded and sealed—then covered her arm again. My horse stepped back nervously and I patted his neck to calm him.

"That bears my lord Aelius' seal," she said. "He and I were the only ones who knew the truth. He wanted to tell Canthara, but fear of his wives and his need for their money kept him silent. He treated the girl as well as he could. He planned all along to emancipate her someday. He wrote that and left it with me so, if something happened to him, Canthara could still know the truth. About her father."

"So that's why he freed her and gave her some money instead of selling her," I said.

"Yes, my lord. It hurt him so badly to send her away, but he knew my lady Fabia would never forgive him if the truth came out."

"Why would it matter to her? Fabia told us that she suspected Canthara was his daughter. And she had her own daughter by Aelius."

"Yes, my lord, but Canthara was the daughter of a servant woman."

"That does happen in large houses, more than we care to admit."

"And most wives tolerate it," Tacitus said.

Xanthippe gave us a less than kindly look. "My lady Fabia would not. If Canthara had known who she really was, my lord, she would have been absolutely insufferable to Fabia. She was a livelier, more intelligent girl than Fabia's daughter, and she was arrogant and strong-willed enough as it was, just like her mother."

By "mother" she was talking about the woman who was now Domitian's wife, I reminded myself. Though such traits were no proof of Canthara's ancestry, they were characteristic of any imperial woman I'd ever encountered.

"Do you know where Canthara is now?" I asked.

"No, my lord, but I doubt she's far from here. She swore she was going to get her brother freed, and that she would get even with Aelius and Calpurnius. Swapping him for a horse—that made her furious. I heard her say it many a time, 'They traded him like he was an *animal*.'"

"How did she plan to free her brother—or the man she thought was her brother—and take vengeance on Aelius and Calpurnius? That's an ambitious plot for a single slave."

"She didn't say, my lord, but she said she had a plan, and she wouldn't leave this area until she'd done it."

I wondered if she had given information to Domitian that had led him to execute Aelius—unknowingly condemning her own father. "Do you know if anyone in this house has heard from her since she was emancipated?"

"No one has, my lord. My lady Fabia forbade anyone to have contact with her, but that wasn't necessary. She had no friends among the servants here. She treated us all as though she knew her lineage and considered us beneath her."

Voices sounded from inside the house. "They're looking for me," Xanthippe said. "I must go."

"I have one more question," Tacitus said. "Why has the lady Fabia sealed up her house? Is she really devoting herself to some god?"

Xanthippe bit her lip and finally said, "It's the…the leprosy, sir."

"Leprosy?" I said. "There hasn't been any leprosy in Italy since the Republic collapsed."

"It comes from Egypt, doesn't it?" Tacitus said.

"Yes. I remember my uncle commenting on that when he was writing his *Natural History*. He thought it ironic that leprosy disappeared from Italy about the time Cleopatra died. It was as though she was the source of the disease, as she was of so much evil for Rome."

"Well, sad to say, my lord, it's in this house. Just before my lord Aelius was…that is, just before he died, he acquired two servant women from Egypt. Shortly after his death my lady Fabia realized that these two women had leprosy and had spread it to other women in the household. She sent the servants who weren't afflicted to friends and family of hers and shut the rest of us up in the house. There were ten of us. Two have died."

"Does Fabia have it?"

"Not yet, my lord. But she is caring for the rest of us as best she can. She is truly a noble lady. There is nothing anyone can do, though, but wait."

I looked with dread at the document that she'd passed from her hand to mine. "You have it, don't you?"

"Yes, my lord, but you won't get it just from touching that. I know there's no hope for me, but I decided this would be my last chance to tell anyone the truth about Canthara, and I believe I can depend on you to know what to do with this secret. It's out of my hands now." She stepped into the woods and almost vanished as her featureless clothing blended in with the brush.

Before we rejoined our servants I asked Tacitus, "How do you think Longina would react if she found out her 'wretched' daughter is still alive, given that she and Domitian have no children?"

"I'm more concerned about what she'd do if she knew that we suspect that daughter of blackmail and murder. Are you going to open that document?"

"Let's get away from here first." I held the papyrus between two fingers, touching as little of it as possible.

†

Once we were out of sight of the house Tacitus and I told the servants to keep riding and we pulled our horses over to read Aelius' document.

Trying to reassure myself that I was not going to become a leper, I noticed that Tacitus did not reach for the papyrus to snatch it from me, as he often does when we have something to read. I broke the seal gently so we could preserve the two parts of it. The note confirmed everything Fabia's servant had told us:

> I, *Lucius Aelius Plautius Lamia Aelianus, do hereby acknowledge that the slave Canthara, known by her misshapen left foot, is my daughter, by my wife Domitia Longina. When circumstances allow, I will emancipate her, even if I cannot reveal the full truth of her birth to her. I swear to the veracity of this statement before the almighty gods and affix my seal as a further witness.*
>
> *Written by my own hand on the fourth day before the Kalends of March in the eleventh year of Nero Caesar Augustus.*

Aelius had pressed his seal ring into a glob of wax at the end of the note. It matched the seal on the exterior of the papyrus.

"I think this does answer one question," I said.

"Which one?"

"Isn't it odd for a girl—even a slave—to have a name taken from a drinking cup?"

Tacitus thought for a moment, then recognition dawned. "Canthara. Yes, one of those old Greek cups that usually has two women's faces on the base, one Greek and the other barbarian. Your uncle had one, didn't he?"

"Yes. Which woman you're seeing depends on which side of the cup you're looking at."

"And how much you've had to drink out of that cup."

I held the papyrus up, still by only two fingers. "I think Aelius left a clue in the girl's name—Canthara, a woman with two faces. If you look at her from one side she's his slave, but look from the other side and she's a descendant of Augustus."

"Now all we have to do is locate her," Tacitus said. "A woman with a misshapen left foot shouldn't be that difficult to find, especially with a name like that."

"She still has the foot, I'm sure, but I doubt if anyone calls her

Canthara now. I think Aelius has given us another clue—his full name: Lucius Aelius Plautius Lamia Aelianus. As a freed slave, don't you suspect she took part of her former master's name?"

"Of course!" Tacitus slapped his thigh, startling his horse. "The book shop in Naples! The scribe said the owner's name was Plautia."

"And she owns the entire *insula* in which the book shop is located. Aelius must have been very generous when he emancipated her. No wonder Calpurnius never saw anyone leave with the blackmail money. She also had a perfect vantage point to see if he was watching the shop. He could have seen her looking out a window and never would have suspected who she was."

†

By the time we got back to Naples the book shop was closed for the midday rest, which a number of people seemed to be taking at a *taberna* at the end of the block. We left our servants with the horses. Thamyras would get them some food and bring it out to them. I have no objection to sharing a meal with a servant, but in this neighborhood it seemed smarter to have them guard the horses. I didn't want to walk the rest of the way back to Aurelia's villa.

"Let's get something to eat," I said, "and see what we can learn about…Plautia. I guess that's what we should call her now."

"Shouldn't we be asking about Sychaeus? We know where Plautia is."

I patted the neck of the gelding I'd been riding, a gentle animal. "I suppose you're right. One glimpse of the owner of the book shop and we should know if we've found the right person. But I'll bet Sychaeus isn't going by that name anymore either."

"It's almost too convenient," Tacitus said, "that they've both got some mark by which we can identify them, like a device from a Greek comedy. Otherwise they could change their names and disappear."

"But I'll bet there's more than one man in that *taberna* right now with a missing little finger."

The noise of loud conversation drifted out through the open door of the *taberna*. It fell to a murmur when we stepped into the place. The sight of a stripe on a tunic usually has that effect in places like this. The only activity that continued without a pause was on the far side of the room where a man was throwing darts at a board. He held the missiles in his right hand, with his small finger straight up.

"He's not our man," Tacitus observed.

"But he's very good," I said.

"Probably learned to use the things in the army."

The Greeks developed the dart—which we call *plumbata*, from the lead tip—as a weapon centuries ago. While it's not a standard weapon in our armies, some soldiers use it when they are attacking stealthily. It's quiet, effective from a considerable distance, and easy to make.

"It probably helps his aim," Tacitus said, "to have a target like that. Easy to focus on."

The board was decorated with a painting of a nude woman, provocatively posed. Points could be won by hitting certain strategic areas.

There were no empty tables in the *taberna*, but the owner took one look at us and stepped to a corner where two men were bent over a *latrunculus* board.

"All right, you louts," he said, "you been nursin' them drinks for an hour. Pack up that game and clear the table for some payin' customers."

From the glares on the faces around the room I could sense that we wouldn't get any information out of anyone if we allowed the owner to commandeer a space for us like that. "That's all right," I said. "We can wait until they finish. In fact, let me buy them another drink. Your best vintage."

"Suit yourselfs," the owner grunted and turned away to get some more wine.

"Do you mind if we watch?" I asked the two men. "I love the game."

"Not at all," the man playing the white stones said. "And thanks for the drink, but the best vintage around here is going to be last month's instead of this month's."

While Tacitus gave Thamyras some money to buy lunch for himself and the servants outside, I turned my attention to the game. They were playing with a set of white stones on one side and reddish ones on the other, instead of the usual black. I soon saw that one reason they'd been playing for so long was that neither one understood the strategy well enough to conquer the other.

"You're new here, aren't you?" the man playing white asked. He seemed the more garrulous of the two, a large man with inky black hair and almost no neck supporting his pockmarked face. His opponent was shorter and leaner with thin brown hair and a scar on his right cheek.

"Yes. We're friends of the lady Aurelia and her husband Calpurnius."

"Seems they've run into a spot of trouble lately," the black-haired man said.

"We hope to have that sorted out soon," I said. Without seeming too curious, I hoped, I confirmed that they had twenty fingers between them.

The man nodded. "They're good folks, from what I hear."

Tacitus rejoined me as the owner of the *taberna* brought two fresh cups of wine. As he placed them on the table I noticed he was missing the tip of the first finger on his left hand. Probably an occupational hazard for a man who spent his life cutting and chopping food. I hoped it didn't end up in a stew.

"Would you gents like anything?" the owner asked.

"Some of that wine and a portion of whatever you're serving today," I said.

"Right away."

I turned my attention back to the table, not so much to the game as to the men playing it. I had the feeling that I could get some information out of the black-haired man if I could get the brown-haired fellow out of the way. I pointed to the *latrunculus* board. "Could I offer a suggestion?"

The black-haired man sat back. "Sure. It's my turn. Go ahead."

I moved one of the white stones. The man playing the red stones looked up in surprise and moved one of his pieces, but it was too late. The man playing white was clever enough to pick up on my hint and in three moves had his opponent's *dux* surrounded and beaten.

"There!" he cried. "That's five *sesterces* you owe me, Murinus."

"I'll not pay you an *as*, Gaeton," the loser said. "You had help. Two against one's not fair." He swung a hand at the game board, scattering pieces in all directions, and started to get out of his chair.

"I'll pay the wager," I said, holding out a hand to calm everyone. "You're right. I did interfere."

Murinus, mollified and slightly drunk, got to his feet and left. Gaeton started to pick up the game pieces and put them in a bag. "Damn him," he muttered. "Where's my *dux*?"

I got down on one knee and helped him look under the table for the most crucial piece in the game. "Here it is," I said, handing him the polished blue stone.

"Thank you, sir. My grandfather gave me that stone when he taught me to play. It would grieve me deeply to lose it." He went back to putting the pieces in his bag, but I laid a hand on his arm.

"Would you be willing to play me?"

"What would the wager be, sir?" Gaeton asked. "Nothing involving my *dux*, I hope."

"No, I would never expect a man to risk something that important to him." I touched the Tyche ring on its strap under my tunic around my neck. "Ten *sesterces*."

Gaeton eyed me, probably reckoning whether he could beat the man without whose help he would not have just won.

"Ten *sesterces*," I repeated, "and I'll buy you lunch, regardless of who wins."

"Done." He gathered up the stones and began setting up the game as I sat down across the board from him.

Tacitus took the chair between us. "This is like having a front row seat in the arena," he chuckled. "I may even get spattered with some blood. Fair warning, Gaius Pliny plays this game like a Thracian gladiator."

Strangers asking about someone, I've learned by now, need to ease into the conversation, like a man wading into a cold mountain stream, and not plunge in all at once, the way some men do in the warm waters of the baths. I stuck my toe in. "So, Gaeton, is it? I'm Gaius Pliny and this is Cornelius Tacitus."

Gaeton looked from one of us to the other until he seemed satisfied. "You're not from around here, you said. Friends of Calpurnius and Aurelia?"

As far as I could tell, he was a freeborn man, but he did not offer the kind of deference plebeians usually display in the presence of a tunic with a stripe on it.

"That's correct."

"Well, as I said, they're good folks. I'm sorry to hear about their trouble."

"What exactly do you hear?" I wondered how much gossip Aurelia's servants or the men from the *vigiles* had spread by now.

"I hear Calpurnius cut up one of his servant women." He made his first move on the board. "Somebody said he cut her heart out and ate it, but I don't believe that. At least, not the eating part."

"No sensible man would. I've seen the woman's body and I can assure you it's in one piece and the heart is still in it."

"But it's been several days," Gaeton said. "How could you—"

"Gaius Pliny has a very strong stomach," Tacitus said. "Or no soul. I haven't yet figured out which."

I made my first move. Tacitus raised an eyebrow but said nothing. He doesn't play the game very well, but even he knew it was a poor way to open.

Gaeton made a countermove, not a brilliant one but effective enough. "Are you going to defend Calpurnius in court?"

"I'm just here to give what help I can to Aurelia." I made another indifferent move. "She's a friend of mine from some time back."

A serving girl brought our lunch, a pastry stuffed with meat and vegetables that actually smelled quite good, and a jug of wine. Tacitus patted her bottom and she tugged his ear affectionately. Gaeton moved one of his stones. I had to suppress a groan at the stupidity of his strategy and think for a moment how I could make a move without bringing the game to an abrupt end. While I was doing that, I decided my toe had been in the water long enough and I could risk getting in deeper.

"We're hoping while we're here to visit the book shop up the street. Do you know anything about it?"

"It's a good one, I'm told. Don't have much time for reading myself." That was as close as he would come, I imagined, to admitting that he couldn't read. "The store's nicer than her that owns it—the lady Plautia. That much I've heard. If you want to know anything about the place, ask that fellow by himself over there." He pointed to a young blond man with a scraggly philosopher's beard eating alone two tables over from us.

I took a bite of my lunch and a sip of wine. The stuffed pastry was a bit too salty for my taste, but otherwise unexpectedly good for an establishment of this sort. The less said about the wine, the better. It must have come from the same dealer Calpurnius was buying from these days.

Gaeton moved a stone in front of his *dux*. He apparently thought

he was going to protect his most important piece, but he was just setting it up to be trapped.

"What does that fellow know about the book shop?" I passed up
an obvious move and made a meaningless play on the other end of the
board.

"He's one of their scribes," Gaeton said, showing no awareness of
how bad my move had been as he moved a stone to the other side of
his *dux*.

"Then I definitely should have a word with him." I put a hand on
Tacitus' shoulder. "Would you sit in for me?"

"From spectator to gladiator? Gladly. Double or nothing, my
friend?"

I rolled my eyes. "Gaeton, don't beat him too badly."

Figuring that the players were now evenly matched enough to pro-
long the game, I stepped over to the scribe's table. "May I buy you a
drink?" I asked.

He merely nodded. When I sat down he looked up and said, "Oh,
I didn't realize you meant to join me."

"For a moment, if I may."

"Suit yourself."

"I'm Gaius Pliny."

"I'm called Capsius," the young man said. It was an odd name, one
I'd never heard before.

As the serving girl brought our wine I noticed Capsius' left hand.
It was missing the thumb and the small finger, leaving him with the
three middle fingers that made the Greek letter *psi*, like Neptune's
trident.

"I was born this way," he said.

"I'm sorry. I didn't realize I was staring."

"Everybody does at first. My father thought he was being clever to
give me a name with my deformity in it."

"I would say more cruel than clever."

Capsius nodded appreciatively. "You sound like you knew my father. He told me if it had been my right hand, he would have put me
out to die. He wanted to anyway, but my mother wouldn't let him." He
paused as though savoring a memory. "She taught me to do all sorts of
things with one hand that most people need two for."

"From the ink stains on your right hand I gather you're a scribe."

"Just about the only job for a man with this." He held up his left hand and looked at it, not just as though he'd never seen it before but as though he was completely baffled by it.

"Do you work in Plautia's book shop?"

"That I do." He took a long drink of wine.

"Do you know when it will open again?"

"Not any time soon. My lady Plautia told us today that she's thinking of selling the place—the whole *insula*, in fact." His eye ran up and down the stripe on my tunic. "Would you be interested in buying?"

I nodded without any hesitation. I didn't want to acquire a building, but this might be an opportunity to come face-to-face with the woman without arousing her suspicion. "I might. Yes, I would like to talk to her. Where would I find her?"

"The last few days she's been in and out of the shop quite a bit. I'll get word to her that you're interested. I'm sure she'll find you."

"Is she sharp at business? What do you think she'll be like to deal with?" Men often think women aren't astute enough to stand up for themselves in financial matters. The man who had cheated my prospective mother-in-law was finding out what a mistake that was.

Capsius peered into his cup as he pondered his answer. "Let's just say that the book shop is a more pleasant place when she's somewhere else. She's smart and she's beautiful, but if you cross her, she has a temper like one of the Furies."

"Is she often angry?"

"Quite often. Speaking as one with a similar experience, I think she resents her deformity—that misshapen foot of hers. I've seen her kick things with it, like she was angry at her foot, not at the thing she was kicking. In my worst moments, I've done the same." He rubbed his right hand over his left.

Tacitus joined us, pulling up a chair from another table. "I lost," he said.

"Against Gaeton?" Capsius said with a snort. "That must have been hard to do."

"Probably not for Tacitus," I said. "*Latrunculus* isn't his best game. Did you pay off the wager?"

"It's all taken care of. You can pay me back later." In response to my grimace he said, "Well, it was your wager. I just added the…the double-or-nothing part."

"Why—"

"I was sure I could beat him, but that move you showed him must have gotten him to thinking."

I looked over my shoulder to see Gaeton setting up for another game. His face showed his pleasure at his winning streak and the wine I had bought him.

"Whatever you let him win won't last long," Capsius said. "He's a pleasant enough fellow, but he doesn't know how much he *doesn't* understand about that game. I'd better go play him and get my share before it's all gone." He pushed his chair back and was about to get up. "Is there anything else you need?"

"There is one more thing, as a matter of fact," I said. "A couple of days ago we ran into a man whom we would like to see again. We didn't have time for formal introductions, but he had dark hair and was missing the small finger on his right hand. Have you seen anyone like that around here lately?"

Capsius narrowed his eyes and gave me a steady stare. "I have seen such a fellow once or twice. I suppose I notice things like that—hands and fingers, I mean—more than most people." He indicated his left hand. "He's been in and out of the *insula*. Seems to be a friend of Plautia. I've seen them talking."

"Is he by any chance in here now?"

Capsius swept his eyes over the room slowly and shook his head. "Should I tell Plautia that you're looking for him as well?"

"No," I said quickly. "We'd like to see him, but I don't think he wants to see us, so it would be better if you didn't say anything about this conversation. What you've told us has been most helpful and I appreciate it." I put enough money on the table to buy an entire amphora of Falernian. "Have another cup on me."

XVIII

A S WE MOUNTED our horses, Tacitus took me to task. "You were awfully generous in there."

"Me? You were the one who played double or nothing."

"Well, you threw a lot of money around and you could have kept your voice down. In a place like that, you never know who's listening."

"I hope Sychaeus, or someone who can contact him, was listening. We need to draw him out. As long as he thinks he's getting away with something, *we* have to look for *him*. We don't have time for that. Let's make him come to us."

"He's already come to us, if you'll recall, and nearly kidnapped Aurelia."

"We've got her protected now." I leaned back on my horse and studied Plautia's *insula*. Three floors high, it wasn't large by the standards of Rome, but for any other city it was substantial.

"What's your interest in this place?" Tacitus asked.

"Capsius said Plautia wants to sell it. I'm going to try to talk to her as an interested buyer. I think I should know something about it so I can ask intelligent questions."

"That's the only kind I've ever heard you ask."

Accepting the compliment with a nod, I turned my horse to ride around to the other side of the *insula*, followed by Tacitus and our servants. The street on that side was as clean as the street in the front. Four shops opened off the ground floor, all of which appeared to be occupied.

"Looks like it would bring in some steady rental income," Tacitus said.

"It might, if it doesn't collapse in the next earthquake."

"That's always a possibility around here, I suppose. This one looks solid, though. Not like that *insula* Cicero mentioned in his letter, when he couldn't decide whether to repair it or just cover the cracks and hope no one noticed."

I slipped off my horse. "Let's take a look upstairs."

Tacitus joined me and we climbed a set of stairs leading to part of the second floor.

"Wooden stairs," I pointed out. "That's a sign of cheap construction. And the tenants could be trapped in the event of a fire."

But the wooden stairs were the only negative feature I noticed. We did not knock on any doors or try to look into any of the living quarters, but the place seemed clean and well-maintained. The fact that the stairwell did not reek of human waste put it in a class above most such buildings.

"Would you say it shows a woman's touch?" Tacitus said.

"At the very least, the hand of an owner who cares about the place." I ran a hand over the plaster. "This is fresh."

"How many people do you think live here?"

"That's hard to tell. A family will rent an apartment and then rent one room of it to another family. There could be four or five hundred people living here. The new owner would have to take a census, I suppose, to be sure he was getting full value."

Tacitus shook his head. "You're starting to think about buying it, aren't you?"

"I can't entirely rule out the possibility."

"It must be nice to ride past some random building one day and think, 'Oh, I might buy that,' like buying a loaf of bread." He stroked his chin like a man pondering a weighty question.

Tacitus' fortune is sufficient to qualify him for membership in the equestrian order, but it comes nowhere near to equaling mine. I inherited my father's estate and then my uncle's, both of them quite large. In financial matters I am somewhat cautious—I prefer to think of myself as judicious—and I have added substantially to my holdings in the five years since my uncle's death, partly by selling two *insulae* that were costing me more than they were earning. I regretted any instance when my wealth became an issue between Tacitus and me.

"I've seen all I need to," I said. "Let's get back to Aurelia's."

†

We mounted our horses again and soon passed through the city gate, which could no longer be closed because of damage from the last earthquake. I prodded my horse to pick up the pace. In a few moments we were passing the Necropolis—which seemed to stretch halfway to Vesuvius. The road dipped a bit, making me feel that the tall monuments on either side were rising above a little valley. I was about to joke with Tacitus about whether he needed to step behind a tombstone and relieve himself again when something whistled past my head and the servant riding behind Tacitus cried out in pain.

I turned to see the man clutching at a dart sticking out of his shoulder. Blood ran through his fingers and down onto his tunic.

We had ridden into an ambush!

The horses reared, throwing two of our men off and galloping away. I bent over, my face in my horse's mane, as another dart flew over my head and clattered against a tombstone on the other side of the road. If we tried to ride out of the trap, we could be picked off one by one, and we couldn't leave the men who had lost their horses. I had no choice.

"Quickly, men! Dismount! Scatter among the tombs."

A shower of stones began to rain down on us from both sides. Tacitus' horse reared when a dart struck him in the neck. I heard his leg snap as he fell to one side, nearly trapping Tacitus under him. The rest of us dropped from our horses and scrambled for the tombs on each side of the road. Tacitus and I dove behind the first monument we could reach, a low sarcophagus that wouldn't offer protection for long. I pointed ahead of us and we crawled on our elbows and knees to hide behind a taller mausoleum. The spot offered better concealment but the arrangement of the tombs meant we were boxed in on three sides.

"Any idea where they are?" I whispered.

"None. They're on both sides of the road, though." His head jerked as he looked to each side and above us.

Tacitus reached under his tunic and drew out his knife. I unsheathed my sword. Handle and all, it was the length of my forearm and sharper than a butcher's cleaver. I hoped it would be to our advantage if our attackers assumed that we were typical unarmed aristocrats, separated from our servants, who—as luck would have it—had all found cover on the other side of the road, except for the one lying in the road, moaning and clutching his wound.

We listened and tried to determine where scuffling noises were coming from. The tall marble tombs and the narrow passages between them distorted sounds, bouncing them around in all directions. A Necropolis is truly a *city* of the dead. We were hiding behind small-scale houses with the streets between them reduced to the appropriate width, and the streets were not laid out in a grid pattern. It was as confusing as being lost in the maze of streets and alleys that winds through Rome once you get away from the center of town.

I was gathering my courage to peek over the top of our hiding place when I heard a voice that seemed to come from right around the corner from where we were.

"I think they went in about here."

The depth of the voice made me expect a large man. My grip tightened on the handle of my sword as I held it slightly behind me, out of view, to save the surprise for the best possible moment. A cry of pain rang out from across the road. Tacitus and I exchanged a glance. One of ours or one of theirs? Our men, though not skilled fighters, were armed with knives. But those damnable darts could be thrown effectively from a considerable distance, as we had seen in the *taberna*.

Metal clinked against marble and one of the would-be assassins stepped into view. He wasn't as big as I expected, but his sword was large and heavy. He had the air of a former legionary. "Found 'em!"

"Where are you?" the dart-thrower responded. Although I had heard only a few words from the men who tried to kidnap Aurelia, I recognized that voice, now that I heard it without the distraction of the crowd in the *taberna*. He was the man who had been holding Aurelia's feet.

"To your right, I think."

"On my way," the disembodied voice promised.

I concluded that there were only two men on this side of the road. I could see that the man clutching the sword in front of us had the small finger on his right hand, and the dart-thrower had shown that particular digit in the *taberna*, so neither of them was Sychaeus. If Sychaeus was involved in this attack, he must be on the other side of the road. If we could deal with these two, we would probably have good odds against those on the other side, as long as they weren't throwing darts. We backed up against the tomb that blocked our retreat, and at the same time, protected us against assault from that direction.

"Sniveling cowards," the brute said, taking a step toward us. "Just like all you narrow-stripers. Two against one, but the odds are still in my favor." Holding his sword with both hands, he drew it back over his head.

I lunged and thrust my sword into his stomach all the way to the hilt. Angling it upward, I hoped to hit his heart. He gasped and looked down at it in surprise, his eyes bulging. I pulled the blade out and he sank to his knees. His weapon clattered to the ground behind him and a pool of blood gathered around him as he toppled over on his side.

"Watch out!" Tacitus cried.

The dart-thrower appeared on top of the house-shaped tomb to our left. "Bastards!" he snarled, hurling a dart.

Tacitus yelped as the weapon struck him in the leg. Before I could react, the man threw another dart, at me. The thing struck me in the chest, hitting the Tyche ring. Deflected, it fell to the ground.

The man heaved himself over the roof of the tomb and dropped in front of me, with a sword drawn. As he made his move, I picked up the dart and clutched it in my left hand and a little behind me, holding my sword out to draw attention away from my hidden weapon.

"How did I miss you?" he sneered.

"Do you want to try again?" I flung the dart at him. Underhanded and with my left hand, it was an awkward throw but accurate enough to strike him on the right shoulder.

His reaction startled me. Panic spread over his face as he tore the dart out, making the wound even larger. "Oh, gods! No!" he gasped.

Suddenly I realized—the darts had poisoned tips. Even with his minor wound, Tacitus was going to die if I didn't do something right away.

The dart-thrower sank to his knees, dropping his sword, and tried to suck at his wound, but he couldn't get his mouth over it. I looked at Tacitus, clutching the wound in his thigh, his face pleading.

"Gaius Pliny! It's starting to burn."

I sheathed my sword. As unpleasant as the prospect was, I knew what I had to do. First I picked up the dart-thrower's sword and heaved it over a tomb, then did the same with the first man's weapon. I knelt and sucked as much blood out of Tacitus' leg as I could hold in my mouth without swallowing or vomiting. When I spat it out and was about to resume, Tacitus cried, "Look out!" He pushed me away from him and rolled over in the opposite direction. The dart-thrower's blow—with a knife he must have had hidden under his tunic—fell between us, the weapon clattering on the marble.

"I'm going to kill you," the man said, scrambling to his feet and breathing hard. "That's what I was…paid to do. Then I'll watch your friend die…while I die. Some consolation, at least."

"But not just yet," I said, pointing behind him.

"Do you think I'm that big a fool?" the dart-thrower said.

"You are if you don't drop that knife," Novatus, the commander of the *vigiles* said, causing my attacker to jerk around.

He found himself facing Novatus and three of his men, all with swords drawn. To judge by the sounds coming from across the road, other *vigiles* were rounding up the rest of the bandits. Novatus walked up to the man, and without a word, plunged his sword deep into his chest.

†

Leaving several of the *vigiles* to recover our horses and stand watch over the dead bandits, we borrowed their mounts and set out for Aurelia's house. The sun was low over the bay by the time we arrived and got Tacitus and the wounded servant, Antullus, settled. Both were in considerable pain, sweating and beginning to babble. I was riding the same horse as Tacitus, holding him in front of me. Most of what he was muttering was incoherent, but I caught a few words about his father-in-law, Agricola. I just hoped he didn't start talking about how much the two of them hated Domitian. I decided to keep close to him when we got back to the house. His delirious ravings could get us all into trouble if they came to the wrong ears.

Philippa, taking her duties in the stable very seriously, met us even before Aurelia's groomsman came out. "Where are our horses, my lord?"

Since she'd been on the premises for only two days, I was amazed she could recognize that these weren't our horses, something I wouldn't have been able to do. As far as I can tell, a horse is a horse. "We were attacked. One of our horses was killed and the others ran away. We borrowed these from the *vigiles*. They're looking for ours back up the road."

"These have been ridden hard, my lord," Philippa said, patting my mount on the neck. "We'll feed and water them."

When we got into the house I was more disappointed than surprised to find Bastet in charge. She had ridden back from the ruins with a servant who brought food and water to Calpurnius. In the morning she would return on a horse, so that she could come and go as needed. She had ordered Aurelia to stay in her bed and had virtually taken over the household in the few hours she'd been there.

"Do you know what kind of poison was used, my lord?" she asked.

"No, we don't. I didn't have time to ask the man any questions before Novatus here killed him."

The watch commander's annoyance was evident. "As I told you on the way down here, sir, he made a motion toward me with his knife. You couldn't see it because you were trying to help Cornelius Tacitus. I had no choice."

"It might have been just a spasm caused by the poison. He was dying and he knew it."

"I saved him some misery then, I guess."

"Never mind all that," Bastet said. "If I knew what sort of poison he used, I might be able to make an antidote."

The last thing I wanted was for this witch-princess to put some concoction in Tacitus' mouth, but I couldn't let him die without trying something, no matter how futile or risky. "We did bring along the man's bag," I said. "He kept his darts in it, and there's a small vial of some sort in here."

I gave the leather bag to the Nubian, who retrieved the vial, pulled the stopper out of it and sniffed it. Then she put a minute drop on the tip of her finger, touched it to her tongue and immediately spat it out. "Scorpion's venom," she said, wiping her tongue on the back of her hand, "with aconite mixed in. It's powerful, but it takes longer to work than some poisons. I think I know what might stop it." She took the vial and headed toward her room.

"Well, if that's all, sir," Novatus said, "I'll be going back. We've got a bit of a mess to clean up before dark. You've got our horses. We'll keep yours when we round them up. Easier for everybody that way."

I offered my hand to close the deal. "All right, and thank you again for your help."

"Just sorry we didn't get there a bit sooner, sir."

"Any time before we were dead was soon enough." I hoped that was true for Tacitus. "Remember to keep an eye on Plautia's *insula*. If Sychaeus was involved in this attack, he'll go back there."

"I'll do that, sir, and I'll make an offering to Asclepius for his help in saving your friend and your servant."

"The gesture will be appreciated," I said. *No matter how useless.*

Novatus turned on his heel and left the garden.

I entered Tacitus' room, picked up a cloth and begin wiping his legs and feet. The wound where the dart had pierced his skin was inflamed, growing redder and spreading, even as I watched, it seemed. I heard him say, "Julia, Julia."

"That's his wife," I told the servant woman. "He doesn't really know what he's saying."

"Yes, my lord. A fever can make people say the strangest things. You can't pay it any notice."

"Do you think he might survive?"

"There's really nothing we can do until Bastet finds a potion."

"Do you think she will?"

The woman pulled up the blanket that Tacitus kept kicking off. "Yes, my lord. She has those skills."

"Do you trust her?"

She looked at me, then turned her attention back to Tacitus. "My lord Calpurnius does. Now, if I may speak freely, my lord, you are in my way. Why don't you wait outside? I'll call you if there's any change."

"For better or for worse."

"Any change at all, my lord."

I sat on a bench outside Tacitus' room. Now that I was still, a wave of fear and sorrow washed over me at the prospect of losing Tacitus. In less than two years he had become one of the three most important people in my life. I could not imagine waking up and knowing that I would never again see my mother or Aurora, or Tacitus. I loved each of them in different ways, and my life would be diminished in different, but equal, ways by the loss of any of them.

I put my head in my hands and began to weep.

†

A servant brought me the wine I had requested. With enough spices added to it, it was drinkable, as long as I reminded myself there was nothing better available in the house. Like the wine, the garden before me was a sad reminder of the deterioration of the house. It would cost money to procure a better vintage and it would cost even more money to restore the garden to what it must have looked like before the eruption.

I was facing Aurelia's room, which was still being guarded by two of my men. Given some calm, I needed to think through the events of the day and decide what they meant and what I should do next. Trying to blot everything out, I lowered my head and closed my eyes. When I opened them and looked up, Aurelia was standing in front of me, making adjustments to her blond wig.

"I thought Bastet sent you to bed," I said, moving over so she could sit beside me.

"She thinks so, too. I want to know what's going on, Gaius Pliny. Everyone says I shouldn't know so it won't affect the baby, but *not* knowing just makes me that much more anxious, and that can't be good for the baby. Please tell me everything, no matter how bad it is."

And so I told her all I knew—starting with what I'd said before about Calpurnius being blackmailed, and going into detail about how much money he had paid the blackmailers and how little money they now had (and why they had to drink such wretched wine).

She was quiet as I talked, her hand going to her mouth as the enormity of it hit her. "Do we have...anything left?"

"Whatever you inherited from your father. I suppose Calpurnius hadn't figured out how to get to that without you finding out, but he had run out of his own funds. He couldn't pay the blackmailers last month."

"So they killed Amalthea, as a warning to him."

"I believe that, but I can't prove it yet."

"I knew my husband couldn't have done it. It must have been someone who knew this house well enough to know she would be out there every morning."

"You were aware of what she was doing?"

Aurelia nodded. "I saw no harm in it. One can't pray to too many gods."

"Amalthea's prayers didn't do her much good."

"It's such a shame that she had to die merely as a warning."

"And two of the blackmailers tried to kidnap you for the same reason. One was a former servant of yours, a man named Sychaeus."

Her lip curled in distaste. "Calpurnius sold him about six months ago. A very disagreeable man. He was missing a finger, wasn't he?"

I nodded. "The small finger on his right hand."

"Was he the one who attacked you on the road?"

"We don't know. We killed two of them, but two escaped."

"It's fortunate that Novatus came along when he did."

"I suppose so."

Aurelia turned to face me and rested a hand on her belly. "Why do you sound dubious?"

"Novatus says he had an informant in the *taberna*. He supposedly heard a man say something about narrow-stripers and setting a trap, and he told Novatus."

"We're surrounded by spies, aren't we?"

I was more aware of the truth of her statement than she could ever know. "But I find it difficult to believe that anyone planning an ambush would have revealed enough details that Novatus could come right to the spot."

"He would have reasoned that you were coming back here, wouldn't he? There's only one road from Naples that you could take. He was bound to find you."

"I suppose so, but why did he kill the dart-thrower before I had a chance to question him? Before I had a chance to even learn his name?"

"Do you think the man knew something Novatus didn't want you to know?"

I looked at her with a new degree of respect. She was asking more pointed questions than Tacitus would have. He blunders around and often says something helpful, mixed in with a lot of nonsense. Aurelia had hit the target as deftly as the dart-thrower had in the *taberna*. "I hate to admit it, but you're probably right. And his men couldn't catch the attackers on the other side of the road. He rounded on them because of their 'ineptitude,' but maybe they weren't really trying to catch them. I simply don't know how much we can trust Novatus."

"I wish I knew how much we can trust *her*," Aurelia said softly, nodding toward Bastet as she made her way across the garden, holding two cups. Her gait was as stately as a priestess approaching the altar of her god.

"My lady," the Nubian said sternly, "I told you to stay in bed."

Aurelia didn't answer. "Do you have something that will help these men?"

"I believe so, my lady."

Aurelia turned to me. "Shall we try it on your slave first, to see how he responds?"

"I don't think we have time for that. Let's give it to both of them. They're going to die without it." And probably with it, I thought.

Tacitus and Antullus were in neighboring rooms. I reached for one of the cups, but Bastet, with a barely perceptible shift of her hands, held the other one toward me. I took the cup I had originally intended to and signaled for Bastet to go to the servant's room. Aurelia and I entered Tacitus' room.

"How is he?" Aurelia asked the servant woman who was tending to him.

"He's very hot, my lady. I think he's getting worse. He's not saying much of anything now."

I would have been glad to hear of Tacitus' silence if it hadn't been a possible omen of his imminent death. Standing over the bed, I put a hand on his shoulder. "Cornelius Tacitus, can you hear me? It's Gaius Pliny. I need for you to drink something, to make you feel better."

Tacitus' eyes opened and the irises rolled back under his lids. His body shook, drenched with sweat. Aurelia held his head up and still while I poured Bastet's potion into his mouth.

"A little at a time," she said. "Give him a chance to swallow it." She smoothed his hair, glistening with sweat, away from his face.

When Tacitus had consumed the entire contents of the cup, I hoped to see some immediate improvement in his condition, but he continued to breathe hard and to sweat profusely. Sending the servant

woman to get more water and cloths, Aurelia began sponging Tacitus'
head and chest herself. I took a cloth to his legs, trying to avoid being
kicked. About half an hour later his breathing slowed and he stopped
thrashing around on the bed.

"Is he dying?" I asked.

"No, I think he's past the worst of it." She took a dry cloth and
wiped his forehead. "See, he's not sweating now."

"Can you stay with him for a moment? I want to see how Antullus
is doing."

Bastet and the servant woman assisting her were standing in the
garden when I emerged from Tacitus' room. From the expressions on
their faces I knew the answer to my question before I asked it. "Is he—"

"He died, my lord," Bastet said. "I'm very sorry."

I grabbed the cup she was holding. There was still about a quarter
of the potion in the bottom.

"Why didn't you give him all of it?"

"He died before he could finish it, my lord."

"Drink the rest of it," I ordered her.

"Why, my lord?"

"Don't question me, woman. Just drink it."

Bastet put the cup to her lips and appeared to drink the rest of the
potion. Then she turned the cup upside down.

"I want to see you swallow it," I said. When she had appeared to
swallow the liquid I said, "Now open your mouth."

She complied and I ran my finger around the inside of her mouth,
daring her with my eyes to bite me. She had indeed swallowed the
potion.

"Why are you humiliating me this way, my lord? Inspecting me
like a man looking at a horse's teeth?" She spat, barely missing my feet.

"You tried to give me that cup," I said.

"It was the one nearest to you, my lord. Both cups contained the
same potion."

"Then why is Tacitus alive and Antullus dead?"

"Which man was struck first, my lord?"

"Antullus was."

"He was also the smaller man, my lord. The poison had more time
to spread and less of an area over which to spread." She drew herself

up and set her chin. "Let us speak frankly. Do you suspect me of some wrongdoing? Do you have any proof?"

I held her gaze. Suspect? Yes. Able to prove? "No."

She snorted derisively. "I should hope not. I have been a loyal servant of my lord Calpurnius for over twenty years. I nursed his mother through her last years and I've seen my lady Aurelia through a difficult pregnancy, even though she ignores much of my advice."

What could I say? I barely knew the woman. My mistrust of her was based on instinct—a dislike of her regal manner, her general demeanor—not on rational thought, and I had adopted Aurelia's misgivings. Bastet had swallowed whatever was in the cup without any hesitation. But, a part of my mind whispered, experts in poison usually take small doses of the stuff over the years, as Nero's mother Agrippina did, building up immunities to doses large enough to kill a person almost instantly.

But what reason would she have to kill Tacitus—or anyone else? No matter how much she hated Rome for enslaving her, she must know what would happen to a slave who murdered a citizen, especially someone of Tacitus' class. The crowds in the arena clamor for entertainment. Exquisite tortures would be devised for someone as exotic as a Nubian princess.

"May I be excused, my lord?"

I had not yet kept her in my presence long enough, I thought. She might be asking to leave so she could make herself vomit and expel what she had drunk, also a common tactic for poisoners. Without arousing her suspicion, I could not detain her any longer. Unless—

"First I want you to take a look at Tacitus. He seems to be doing better, but I'd like your opinion."

"Very well, my lord."

When she entered the room Aurelia stepped back, almost in deference to the Nubian. Bastet felt Tacitus' head, put her ear to his chest for a moment. She lifted the blanket which Aurelia had drawn up over him.

"He seems to be sleeping calmly," she said. "He is much cooler, and he has expelled a large quantity of urine. That's a sign that his body is cleansing itself. He will be better by tomorrow, I think. I'll send someone to clean him up and change his clothes and bedding. I would recommend that he stay in bed for the next day, if my opinion in such matters means anything." She gave Aurelia a glance that spoke volumes. "Is that all you require, my lord?"

"Yes, thank you," I said.

"Then I will prepare to return to my lord Calpurnius in the morning."

As Bastet left the room one of Aurelia's other servants stood at the door. "My lady, my lord, the messengers you sent to Puteoli to inquire about Proxena have returned. They say they have news, both good and bad."

XIX

"CAN WE MEET them in your library?" I asked Aurelia. "I want to be in a closed room so we won't be overheard."

"Don't you want to be in here, where we can keep an eye on Tacitus?" Aurelia said.

"I'd rather be somewhere else right now." I was grateful beyond words that Tacitus seemed to be recovering, but the stench in this small room was becoming unbearable. Aurelia gave the order to bring the messengers to the library and accompanied me there. I stood while she sat on a scribe's bench.

I did not want Thamyras to hear this report. He had no idea that I was trying to find his woman, and I did not want him to hear anything until I'd had a chance to evaluate this information. Hope raised and then dashed is worse than no hope at all.

"You made the trip in good time," I said when the messengers entered the library. "Your effort will be rewarded. What did you learn?"

"We found the man who bought the woman Proxena, my lord."

"Did you ask if he would be willing to sell her?"

"He can't, my lord."

"Why? Has he already sold her?" I didn't have time to keep following a slave's trail from master to master.

"Worse than that, my lord. She died two years ago when an illness swept through that house."

My shoulders sagged. "I'm sorry to hear that."

"It will be devastating news for Thamyras," Aurelia said.

"We'll have to consider how we're going to tell him." I knew we would have to tell him. There are no secrets among servants in a house, no matter how stringently the master insists or what punishments he threatens. "Get yourselves something to eat, and do not say anything to anyone."

"But, my lord," the man said hesitantly, "there is more."

"Oh, yes, the good news. What is it?"

"Proxena had a child, my lord. She gave birth seven months after she arrived in the house."

"Seven months?" Aurelia sat up with interest. "So she was already pregnant when she left here."

"It seems so, my lady."

"Then the child must be Thamyras'. Is it a boy or a girl?"

"A boy, my lady—a handsome little fellow."

We thanked the messengers again and sent them off to get something to eat.

"You know what we have to do, Gaius Pliny," Aurelia said, "or at least what you have to do. After what you've told me about Calpurnius spending all our money, I'm not sure what I can afford."

I nodded. "Don't worry about anything. It shouldn't cost much to purchase the boy. Raising a slave child costs money and you never know if he's going to be a good enough worker to justify the investment."

"Is the master more willing to invest if the slave is his own child?"

"Well…I'm sure your father…I didn't mean…." Aurelia seemed so natural in her current status as my equal that I kept forgetting that she'd been a slave when I met her.

"And what if the master is in love with the slave?" A smile played on her lips.

The room suddenly seemed warm and close. "I…that is…."

Aurelia stood, with some effort, and put a hand on my arm. "Why, Gaius Pliny, I didn't think you were ever at a loss for words. I wasn't really sure how you felt, but there's something about the way you react when anyone mentions her. And you keep touching something on that strap around your neck that I suspect has some connection to her."

"How I may, or may not, feel doesn't matter." I could not look Aurelia in the eye. She had already guessed too much. One more glance and I was afraid I would tell her everything. "There's...nothing that... can be done." Stating it passively took the responsibility off me.

"Oh, dear Gaius, there's always something that can be done. The only question is whether you'll do it in time."

"Now is not the time." I took her hand off my arm and straightened my tunic, resisting the urge to touch the Tyche ring as I did so. "We were talking about Thamyras and his son. I'll purchase the boy and give him to Thamyras. Or I could free him, if you—"

"By all means, I'll free Thamyras. That won't cost me anything. He and the child can stay here and continue to mind the garden for us, if that's what he wants."

"I can see a certain justice in it. We took Philippa's father away from her, so we should seize on the opportunity to bring a father and his son together."

"Yes, there is a kind of balance about that," Aurelia said, holding her hands up like a scale. "As much as there can be in such an imperfect world as ours."

"I'll send someone tomorrow to see if we can make the arrangements."

"And I'll draw up the document for Thamyras' emancipation. Calpurnius will have to approve it."

"Let's not say anything to Thamyras until everything is in place." I took her by the elbow and guided her to the door. "Now, you're obviously uncomfortable and you really should get back to bed. Don't ignore good advice just because it comes from Bastet."

†

The house was busy as the sun set. Under Thamyras' direction, the bodies of Antullus and Amalthea were carried down close to the bay and a large pyre erected. It would burn all night. The evening breeze blowing toward the bay would fan the flames, and keep the odor of charred flesh away from the house. I was glad to have something to keep Thamyras busy and away from Aurelia and me. The temptation to tell him what we'd learned was enormous.

I checked in on Tacitus every time I passed his room. The servant woman sitting with him reported he was sleeping quietly. I was relieved that he had stopped talking. I wondered what he might have said in his delirium but did not want to draw attention to it by asking the woman who had taken care of him. People can remain unaware of the importance of something they know if no one makes an issue of it.

I was having a late supper alone when Capsius arrived. The door-keeper brought him into the garden. He removed the soft cap he was wearing and stood before me with his right hand, holding the cap, crossed over his left, no doubt a lifelong habit to cover his deformity.

"I'm sorry to disturb you, sir," he began, "but my lady Plautia sent me to ask if you can come to Naples tomorrow to discuss the possible sale of her *insula*."

"Can she wait until the next day?" I did not want to make this trip without Tacitus.

"Well, sir, she is planning to leave on a long business trip and would like to get this matter settled, if at all possible."

She was planning to flee, and probably Sychaeus with her. "I guess it will have to be tomorrow, then, won't it?"

"If you don't mind, sir. May I report that to her?"

"You may stay here tonight and ride back with me in the morning." I was already wondering if I was being lured into another ambush.

"But, sir—"

"I am inconveniencing myself by going tomorrow. You can accommodate me by accompanying me on the ride."

"Yes, sir."

"Besides, it's almost dark and I don't want you exposed to the dangers of travel at night. That road is perilous enough in the daytime, as I learned today."

"As you wish, sir."

I suspected that, if this was a trap, he would find some roundabout way to avoid the main road. "Now, get yourself something to eat and tell the steward to show you to a room." There was at least one empty room off the garden, the one where Antullus had died. I hoped the bedding had been changed.

†

The events of the day had left me exhausted but too agitated to sleep. I decided this would be a good opportunity to take a longer look at Calpurnius' financial records. Tacitus and I had made only a cursory examination. I wanted to see if Calpurnius had *any* money left and if he had begun to sell his wife's property. I found Diomedes and had him unlock the treasury room and the strongbox and light some lamps. This time I did not offer to let him wait outside, nor did he insist on doing so. He seemed to accept that the room's "virginity" had been violated and left me alone to have my way with the contents.

Diomedes had returned the documents to their places on the shelves, so I had to lay them all out on the table again. In the strongbox I noticed a couple of scrolls that Tacitus and I had overlooked earlier. One proved to be a list of property belonging to Aurelia's father, and now to her. The two most distant pieces had VEND in small letters written beside them, making me suspect Calpurnius was trying to figure how he could begin selling them. He was desperate enough to ruin his family in order to keep his secret. Considering that it would cost him his life if Domitian ever found out that Calpurnius had entertained— even for a moment or even in jest—the idea of killing him, I could find a dollop of sympathy for the man. But only a dollop.

The other scroll was sealed. I decided that I had endured enough on Calpurnius' behalf in the last few days to claim the right to break that seal.

The document proved to be not a list but some kind of family history, the sort of thing we Romans have been writing since the days of Fabius Pictor, three hundred years ago. At first I thought Calpurnius intended it as part of a eulogy for his father. I had delivered such a speech at my uncle's funeral. It lasted only two hours because my uncle's death had come so unexpectedly and I'd had precious little time to write it, but it was well received. I assumed Calpurnius was preparing for that inevitable day—a wise thing to do, considering Fabatus' age.

But this family history, I realized after reading only a few pages, had a different purpose, a darker side. It detailed the accusations that were leveled against his father in Nero's time. Since my mother was a friend of Fabatus' daughter and I had made a solemn pledge to marry the man's granddaughter, I had more than a passing interest in the story. Once a family bears this kind of stain—accusations from one *princeps*, a plot to kill another—it becomes permanent, and anyone who comes into contact with them risks being marked by it as well.

I had to read the document several times because the story was so convoluted, and made even more so by the fact that there were so many descendants of Augustus by Nero's day. Any one of them had as valid a claim to be *princeps* as Nero did. His mother eliminated several and Nero kept up the onslaught. The object of his wrath in this case was Junia Lepida, the great-granddaughter of Augustus. Nero suspected Lepida of plotting to place her nephew, Junius Silanus—another Augustan descendant—in power. He accused her, however, of taking part in bizarre religious rituals and committing incest with her nephew, things that even Nero's worst enemies should find abhorrent.

Along with several others, Calpurnius Fabatus was charged as an accomplice. I could understand how, given his interest in Egyptian customs, Nero might have seized on him as an easy target. Having seen his house and his relationship with his great-niece, I would need little evidence to consider him guilty. He proved to be too insignificant, though—in other words, not directly related to Augustus—for Nero to bother with and the case was never prosecuted. Lepida, her husband, her nephew, and other, more prominent people were executed or exiled.

Junia Lepida was married to G. Cassius Longinus. Their granddaughter was Domitia Longina, first the wife of Aelius Lamia and now the wife of Domitian, and the reason Calpurnius had plotted to kill Domitian fifteen years ago. Longina's daughter, Canthara/Plautia—a direct, but unsuspecting, descendant of the deified Augustus—was the woman I was planning to meet in Naples in the morning.

What did I expect her to do? She knew nothing of her true ancestry, and I had no intention of telling her. She would never admit, I knew, to any involvement in blackmailing Calpurnius or killing his servant or trying to kidnap his wife. I was certain she was an accomplice—probably the instigator—in all those acts, as well as being behind the attack on Tacitus and me. But I couldn't prove anything against her. And until I could, Calpurnius and his family would never be safe.

†

Tacitus was awake the next morning but in no condition to bestir himself. His limbs felt weak, he said, and his head ached. Sitting up to use a chamber pot was the most vigorous activity he was capable of. I assured him that I had everything under control.

"That's what a driver in the Circus Maximus will tell you," he snorted, "when he's really just hanging on for his life." Having described my situation so succinctly yet vividly, he rolled over and was asleep again before I left the room.

The ride to Naples did prove uneventful. I was glad to have misjudged Capsius. Or perhaps, when one tactic failed, Canthara and Sychaeus switched to a different one. I could not let my guard down, though. The four armed servants riding with us made me feel somewhat more secure.

Naples was humming with building activity, reminding me of Virgil's description of Carthage when Aeneas first sees it, with two important differences. In this case it was *rebuilding* activity, and I wasn't covered with the cloud which Venus had dropped over her son to make him invisible. How useful that would be at times! But as Virgil said, men were wrestling stones into place, measuring lines for walls, and setting up gates. They weren't quarrying stone from the earth, though. Their quarries were the buildings which had been most heavily damaged in the last couple of earthquakes.

With my servants stationed where they could see into the book shop and be seen from inside, Capsius led me in to where Plautia—I decided I'd better accustom myself to calling her that—was seated at a table, apparently checking a scroll for mistakes. Her feet were out of sight under the table. "My lady, this is Gaius Pliny."

"Thank you, Capsius. Please leave us." When the scribe was gone, she turned to me. "I understand that you might be interested in buying this building."

That was it. No welcoming comment. No easing into the conversation. Her gruff manner fit her appearance. She was somewhat plump, with a round face. Her hair was dark, her skin pale, like someone who spent most of her time indoors. Even with her sitting down, I could tell that she was short. Her stubby fingers showed the calluses of a working woman but no ink stains. She had none of the aura one would expect of a descendant of the deified Augustus. But then Nero probably didn't either. On his coins he looks like a bloated frog, with a growth on his throat. Even the most royal blood can get thinned out over the course of time. And what does "royal blood" mean anyway? In spite of their claim to be descended from Venus, the Julian family were nothing more than opportunistic adventurers who had seized power by defeating other, less opportunistic, adventurers. No one is born with an innate "majesty." Augustus was so short, I've read, that he received people sitting down so they couldn't accurately gauge his stature.

"I might be interested in buying it. What is your price?" I could be as blunt as she was.

"One hundred thousand *sesterces*."

"That's a reasonable price…if I were buying the nicest *insula* in Rome. My offer is sixty thousand."

The woman shook her head. "That's not acceptable."

"Perhaps we could agree on a price if your mistress would come out and bargain with me instead of having a servant pretend to be her."

The woman blinked her eyes, helpless, and looked over her shoulder. From a doorway behind her stepped a tall, elegant woman, the very embodiment of imperial dignity except for her misshapen foot and her limp. Her brown hair was swept up and piled in front in the current fashion, adding to the sense of her height.

"How did you know, Gaius Pliny?"

"First, she said 'thank you' to a servant. Then, her fingers have no ink stains on them. I've been told that you write alongside your scribes. There would have to be some traces of ink on your fingers."

Plautia looked down at her hands, rubbed the tips of her fingers, and chuckled. "And I thought my foot would betray me. I can't get these damned spots out."

"I'm sorry, mistress," the dark-haired girl said. "I tried. Really, I did. I did just what you told me."

"It's not your fault. Go on back to your work." The girl hurried out of the shop. Plautia sat down in her place. "She cleans for me. I thought I might be able to avoid confronting you if I coached her carefully."

"Why would you not want to confront me?" We faced one another like two gladiators in the arena, swords still not raised, circling and assessing one another to find an opening.

"I wanted to see if you could spot the fraud. If you couldn't, I had no need to be worried about you."

"What makes you think you have reason to be worried about me?"

"You've shown a great deal of interest in me these last few days.

You've been asking questions all over Naples, inspecting my property. I don't like it when people pry into my business."

That felt like the first thrust, so I parried. "When they do pry, do you always set up ambushes for them?"

"Was that you who was attacked yesterday? I heard about it. Was anyone hurt?" The slight raise of her eyebrows was neither an admission nor a denial of her guilt.

"Yes. One of the servants with me was killed, and my friend Tacitus was gravely wounded."

"I'm sorry to hear that. Have they caught the men who did it?"

It was time to take the offensive. "I killed one at the scene. Novatus, commander of the watch, killed another. At least two others escaped."

I could almost see her step back to reconsider her strategy. "Well, I'm sure the magistrates will catch them soon. But what is your interest in me and my business?"

"I'm trying to help my friends Calpurnius and Aurelia. Your name has come up and I've tried to learn why." I decided to play the role of the *retiarius*, the gladiator who uses a fisherman's net to snare his opponent, then spears him with a trident. His movements have to be more subtle until he has his opponent entangled.

"People talk about me because they're envious of a woman who has been successful."

"Especially one who has risen so far, so fast."

"How much do you know about me?"

"As much as there is to know, Canthara." *And a bit more, which I'm not going to tell you.*

She slapped her hand on the writing table. "Don't call me by that slave name! I was emancipated and took on my former master's name. It's all legal. My name is Plautia."

When your opponent becomes angry, you have to press your advantage. "Your former master must have been exceptionally generous when he freed you, if you were able to buy this place."

"He said he wanted to be sure I was taken care of, but I don't see how that's any of your business." She regained control of herself and sidestepped me neatly. "And you're not here to talk about buying this building, are you? You just used that as a pretext to get in here."

"You invited me to come and talk to you this morning."

Plautia stood and drew herself up to her full height. "There's no point in pursuing this any further. Good day, Gaius Pliny." She turned toward the doorway behind her.

I cast my net and stopped her. "Did Sychaeus come back here after the ambush yesterday?"

"I haven't seen him in several days," she said without turning around. "He's a free man now and answers to no one."

"Are you saying it was his idea to kill Calpurnius' servant woman Amalthea?"

"I had nothing to do with that."

I tugged on my net, trying to throw her off-balance. "You know, you wasted the money you spent to buy his freedom. He isn't your brother."

With her back to me, I couldn't gauge her initial reaction, except for a sharp intake of breath. By the time she turned to face me, she had composed herself.

"What are you talking about? Of course he's my brother. Well, my half-brother, if you want to be precise."

"How do you know that?"

Her brow furrowed. "It's what we were told as we grew up. Our mother died soon after I was born. I never knew her, but others in the household told us about her."

That was convenient, I thought. If the woman had lived, would she have been able to tell that her child had been switched with Longina's? Would others have noticed a resemblance between Longina's supposed child and the slave woman who was her real mother? Did Aelius resort to murder to protect his secret?

"Why are you looking at me like that?" Plautia demanded.

"I was…just realizing that you must have had a difficult life."

She sneered, looking down at her crippled foot and back up at me. "Don't waste any pity on me. Sychaeus watched out for me, like a brother. He was all I had. He *is* all I have."

"And, from what I've heard, you were very angry when he was sold."

"He wasn't sold. He was traded for a horse, like he was an animal." She could barely control the rage that the memory evoked.

"So you vowed to take revenge on Aelius and Calpurnius. But

Domitian got Aelius first. That left only Calpurnius for you to deal with." For some reason I felt we were being watched. I could not see anyone in the other room of the book shop or in the darkened room from which Plautia had emerged, but I had a definite sense that someone was there. I glanced over my shoulder to assure myself that my armed defenders were still in view.

"You're talking rubbish," Plautia said. "You have no proof of *any* of this…. Do you?" In a moment of doubt, she had lowered her shield and left herself vulnerable.

"Yes, I do."

The shield went back up. "Then let me see it, at once. I won't believe a word of what you've said until I've seen your so-called proof."

Now I could imagine myself standing before an emperor. Her chin was lifted and set, her eyes drilling into me. Augustus, so I've read, was proud of his ability to hold people with his gaze. Could a trait such as that be inherited?

"I'm not going to show you anything until I know who is threatening Calpurnius and his family."

"Then we have nothing more to discuss. I'm sorry your trip up here was a waste of time—for both of us."

"I do want to know one thing, which you can tell me without admitting to any wrong-doing. You were emancipated six years ago. Why did you wait so long to purchase Sychaeus' freedom?"

"I couldn't purchase him from Calpurnius without arousing suspicion. He knows Sychaeus has a sister."

"He actually didn't know until two days ago."

"How could he not know? I wrote letters to Sychaeus."

"Others in the house knew, but not Calplurnius."

"Well, I thought he must know, so I had to wait until Sychaeus had been sold to another house."

"How could you be sure that would happen?"

"Sychaeus made himself obnoxious so that Calpurnius would be eager to sell him."

"From what I've heard of him, that didn't take much effort on his part."

Plautia took a limping step toward me. "Have you ever been a slave, Gaius Pliny? Don't even bother to answer. Until you have been, you have no idea what a horrible thing it is, no matter how kind and indulgent your master may be."

Was that how Aurora felt? I wondered. I tried to go back on the attack. "You also needed someone in Calpurnius' house, didn't you? To keep an eye on things once you started blackmailing him."

"You may interpret my actions any way you like. I have nothing further to say to you. I hope you have a safe journey home."

I couldn't miss the sarcasm in her last statement. Or was it a threat?

XX

G AIUS PLINY, I want to see my husband." Aurelia voiced her demand quietly, but the determination in her tone could not be missed. "I must know that he's all right, and I have to talk to him about...all of this."

The morning had begun well. Tacitus was up and around again, with only slight discomfort where the poisoned dart had pierced his leg—hardly more troublesome than an insect bite, as he described it. As we sat in the garden he was telling me how he now adored Bastet with all the fervor of a devotee of Isis or Cybele.

The funeral pyre had burned itself out. When it cooled later today, the ashes would be collected. Amalthea and Antullus would have to share an urn, but we would inscribe both names on the stone. Bastet had left to tend to Calpurnius, and the entire household seemed more relaxed with her gone. Her absence may have been what prompted Aurelia to raise the issue of seeing her husband.

"I don't think that's advisable," I told her. "I'm sure Bastet would tell you that travel at this stage of your pregnancy could be dangerous."

"I have to see him, Gaius Pliny. I have to forgive him for the mess he's gotten us into and let him know that I still love him. I'll have an easier time in the birth if my mind is at ease about Calpurnius. Please take me out there."

If her own safety didn't matter to her, I had to find another argument. "It could be dangerous for Calpurnius. Someone—probably in this household—is aware of your movements and could threaten Calpurnius if they find out where he is."

She folded her arms and rested them on her belly. "If you don't take me out there, I will get on a horse and go by myself."

"Aurelia, please don't—"

"I swear to you, Gaius Pliny, I'll do it." She turned and started walking away.

"Are you going to let her become the first woman to give birth on horseback?" Tacitus said. "Or do you want her to do it on the side of the road, like Virgil's mother?"

I shook my head. "I guess we'll have to take her in the *raeda*. We'll tell the driver to go as slowly as possible so we don't jostle her too badly."

"Just be ready to catch the baby when it comes."

†

It took almost an hour to get the *raeda* hooked up and enough cushions arranged to soften the ride for Aurelia. Bastet had taken some food with her, but Aurelia insisted on taking more. As we were getting into the carriage Philippa asked, "Will you take me with you, sir? I know that place as well as anybody, and I can help with the horses."

"The child's right," Tacitus said. "We need one person to stay with the *raeda* and one to stand watch for us at the entrance."

"Very well," I said. "Ride with the driver." Now that she was bathing regularly and had clean clothes to wear, I wouldn't have minded having Philippa in the *raeda* with us, but I knew she would get more pleasure out of watching the horses and I wasn't sure she was old enough to be present at a birth, if worse did come to worst.

"How are you doing?" I asked Aurelia as we bounced along.

"I feel fine," she said. "Please don't worry about me. This is what I need to do."

Aurelia closed her eyes and lay back on the cushions. As I watched her I couldn't help but be in awe of her devotion to her husband, a man she hadn't even known a year ago. Would my bride-to-be develop such feelings for me? Could I return them? Marriages do turn out happily for many people. Tacitus dotes on his Julia, for all his jokes about her flightiness. My mother still mourns the loss of my father, after all these years. But, I reminded myself, my uncle never married and was content with the love of a slave woman. Could that woman's daughter play the same role in my life?

When the *raeda* came to a halt Tacitus and I got out and looked to see if anyone had followed us. Even as we climbed up on the banks of ash on each side of the road, though, I wondered if we were wasting our time. There were so many places a person could hide. If his tunic was the right dingy shade, he would blend in with the bleak landscape, no more noticeable than the pile of ash he was hiding behind.

"I don't see anyone," Tacitus said. "Do you?"

"No. Still, let's get Aurelia down into the tunnel before someone spots us."

Aurelia inhaled sharply and clutched her belly as we helped her out of the *raeda*. "I'm all right," she said, but I wasn't convinced.

Leaving Philippa on guard near the entrance, we walked single-file down the tunnel. Tacitus, in the lead, and I, behind Aurelia, carried torches. With some light, such as it was, and with my attention focused on Aurelia, I was able to squelch my fear of the narrow place for a few moments.

Bracing myself with one hand on the wall of the tunnel, I thought I felt something I hadn't been aware of before—a few cracks here and there. I wasn't sure they'd been there the last time we came through or what they might mean, and I didn't want to say anything to Tacitus, for fear of upsetting Aurelia.

When we reached the bottom of the entrance shaft and turned toward the front of the house, Aurelia began to call, "Calpurnius! Calpurnius! Where are you?"

We heard a muffled sound ahead of us and Aurelia stepped in front of Tacitus and began to walk faster. I'm sure she would have run if she'd been able to. Tacitus and I had to pick up our pace to keep up with her.

We entered the atrium of the ruined house and I was thankful for the somewhat more open space provided by the fallen roof, which had kept the ash from filling the side of the atrium where Calpurnius was holed up.

Bastet met us at the door of Calpurnius's room. "My lady, what are you doing here?" She tried to get hold of Aurelia's shoulders, but Aurelia pushed her aside and barged into the room.

"Calpurnius!" she cried. "Oh, my darling, are you all right?"

When I got to the door I could see Aurelia kneeling beside the makeshift bed Calpurnius was lying on. He kissed her hand and drew her down to him. Bastet had washed him and brought him a clean tunic, so, while he looked gaunt, his appearance should not have dismayed his wife.

"My lord, why did you bring her here?" Bastet snarled, stepping toward us with such vehemence that Tacitus and I both backed up.

"Because she was going to come," I said, "with or without us."

Bastet looked at the couple as they embraced and her face softened. "I suppose it's for the best."

"How is Calpurnius?"

"He's doing all right, my lord. I worry, though, that he thinks he has little reason to live. He won't eat, and that leaves him weak. The earth shook a bit during the night, he says, and I want him to leave this place, but he doesn't seem to want to."

"Well, maybe having Auro—I mean Aurelia—in his arms will remind him of everything he does have to live for." I knew Tacitus had heard me, but he didn't say anything.

"Pliny, Tacitus," Calpurnius called, "come in, please." His voice sounded hearty enough.

We entered the room to find him sitting up, still holding Aurelia close to him. "I'm glad to see you looking so well, my friend," I said.

"I am much better. Thank you for bringing my wife to see me. Have you made any progress in…that matter we were…discussing?"

"You don't have to talk over me," Aurelia said. "I know everything—the blackmail, the properties you've sold. Everything."

Calpurnius looked from me to his wife in dismay. "You know? Then…why are you here?"

"Where else would I be? You're my husband and the father of our child. You should never have kept anything from me."

"My darling, I am so sorry. I would never do anything to hurt you. I only wanted to protect you."

"I know. I know. It's all forgiven. When we get out of here, we'll make a fresh start."

"I don't deserve…your forgiveness." Calpurnius lowered his head and began to weep, long wrenching sobs.

Tacitus and I stood back, leaving Aurelia to comfort her husband. We placed our torches in the wall brackets. I touched the one right outside Calpurnius' room with particular care, remembering my experience at Fabatus' house. The flickering light bathed the couple in a glow that no painter could hope to capture.

"We have to get him out of here," I said.

Before Tacitus could reply, somebody rushed at us out of the darkness. Because I was standing turned toward Tacitus, I saw a flicker of movement before he did and was able to step back, causing the attacker to miss me and stumble. But another man grabbed Tacitus from behind. They struggled until the attacker threw Tacitus, who was still not at full strength, against the wall. His head struck with a thud and he fell to the floor in a heap. I pulled out my sword and was ready to face my assailant when he regained his footing and turned around. He had a knife, but it was no match for my weapon. One quick thrust left him gasping out his life at my feet.

By the time I could turn my attention to what else was going on, the other attacker was advancing on Aurelia. Bastet threw herself in his path and the man stabbed her. "You meddlesome bitch," he muttered. "I've wanted to do that for a long time."

"Sychaeus!" Calpurnius said. "What are you—"

Sychaeus hit his former master in the face with the butt end of his knife and yanked Aurelia away from him. He was almost as tall as Tacitus, with a slim face, almost handsome except for the large ears.

"Don't hurt her," I ordered him.

"I don't intend to unless I have to. Things haven't gone as I planned, so she could be my passage out here." He put his left arm around her throat, and with the other hand, held his knife poised over her.

"Are you mad?" I said. "What do you hope to accomplish? There's not going to be any more blackmail money, no matter what you threaten us with."

"Oh, I figured that. I just need to clean up. You're the only ones who know what I've done. We've been watching and when we saw all of you coming out here together, it was too good a chance. If I kill you and leave you down here to rot, no one will ever know. Canthara and I can leave here and start over again somewhere else."

"But you're badly outnumbered—four against one."

"That's not how I count it. One of yours is out on the floor and the princess there is wounded." Sychaeus jerked his head in Calpurnius' direction. "And he's useless, like he always has been. It's really just you and me, *sir*. But I've got the one who matters. You won't make a move against me as long as my knife is at her throat."

"That's the way you killed Amalthea, isn't it? You grabbed her from behind and plunged your knife into her heart." I made a motion with my own weapon. "But you left your knife beside the body."

"I figured Calpurnius would pick it up if I made a noise of some kind. And that wasn't my knife. It was one I'd stolen from the kitchen." Sychaeus raised the weapon he was holding. "This is mine." He pressed the blade closer to Aurelia's throat.

"And I'm sure I would find scratch marks on your left arm."

Glancing at his arm, Sychaeus tightened his hold on Aurelia. "You're a smart fellow."

The words had never felt less like a compliment.

"Yeah, that's how I did it. But it was Canthara's idea. There's no harm in you knowing that now, I guess, since you won't live to tell anybody."

"How did she know about Amalthea's habit of coming out into the orchard every morning?"

"She didn't. She said we should throw a good scare into Calpurnius because he hadn't paid for this month. We couldn't let him get away with that. I told her about Amalthea. I thought we could tie her up and knock her around, but Canthara told me to kill her."

Aurelia groaned and wriggled in Sychaeus' grasp as he backed her away from Calpurnius.

"Don't worry, my lady. I'm not going to hurt you as long as you don't give me any trouble. You wouldn't want *anybody* to get hurt, would you?" He slid the knife down and pressed it against Aurelia's belly, wiping Bastet's blood on her gown. "I'm going to have to change my plans a bit and take you with me as a hostage."

From behind us a thin voice echoed through the tunnel. "My lord, Gaius Pliny, watch out!"

Sychaeus instinctively turned his head when he heard Philippa's warning. In that instant Calpurnius lunged at him, grabbing the hand that held the knife and flinging Sychaeus to the floor. The knife clattered away from them. I was amazed to see Calpurnius display so much strength—the fury of a man pushed to madness. I took Aurelia's hand and pulled her away from the two of them. She doubled over, as though in severe pain, and grabbed my arms in a grip that I couldn't break.

Calpurnius had thrown Sychaeus back into the room where he was holed up. Now he began pummeling him with his fists. Sychaeus, the stronger man, fought back, but Calpurnius attacked him like a wild animal, falling on top of him and pinning him down. I tried to loosen Aurelia's grip on me so I could help him.

"Gaius Pliny," Calpurnius yelled in Greek, "grab the torch bracket…beside the door. When I tell you to…push it down, to the right!"

Of course! Calpurnius' father—lover of all things Egyptian—had built this house before he moved to the villa where he now lived. I got one arm free from Aurelia and reached for the bracket. "By the gods, man," I called. "Do you know what you're doing?"

"It will take…precise timing. Get ready." He mustered enough strength to push Sychaeus toward the back of the room where he'd been hiding. "Now!"

Calpurnius turned and I put my full weight on the bracket. Just as the lever moved and Calpurnius lunged toward the door, Sychaeus recovered enough to grab the hem of Calpurnius' tunic. As the giant block of stone crashed to the floor, he pulled Calpurnius back. Aurelia screamed. Letting go of my arm, she ran to the blocked door and began slapping her hands against it. "No! No! No!"

I pulled her away and tried to comfort her. "We can get some men out here to raise the stone. It can be done. That's the way Fabatus engineered it." *Though I was sure he hadn't figured on two mortal enemies being trapped behind the stone with one knife between them. Which of them would still be alive by the time I could get enough men down here to—*

Then all around us I heard and felt a rumble. Pieces of the hardened ash began falling to the floor. The sudden shifting of all that weight had jarred everything loose. As if the keystone of an arch had been removed, the whole structure was collapsing.

"We have to get out of here!" I cried. "Philippa, help her."

"But, my lord—"

Then I noticed that the girl's hands were tied behind her back. Her face showed bruises where she must have fallen while running down the tunnel in the dark with no way to brace herself. I sliced the ropes. "Get one of those torches."

I got Tacitus to his feet and put his arm over my shoulder and my other arm around his waist. It was going to be difficult to drag a heavier man up that shaft, but it was the only way we could get out. Bastet staggered to her feet, holding the spot in her shoulder where she had been wounded. As best she could, she helped Philippa support Aurelia.

"Leave me here," Aurelia cried, shaking her head so vehemently that her wig fell off, showing her own hair, barely longer now than mine. "I want to die with my husband." She looked back over her shoulder and tried to pull away.

"No," I said. "You're going to live with your child. Remember, I promised Calpurnius I would marry her."

We hurried out the way we had come in, but when we reached the entry shaft I took one look and could not see light at the other end, as I had been able to the other times I had peered up there. Dust and clumps of ash rolled down it.

"It's already collapsing," I said.

"What will we do, my lord?" Bastet wailed.

"We can't go back and we can't go up this shaft," I said. "The only thing we can do is follow this tunnel toward the back of the house."

"What's down there?" Bastet asked.

"Besides rats, I don't know. I've only been part way."

"You said someone was living down there, didn't you, sir?" Philippa asked. "People who live in these ruins always have a second way they can get out."

"Did you and your father?"

"Yes, sir. We lived like animals, he said, so we needed to think like animals. It wasn't a very big hole and it was covered up, but we had one."

"Then let's find this one. And we'd better be quick about it." I touched the Tyche ring under my tunic. A cloud of dust came roiling up the tunnel behind us as the thunder of collapsing ash grew louder. The earth beneath our feet shook.

We were almost to the point where the tunnel turned when Aurelia made a strange, gasping noise and Bastet said, "My lord, her gown is all wet."

"Is she bleeding?"

Bastet grabbed Philippa's arm and pulled the torch down so that she could see by the dim light. "No, my lord. It's the first sign that the baby is coming. The baby is in a sack in her belly. When that sack breaks, water flows out. Then the baby is born."

"Now?"

"It could be very soon, my lord, or it could be hours yet."

I wondered if we could pray to Juno to prevent the birth for a while, as she had done when Alcmene was in labor with Heracles. It wouldn't have to be long—not the seven days Alcmene suffered through—just until we could get back to the villa. From Aurelia's gasps and cries of pain, though, I suspected something was going to happen much sooner.

We turned the corner in the tunnel and Philippa immediately cried, "I see light ahead."

The denizens of the place had already bolted out of their hiding place, leaving the door open behind them. In the darkness it was hard to tell how far we had to travel. We couldn't run, but we did walk faster. As soon as we exited the tunnel Bastet started to put Aurelia down on the ground.

"No," I said. "We need to get farther away, some place where we're not directly over the house. There's no telling how much of this ash may cave in. We need to be on solid ground."

Bastet encouraged Aurelia and I dragged Tacitus about twenty paces farther, enough I thought, to get us over the back wall of the house. His groans and mumbling told me he was regaining consciousness. Behind us dust erupted from the exit we had just used. Then an eerie calm settled over the place.

"I think we're safe now," I said, laying Tacitus on the ground. "I don't feel any shaking."

The sun was at its highest point, but there was no shade nearby in the barren landscape, and no time to move anywhere else. Aurelia began to pant rapidly.

"The baby's coming, my lord," Bastet said. "I need some help."

"What can we do?" I asked.

"I wish we had a birthing stool, but we'll just have to work with what we have. My lord, you need to get behind her and let her rest against you. When she pushes, you must be strong and give her something to push against. Little one"—she turned to Philippa—"I know you hate me for what I did, but please, for the sake of our lady and her child, assist me."

Philippa knelt down beside Bastet without saying anything, and I took the position Bastet indicated for me, wrapping my arms around Aurelia as she leaned against my chest. Bastet lifted Aurelia's gown to her knees and she and Philippa peered under it. I could see that the gown was indeed as wet as if Aurelia had plunged into a pool. As another wave of pain swept over her, she cried out and gripped my arms so hard I feared she might break them.

"That's good, my lady," Bastet cooed. "Very good."

"I see a head!" Philippa squealed.

"That's good," Bastet said. "It's going to be a normal birth. Child, you're going to have to take the baby when she comes out. With this wound, my arm is weak. I'm afraid I might drop her. I just wish we had something to wrap her in." Philippa glanced at the head scarf Bastet wore and the Nubian put her hand to her head and began unwinding the cloth. "It's the cleanest thing we have."

My mouth fell open when I saw her bare head. She had only tufts of hair, with long scars between them.

"When I was captured," she said without meeting my eyes, "Roman soldiers, after doing what they do to women, amused themselves by taking the jewels out of my crown, turning it upside down on my head, and twisting it back and forth. My lord Calpurnius was their tribune, but he was away from the camp at that time and had no control over them. In his remorse, he took me as his only spoils of the battle."

She folded the cloth and handed it to Philippa. "Get ready, child. We don't want this baby to fall to the ground. Now, my lady, push as hard as you can."

†

"Did you really promise Calpurnius that you would marry her?" Aurelia asked as she cradled her daughter in her arms. The baby was still wrapped in Bastet's colorful scarf.

"Yes, he did promise," Tacitus said, "in front of a witness. I intend to hold him to it."

Aurelia managed a slight laugh, the first sign of any emotion except the grief she had been expressing for Calpurnius. "How odd it will be to have you as my son-in-law."

"Well, there is the complication of the woman I'm engaged to," I reminded them.

"And the further complication," Aurelia said, "of the woman you're really in love with."

We were resting and recovering after the most exhausting morning I could remember. And I wasn't the one who gave birth to a child—a fairly easy birth, according to Bastet. And it wasn't just the baby that came out. To think that was what my mother had gone through to bring me into the world. I would never look at her the same way again. I wasn't sure I would ever look at any woman the same way again. There's a good reason why this sort of thing is confined to the women's part of the house.

Philippa had told us what happened after we went into the tunnel. Sychaeus and the other man, accompanied by a woman, took her by surprise. Sychaeus wanted to kill her but the woman wouldn't let him. Instead she tied Philippa up. Sychaeus didn't want the woman to go into the tunnel with them because of her foot. He was afraid she couldn't move fast enough. Once the men were in the tunnel, Philippa tripped the woman and broke away from her. She was sorry she hadn't gotten to us sooner, but she had fallen several times because her hands were tied behind her back.

I knew already that I would not make any inquiries about the family that had owned her and her father before the eruption. Her freedom would be a small reward for all she had done for us and endured from us.

"Do you think you can make it back to the *raeda?*" I asked Aurelia. I wasn't even sure the carriage would still be there. Canthara might have driven it off. What had become of the driver? Since he'd made no effort to warn us or help us, I feared the worst for him.

"I believe so," Aurelia said. "I'll have to at some point, and it might as well be now. Can you carry Calpurnia so I can lean on you?"

I took the baby in my arms and Aurelia slipped her arm through mine.

"She is a beautiful child," I said. "If she turns out to be half as beautiful and charming as her mother, the wait will be worth it."

Tacitus walked with Philippa as his guide. He was complaining of not seeing clearly, probably as a result of having his head bashed against the wall. Instead of taking us over the ruins of the house—which would have been the shorter route—I led the party straight up to the road and then turned toward the *raeda*. It was still there, but the driver's dead body lay in the road. We placed him in the *raeda* and covered him with a blanket.

"I guess I'll drive," I said.

"You'll have to," Tacitus said. "I can't handle four horses."

"But, my lord," Philippa said, "there are only two."

"Gaius Pliny," Aurelia said, "I wish you could ride in the back with me."

I put a hand on Philippa's shoulder. "I need you to be Tacitus' eyes, and he will be your strength. Between the two of you, driving slowly, I think we can make it back to the villa. We'll get some men and get back down here to—"

Aurelia patted my arm. "You don't need to give me false hope, Gaius Pliny. I know my husband is dead. There's no way anyone could have survived down there. It would take weeks—possibly months—just to get back to where he was hiding."

"But shouldn't we try?" I knew there was no real hope, but I wanted to keep Aurelia's spirits up.

"We would only risk injury or death to others. I'm glad I got to see him and let him know that I love him. I just hope he died quickly and that Sychaeus was left to a lingering death. Am I horrible for thinking that?"

XXI

TACITUS WAS TOO GROGGY to ride into Naples with me and several servants, shortly after midday. I left the servants with the horses a block away from Plautia's *insula* with orders to come running at the first sound of trouble. Knowing Sychaeus wouldn't be there, I didn't expect any problem. When I saw that the door of the book shop was open I stood quietly in it for a moment, in awe again at the number of scrolls in the shop. Could it be two thousand or more?

Plautia looked up from the scroll she was correcting. Except for a quick intake of breath she displayed remarkable calm. She said nothing for a moment, re-evaluating her situation, I suspected.

"Why, Gaius Pliny," she finally said, "I didn't expect to see you again. I thought we concluded that we had no further business to discuss."

"You mask your surprise well." I stepped into the shop. "Seeing me here must be quite a shock, considering that you must have believed I was dead."

She cocked her head. "Why would I think that?"

"Because you didn't believe anyone could have survived the collapse of the ash over Calpurnius' house. That's why you're still here, instead of taking flight. You thought that everyone who knew what you'd done was dead."

"I have no idea what you're talking about." Her hands shook as she rolled up the scroll.

"I'm in no mood to bandy words. You were there, with Sychaeus and another man. Philippa told us."

Plautia shoved the scroll into a cloth bag. "Sychaeus wanted to kill that brat. I should have let him."

242

"The fact that you spared her is the main reason I didn't bring Novatus and his guards with me to arrest you."

"Arrest me? On what charge?"

"Blackmail and murder."

"Ridiculous. You have no proof of anything."

"I have Sychaeus' confession, in front of witnesses, that you told him to kill Calpurnius' servant woman."

"And where are those witnesses?"

"They are at Aurelia's villa." On this point she had the upper hand. Tacitus had been only half-conscious when Sychaeus admitted to the murder, and Bastet's testimony would not be accepted unless she was tortured first, which I would never permit. Given Aurelia's state of mind at that time and the fact that she was a woman, any good advocate could discredit her testimony—I certainly could.

"Where is Sychaeus? Can he corroborate what you say?"

"Sychaeus is buried in the ruins of the house along with Calpurnius."

Her voice softened. "But you've risen from the ashes, it seems. And I thought the Phoenix was only a legend."

"You don't seem surprised—or distraught—to hear that Sychaeus is dead."

"As you say, let's not bandy words." She turned on her stool to face me. "I heard the noise, felt the earth shake, and saw the ash collapsing and dust blowing up the shaft. I could only assume that everyone down there was dead. As a slave, one learns that things are beyond one's control. Being freed doesn't erase that lesson. There was nothing I could do, so I left. How did you get out?"

"There was another entrance. We got out just before it collapsed, too."

"So that brings us back to the question of why you're here."

"You may be right that I can't prove anything against you, but we both know what you did and you're going to have to make that right, as far as you can."

"How do I do that? I can't bring Calpurnius back to life, or my brother. By the way, I reject your claim that he is not my brother." She stacked several loose pieces of papyrus.

"We all make ourselves happy with our delusions. Yours don't

matter to me. What does matter to me is some degree of justice for
Aurelia and her child."

"So the bitch whelped? That must have been exciting." She met my
eyes, daring me to react to the insult.

I clenched my fists. I could not let her make me angry, nor could
I strike a woman. "You and your—and Sychaeus—have left Aurelia
nearly destitute. In return for my not bringing a charge against you,
you are going to repay her the money that Calpurnius paid you in
blackmail."

"You can't prove that I had any connection to the blackmail or to
the murder of Amalthea."

"You know her name. I didn't tell you that."

She stumbled and caught herself. "Sychaeus must…must have
mentioned it. Killing her was all his idea."

"That's not what he said."

"Bring him in here. Let's hear his testimony."

I stepped toward her and tapped my finger on her table. "The blackmail payments were dropped off here."

She shrugged. "One of my scribes could have been collecting them.
I'm not here every moment the shop is open."

"The letter you used for the blackmail was written in Greek, which
Sychaeus couldn't read, and it was taken from Aelius' library, to which
Sychaeus did not have access. Aelius trained you from childhood to
work with him there. He spared your life when you were born."

Plautia looked at her foot, twisting it back and forth. "He was a
kind man, even if he was a fool. From the way he doted on me and
gave in to anything I asked for, you'd have thought he was my father."

I must have hesitated an instant too long.

"He was my father, wasn't he?" she said. "You know it."

"Yes, he was your father." That bit of information didn't really matter. It was her mother's identity that I would not reveal.

"I sometimes heard whispers among the servants. I asked him once
who my father was. All he said was that that secret had died with my
mother." She got up and returned a scroll to a niche. Even with her
limp, I would have to describe her movement as somewhat graceful.
Like Capsius, she had learned to compensate for her abnormality.

"So, you suspected he was your father, and yet you seized on the first opportunity you got to betray him. Did you inform on him to Domitian?"

"No. I never got the chance. I think his wife, that whore Longina, nagged him to do it."

She considered her father a fool and her mother a whore. The irony of that gave me some satisfaction.

"I had to settle for punishing Calpurnius," she continued with venom, "for trading my brother for a horse."

"And that brings us back to the money. I've studied Calpurnius' financial records. I know how much property he sold in order to pay your blackmail demands. I want you to give that money back to Aurelia."

"And what if I refuse?"

"The arena has an insatiable demand for victims. No matter how long it takes, I will see that you end up there."

"How much money do you think Calpurnius paid us?"

"At least four hundred thousand *sesterces*."

She raised her eyebrows. "Enough to qualify a man for the equestrian order. If I pay that, you're going to leave me with nothing."

"I'm not going to leave you with blood money you've extorted from Calpurnius and Aurelia."

"You nobles are all alike." Her voice dropped to a snarl. "Have you made your money any more honestly than I have? How much money did your ancestors extort from the provinces where they were governors? You can't bear to see someone rise to equal you."

"Having money doesn't make you my equal."

She looked at her ink-stained fingers. "Once a slave, always a slave, is that it?"

"No. Once a scoundrel, always a scoundrel."

She stood and drew herself up to her full height. "Gaius Pliny, I don't have all the money that Calpurnius paid us. I bought Sychaeus' freedom, and there are expenses involved in keeping this place up. I could pay…two hundred thousand *sesterces*."

I knew she was lying. She must have had a considerable sum of money set aside, but I couldn't get access to her financial records to prove it. I had to get as much for Aurelia and Calpurnia as I could while I had some leverage. "I'll settle for three hundred thousand, and you're going to deed this *insula* and all its contents over to Aurelia."

She laughed. "I'm not going to *give* her the place."

"The government will confiscate it when you're arrested. You'll get nothing then."

She sat down and studied my face. "I almost believe you, Gaius Pliny. Why are you so determined to punish me?"

"You have harmed people I love. If you don't already know the meaning of the words 'implacable enemy,' you soon will."

"Are you going to hound me like the Furies for the rest of my life?"

I nodded slowly. "Your only escape from me is to make restitution to Aurelia and then get away from here, as far and as fast as you can. I would recommend Alexandria. It's a large city, where you could become whomever you choose. Perhaps even rise from the ashes, like the Phoenix."

A faint smile played on her lips. "All right, then. I'll send the money to Aurelia this evening."

"No. You'll bring it to her and apologize to her face."

"What?" She slapped the table.

"And you'll bring the deed to this place, made out to Aurelia, with your signature and whatever seal you use on it."

"You keep adding to your demands. I might be better off just to take my chances with the Furies."

"I've given you my final conditions. In return, in spite of all the evidence I could marshal against you, I'm willing to forgo a prosecution as long as you disappear from Naples."

"That's what puzzles me," Plautia said. "You have this over-inflated sense of protecting others of your class—what you call justice—and yet you don't want to prosecute me, in spite of all I've done. There must be something else behind that decision."

Of course there was something else. I wasn't sure I had enough evidence to convict her, especially of the murder of Amalthea. Bringing her into court would make her into a public figure. Someone might find out that she was a descendant of Augustus. As things now stood, she was just one more former slave who could lose herself in a place like Alexandria, where Romans, Greeks, Jews, Egyptians, and peoples from the farthest reaches of the world mingled. It wasn't an entirely satisfactory resolution—nothing short of bringing Calpurnius back to life would be—but it would have to do.

"Those are the conditions. I'll see you before dark tonight."

As I walked out the door, she called after me, "Can I expect to be invited to dine with you?"

†

Emancipation ceremonies can be festive occasions for an entire household. Given the death of Calpurnius, however, we decided to make Thamyras' manumission ritual brief, with only Tacitus, Aurelia, Bastet, and myself in attendance. We might have put the entire thing off for a few days if Thamyras' son had not arrived at about the ninth hour, sooner than we expected, in the care of the two servants I'd sent to purchase him and bring him back. The boy was frightened and needed some reassurance.

He found comfort from a source I would never have anticipated. When Philippa came out to tend the horses, the boy took an instant liking to her, clinging to her tunic and staying in her shadow. She must have reminded him of the nurse he'd had back in Puteoli. Girls of Philippa's age are often assigned the task of caring for the younger children in a house. It frees the older servant women for heavier work and prepares the girls for their roles as mothers.

"Why don't you let the regular groomsman tend to the horses?" I told her. "It looks like you're needed here for the moment."

She looked at the boy as though he was some exotic animal that ought to be on display in the arena. "What should I do with him, my lord?"

"Show him around the stables and the grounds. I don't think it much matters as long as he's with you. We'll call you shortly when we've got Thamyras ready."

Thamyras must have known something was afoot. He'd been told to clean himself up and present himself to his mistress in the garden. Aurelia was seated in a shady corner, the least damaged part of the garden, with Calpurnia in her arms. Bastet, with one arm in a sling, sat beside her, a different but still magnificent scarf wound around her head. She seemed unable to take her eyes off the baby. Tacitus and I stood behind Aurelia.

Head bowed, Thamyras stood in front of Aurelia, uncertain exactly what was about to transpire. He glanced at the shrubbery on either side of her, probably planning how he would trim it when all of this business—whatever it was—was over.

"Thamyras," Aurelia began, "this day has brought sorrow and joy to our house. My husband, whom you served so faithfully for so many years, died this morning." She paused to collect herself and hold Calpurnia a little closer. "And yet we've been blessed with the birth of his child."

Dropping to one knee, Thamyras looked at the ground as he spoke. "My lady, I don't know the words to tell you how grieved I am and yet how happy for you at the same time."

Aurelia fought back tears. "Thank you. It is a…difficult time…for us all. But it will be a day of joy…for you." Unable to go on, she looked up at me.

I stepped out from behind Aurelia's chair and handed a sheet of papyrus to the kneeling slave. "This is the certificate of your manumission. Thamyras, you are now a free man. It is the lady Aurelia's hope that you will remain here as a part of her household, but you may decide what you want to do."

Thamyras looked at the document like an initiate who's just been given the darkest secret of some mystery cult. He mumbled as he read what it said, then looked up at us. "My lord, my lady…I don't know what to say except thank you. Thank you." He fell forward and kissed Aurelia's feet. "You know I will do anything for you. If you're willing, I would like to stay here."

"We would be happy for you to stay," Aurelia said, wiping her eyes. "Now, it is the custom to give a servant a gift when he is freed."

"Oh, my lady, that isn't necessary. You've given me the greatest gift I could ever hope for."

"You may think differently about that in a moment. Philippa, dear! Come on in."

Philippa and the boy had been sitting in the nearest room off the garden, with the door partly open. Philippa had kept him quiet by telling him they were playing a game, seeing how long they could hide without being found. I guess the honeycakes she'd been feeding him had also helped pacify him. She now stepped into the garden, with her charge clinging to her leg. Thamyras' face showed utter confusion.

"Thamyras, this is your son," Aurelia said. "Proxena's boy."

"My…son? How could it be?"

"Proxena was bearing your child when she was sold."

Philippa led the boy to his father and joined their hands.

"And this," I said, handing the speechless man another piece of papyrus, "is his certificate of manumission."

†

As darkness came on, Tacitus and I looked up the road toward Naples. "She should have been here by now," I said.

"You put a lot of trust in someone who hasn't shown that she deserves an iota of it."

Before I could think of a rejoinder—if one were possible—a pair of riders accompanying a wagon appeared around a bend in the road. They weren't in any real hurry.

"That doesn't look like a woman on either horse," Tacitus said, canceling the sense of relief I had felt at first. "Or driving the wagon."

We waited in silence until the riders pulled up in front of Aurelia's house. One of them was Capsius.

"What's the meaning of this?" I demanded. "Where is Plautia?"

"She sends her regrets, sir," Capsius said, "along with the money you demanded and the deed to the *insula*." He pointed to a large chest in the wagon.

I grabbed the reins of his horse. "This is not acceptable. I told her that she had to come down here herself. That was an important condition of our agreement."

"I'm sorry, sir. I am only doing as I was ordered. She did send this." Capsius took a piece of papyrus from a leather pouch on a cord around his neck and handed it to me. It was folded and sealed and addressed to Gaius Plinius Caecilius Secundus. All four of my names—a touch of sarcasm, I thought, apparently a specialty of hers. I opened it and read: *Gaius Pliny, your suggestion inspired me. The Phoenix must have ashes from which to rise.*

"By the gods!" Tacitus said. "She wouldn't—"

"Get me a horse!" I grabbed the first servant I saw and pushed him toward the stables. "Two horses. At once."

In a few moments that felt like hours Philippa led two horses to us, bridled and ready to ride. Tacitus and I mounted, and Capsius and his companion turned their horses to accompany us. The man driving the wagon was left to unload the chest with the help of some of Aurelia's servants.

"Guard that with your lives," I told the servants, "but don't open it.

Have Diomedes lock it up in the storeroom. Tell your lady I'll explain when I get back."

"Where are we going?" Capsius asked.

"Just ride!" I told him, digging my heels into my horse's flanks.

Even before we got to the south gate of Naples we could see the flames stretching into the sky. Our horses refused to go the last two blocks, and we couldn't have gotten through the crowd anyway. The *insula* was fully ablaze and sending sparks flying in all directions. Men on the roofs of neighboring buildings were dousing embers as they landed. People leaned out the windows of the burning *insula*, begging for help. Novatus and his *vigiles* had given up trying to put out the fire and were concentrating on getting what few ladders they had up to people who were trapped.

"There are hundreds of people in there," I said, hardly able to look at the disaster. "They'll never get to all of them in time."

In their desperation some people dared to run down the stairs. A few staggered out into the street, their clothes and hair in flames. Bystanders threw water on them or smothered the fire in blankets. Others never got that far. Their dying screams and the crashing of the staircases were the only testimony to their effort.

Novatus paused beside us and took a drink of water.

"How did this happen?" I asked him.

"The fire started in the book shop. It looks like someone spread oil on the steps and anywhere else there was wood. Nobody had any warning. They were getting ready for supper." He ran a hand over his smoke-stained face. "Two rooms full of papyrus documents and those wooden stairs and floors—the place was an inferno before we could get here."

I looked around at the crowd of people watching the "entertainment" that a fire always provides. They were urging the trapped people to jump. The spectators didn't seem to understand that they could as easily be the ones in the building. No one made any effort to help.

"Don't just stand there!" I yelled. "Those are your friends and neighbors. Do something."

"What can we do, sir?" one woman said. "We'd have to risk our own lives to go in there."

Tacitus pulled me into the rear of the crowd. "There's nothing anyone can do, Gaius Pliny. Sometimes we just have to accept what's happened."

"This didn't 'happen.' Somebody *did* it." I began looking around.

"Are you looking for someone in particular?" Tacitus asked.

"Yes, a woman with a misshapen foot."

"Surely you don't think she's still here."

"I don't doubt it for a moment. To get the full satisfaction from this, she would have to see me looking at it and know how much it hurts me—to think that I goaded her to do this."

An ominous creak emanated from the *insula*, growing louder until the building collapsed in on itself. The screams of the dying as well as the excited shouts of the spectators were drowned by the roar.

Putting my hands over my ears to block out as much of the sound as I could, I turned away from the sight. Tacitus put his arms around me and held me to his chest. Plautia would learn the meaning of "implacable enemy," I vowed to myself.

XXII

SADLY, THE *JUPITER* wasn't available for our return trip. The current commander of the fleet at Misenum had sent Decius and his crew to investigate a problem with pirates off the coast of Sicily, so we had to book passage on a commercial ship. Even though it took a day and a half, the trip wasn't as bad as I feared it might be.

Our ride on horseback from Ostia back to Rome was almost leisurely. We still had two days before the Ides, giving me ample time to go over my speech for Pompeia's case. I was thinking about rewriting it *de novo*, now that I knew I would be facing Regulus. I was determined to make the man pay for his hubristic error in giving up a victory by default just so he could seize an opportunity to humble me.

"Arrogant ass," I muttered.

"Got Regulus on your mind again?" Tacitus asked.

I nodded. It was a relief to have anything on my mind other than the horrible scene of that collapsing *insula* and the people trapped in the flames. The last two nights I had slept only after reaching a point of utter exhaustion, and my sleep was restless, bringing no relief to mind or body. Tacitus kept reassuring me—and I knew it with some part of my mind—that I was not responsible. Plautia did it because she was an evil, uncaring person, the same reason that she had ordered Sychaeus to kill Amalthea. One victim or hundreds, the blame lay on her and her indifference to other human beings.

But who would make her pay for her crime? Novatus and his men had searched as much of Naples as they could. It was an empty gesture. She wasn't in the city any longer, I was sure. She had the money

252

to go wherever she chose, even after paying Aurelia the full sum I had demanded, I guess because she thought that would make me leave her alone. What frustrated me was that she could be tracked. Her foot was not an easy thing to hide. Someone, somewhere, would inevitably notice her. But how could I learn of it? They wouldn't know the evil they were looking at. They would probably just pity her because of her deformity.

We had sent a servant ahead as soon as we got off the boat, and since we weren't rushing, my household would have about an hour's advance notice of my arrival. As we entered the Ostian Gate, Tacitus said his good-byes and turned to his own house.

"I hope Julia is feeling better," I said.

"I'm afraid the loss of the child will be with her for a long time, as it has been with your mother all these years." As he and his servants started up the street to his house he called over his shoulder, "Let me know how the plans for your wedding are progressing."

He might as well have slapped me in the face. The prospect of confronting Regulus in court was one I could deal with, even look forward to. I knew I had the oratorical ability to stand toe-to-toe with him. The prospect of confronting the fifteen-year-old girl who was supposed to become my wife made me want to turn around and ride to…anywhere but home. I had no confidence in my ability to be a husband to a woman I did not love.

And there was the question of Aurora. Or rather the questions of Aurora. Would I find her at home? If so, where had she been? If not, where was she now? Would I have to go looking for her? Could I punish her if I had to?

That last question I could answer. The rest were as unclear to me as the waters of the Tiber after they've been roiled by a storm.

†

When Demetrius opened the door and welcomed me home, the first thing I saw was my mother waiting in the atrium, huddled with Naomi. The door was hardly closed behind me when Mother assailed me. There was no other word for the manner in which she approached me. Naomi trailed after her, as powerless to rein her in as a groomsman chasing a runaway horse.

"There you are," Mother said in the voice she usually reserved for scolding a delinquent servant. "It's time you returned. Long past time, for that matter."

"Good day, Mother. I'm happy to see you, too." I leaned in and kissed her on the cheek.

"Don't get sarcastic with me, Gaius. You have responsibilities here, and you've been evading them. Pompeia Celerina and Livia will arrive at any moment."

"Already? I've hardly set foot in the house." Something was clearly bothering her. Something that she considered serious.

"I sent for them as soon as the servant that you sent told us you were on your way from Ostia. We've got to get the plans for the wedding settled."

"You mean *you've* got to get the plans settled. I see no need at all to rush."

Mother wrung her hands. "Now that we've announced the engagement, Pompeia is concerned that people will begin to talk if the wedding doesn't take place soon. They'll think something is wrong with Livia."

"Tell them something is wrong with me." I sat on a bench beside the *impluvium* and accepted a cup of wine from a servant, who then scampered away. As I glanced around, I thought the atrium seemed oddly quiet and deserted. The servants, I suspected, had gone to their hidey-holes, like animals taking shelter before a storm. Only Demetrius and Naomi were brave enough to face whatever was coming.

"Is there something wrong with you?" Mother asked. "Is that why you spend so much time with Tacitus?"

I stopped in mid-drink. "What—"

"I've recently heard stories about that man—vile, disgusting stories. I might believe you were like that if I didn't know you were in love with that servant girl." She jerked her head toward the servants' quarters.

Standing up, I took a step toward her, my eyes narrowing. "How can you know how I feel when I don't even know?"

"I'm your mother, and I won't have it." She shook her finger at me. "If you think I'm going to let you carry on with that…trollop, the way my brother did with her mother—"

I slammed my cup to the floor, shattering it and splattering wine on my mother's feet. "If you *ever* refer to her again with that word—or in that tone—I will move you as far from Rome and as far away from me as I possibly can. Don't force me to make a choice, Mother."

Demetrius cleared his throat behind us. "My lord, my lady, the lady Pompeia Celerina and the lady Livia have arrived. Shall I show them in?"

"I'll let you greet your guests," I told my mother. "Demetrius, I need you! I'll be in the library."

When Demetrius and I had some privacy, I asked, "Do you know where Aurora is?"

"She's in her room, my lord."

"In her room?" That was the last answer I'd expected.

"Yes, my lord. She returned last night."

"Last night? Where had she been?"

"She refused to tell us, my lord. She said she would talk only with you."

I ran my hand over the scrolls that lay on the table—the book Martial had given me, a book of Livy which Phineas seemed to be copying. "I can only imagine how my mother reacted to that."

Demetrius looked down, then back up at me. "No, my lord, you can't."

"What do you mean?"

"Your mother…slapped her, my lord, and told me to put her in chains."

"You didn't—"

"No, my lord. I knew you would take a whip to me if I did. I locked her in her room. I hope you'll forgive me, but I had to keep peace with your mother."

I looked at Demetrius with a new appreciation for a man who, every day of his life, had to navigate a narrow, often treacherous, channel between two powerful forces. Perhaps it would be better for everyone if Mother lived in one of my other houses—at least for a while.

"Will you talk to the ladies now, my lord?"

"Not just yet. Give me the key to Aurora's room."

"I'll get it, my lord."

As he left the room I heard my mother's voice and Demetrius' reply. "He'll be with you in a few moments, my lady. Why don't you wait in the *exhedra*. It's such a pleasant day. I'll have some food and drink brought to you."

Clever of him, I thought. That would keep me out of their sight when I went to Aurora's room. The man had developed more of an ability to manipulate us than I had realized.

As soon as Demetrius handed me the key, I hurried to Aurora's room, taking the stairs off the atrium two at a time. I unlocked the door and called her name. When she responded, I opened the door and found her sitting on her bed, her legs drawn up and her arms clasped around her knees. She was still wearing the robe in which she'd disguised herself for her trip to Ostia and the dark makeup she had applied, though it was beginning to smear. Her hair hadn't been washed or combed in days.

She was the most beautiful woman I'd ever seen.

"My lord." She bowed her head. The warmth I was accustomed to hearing in her voice was gone. And whose fault was that? "What do you want, my lord?"

You, I thought. I sat in the chair beside her bed. She should have stood when her master came into the room, but I knew we were far beyond such niceties.

"I want to know where you've been the past few days and why you didn't come straight home from Ostia. You know, the penalty for a runaway slave—"

"I didn't run away. After we…talked in Ostia I started back to Rome." Her eyes pleaded with me. "Don't you understand? I came back."

I did understand, but I couldn't let myself admit what it meant— for her, for me, for us. "I came back, too."

"You had to."

"You would have suffered a great deal if you hadn't come back."

"You're suffering because you did come back." Now I felt the warmth returning, like a fire that grows from fanning just a few embers.

I drew my chair closer to the bed and took her hand. "It was already dark when you left Ostia. Someone could have attacked you."

"I didn't care. I didn't care about much of anything at that point." She shook her head and ran her fingers through her hair, as I longed to do.

I hung my head, unable to say anything, unable to feel anything except the ache in my heart. I'd had the chance to tell her how I felt and had let it slip away. No, it hadn't slipped away. I had thrown it away.

"I was riding hard," she went on, "not paying attention to anything around me, when I heard someone call for help."

"Please tell me you didn't stop. It could have been a trap." But I knew she had. And part of me was glad she wanted to help. It's what those heartless people in Naples should have done.

"Of course I stopped. That's what you and I have always done." She squeezed my hand.

"Who needed help?"

"A woman with a child. She said her husband had gone missing. She knew where he was headed when he left home, but no one had seen or heard of him for several days. They were on the road, looking for him."

"What did you do?"

"I got them a room in an inn and tried to find some trace of the man, without any luck. You had the Tyche ring. After a few days I came home to see if you were here yet and if you could—"

"Gaius! Gaius!" My mother's voice rang through the atrium and up the stairs. "Where are you? As if I didn't know."

I put my hands on my legs and lowered my head, then looked back up at Aurora. "I want to hear all of that story. But now I have to talk to Pompeia Celerina about her case."

"And about your marriage to her daughter," Aurora said softly, patting my arm.

Thinking about her lips, I kissed her on the forehead. "Well, yes, there is that, too."

CAST OF CHARACTERS

Unless otherwise indicated, numbers in parentheses refer to Pliny's letters (e. g., 6.16 means book 6, letter 16). The letters are available in a Penguin translation by Betty Radice. The older translation by William Melmoth is on the Internet, but it is cumbersome and severely dated. Selected letters appear on various websites. Unless otherwise indicated, all dates are A.D.

HISTORICAL PERSONS

Aelius Lamia His name really was Lucius Aelius Plautius Lamia Aelianus. (Try putting that on a name tag at the family reunion.) He was married to Domitia Longina, a descendant of Augustus, until Domitian took her away from him in 69/70. He was executed at either the beginning or the end of Domitian's reign (81 or 96). Scholars can't seem to decide which. For the purposes of this story the earlier date worked better.

Agricola Gnaeus Julius Agricola, father-in-law of Tacitus. He does not appear in this book, but he is mentioned several times as a symbol of opposition to Domitian. He solidified the Roman conquest of Britain in the early 80s and aroused the envy and suspicion of Domitian. Agricola plays a significant role in the second book in this series, *The Blood of Caesar*. Tacitus reports the rumor that Agricola was poisoned: "We have no definite evidence. That is all I can say for certain." He died in 93.

Calpurnia Pliny's third (or perhaps second) wife appears only as an infant in this book. The question of how many wives Pliny had arises from his statement to the emperor Trajan that he had "married twice" (10.2). But was that written before or after he married Calpurnia? We do not know the names of any other wives. Calpurnia was raised by her grandfather, Calpurnius Fabatus, and her aunt, Calpurnia Hispulla, a friend of Pliny's mother. We know nothing about the parents of Pliny's wife, except that her father's name would have been Calpurnius.

Calpurnius Fabatus Grandfather of Pliny's wife, Calpurnia, and a native of Comum, Pliny's home town. Tacitus (*Annals* 16.8) says that Calpurnius Fabatus was accused of participating in, or knowing about, crimes of adultery and magic involving Nero's aunt, Junia Lepida, but the case was never prosecuted. Pliny writes a letter to Fabatus promising to make repairs to Fabatus' villa in Campania (6.30), and writes moving letters to Fabatus and to Calpurnia Hispulla, after his wife Calpurnia suffered a miscarriage (8.10; 8.11). Fabatus lived to be quite old. The penultimate letter in Pliny's collection informs Trajan that Pliny used the imperial post to send his wife home from the province of Bithynia when her grandfather died (112/113).

Domitia Longina The wife, first of Aelius Lamia, then of the emperor Domitian, who took her from Aelius during the turmoil of the Year of the Four Emperors and married her in 69/70. As the first dynasty after the Julio–Claudians, Domitian and his family—the Flavians— needed some way to legitimize their rule. Longina was the great-great-great-great-granddaughter of Augustus, so her children would be descendants of that first dynasty. She lived at least twenty-five years after Domitian's death in 96 and continued to refer to herself as "Domitia, wife of Domitian," even though he had suffered *damnatio memoriae* by the Senate.

Domitian Emperor 81–96, younger son of Vespasian (69–79) and brother of Titus (79–81). He may not have been as bad an emperor as Pliny and Tacitus would have us believe, but he did show a tendency toward paranoia and had people executed or exiled on the slightest suspicion of plotting against him. The biographer Suetonius says Domitian lamented that no one would believe an emperor's claim of plots against his life until he was murdered (*Domitian* 21). He was assassinated in September of 96. He is a significant character in my historical novel *The Flute Player*, an e-book.

Fabia Second wife of Aelius Lamia. Nothing else is known about her.

Martial Marcus Valerius Martialis was one of the most popular poets of the 80s and early 90s. His witty, often salacious, epigrams survive today in fourteen books. When Roman society became more puritanical after the death of Domitian (96), Martial's poetry fell out of favor and he returned to his native Spain. Pliny gave him travel money and complimented his poetry. He expresses his sadness over Martial's death and his appreciation of the epigrams, especially one (10.19) in which Martial flattered Pliny, but there is no evidence of any close connection between them (3.21). Martial is a major character in *The Flute Player*, in which Pliny also appears.

Plinia Mother of Pliny the Younger and sister of Pliny the Elder. Pliny mentions her in the letters he writes to Tacitus about the eruption of Vesuvius (6.16; 6.20), but we know little else about her. She is referred to in the past tense in 4.19, which was written ca. 101–104, so scholars assume she was dead by then.

Regulus Marcus Aquilius Regulus, a legal advocate and informer whom Pliny loathes. Informers (*delatores*) had networks of spies in the homes of the wealthy and reported even the most innocuous comments to the emperor. They were rewarded handsomely. The only sympathy Pliny could muster for the man was when his son died. "Even Regulus did not deserve that," Pliny said (4.2). When Regulus died, Pliny told a friend he "did well to die, and would have done better to die sooner" (6.2). The elder Pliny held Regulus in contempt, so the animosity between Regulus and the Pliny family had a long history. That antagonism is a major element in *The Flute Player*.

Tacitus Cornelius Tacitus, whose first name (*praenomen*) may have been Publius or Gaius, but we aren't certain. Like Pliny, he was from a wealthy family from either northern Italy or southern France. He was one of the leading orators of Rome in the 90s. He survived Domitian's reign, but Domitian's attack on the Senate left him with an abiding hatred of Rome's imperial system. His *Annals* and *Histories* cover the period from Augustus' death to the death of Domitian (14–96), though large chunks are now missing. He also wrote shorter works on oratory, on the Germans, and a biography of his father-in-law, Gnaeus Julius Agricola. His request for information about the eruption of Mt. Vesuvius in 79 prompted Pliny to write two of his most famous letters describing that catastrophe. Pliny's collection contains a number of letters to Tacitus.

FICTIONAL CHARACTERS

Aurelia A young woman whom Pliny met and rescued in the first book in this series, *All Roads Lead to Murder*. Now the wife of Calpurnius, she is about seventeen, a typical age for Roman girls to be married. (Pliny later married Calpurnia when she was about fifteen.) Aurelia's name means "golden-haired." The Romans prized blond hair so much that they shaved the heads of captive German women to make blond wigs.

Aurora Pliny's slave, and for my purposes, the love of his life. In his letters Pliny comes across as a rather straitlaced type, but Roman aristocrats often had relationships with slave women or freedwomen in their households.

Bastet Calpurnius' slave. Bastet is an ancient Nubian name. Nubia lay on the southern border of the Roman province of Egypt. The incident of decapitating a statue of Augustus referred to in Chapter XIII actually happened. Nubian slaves were highly prized in Rome.

Canthara/Plautia Unacknowledged daughter of Aelius Lamia and Domitia Longina. Aelius raised her as a slave and finally emancipated her.

Capsius Scribe with an oddly shaped left hand. Missing a thumb and little finger, he has only three fingers, giving the appearance of the Greek letter ψ (*psi*). Instead of putting him out to die, his father created a name with *-psi-* in the middle of it. The "p" in *psi* is pronounced here, so his name becomes "CAP-see-us."

Decius Captain of the trireme *Jupiter*, the ship on which Pliny the Elder set out to rescue survivors from the eruption of Mt. Vesuvius. Not all ships in the ancient world had names, but enough did that I felt comfortable christening this one.

Naomi A Jewish slave who is the close confidante of Pliny's mother. She is also the mother of Phineas. Both are important characters in the second Pliny mystery, *The Blood of Caesar*.

Novatus Commander of the *vigiles* in one district in Naples. Cf. *vigiles* in the Glossary of Terms.

Phineas Pliny's scribe and son of Naomi.

Thamyras A servant of Calpurnius, born and raised in the house. The term for such slaves was *vernae*, from which we get the word "vernacular," a dialect used in one's own home town, or something that is native or indigenous to an area.

GLOSSARY OF TERMS

amicitia Latin for friendship. Upper-class Romans extended an *official* recognition of friendship to certain persons, recognizing an obligation to assist them and expecting to be able to call on them in a time of need.

atrium The front part of a Roman house (*domus*). It consisted of rooms arranged around a pool (*impluvium*) which was originally used to collect rain water through the roof opening. The atrium was the business part of a house, where a wealthy man met his clients each morning.

calendar From the word "Kalends," the Latin name for the first day of a month. The Romans used the same names for the months that we do, but counted the days in relation to the Kalends, the Nones, and the Ides. The Nones was approximately the eighth day of a month and the Ides was the thirteenth or fifteenth, depending on the month. After the Kalends, all dates were given as "before the Nones." After the Nones, all dates were given as "before the Ides." After the Ides, dates were given as "before the Kalends" of the next month.

client From a Latin word meaning to lean or rely on someone. A wealthy Roman (patron) took on as many clients as he could afford, since they were a visible measure of his standing. His *clientela* were expected to come to the patron's house each morning at dawn to greet him, receive a small daily allowance, and accompany him as he went to the Forum.

exhedra Given how warm the climate of Italy can be for much of the year, the Romans created outdoor eating areas, especially in the southern part of Italy. These alcoves were usually on the back wall of a garden. The ones in Pompeii and Herculaneum have concrete sloped benches for diners to recline on around three sides, with an opening on the fourth side where servants brought in food.

hours The Romans divided the day into twelve segments, called *horae*. As the length of the day varied with the seasons, the length of an hour would vary. Even with water-clocks and sundials, precision in time-keeping was impossible.

insula Large apartment house in ancient Rome and other cities in the Empire. The largest stood five stories high and housed as many as two thousand people. They were unheated and had no running water. Wealthy men often owned a number of these tenement houses, which were notorious firetraps. The Romans did not build houses with hall-ways, so one set of stairs in an *insula* would lead to part of an upper floor with a few apartments around a landing, while another set would lead to a different part of the same floor and other apartments.

latrunculus A popular board game, a mixture of chess and Othello. The objective was to surround the opponent's primary piece, the *dux* (leader).

Necropolis Since the area inside a city's walls was sacred to a god, the dead had to be buried outside the walls. The tombs could be rather large and were often shaped like houses. They lined the roads outside any city. Families often went out for picnics on the deceased's birthday or anniversary of his or her death. Messages on the tombs were often composed as though the dead person was talking to passersby. Step-ping behind one of the large monuments to relieve oneself was a common practice, as seen in the werewolf story in Petronius' *Satyricon* 62.

names Roman nomenclature, among the upper classes, was based on a man's family name (*nomen*), along with a first name (*praenomen*) and a third name (*cognomen*), e. g., Gaius Julius Caesar or Marcus Tullius Cicero. When a man was adopted into a family, he kept his biologi-cal father's *nomen* as part of his name. When Octavius was adopted by his great-uncle, he became Gaius Julius Caesar Octavianus (and eventually Augustus). Pliny's family name by birth was Caecilius, so when he was adopted by his uncle, Gaius Plinius Secundus, he became Gaius Plinius Caecilius Secundus. A woman was given a feminine form of her father's *nomen*. Any daughter born to Julius Caesar was Julia. Younger daughters were sometimes referred to as Secunda or Minor. Among the lower classes, names could vary tremendously, reflecting ethnic origin, place of birth, or numerous other factors. We are somewhat whimsical in our anglicizing of Latin names. Tacitus remains Tacitus, but Plinius becomes Pliny.

October Horse One of the least understood of Roman religious rituals. On October 15 a race was held between two chariots, each drawn by a pair of horses. The right-hand horse on the winning chariot was sacrificed to Mars. Its head was cut off and residents from two districts of Rome fought to see who would have the honor of displaying the head in their district. The tail was also cut off and the blood dripped over a sacrifice to Mars. (It is possible that "tail" is a euphemism for penis, since the tail would not have much blood in it.) The Romans did not typically sacrifice animals they didn't eat, and they did not eat horses, so this whole ritual stands out as bizarre. It was still being practiced as late as 354.

princeps This term, meaning "chief citizen," was commonly used by Pliny in his earlier letters to designate the emperor. *Imperator* was a military term. While that title was given to the emperors from the beginning of Augustus' reign, *princeps* was more of a civilian concept, helping to mask the fact that the emperors were military dictators.

raeda An enclosed four-wheeled wagon, the "station wagon" of ancient Rome.

salutatio The "morning greeting." Clients were expected to gather at their patron's home each morning to demonstrate, by their numbers, his importance. The poet Martial says he doesn't mind walking two miles to his patron's home, but it does rile him to learn that his patron isn't there that day.

sinus A toga was draped over and around the body in such a way that a "pocket" was created on the man's left side, between his arm and his ribcage. When Julius Caesar was on his way to the Senate house on the Ides of March, he was given a note warning him of the planned assassination. He dropped it into his *sinus* to read later.

slave/servant The Romans used the word *servus* to mean a slave or a free servant. Many servants were freed slaves who remained in their former master's household. I have not tried to observe a strict rule about applying "slave" or "servant" to any particular character in this novel. In Pliny's mind, Aurora, for example, was his *serva*, whatever that might mean.

taberna Obviously the origin of our "tavern," but in ancient Rome it meant any kind of shop. Many were little more than "fast-food" places with no room to sit down. Others were more like taverns. In Pompeii we find graffiti in *tabernae* recording how much customers owed, the services available from prostitutes, and other pertinent information.

Tironian notation A system of shorthand devised by Tiro, Cicero's scribe, to make it possible to take down what a person was saying as he spoke. Tiro's system used 4,000 signs. The system was modified in the Middle Ages and eventually reached 11,000 signs.

Tyche Goddess of fortune, called Fortuna by the Romans. In the Hellenistic and Roman periods the concept of fortune loomed large, as people's destinies were controlled by monarchs whom their subjects rarely saw. Temples were built to the goddess embodying the idea of luck or blind chance. The temple of Tyche in Alexandria was one of the largest in the Hellenistic world.

vigiles No ancient city had what we could consider a police or fire department. The *vigiles* (watchmen) patrolled the streets at night, primarily to awaken people and get them out of a burning building. Over time they took on the functions of a police force.

ABOUT THE AUTHOR

ALBERT A. BELL, JR. is a college history professor and novelist who lives in Michigan. He and his wife have four adult children and a grandson. In addition to his Roman mysteries, Bell has written contemporary mysteries for children and adults, as well as nonfiction. Visit him at www.albertbell.com and www.pliny-mysteries.com, and also on Facebook.

More Traditional Mysteries from Perseverance Press
For the New Golden Age

Albert A. Bell, Jr.
PLINY THE YOUNGER SERIES
Death in the Ashes
ISBN 978-1-56474-532-3

The Eyes of Aurora *(forthcoming)*
ISBN 978-1-56474-549-1

Jon L. Breen
Eye of God
ISBN 978-1-880284-89-6

Taffy Cannon
ROXANNE PRESCOTT SERIES
Guns and Roses
Agatha and Macavity awards nominee, Best Novel
ISBN 978-1-880284-34-6

Blood Matters
ISBN 978-1-880284-86-5

Open Season on Lawyers
ISBN 978-1-880284-51-3

Paradise Lost
ISBN 978-1-880284-80-3

Laura Crum
GAIL MCCARTHY SERIES
Moonblind
ISBN 978-1-880284-90-2

Chasing Cans
ISBN 978-1-880284-94-0

Going, Gone
ISBN 978-1-880284-98-8

Barnstorming
ISBN 978-1-56474-508-8

Jeanne M. Dams
HILDA JOHANSSON SERIES
Crimson Snow
ISBN 978-1-880284-79-7

Indigo Christmas
ISBN 978-1-880284-95-7

Murder in Burnt Orange
ISBN 978-1-56474-503-3

Janet Dawson
JERI HOWARD SERIES
Bit Player
Golden Nugget Award nominee
ISBN 978-1-56474-494-4

Cold Trail *(forthcoming)*
ISBN 978-1-56474-555-2

What You Wish For
ISBN 978-1-56474-518-7

Death Rides the Zephyr
ISBN 978-1-56474-530-9

Kathy Lynn Emerson
LADY APPLETON SERIES
Face Down Below the Banqueting House
ISBN 978-1-880284-71-1

Face Down Beside St. Anne's Well
ISBN 978-1-880284-82-7

Face Down O'er the Border
ISBN 978-1-880284-91-9

Elaine Flinn
MOLLY DOYLE SERIES
Deadly Vintage
ISBN 978-1-880284-87-2

Sara Hoskinson Frommer
JOAN SPENCER SERIES
Her Brother's Keeper
ISBN 978-1-56474-525-5

Hal Glatzer
KATY GREEN SERIES
Too Dead To Swing
ISBN 978-1-880284-53-7

A Fugue in Hell's Kitchen
ISBN 978-1-880284-70-4

The Last Full Measure
ISBN 978-1-880284-84-1

Margaret Grace
MINIATURE SERIES
Mix-up in Miniature
ISBN 978-1-56474-510-1

Madness in Miniature *(forthcoming)*
ISBN 978-1-56474-543-9

Wendy Hornsby
MAGGIE MACGOWEN SERIES
In the Guise of Mercy
ISBN 978-1-56474-482-1

The Paramour's Daughter
ISBN 978-1-56474-496-8

The Hanging
ISBN 978-1-56474-526-2

The Color of Light *(forthcoming)*
ISBN 978-1-56474-542-2

Diana Killian
POETIC DEATH SERIES
Docketful of Poesy
ISBN 978-1-880284-97-1

Janet LaPierre
PORT SILVA SERIES
Baby Mine
ISBN 978-1-880284-32-2

Keepers
Shamus Award nominee, Best Paperback Original
ISBN 978-1-880284-44-5

Death Duties
ISBN 978-1-880284-74-2

Family Business
ISBN 978-1-880284-85-8

Run a Crooked Mile
ISBN 978-1-880284-88-9

Hailey Lind
ART LOVER'S SERIES
Arsenic and Old Paint
ISBN 978-1-56474-490-6

Lev Raphael
NICK HOFFMAN SERIES
Tropic of Murder
ISBN 978-1-880284-68-1

Hot Rocks
ISBN 978-1-880284-83-4

Lora Roberts
BRIDGET MONTROSE SERIES
Another Fine Mess
ISBN 978-1-880284-54-4

SHERLOCK HOLMES SERIES
The Affair of the Incognito Tenant
ISBN 978-1-880284-67-4

Rebecca Rothenberg
BOTANICAL SERIES
The Tumbleweed Murders
(completed by Taffy Cannon)
ISBN 978-1-880284-43-8

Sheila Simonson
LATOUCHE COUNTY SERIES
Buffalo Bill's Defunct
WILLA Award, Best Softcover Fiction
ISBN 978-1-880284-96-4

An Old Chaos
ISBN 978-1-880284-99-5

Beyond Confusion
ISBN 978-1-56474-519-4

Shelley Singer
JAKE SAMSON & ROSIE VICENTE SERIES
Royal Flush
ISBN 978-1-880284-33-9

Lea Wait
SHADOWS ANTIQUES SERIES
Shadows of a Down East Summer
ISBN 978-1-56474-497-5

Shadows on a Cape Cod Wedding
ISBN 1-978-56474-531-6

Shadows on a Maine Christmas
(forthcoming)
ISBN 978-1-56474-531-6

Eric Wright
JOE BARLEY SERIES
The Kidnapping of Rosie Dawn
Barry Award, Best Paperback Original. Edgar,
Ellis, and Anthony awards nominee
ISBN 978-1-880284-40-7

Nancy Means Wright
MARY WOLLSTONECRAFT SERIES
Midnight Fires
ISBN 978-1-56474-488-3

The Nightmare
ISBN 978-1-56474-509-5

REFERENCE/MYSTERY WRITING

Kathy Lynn Emerson
How To Write Killer Historical Mysteries:
The Art and Adventure of Sleuthing
Through the Past
Agatha Award, Best Nonfiction. Anthony and
Macavity awards nominee
ISBN 978-1-880284-92-6

Carolyn Wheat
How To Write Killer Fiction:
The Funhouse of Mystery & the Roller
Coaster of Suspense
ISBN 978-1-880284-62-9